*From the world's number one bestselling
crime writer comes the extraordinary
twentieth Kay Scarpetta novel.*

A woman has vanished while digging a dinosaur bone bed in the remote wilderness of Canada. Somehow, evidence has made its way to the in-box of Chief Medical Examiner Kay Scarpetta, more than two thousand miles away in Boston. She has no idea why.

But as events unfold with alarming speed, Scarpetta begins to suspect that the paleontologist's disappearance is connected to a series of crimes much closer to home: a gruesome murder, inexplicable tortures, and trace evidence from the last living creatures of the dinosaur age.

When she turns to those around her, Scarpetta finds that the danger and suspicion have penetrated even her closest circles. Her niece, Lucy, speaks in riddles. Her lead investigator, Pete Marino, and FBI forensic psychologist and husband, Benton Wesley, have secrets of their own. Feeling alone and betrayed, Scarpetta is tempted by someone from her past as she tracks a killer both cunning and cruel.

"The tight plot keeps a local focus, the disconnected deaths are neatly tied together . . . and there are plenty of stomach-churning autopsies performed with cutting-edge equipment."
—*The New York Times Book Review*

"An ingenious murder method, more hours in the mortuary and forensics lab than usual, an uncharacteristically muffled killer, and all the trademark battles among the regulars and every potential ally who gets in their way."   —*Kirkus Reviews*

"The story is nail-bitingly violent and suspenseful, and it highlights Scarpetta's signature survival instinct, brilliant logic and attention to personal relationships."   —*The City Paper*

co

BOOK OF THE DEAD

"Compelling."   —*Richmond Times Dispatch*

"What a walloping, riveting mix of . . . adventure and psychology. Author Cornwell certainly is skilled at dissecting the not always attractive innards of human nature."   —*Forbes*

PREDATOR

"A fine psychological thriller."   —*The Denver Post*

"Sensationally plotted, with a twist at the end that will leave you gasping for breath."   —*Daily Express* (U.K.)

TRACE

"Cornwell gets her Hitchcock on . . . [She] can generate willies with subtle poetic turns."   —*People*

"Fun [and] flamboyant."   —*Entertainment Weekly*

BLOW FLY

"[A] grisly fast-paced thriller . . . utterly chilling."
                                            —*Entertainment Weekly*

"A story so compelling that even longtime readers will be stunned by its twists and turns."   —*Chicago Tribune*

THE LAST PRECINCT

"Ignites on the first page . . . Cornwell has created a character so real, so compelling, so driven that this reader has to remind herself regularly that Scarpetta is just a product of an author's imagination."   —*USA Today*

"The most unexpected of the Kay Scarpetta novels so far . . . Compelling . . . Terrific."   —*The Miami Herald*

TITLES BY PATRICIA CORNWELL

SCARPETTA SERIES

ANDY BRAZIL SERIES

WIN GARANO SERIES

NONFICTION

BIOGRAPHY

OTHER WORKS

the bone bed

Patricia Cornwell

BERKLEY BOOKS NEW YORK

THE BERKLEY PUBLISHING GROUP
Published by the Penguin Group
Penguin Group (USA) Inc.
375 Hudson Street, New York, New York 10014, USA

USA I Canada I UK I Ireland I Australia I New Zealand I India I South Africa I China

Penguin Books Ltd., Registered Offices: 80 Strand, London WC2R 0RL, England
For more information about Penguin Group, visit penguin.com.

THE BONE BED

A Berkley Book / published by arrangement with Cornwell Entertainment, Inc.

BERKLEY® is a registered trademark of Penguin Group (USA) Inc.
The "B" design is a trademark of Penguin Group (USA) Inc.

For information, address: The Berkley Publishing Group,
a division of Penguin Group (USA) Inc.,
375 Hudson Street, New York, New York 10014.

ISBN: 978-0-425-26767-7

PUBLISHING HISTORY
G. P. Putnam's Sons hardcover edition / October 2012
Berkley international edition / May 2013

PRINTED IN THE UNITED STATES OF AMERICA

10 9 8 7 6 5 4 3 2 1

Cover design by Richard Hasselberger.
Title page photograph by Patricia Cornwell © 2012
by Cornwell Entertainment, Inc.

ALWAYS LEARNING   **PEARSON**

To Staci—

You make it possible and fun.

prologue

Where the Red Willow and Wapiti Rivers merge in the Peace Region of northwestern Alberta, dark green waters tumble and foam around fallen trees and gray sandy islets with white pebble shores.

Black spruce and aspens are thick on the hillsides, and saplings grow at steep angles on riverbanks and cliffs, the slender boughs straining toward the sun before gravity bends them and snaps them in half.

Dead wood litters the water's edge and collects in nests of split trunks and splintered branches that rapids boil around and through, the debris moving downstream in the endless rhythm of life thriving and dying, of decay and rebirth and death.

There is no sign of human habitation, no man-made trash or pollution or a single edifice I can see, and I imagine a violent catastrophe seventy million years ago when a herd of migrating pachyrhinosauri perished at once, hundreds of them thrashing and panicking as they drowned while crossing the river during a flood.

Their massive carcasses were fed upon by carnivores, and decomposed and disarticulated. Over time, bones were pushed by landslides and currents of water, becoming glacial deposits and outcrops almost indistinguishable from granitic bedrock and loose stones.

The scenes flowing by on my computer screen could be of a pristine wilderness that has remained untouched since the Cretaceous Age, were it not for an obvious fact: The video file was made by a human being holding a recording device while skimming over shallow water, careening at precarious speeds around sandbars and semi-submerged boulders and broken trees.

No recognizable details of the jetboat's exterior or interior or the pilot or passengers on board are shown, only the aft deck's metal rail and the shape of someone blacked out by the sun's glare, a sharply outlined solid shadow against bright rushing water and an open blue sky.

one

I CHECK MY OVERSIZED TITANIUM WATCH ON ITS RUB-
ber strap and reach for my coffee—black, no sweetener—as
distant footsteps sound in the corridor of my bullet-shaped
building on the eastern border of the Massachusetts Institute of
Technology's campus. It isn't light out yet this third Monday
of October.

Seven stories below my top-floor office, traffic is steady on
Memorial Drive, rush hour in this part of Cambridge well under
way before dawn no matter the season or the weather. Headlights move along the embankment like bright insect eyes, the
Charles River rippling darkly, and across the Harvard Bridge
the city of Boston is a glittery barrier separating the earthbound
empires of business and education from the harbors and bays
that become the sea.

It's too early for staff unless it's one of the death investigators, but I can't think of a good reason for Toby or Sherry or
whoever is on call to be on this floor.

Actually, I haven't a clue who came on at midnight, and I
try to remember what vehicles were in the lot when I got here
about an hour ago. The usual white SUVs and vans and one of
our mobile crime scene trucks, I dimly recall. I really didn't
notice what else, was too preoccupied with my iPhone, with

alert tones and messages reminding me of conference calls and appointments and a court appearance today. Poor situational awareness caused by multitasking, I think impatiently.

I should pay more attention to what's around me, I chastise myself, but I shouldn't have to wonder about who's on call, for God's sake. This is ridiculous. Frustrated, I think of my head of investigations, Pete Marino, who can't seem to bother updating the electronic calendar anymore. How hard is it to drag-and-drop names from one date to another so I can see who's working? He's not kept up with it for quite some time and has been keeping to himself. Probably what I need to do is have him over for dinner, cook something he likes, and talk about what's going on with him. The thought of it tries my patience, and at the moment I seem to have none.

Some mentally disturbed person, or maybe evil is the word.

I listen for whoever might be prowling around but hear no one now as I search the Internet, clicking on files, pondering the same details repeatedly as I realize how defeated I feel and how angry that makes me.

You got what you wanted this once.

There really isn't anything gory or gruesome I've not seen or can't somehow handle, but I was caught off guard last night, a quiet Sunday at home with my husband, Benton, music playing, the MacBook open on the kitchen counter in case anything happened that I should know about immediately. In a mellow mood, I was preoccupied with making one of his favorite dishes, *risotto con spinaci come lo fanno a sondrio,* waiting for water to boil in a saucepan, drinking a Geheimrat J Riesling that made me think of our recent trip to Vienna and the poignant reason we were there.

I was lost in thoughts of people I love, preparing a fine meal and drinking a gentle wine, when the e-mail with its attached video file landed at exactly 6:30 Eastern Standard Time.

I didn't recognize the sender: *BLiDedwood@stealthmail .com.*

There was no message, just the subject heading: ATTENTION CHIEF MEDICAL EXAMINER KAY SCARPETTA, in a bold uppercase Eurostile font.

At first I was simply puzzled by the eighteen seconds of video with no audio, a cut-and-pasted jetboat ride in a part of the world I didn't recognize. The film clip seemed innocent enough, and meant nothing to me as I viewed it the first time. I was sure someone had e-mailed it by mistake until the recording suddenly stopped, dissolving into a jpg, an image meant to shock.

I launch another search engine into cyberspace, unable to find much useful about the pachyrhinosaurus, a thick-nosed herbivorous dinosaur with a horned bony frill and flattened boss likely used to butt and gore other animals into submission. A uniquely strange-looking beast, somewhat like a two-ton short-legged rhino wearing a grotesque bony mask, I suppose, as I look at an artist's rendering of one. A reptile with a face that's hard to love, but Emma Shubert did, and now the forty-eight-year-old paleontologist is missing an ear or dead or both.

The anonymous e-mail was sent directly here to the CFC, the Cambridge Forensic Center, which I head, the point I can only assume to taunt and intimidate me, and I imagine a jetboat skimming over a river thousands of miles northwest of here in what looks like a lost part of the world. I study the overexposed ghost-like shape sitting in back, possibly on a bench seat, directly facing whoever was filming.

Who are you?

Then the steep rocky slope, what I now know is a dinosaur dig site called the Wapiti bone bed, and the image dissolves into a jpg that is violent and cruel.

two

THE SEVERED HUMAN EAR IS WELL DEFINED AND DELI-
cate, the curved cartilage devoid of hair.

A right ear. Possibly white. Fair-skinned is as definitive as I
can get. Possibly a woman's ear, for sure not an adult male's or
a young child's ear, but I can't rule out an older girl or boy.

The lobe is pierced once directly in the center, the bloodstained section of newspaper the ear was photographed on easily identifiable as the *Grande Prairie Daily Herald-Tribune,*
which would have been Emma Shubert's local paper while she
was working in northwest Canada's Peace Region this past
summer. I can't see a date, just a portion of a story about moun-
tain pine beetles destroying trees.

What do you want from me?

I'm affiliated with the Department of Defense, specifically
with the Armed Forces Medical Examiners, or AFME, and
while this expands my jurisdiction to the federal level, that certainly doesn't include Canada. If Emma Shubert has been murdered, she won't be my case, not unless her dead body ends up
thousands of miles southeast of where she disappeared and
turns up in this area.

Who sent this to me, and what is it supposed to make me

think or do? Maybe what I've already done since six-thirty last night.

Alert law enforcement and worry and feel angry and rather useless.

A biometric lock clicks free at the forensic computer lab next door. Not Toby or some other investigator but my niece, Lucy, I realize, and I'm surprised and pleased. I thought she wasn't coming in today. Last I heard she was heading out in her helicopter, maybe to New York, but I'm not sure. She's been very busy of late, setting up her *country home*, as she calls the big spread she purchased northwest of here in Lincoln. She's been back and forth to Texas getting certified in the new twin-engine helicopter that recently was delivered. Busy with preoccupations I can't help her with, she says, and my niece has secrets. She always has, and I can always tell.

That U? I text her. *Coffee?*

Then she is in my open doorway, slender and remarkably fit in a snug black T-shirt, black silk cargo pants, and black leather trainers, the veins standing out in her strong forearms and wrists, her rose-gold highlighted hair still damp from the shower. She looks as if she's already been to the gym and is headed to a rendezvous with someone I don't know about, and it's not even seven o'clock in the morning.

"Good morning." I'm reminded of how nice it is to have her around. "I thought you were flying."

"You're here early."

"I have a backlog of histology I need to put a dent in but probably won't," I reply. "And I've got court this afternoon, the Mildred Lott case, or maybe I should call it the Mildred Lott spectacle. Forcing me to testify is nothing more than a stunt."

"It could be more than that." Lucy's pretty face is intensely preoccupied.

"Yes, it could be embarrassing. In fact, I fully expect it will be." I watch her curiously.

"Make sure Marino or someone goes with you." She has stopped midway on the gunmetal-gray carpet and is looking up at the geodesic glass dome.

"I guess it's you I've heard wandering around for the past hour," I continue to probe. "I was getting a little worried we might have an intruder." It's my way of asking what's going on with her.

"It wasn't me," she says. "I just got here, stopped by to check on something."

"I don't know who else is in, who's on call," I add. "So if it wasn't you I heard? Well, I'm not sure why anyone on call would be wandering around on this floor."

"Marino, that's who. At least this time. I'm surprised you didn't notice his gas guzzler in the lot."

I don't mention that she's one to talk. My niece won't drive anything with less than five hundred horsepower, usually a V12, preferably Italian, although her most recent acquisition is British, I think, but I could be wrong. Supercars aren't my area of expertise, and I don't have her money and wouldn't spend it on Ferraris and flying machines even if I did.

"What's he doing here this early?" I puzzle.

"He decided to be on call last night and sent Toby home."

"What do you mean he decided to be on call? He just got back from Florida last night. Why would he decide to be on call? He's never on call." It makes no sense.

"It's just a good thing no big cases came in that required someone to go to the scene because I'm guessing Marino slept. Or maybe he was tweeting," she says. "Which isn't a good idea. Not after hours, when he tends to be a little less inhibited."

"I'm confused."

"Did he tell you he's moved an inflatable AeroBed into Investigations?" she says.

"We don't allow beds. We don't allow people on call to sleep. Since when is he on call?" I repeat.

"Since he's been having fights with what's-her-name."

"Who?"

"Or he's ornamenting and doesn't want to drive."

I have no idea what Lucy is talking about.

"Which is rather often these days." She looks me in the eye. "What's-her-name he met on Twitter and had to unfollow in more ways than one. She made a real fool of him."

" 'Ornamenting'?"

"Minis he turns into ornaments. After he drinks what was in them. You didn't hear it from me."

I think back to July eleventh, Marino's birthday, which has

never been a happy occasion for him and is only worse the older he gets.

"You need to ask him yourself, Aunt Kay," Lucy adds, as I recall visiting him at his new house in West Cambridge.

Wood-sided on a sliver of a lot, it has working fireplaces and *genuine hardwood floors,* he likes to boast, and a finished basement, where he installed a sauna, a workshop, and a speed bag he loves to show off. When I drove up with a birthday basket of homemade asparagus quiche and white chocolate sweet salami, he was on a ladder, stringing strands of lighted small glass skulls along the roofline, Crystal Head vodka minis he was ordering *directly from the distillery and turning into ornaments,* he volunteered before I could ask, as if to imply he'd been buying empties, hundreds of them. *Getting ready for Halloween,* he added boisterously, and I should have known then that he was drinking again.

"I don't remember what you're doing today except maybe another pig farm somewhere that you intend to put out of business," I say to Lucy, as I push away every horrible thing Marino's ever done when he's been drunk.

"Southwest Pennsylvania." She continues looking around my office as if something has changed that she should know about.

Nothing has. Not that I can think of. The juniper bonsai on my brushed-steel conference table is a new addition, but that's all. The photographs, certificates, and degrees she's glancing over are the same, as are the orchids, gardenias, and sago palm. My black-laminate-surface bow-shaped desk she is staring at hasn't changed. Nor has the matching hutch or the black granite countertop behind my chair, where she's now wandering.

Not so long ago I did get rid of the microdissection system, replacing it with a ScanScope that allows me to view microscopic slides, and I watch Lucy check the monitor, powering it off and on. She picks up the keyboard and turns it over, then moves on to my faithful Leica microscope, which I'll never give up because there isn't anything I trust more than my own eyes.

"Pigs and chickens in Washington County, more of the same," she says, as she continues walking around, staring, touching things, picking them up.

"Farmers pay the fines and then start in again," she adds. "You should fly with me sometime and get an eyeful of sow stalls, piggeries that cram them in like sardines. People who are awful to animals, including dogs."

A whoosh sounds, a text message on her iPhone, and she reads it.

"Plumes of runoff going into streams and rivers." She types a reply with her thumbs, smiling as if whoever sent the message is someone she's fond of or finds amusing. "Hopefully we'll catch the assholes in flagrante delicto, shut them."

"I hope you're careful." I'm not at all thrilled with her new-found environmentalist vigilantism. "You start messing with people's livelihoods and it can get mean."

"Like it did for her?" She indicates my computer and what I've been watching on it.

"I have no idea," I confess.

"Whose livelihood was Emma Shubert messing with?"

"All I know is she found a tooth two days before she disappeared," I reply. "Apparently it's the first one unearthed in a bone bed that's a rather recent discovery. She and other scientists had just started digging there a few summers ago."

"A bone bed that may end up the most productive one anywhere," Lucy says. "A burial ground for a herd of dinosaurs that died all at once, really unusual, maybe unprecedented. It's an incredible opportunity to piece together entire skeletons and fill a museum, attract tourists and dino devotees and outdoors lovers from all over the world. Unless the area is so polluted nobody comes."

One can't read about Grande Prairie and not be aware of the economic importance of its natural gas and oil production.

"Seventeen hundred miles of pipeline carrying synthetic crude from the tar sands of Alberta to refineries in the Midwest and all the way to the Gulf of Mexico," Lucy says, disappearing inside my bathroom, where there are a Keurig and macchinetta on the counter by the sink. "Pollution, global warming, total ruination."

"Try the Illy MonoDose. The silver box," I call out to her. "And make mine a double shot."

"I believe this is a café Cubano kind of morning."

"The demerara sugar is in the cabinet," I let her know, as I finish my last sip of cold coffee and select play again.

What is it I've missed? Something.

I can't shake the gut feeling, and I focus again on the overexposed figure whose features are blown out by the glaring sun. The person doesn't appear to be very large, could be either a woman or a small man or possibly an older child wearing a sun cap with a veil around the sides and a wide brim that he or she appears to be holding with two fingers of the right hand, perhaps to keep the cap from blowing off. But again, I can't be certain.

I can't make out a single feature of the darkly shadowed face or what the person is wearing except for a long-sleeved jacket or baggy shirt and the sun cap, and there is a barely noticeable glint near the right temporal area that suggests glasses, possibly sunglasses. But I can't be sure of anything. I don't know much more now than I did when the attachment was e-mailed to me some twelve hours ago.

"I've heard nothing further from the FBI, but Benton's arranged a meeting for later today, assuming I'm out of court in time," I say, above the macchinetta's steamy blasts. "More of an informal discussion, since nothing's happened yet beyond the film clip being sent to me."

"Something's happened." Lucy's voice sounds from inside the bathroom. "Someone's ear has been cut off. Unless it's fake."

three

THE EXTERNAL PART OF THE SEVERED EAR, THE PINNA, appears to have been cleanly excised from the fascia of the temporalis muscle.

I've magnified the image as much as I can without its deconstructing into a blur, and the visible edges of the incised wound appear sharp and regular. I see no paleness or any hint that the incised tissue is everted or collapsed, which is what I might expect in a dismemberment that occurs long after death—if the ear was removed from an embalmed body, from a medical school cadaver, for example. What I'm seeing doesn't strike me as something like that. The ear and the blood on the newspaper don't look old.

But I can't know if the blood is human, and ears are difficult. They aren't particularly vascular, and it's not inconceivable one could cut off an ear ante- or postmortem and refrigerate it for weeks, and it might look fresh enough in a photograph to make it impossible for me to determine if the injury happened when the victim was alive or dead.

In other words, the jpg is far from adequate for my purposes, I'm explaining to Lucy. I need to examine the actual ear, to check incised edges for a vital response, to run the DNA in the National DNA Index (NDIS), and also the Combined DNA

Index System (CODIS), in the event the profile is connected to someone with a criminal record.

"I've already located fairly recent photos of her, plenty of them on various websites, including a few taken of her while she was working in Alberta this summer," Lucy says from my office bathroom, as we continue to talk loudly enough to hear each other. "But obviously we can't do a proper one-to-one. I have to adjust for size, angle it just right, but the good news is the overlay is at least helpful because she's definitely not a rule-out."

Lucy explains that she's been comparing the jpg with photographs of Emma Shubert, attempting to overlay images of her ears with the severed one. We can't rule out a match, but unfortunately a visual comparison isn't conclusive, either.

"I'll send you the file," she adds. "You can show the comparisons to whoever comes to your meeting."

"Will you be back around five?"

"I wasn't aware I was invited." Her voice sounds over the noise of another espresso brewing.

"Of course you're invited."

"Along with who else?"

"A couple of agents from the Boston Field Office. Douglas, I think." I refer to Douglas Burke, a female FBI agent with a confusing name. "I'm not sure who else. And Benton."

"I'm not available," Lucy answers. "Not if she's coming."

"It really would be helpful if you'd be there. What's wrong with Douglas?"

"Something is. No, thanks."

Banished by both the FBI and ATF in her earlier law-enforcement life, my niece's feelings about the Feds generally aren't charitable, which can be awkward for me, since my husband is an FBI criminal intelligence analyst, or profiler, and I have a special reservist status with the Department of Defense. Both of us are part of what she resents and disrespects, the Feds who rejected her, who fired her.

Simply put, Lucy Farinelli, my only niece, whom I've raised like a daughter, believes rules are for lesser mortals. She was a rogue federal agent and is a rogue technical genius, and my life would feel shattered and vacant if she wasn't around.

"We're dealing with somebody pretty clever." She emerges

from the bathroom carrying two shot glasses and a small steel pitcher.

"That's not a good sign," I reply. "You rarely think anyone is clever."

"Someone cunning who is smart on some fronts but too smug to realize how much he doesn't know."

She pours espresso, strong and sweet, with a light brown foamy layer on top, coladas that became a habit when she was with ATF's Miami Field Office years ago, before she got into a *bad shooting.*

"The address *BLiDedwood* is rather obvious." She sets a shot glass and the pitcher next to my keyboard.

"It's not obvious to me."

"Billy Deadwood." She spells it out.

"Okay." I let that sink in. "For my benefit?"

Lucy comes around to my side of the desk and taps the granite countertop behind me, waking up the two video displays on it. Screensavers materialize in vivid red, gold, and blue, the CFC's and AFME's crests side by side, a caduceus and scales of justice, and playing cards, pairs of aces and eights, the *dead man's hand* that Wild Bill Hickok supposedly was holding during a poker game when he was shot to death in 1876.

"The crest for the AFME." She indicates the *dead man's hand* on the computer screens. "And Wild Bill Hickok, or *Billy,* was murdered in *Deadwood*, South Dakota. For your benefit? Yes, Aunt Kay. I just hope it's not someone in our own backyard."

"Why would you entertain the slightest suspicion that it might be?"

"Using a temporary free e-mail address that self-destructs or deletes itself in thirty minutes?" Lucy considers. "Okay, not all that unusual, could be anyone. Then this person routes the e-mail to you through a free proxy server, this particular one a high-anonymity type with an unavailable host name. Located in Italy."

"So no one can respond to the e-mail because the temporary account is deleted after thirty minutes and is gone."

"That's the point."

"And no one can track the IP and trace where the e-mail was actually sent from." I follow her logic.

"Exactly what the sender is banking on."

"We're supposed to assume the e-mail was sent by someone in Italy."

"Specifically, Rome," she tells me.

"But that's a ruse."

"Absolutely," she says. "Whoever sent it definitely wasn't in Rome at six-thirty last night our time."

"What about the font?" I return to the e-mail and look at the subject line.

ATTENTION CHIEF MEDICAL EXAMINER KAY SCARPETTA

"Is there any significance?" I ask.

"Very retro. Reminiscent of the fifties and sixties, big squarish shapes with rounded corners supposedly evocative of TV sets from that era. *Your* era," she teases.

"Please don't hurt me this early in the morning."

"Eurostile was created by Italian type designer Aldo Novarese," she explains, "the font originally made for a foundry in Turin, Nebiolo Printech."

"And you think this means what?"

"I don't know." She shrugs. "They basically manufacture paper and high-end technologically advanced printing machines."

"A possible Italian connection?"

"I doubt it. I think whoever sent the e-mail to you assumed you couldn't trace the actual IP," she says, and I know what's next.

I know what she's done.

"In other words," she continues, "we wouldn't figure out the actual location it was sent from—"

"Lucy," I interrupt her. "I don't want you taking extreme measures."

She's already taken them.

"There are a ton of these anonymous freebies available," she continues, as if she's not done what I know she has.

"I don't want you helping yourself to some proxy server in Italy or anywhere else," I tell her flatly.

"The e-mail was sent to you by someone who had access to Logan's wireless," she says, to my astonishment.

"It was sent from the airport?"

"The video clip was e-mailed to you from Logan Airport's wireless network not even seven fucking miles from here," she confirms, and it's no wonder she's entertaining the possibility it might be someone in our own backyard.

I think about my chief of staff, Bryce Clark, of Pete Marino, and several forensic scientists in my building. Members of the CFC staff were in Tampa, Florida, last week for the International Association for Identification's annual meeting, and all of them flew back into Boston yesterday around the same time this e-mail was anonymously sent to the CFC.

"At some point prior to six o'clock last night," Lucy explains, "this person logged on to Logan's free wireless Internet. The same thing passengers do thousands of times a day. But it doesn't mean the person who sent the e-mail was physically in a terminal or on a plane."

Whoever it is could have been in a parking garage, she says, or on a sidewalk, possibly in a water taxi or on a ferry in the harbor, anywhere the wireless signal reaches. Once this person was connected, he created a temporary e-mail account called *BLiDedwood@Stealthmail*, possibly using word-processing software to write the subject line in Eurostile, and cutting and pasting it into the e-mail.

"He waited twenty-nine minutes before sending it," Lucy says. "Just a shame he has the satisfaction of knowing it was opened."

"How would this person know I opened the e-mail?"

"Because he didn't get a bounce-back *nondelivery* notification message," she replies. "Which he would have gotten just seconds before the account self-destructed. He has no reason not to assume the e-mail was received and opened."

Her tone is different. What she's saying sounds like a reprimand.

"The bounce-back is instant and automatic for harassing or virus-infected communications sent to the CFC's main address," she reminds me. "The purpose is to give the sender the impression that the e-mail couldn't be delivered. But in fact with rare and unfortunate exception, suspicious e-mails go directly into what I call quarantine so I can see whatever it is and assess the threat level," she emphasizes, and I realize what she's getting at. "I didn't see this particular e-mail because it wasn't quarantined."

The rare and unfortunate exception she's talking about is myself.

"The firewalls I've set up recognized the e-mail as legit because of the subject heading *Attention Chief Medical Examiner Kay Scarpetta*," she says, as if it's my fault, and it is. "Something directed to your personal attention doesn't get spammed or temporarily outboxed in quarantine because that's been your directive to me. Against my wishes, remember?"

She holds my gaze, and she's right, but there's nothing I can do about it.

"You see the consequences of my allowing you to cheat what I've secured?" she asks.

"I understand your frustration, Lucy. But it's the only way a lot of people, particularly police and families, can reach me when they don't know my direct CFC contact information." I say what I've said before. "They send something to my attention and I certainly don't want it spammed."

"It's just too bad that you're the one who opened it first," Lucy says. "Of course, typically Bryce probably would have before you had the chance."

"I'm glad he didn't." My chief of staff is very sensitive and more than a little squeamish.

"Right. He didn't because he was on his way back from a trip. He and several others had been out of pocket for a week," Lucy says, as if the timing wasn't an accident.

"Are you worried that whoever sent the e-mail knows what's going on at the CFC?" I ask.

"It worries me, yes."

She rolls a chair close, refills our shot glasses, and I smell the fresh grapefruit scent of her cologne, and I always know when my niece has been on the elevator or has passed through a room. I can close my eyes and recognize her distinctive fragrance anywhere.

"It would be foolish not to consider someone might be paying attention to all of us and what we're doing," she is saying. "Someone into games who thinks he's smarter than God. Someone who gets off on traumatizing people and jerking them around."

I have no doubt about why she's been snooping around my office this morning. She stopped by *to check on something* because she's overly protective of me, vigilant to a fault. Since Lucy was old enough to walk she's demanded my attention and watched me like a hawk.

"Are you worried Marino's involved? That he's spying on me or trying to hurt me somehow?" I log in to my e-mail.

"He sure as hell does stupid things," she says, as if she has specific ones in mind. "But he's not that savvy, and what motive could he have? The answer's none."

four

I SCROLL THROUGH MY IN-BOX, LOOKING FOR AN E-MAIL from Bryce or Assistant U.S. Attorney Dan Steward, as I continue to hope my appearance in court won't be needed.

"What about image clarification? Maybe we can figure out who's on the jetboat?" I'm talking about the video clip while I'm fretting about Mildred Lott.

"Forget it," Lucy says.

"It's so ridiculous," I mutter, when I find no message that might grant me a reprieve.

It used to be that my autopsy report was enough for the defense, my appearing in court not necessary or even desirable, but since the Melendez-Diaz decision by the U.S. Supreme Court, life has changed for every forensic expert in America. Channing Lott wants to confront his accuser. The billionaire industrialist faces a murder charge for allegedly placing a contract on his now presumed dead wife, and he's demanded the pleasure of my company this afternoon at two.

"What you see in that video file is all you'll ever see." Lucy empties her shot glass. "What you're looking at is as good as it's going to get."

"We're sure there's no software out there that might be more sophisticated than what we're using here at the CFC?" I don't want to accept it.

"More sophisticated than what I've engineered?" She gets up and moves closer to my computer screen. "Nothing holds a candle to what we've got. The problem is the footage is hot."

She clicks the mouse to show me, a heavy gold ring she's recently started wearing on her index finger, a steel chronograph watch around her wrist. Pausing the recording on the faceless image in the back of the boat, she explains that she made multiple layers of the same video clip, dropping the brightness, using sharpness filters, and it's hopeless.

"Whoever did the filming was directly facing the sun," she says, "and nothing is going to *restore* the blown-out parts. The best we can do is suspect who the person on the boat might be based on context and circumstances."

Suspecting isn't good enough, and I replay the clip, returning to a stretch of river an hour by jetboat from a sheer barren hillside where American paleontologist Dr. Emma Shubert was digging with colleagues from the University of Alberta when she vanished almost nine weeks ago. According to statements made to the police, she was last seen on August 23 at around ten p.m., walking alone through a wooded area of a Pipestone Creek campsite, headed to her trailer after dinner in the chow hall. The next morning her door was ajar and she was gone.

When I talked with an investigator from the Royal Canadian Mounted Police last night I was told there was no sign of a struggle, nothing to indicate Emma Shubert might have been attacked inside her trailer.

"We must find out who sent this to me," I say to Lucy. "And why. If it's possible the figure in the jetboat is she, what was going on? What's the expression on her face? Happy? Sad? Frightened? Was she on the boat willingly?"

"I can't tell you that."

"I want to see her."

"You're not going to on this video clip. There's nothing more to see."

"Was she on her way to the bone bed to dig or returning from it?" I ask.

"Based on the position of the sun and satellite images of that part of the river," Lucy says, "the jetboat likely was traveling east, suggesting it was morning. Obviously the day was a sunny one, and there weren't many of those in that part of the world this past August. Not so coincidentally, two days before she vanished, the day she found the pachyrhino tooth, it was sunny."

"So you're thinking the video was taken on August twenty-first, based on the weather."

"Apparently she did go to that site that day, traveled by jetboat to the bone bed on the Wapiti River." Lucy repeats information that's been in the news. "So the video might have been recorded on an iPhone during the boat ride there that morning. She has an iPhone. Or did. As you know, it was missing from her trailer. It may be the only thing that's missing, since other personal effects allegedly were undisturbed."

"The footage was filmed on an iPhone?" This is new information.

"And the photo of the severed ear," Lucy says. "A first-generation iPhone, which is what she had."

I'm not going to ask Lucy how she managed to acquire these details. I don't want to know.

"She still had the first one she'd gotten, didn't bother upgrading, probably because of the contract she had with AT and T." Lucy gets up and returns to the bathroom to rinse our shot glasses, and I detect distant voices down the corridor.

Then I hear the recorded sound of a police siren, one of Pete Marino's ringtones. He's with someone. Bryce, I think, and they're headed in this direction. Both of them are on their cell phones, only the sounds of their words coming through, and I can tell by the energy in their voices that something has happened.

"I'll call you later, will be back before the weather moves in," Lucy adds, as she leaves. "It's going to be really bad later in the day."

Then Marino is in my doorway. His khaki field clothes are rumpled as if he's slept in them, his face flushed, and he walks in as if he lives here, talking loudly on his phone. Bryce is behind him, my delicately handsome chief of staff, wearing designer sunglasses on top of his head and faded denim drainpipe jeans and a T-shirt, as if he just stepped off the set of *Glee*. I notice he hasn't shaved since I saw him a week ago, before he went to Florida, and facial hair or the lack of it always means the same thing. Bryce Clark is stepping in and out of different characters as he continues auditioning for the star role in his own life.

"Well, normally that would be a no," Marino says into his cell phone. "But you're going to need to get the lady from the aquarium on the line so the chief here can tell her directly and make sure everybody's on the same page. . . ."

"We appreciate that and totally get it." Bryce is talking to someone else. "We certainly do realize nobody's going to be fighting over it. Maybe you and the fire guys can flip a coin, just kidding. I'm sure the fireboat's got a Stokes basket same as you. No vacuum bag or cervical collar or whatever needed, *obviously*. Of course the fire guys are better equipped to hose everything off after the fact with those big bad deck cannons of theirs. Point is? Doesn't matter in the least to us, but someone's gotta help get it to shore, and we'll handle it from there." He looks at his watch. "In about forty-five? A little after nine? That would really be fabulous."

"What is it?" I ask Bryce, as he ends the call.

He puts his hands on his hips, scrutinizing me. "Well, we certainly didn't wear the right thing for going out in a boat this morning, did we?" He surveys the gray pin-striped skirt suit and pumps I wore today for court. "I'll just be a minute, gonna grab a few things because you're not going out with the Coast Guard in what you've got on. Fishing out some floater? Thank God it's not July, not that the water's ever warm around here, and I sure as hell hope it's not been in there long, my least favorite thing. I'm sorry, let's be honest. Who can stand it? I realize nobody means to get in such a disgusting condition, can you imagine? If I die and get like that please don't find me."

He's in my closet, retrieving field clothes.

"That's the part the boys with the Guard aren't happy about, because why would they be?" He keeps talking. "Having something like that on their boat, but no worries, they'll do it because I asked them pretty please and reminded them that if you—and I specifically mean you, the chief—don't know how to take care of it, who does?"

He slides a pair of cargo pants off a hanger.

"You'll double-pouch or whatever it takes so their boat doesn't stink to high heaven, just a reminder? I promised. Do you want short sleeves or long?"

He peers at me from my closet.

"I'm voting for long, because it's going to be nippy out there with the wind blowing," he says, before I can even think of answering. "So let's see, your down jacket's a good idea, your rescue-orange one, so you show up a mile away. Always a good idea on the water. I see Marino doesn't have a jacket, but I'm not in charge of his wardrobe."

Bryce carries clothing over to me as Marino continues talking to someone who obviously is out in a boat.

"We don't want anybody cutting through knots or nothing, and any ropes would have to be cleated down," he is saying, as Bryce drapes my CFC uniform across my desk and then returns to the closet for boots. "I'm going to hang up and call you on a landline and maybe have a better connection and you can talk to the doc yourself," Marino adds.

He comes over to my side of the desk as I hear the elevator in the corridor and more voices. Lucy is on her way to her helicopter, and other staff members are arriving. It's a few minutes past eight.

"Some huge prehistoric turtle entangled in the south channel," Marino tells me, as he reaches for my desk phone.

"Prehistoric?" Bryce exclaims. "I don't think so."

"A leatherback. They're almost extinct, have been around since Jurassic Park." Marino ignores him.

"I don't believe there was a *park* back then," Bryce chimes in louder.

"Could weigh as much as a ton." Marino keeps talking to me as he enters a number on my phone, a pair of over-the-counter reading glasses perched on his strong nose. "A waterman checking his lobster pots discovered it at sunrise and called the aquarium's rescue team, which has an arrangement with the fire department marine unit. When the fireboat got there and they started to pull the turtle in, turns out there's an unfortunate attachment on the vertical line . . . Pamela?" he says to whoever answers. "I'm handing you over to Dr. Scarpetta."

He gives me the receiver, folding the glasses with his thick fingers and tucking them into the breast pocket of his shirt as he explains, "Pamela Quick. She's out in the fireboat, so the connection might not be real good."

The woman on the phone introduces herself as a marine

biologist with the New England Aquarium, and she sounds urgent and slightly hostile. She just this minute e-mailed a photograph, she says.

"You can see for yourself we're out of time," she insists. "We need to get him on board *now*."

" '*Him*'?" I ask.

"A critically endangered species of sea turtle that's been dragging tackle and other gear and what's obviously a dead person for who knows how long. Turtles have to breathe, and he barely can keep his nares above water anymore. We need to get him out *right now* so he doesn't drown."

Marino holds his cell phone close to me so I can see the e-mailed photograph he just opened of a young woman, blond and tan, in khaki pants and a green Windbreaker, leaning over the side of the fireboat. She's using a long-handled grappling hook to pull in a line that is entangled with a shockingly massive sea creature, leathery and dark, with a wingspan nearly as wide as the boat. Several yards away from its protruding huge head, and barely visible at the surface of the rolling blue water, are pale hands with painted nails and a splay of long white hair.

Bryce sets down a pair of lightweight ankle-high black tactical boots with polished leather toes and nylon uppers. He complains that he can't find socks.

"Try my locker downstairs," I tell him, as I bend over to slip off my pumps, and I say to Pamela Quick, "What we don't want is to lose the body or cause any damage to it. So normally I wouldn't permit—"

"We can save this animal," she cuts me off, and it's patently clear she's not interested in my permission. "But we have to do it now." The way she says it, I have no doubt she's not going to wait for me or anyone, and I really can't blame her.

"Do what you need to do, of course. But if someone can document it with video or photographs, that would be helpful," I tell her, as I get out of my chair, feeling the carpet under my stocking feet and reminded I never know what to expect in life, not from one minute to the next. "Disturb any lines and gear as little as possible, and make sure they're secured so we don't lose anything," I add.

five

DRESSED IN COTTON FIELD CLOTHES NOW, DARK BLUE, with the CFC crest embroidered on my shirt and on the bright orange jacket draped over my arm, I board the elevator beyond the break room, and for a moment we are alone. Marino sets down two black plastic Pelican cases and stabs the button for the lower level.

"I understand you were here all night," I comment, as he impatiently taps the button again, a habit of his that serves no useful purpose.

"Caught up on some paperwork and stuff. Was just easier to stay over."

He shoves his big hands into the side pockets of his cargo pants, the slope of his belly swelling noticeably over his canvas belt. He's gained weight, but his shoulders are formidable and I can tell by the thickness of his neck, biceps, and legs that he's still pumping iron in that gym he belongs to in Central Square, a fight sports club or whatever he calls it, that is frequented by cops, most of them SWAT.

"Easier than what?" I detect the stale odor of sweat beneath a patina of Brut aftershave, and maybe he drank the night away, went through a carton of Crystal Head vodka mini skull ornaments or whatever. I don't know. "Yesterday was Sunday,"

I continue in a mild voice. "Since you weren't scheduled to work this weekend and were just getting back from a trip, what exactly was easier? And while we're on the subject, I've not been getting updated on-call schedules for quite some time, so I wasn't aware you were taking calls yourself and apparently have been—"

"The electronic calendar is bullshit," he interrupts. "All this automated instant bullshit. I just wish Lucy would give it a rest. You know what you need to know, that someone's doing what they're supposed to. That someone being me."

"I'm not aware that the head of investigations is on call. That's never been our policy, unless there's an emergency. And it's also not our policy to be a firehouse, to sleep over on an inflatable bed while waiting for an alarm to clang, so to speak."

"I see someone's been narking. It's her fault, anyway." He puts his sunglasses on, wire-frame Ray-Bans he's worn for as long as I've known him—what Bryce calls Marino's *Smokey and the Bandit* shades.

"The investigator on call is supposed to be awake at his or her work station, ready to answer the phone." I say this evenly and with no invitation for the argument he is giving me. "And what is whose fault?"

"Fucking Lucy got me on Twitter, and that's what started it."

When he says "fucking Lucy" I know he doesn't mean it. The two of them are close.

"I don't think it's fair to blame her for Twitter if you're the one tweeting, and I understand you have been," I reply in the same bland tone. "And she didn't exactly nark on you, or some things I would have known before now. Anything she's said, it's because she cares about you, Marino."

"She's out of the picture and has been for weeks, and I don't want to talk about it," he says, as we slowly descend through the center of the building.

"Who is?" I puzzle.

"The twat I was tweeting, and that's all I have to say about it. And you really think people don't sleep when they're on call? I didn't miss nothing last night. Every time the phone rang, I answered it and handled it. The only real scene to respond to was the guy who fell down the stairs, and Toby took care of it, a cut-and-dried accident. Then I sent him home. No point in both of us being there. And besides, he gets on my nerves. I can never find him where he's supposed to be, either that or he's on top of me."

"I'm just trying to understand what's going on. That's all. I'm making sure you're okay."

"Why wouldn't I be?" He stares straight ahead at smooth shiny steel, at the illuminated *LL* on the digital panel. "I've had things not work out before."

I have no idea what things or who he's talking about, and now is not the time to press him about some woman he met on the Internet, or at least this is what I suspect he's alluding to. But I do need to talk to him about what I worry could be a breach of professional discretion and confidentiality.

"While we're on the subject, I'm wondering why you went on Twitter to begin with, or why Lucy supposedly might encourage such a thing," I say to him. "I'm not trying to pry into your personal life, Marino, but I'm not in favor of social networking unless it's primarily for news feeds, which is the only thing I follow on Twitter. Certainly we aren't in the business of marketing what we do here or sharing details about it or making friends with the great outdoors."

"I'm not on Twitter as me, don't use anything that can be identified to me. In other words, you don't see my name, just the handle *The Dude* . . ."

"'*The Dude*'?"

"As in *The Big Lebowski* character played by Jeff Bridges, whose avatar I use. Point being, no way you'd know what I do for a living unless you literally do a search for Peter Rocco Marino, and who's going to bother? At least I don't use some generic egg avatar like you do, which is retarded."

"So you represent yourself on Twitter with a photo of a movie star who played in a movie about bowling . . . ?"

"Only the best bowling movie ever made," he says defensively, as the elevator settles to a stop and the doors open.

Marino doesn't wait for me or offer anything further as he grabs up the scene cases, one in each hand, and steps out, his baseball cap pulled low over his tan bald head, his eyes masked by the Ray-Bans. All these years I've known him, more than two decades now, and there's never been a question when he feels slighted or stung, although I can't imagine what

I might have done this time, beyond what I just attempted
to discuss with him. But he was already out of sorts when he
appeared in my office a little while ago. Something else is
going on. I wonder what the hell I've done. What exactly this
time?

He was gone all last week at the meeting in Florida, and so
there wasn't anything I might have done during his time away.
Before that Benton and I were in Austria, and it occurs to me
that's more likely the root of Marino's displeasure. Well, of
course it would be, dammit. Benton and I were with my assistant chief medical examiner, Luke Zenner, in Vienna, at his
aunt's funeral, and I feel frustrated and next I feel annoyed.
More of the damn same. Marino and his jealousy, and Benton,
too. The men in my life are going to be the end of me.

I'm careful what I say to Marino, because there are other
people around. Forensic scientists, clerical and investigative
staff are entering the building from the parking lot in back and
moving along the wide windowless corridor. Marino and I say
little to each other as we walk past the telecom closet and the
locked metal door that leads into the vast mechanical room,
and then the odontology lab, everything in the CFC's round
building flowing in a perfect circle, which I still find tricky at
times, especially if I'm trying to give directions. There is no
first or last office on the right or left, and nothing in the middle,
either.

We wind around to the autopsy and x-ray rooms, our rubber-
soled booted feet making muffled sounds, and then we are in
the receiving area, where there are walls of stainless-steel intake and discharge refrigerators and decomp freezers with
digital displays at the tops of their heavy doors. I greet staff we
encounter but don't pause to chat, and I notify the security
guard, a former military policeman, that we've got a potentially
sensitive case coming in.

"Something that involves what appears to be unusual circumstances," I tell Ron, who is powerfully built and dark-skinned
and never particularly animated behind his glass window. "Just
be aware in the event the media or who knows what shows up. I
can't predict how much of a circus this might be."

"Yes, ma'am, Chief," he says.

"We'll let you know when we get an idea of what might be headed this way," I add.

"Yes, ma'am, Chief. That would be good," he replies, and I'm always ma'am and Chief to him, and I think he likes me well enough even if he doesn't show it.

I check the sign-in log, a big black ledger, and one of the few documents I won't permit to be electronic. Looking over what I recognize as Marino's small snarled handwritten entries for bodies that have arrived since I checked when I first got here around five, I'm reminded that what Lucy reported is only partially true. While there was no need for an investigator to respond to any scenes after hours, there are cases, four of them, that require autopsies. The person who would have decided to have the bodies sent in for postmortem examinations was the investigator on call, who I now know was Toby for the suspected blunt-force trauma from a fall and Marino for the rest of them.

The ones he handled occurred in local hospitals or were DOAs, two motor-vehicle fatalities and a possible drug overdose suicide, and responding to the scenes of the fatal events or actual deaths wouldn't have been necessary unless the police requested it. Marino must have got the information over the phone, and I turn around to ask him about the cases we have so far this day, but the person I sense nearby isn't him after all. I'm startled to find Luke Zenner inches from me as if he traded places with Marino or materialized out of nowhere.

"I didn't mean to scare you." He's carrying his briefcase and wearing a white shirt with the sleeves folded up to his slender elbows and a narrow red-and-black striped tie, sneakers, and jeans.

"I'm sorry. I thought you were Marino."

"I just saw him in the parking lot scouting out one SUV or van and then another, whatever looks the best and has the biggest engine. But thanks for thinking I was him." He gives me an ironic smile, his eyes warm, his British accent belying his Austrian roots. "I'll accept you meant it as a compliment," he adds wryly, and I'm not sure if he dislikes Marino as much as Marino dislikes him, but I suspect their feelings are mutual.

Dr. Luke Zenner is new in more ways than one, recently

board-certified, not even three years ago, and I hired him this past June, much against Marino's wishes, I should add. A talented forensic pathologist, Luke also is the nephew of a friend of mine whose funeral we just attended, Dr. Anna Zenner, a psychiatrist I became close to more than a decade ago, during my Richmond days. That connection is the source of Marino's objection, or at least this is what he claims, although resentment likely is the more accurate reason for why he is blatantly unkind and unhelpful to a very nice-looking young blond-haired blue-eyed doctor who is a citizen of the world with a personal tie to me.

"You heading off? A scene? A SWAT situation? The firing range? A reality show?" Luke notices the way I'm dressed, taking in every inch of me. "No court after all?"

"We've got a case in Boston, a body in the harbor. It may be a difficult recovery because of fishing gear and whatever else it's tethered to," I reply. "I don't know about court, but I'll probably have to be there. There's not much choice these days."

"Tell me about it." He watches a group of forensic scientists heading to the elevator, young women who greet us shyly and can scarcely take their eyes off him. "You so much as initial something and get summoned to appear." His attention lingers on the women, reminding me of what Marino accuses, that Luke takes what he wants, doesn't matter who she is or her marital status. "Much of it is harassment."

"Some of it is," I agree.

"I can go with you if you need some help. What kind of case? A drowning?" His vivid blue eyes are fastened to me. "I remind you I'm a certified scuba diver, too. We can buddy dive. The visibility in the harbor is bound to be quite bad, the water cold as hell. You shouldn't be alone. Marino doesn't dive. I'm happy to go."

"I'm not sure at the moment what we've got, but I think we can handle it," I reply. "I'll trust you to manage morning rounds and oversee the assigning of cases to the other docs. That would be much appreciated."

"Of course. When you've got a moment, can we talk about the on-call schedule or lack of one?"

He stares at me as I open the door that leads into the bay, his keen face so much like his aunt's that I find it unsettling. Or maybe it's the way he looks at me, the way he helps himself to me and how it makes me feel and the difficulties it has caused.

"It's a bit of a problem." He's saying Marino is, and maybe saying something else.

It is the something else I fear, and I'm reminded of Vienna after the service, when Luke guided Benton and me along the graceful tree-lined paths of the Zentralfriedhof to show us the graves of Brahms and Beethoven and Strauss. Benton got palpably unhappy. I could feel his upset like sleet stinging my face.

"I understand, and plan to take it up with him." I promise Luke I will deal with the electronic calendar problem, that if need be I'll have Bryce take it over, and while I'm saying all this I'm remembering what happened.

It was awful. Benton's visible displeasure was triggered by nothing more than Luke's ability to speak perfect English and German and serve as a thoughtful, affectionate guide on a very sad occasion, the burial of his aunt, whom I dearly loved. But Luke, her only nephew, was gracious and brave and unflappably charming, and as we stopped to look at the monument to Mozart, where people had placed candles and flowers on its marble steps, Luke hooked his arm around me to thank me for coming to Vienna for the funeral of Anna, his only aunt and someone I could never forget.

That was all, a hug that pulled me close for a tender moment. But it was enough. When Benton and I returned to our hotel near the Ringstrasse, we drank and didn't eat, and we argued.

"Where is your respect?" my FBI husband began to interrogate me, and I knew what he meant, but I wouldn't own up to it. "You really don't see it, do you, Kay?" He paced the room furiously as he opened another bottle of champagne. "Things start this way, you know." He wouldn't look at me. "The nephew of a friend, and you treat him like family and give him a job and next thing . . . ?" He drank half a glass of champagne in one swallow. "He's not Lucy. You're projecting as if you're his only aunt the way Anna was his only aunt, and somehow that makes you his de facto mother the same way you're Lucy's de facto mother, and next thing . . . ?"

"Next thing what, Benton? I go to bed with him? That's the logical conclusion if I mentor people and am their de facto mother?" I didn't add that I don't sleep with my niece, either.

"You want him. You want someone younger. It happens as we get older, it always does, because we hold on to vitality, fight for it and want it back. That's the problem; it will always be a problem and gets only worse. And young men want you because you're a trophy."

"I've never thought of myself as a trophy."

"And maybe you're bored."

"I've never been bored with you, Benton."

"I didn't say with me," he said.

I walk through the beige epoxy-painted bay, the size of a small hangar, and it crosses my mind as it has a number of times this past week that I don't feel I'm bored with my job or my life, and not with Benton, never with him. It's not possible to be bored with such a complex elegant man, whom I've always found strikingly compelling and impossible to own, a part of him inaccessible no matter how intimate we could ever be.

But it is true that I notice other attractive human beings, and certainly I notice them noticing me, and since I'm not as young as I was, maybe noticing has become more important. But it's simply not true that I don't have insight about it, I certainly do, am insightful enough to know that it's damn harder for women. It's hard in ways men will never understand, and I hate being reminded of our fight and how it ended, which was with Benton's assertion that I'm not honest with myself.

It occurs to me that the person I could be completely honest with is the one who inadvertently caused the problem, Anna Zenner, my confidante of old, who used to tell me stories of her nephew, Luka, or Luke, as the rest of us know him. He left Austria for public school in England, then Oxford, and after that King's College London School of Medicine, and eventually made his way to America, where he completed his forensic pathology residency at the Office of the Chief Medical Examiner in Baltimore, one of the finest facilities anywhere. He came highly recommended and had many prestigious job offers, and I've had no trouble with him and can't see why anyone would question his credentials or feel I hired him as a favor.

The roll-up bay door is retracted, and through the concrete

space and out the big square opening is the tarmac and the clear blue sky. Cars and CFC vehicles, all of them white, shine in the fall morning light, and enclosing the lot is the black PVC-coated anti-climb fence, and over the top of it, rising above my titanium-skinned building on two sides, are brick-and-glass MIT labs with radar dishes and antennas on the roofs. To the west is Harvard and its divinity school near my house, which of course I can't make out above the barricade of dense dark fencing that keeps the world away from those I take care of, my patients, all of them dead.

I emerge onto the tarmac as a white Tahoe rumbles toward me. The air is cool and clear like glass, and I pull on my jacket, grateful that Bryce chose my attire for the day. I'm reminded of how unexpected it is that I've grown accustomed to a chief of staff who cares about my wardrobe. I've come to like what at first I resisted, although his attending to me encourages forgetfulness on my part, a complete disinterest in relatively unimportant details he can easily manage or fix. But he was right, I will need the jacket because it will be cold on the boat and there's a very good chance I will get wet. If anyone has to go into the water, it will be me. I'm already convinced of that.

I will insist on seeing for myself exactly what we're dealing with and making sure the death is managed the way it should be, precisely and respectfully, beyond reproach and in anticipation of any legal accusations, because there are always those. Marino can help me or not, but he's no diver and doesn't do well in a wetsuit or a drysuit, says they make him feel as if he's suffocating, and he isn't much of a swimmer. He can stay on the boat, and I will take care of things on my own. I'm not going to squabble with him or anyone. I've had my fill of squabbling and worrying about the slightest thing that can be misinterpreted. As if I would have an affair with Anna Zenner's nephew, who, even if I were single, would be far more compatible with Lucy, were she inclined that way.

I'm not Luke's de facto mother, and what continues to cut me to the bone about Benton's remark is the suggestion that I'm old.

Old like a Eurostile font evocative of a past era, the fifties and sixties, which I scarcely can recall and don't want to believe I'm from.

I feel Benton's implication like an internal injury that chronically smarts, a depressing symptom of being damaged and not knowing it until he spoke those angry words to me in Vienna. I've perceived myself differently since he said it, and I'm not sure I can get over the deeper wounding it has done.

six

I FLIP UP THE HINGED BOX COVER OF THE BIOMETRIC reader mounted on the side of the building and lightly press my left thumb against the glass scanner. The torque motor purrs, and steel roller chains noisily begin lowering the half-ton sectional shutter bay door.

"The Coast Guard should have drysuits," I say to Marino, as I settle into the Tahoe's front passenger's seat, and I know him.

He picked whatever was most recently washed and filled with gas, which likely was what Luke Zenner observed when he noticed Marino scouting out various vehicles in the parking lot. I smell the pleasant scent of Armor All and notice the dash is glossy, the carpet spotless. Marino likes a V8 engine, the bigger and louder a vehicle the better, and I'm reminded of how much he loathes the new fleet of SUVs I picked, Toyota Sequoias, fuel-efficient, practical, what I drive every day because I don't need to prove anything to anyone.

"We always keep a couple drysuits in the storage lockers. I make sure of it with every scene truck." Marino reminds me of his diligence, and I sense an unpleasant conversation coming on. "There's two in back. I checked."

"Good." I fasten my shoulder harness and find my sunglasses as he backs up. "But hopefully whatever the Coast Guard has on board is better than ours, which isn't saying much. The suits we have are pretty awful, intended for very basic search and rescue, and not evidence recovery."

"Government surplus," Marino complains, and he has something on his mind.

I can always tell.

"Crap that's the lowest bid for Homeland Security or DoD, and then they don't want it and it gets passed down the line at a deal," he says. "Like those cartons for organ sections that said *Fish Bait*? Back in our Richmond days? Remember?"

"It's not exactly something one could forget."

Marino started tweeting, maybe started drinking again, not long after I hired Luke, and I wonder if Luke said something to him in the parking lot a few minutes ago. I wonder if Luke asked where we were going and added the reminder that he is PADI trained and certified at a professional level, is a master instructor and rescue diver.

"Because you needed a shitload of plasticized cartons and it went out on bid?" Marino remembers fondly.

"And we used them, had no choice."

"Yeah, if that happened now a defense attorney would have a field day with it."

I think of Mildred Lott and what I likely face. Court is still on for me, as far as I know. If only I had been more careful. If only I hadn't made a damn stupid comment that I fear will soon be all over the news.

"We may not need to go in at all unless she's no longer close to the surface." Marino stops the Tahoe at the black metal security gate. "In the photo Pam sent it looks like she's within easy reach. Probably we can just pull the lines in and won't even need a drysuit, but who the shit knows."

"We shouldn't assume it's a she."

"Nail polish." He splays his hands as if he's wearing it, then reaches up to the visor and pushes a button on the remote. "You could see it in the pic Pam sent." He refers to the young-looking marine biologist as if they are instant friends. "Definitely nail polish. I couldn't tell what color, though, maybe pink."

"It's best not to assume anything at all."

"Well, we need our own damn dive team. I've been thinking

about it, thinking of getting certified," he says, and that will never happen.

Marino likes to comment that if God meant for us to breathe underwater he would have given us gills. He said it for Luke to hear, and I wonder if Marino has a clue that Luke just volunteered to buddy dive with me, if words were exchanged between the two of them in the parking lot.

"All the bodies we get out of water around here," Marino continues. "Bays, lakes, rivers, the ocean. And the fire guys and the guardsmen and even rescue dive teams, they don't want to deal with floaters."

"That's not what they're in the business to deal with," I remark, and whenever he is full of himself like this and talking nonstop I get ready to find out something I won't be happy about.

"If we just had a boat. I got my captain's license, and it would be nothing to be in business. A Zodiac Hurricane rigid-hull inflatable, a twenty-one-footer, two-forty-horsepower inboard jet would be plenty. Maybe we could try to get grant money for new drysuits and also a boat and keep it back here on a trailer and then we got our own way to handle things," he says confidently. "I could be in charge of that easy. It's what I know like the back of my hand."

Traffic is heavy as we pull onto Memorial Drive, the gate frozen open behind us as other CFC employees turn into the lot.

"I'd make sure everything is stocked and stowed perfectly and deconned," he says. "Would do everything by the book so no worries about some defense attorney saying evidence is contaminated. If you're still going this afternoon, I should be with you. I don't want you alone if it's anywhere near Channing Lott."

"I don't think he'll be in a position to do anything to me inside the federal courthouse, with marshals everywhere."

"Problem is who a scumbag like that might have on the outside," Marino says. "Someone with his money could pay anybody to do anything."

"Apparently he didn't bother paying anything when he decided to have his wife murdered."

"No shit. Probably a good thing for him that he's been locked up all this time. I wouldn't want to promise some hit man a hundred g's and then not ante up."

"Do we have transport?"

"Yeah. Toby will be waiting at the Coast Guard base with one of the vans. I told him he doesn't need to head out until at least an hour from now."

On the other side of the busy street bending around our building, the river flows deep blue and sparkles in the sun, and leaves of hardwood trees along the embankment are beginning to turn yellow and red where the cold water chills the air. Fall is late this year, not a single frost yet, and most of the trees are green on the verge of brown. I fear we will transition straight to winter, which this far north can happen almost instantly.

"I know about the e-mail," Marino finally says, and I figured he would get around to it eventually.

I can't imagine Lucy didn't tell him, and I say as much.

"How come you didn't call me right away?" he asks.

Across the river are the high-rises of downtown Boston, and on the other side of them the inner and outer harbors and the Massachusetts Bay, where a fireboat waits for us. I hope the leatherback made it. I will feel sick to my soul if it drowned.

"I didn't know if you were off the plane or why I should bother you with it," I reply. "Some disturbed person who wanted to get a rise out of me and unfortunately succeeded. I hope it's nothing more than an ugly prank."

"You should have bothered me with it, because it could be interpreted as a threat. A threat to a government official. I'm surprised Benton wouldn't see it that way." Marino's remark is more of a probe, as if he's wondering as usual if Benton is vigilant about my safety or even a decent husband.

"Did Lucy also tell you where it was sent from? The IP?"

"Yeah, I'm aware. Maybe to make it look like it was one of us. Bryce, me, any of us who flew into Logan yesterday right about the time you got the e-mail. You need to ask who might want you to think that, who it might benefit if you don't feel you can trust those you're closest to."

He switches into the right lane to turn onto the Longfellow Bridge, with its central towers that are shaped like salt and pepper shakers, and I think of Lucy searching my office a little while ago. We merge into a long line of cars crossing the river into Beacon Hill, rush hour barely moving, traffic stretching across the water and onto Cambridge Street for as far as I can see. I recall what she said about someone in our own backyard, someone we know, and I imagine Marino and her talking about it, speculating and accusing. It doesn't take much to get her worked up and on the warpath.

"Look, it's no secret I don't have a good opinion of him. I mean, what the hell do we really know about him except he's Anna's nephew?" Marino then says, and I'm really not surprised this is what he's been waiting to confront me with. "Me and Lucy are worried about motives that might not occur to you. We were trying to figure out a connection, and there is one, with his father."

"A connection to what?"

"Maybe a connection to a lot of things. Including that e-mail sent from Logan. Including maybe the two of you having more going on between you than . . . I mean, it's pretty obvious you're under his spell. . . ."

"I wish you wouldn't plant ideas like this with Lucy or anyone else." I won't let him finish such an accusation about my relationship with Luke.

"His father's a big financial tycoon in Austria, right?"

"You really should be careful what you suggest to people."

"You just saw Guenter at Anna's funeral, right?" He won't stop pushing.

Guenter Zenner is Anna's only living sibling. I saw him briefly at her graveside service in Zentralfriedhof, a gaunt old man draped in a long, dark duster, leaning on a cane and immeasurably sad.

"Just so happens one of the things he's into is oil trading," Marino continues, as we crawl across the bridge, the low sun directly in our faces and as bright as the light from a burning lens.

"Lucy found this out?"

"What matters is it's true," he says. "And that pipeline from Alberta to Texas is a huge deal to oil traders. They're counting on it, have huge investments and stand to make millions, maybe billions."

"Do you have any idea how many oil traders there are in the world?" I remind him.

This had to come from Lucy, and I imagine her finding out about Marino staying at the CFC last night because at some point she looked for him. Maybe she went there to talk to him and discovered him drinking and napping on the AeroBed, I don't know, and I reconstruct what happened after I received the anonymous e-mail at 6:30 p.m.

Benton and I spent some time discussing it before I called the Grande Prairie police and next was directed to an Investigator Glenn with the Royal Canadian Mounted Police, who has been working the Emma Shubert case since she disappeared in August. What struck me most was the hesitation I sensed and what it implied, and I mentioned something about it to Lucy when we discussed the e-mail over the phone.

Dr. Shubert was skilled in reconstructing dino skeletons, Investigator Glenn said to me, and he was intimating that anyone who knows how to make molds and anatomically exact casts of bones in a lab might be capable of other types of fabrications, including a severed ear.

"The pipeline's really important to global oil prices," Marino continues, spinning his web, a web he intends to ensnare Luke Zenner in.

"I'm sure it is," I reply.

"A multitrillion-dollar business venture."

"That wouldn't surprise me."

"So how do you know for a fact there's no link?" He glances over at me as he drives.

"Please explain how Guenter Zenner's trading in oil among many other commodities, I can only imagine, would have something to do with Emma Shubert disappearing and my getting the e-mail?" I put it bluntly.

"Maybe she disappeared because she wanted to. Maybe she's in collusion with people who have big money. The picture of the ear, the video are sent to you so we assume she's dead."

"You're basing this on nothing."

"No matter what, you'll stick up for him," Marino says. "That's what worries Lucy and me."

"Did the two of you stay up all night trying to force these

pieces to fit into some puzzle you've devised? You really do want me to get rid of him that badly?"

"All I'm asking is you try to be objective, Doc," Marino says. "As hard as that is in this situation."

"I always do my best to be objective," I reply calmly. "I recommend the same to you, to everyone."

"I know how close you were to Anna, and I really liked her, too. Back in our Richmond days she was one of the few people I was glad as hell you trusted and spent time with."

As if Marino picks my friends for me.

"But her family's got a shady past, and I hate to remind you of that fact," he adds.

"The Zenner family home was occupied by Nazis during the war." I know exactly what he's getting at. "That doesn't make Anna or her family, including Luke, *shady*."

"Well, the blond hair, the blue eyes. He sure as hell fits the part."

"Don't say things like that, please."

"When you look the other way you're just as guilty as the sons of bitches that do it," he says. "Nazis lived in the Zenners' ritzy castle while thousands of people were being tortured and murdered right down the road, and Anna's family didn't do shit."

"What should they have done?"

"I don't know," Marino says.

"A mother, a father, three young daughters, and a son?"

"I don't know. But they should have done something."

"Should have done what? It's a miracle they weren't murdered, too."

"Maybe I'd rather be murdered than go along with it."

"Being held hostage in your own home by soldiers who are raping your daughters, and God only knows what they did to the little boy, doesn't exactly mean you're going along with it." I remember Anna telling me her terrible truths, the wind gusting fiercely and flinging dead branches and brittle brown vines across her backyard as I sat in a carved rocker and felt fear pressing me from all sides.

I could barely breathe as she told me about the *schloss* that had been in the family for centuries, near Linz, on the Danube

River. Day in and out, clouds of death from the crematorium stained the horizon above the town of Mauthausen, where there was a deep crater in the earth, a granite quarry worked by thousands of prisoners. Jews, Spanish Republicans, Russians, homosexuals.

"You don't know where Guenter Zenner got all his money," I hear Marino say, as I look out at a bright morning and am dark inside, reminded of nights in Richmond at Anna's house during one of the most harrowing periods of my life. "Fact is, Guenter was already rich before he went into banking. Him and Anna inherited a shitload of money from their father, who had Nazis living in the family castle. The Zenners got rich off Jewish money and granite quarries, one of them a concentration camp so close they could see the smoke rising from the ovens."

"These are terrible accusations," I say to him, as I stare out my window.

"What's terrible is what Luke reminds you of," Marino says. "A time you don't need to be dwelling on now that things are good. Why the hell do you want a reminder of those old days when everything was fucked up and you were blaming yourself for Benton being dead or at least thinking he was, blaming yourself for everything, including Lucy? She doesn't want it, either. She doesn't want you getting all hung up again about her and how it's somehow your fault."

"I wasn't thinking about such things," I reply, but now I will, since he's managed to remind me.

Lucy's early days at the FBI's Engineering Research Facility in Quantico have not been foremost on my mind for a very long time, but he has conjured up the Lucy from back then and the reminder isn't a happy one. A troubled teenager whose computer skills were savant-esque, she almost single-handedly created the FBI's Criminal Artificial Intelligence Network, CAIN, while falling in love with a psychopath who nearly destroyed all of us.

I got her that FBI internship, I remember saying bitterly to Anna as we sat in her living room close to the fire with the lights out because I've always found it easier to talk in the dark. *I did. Me, her influential, powerful aunt.*

Didn't quite lead to what you intended, did it?

Carrie used her. . . .

Made Lucy gay?

You don't make people gay, I said, and Anna the psychiatrist abruptly got up, the firelight moving on her proud fine face, and she walked away, as if she had another appointment.

"I know you don't want to hear it." Marino keeps talking. "But I'm going to point out that you hired Luke in early July and this dinosaur lady disappeared barely six weeks later from the very area where they're extracting the oil his father's invested in."

The entire region of northwest Canada is dependent on natural gas and oil production, he says, and if the completion of that pipeline gets blocked, Luke's father probably stands to lose a fortune—a fortune that would be inherited by Luke.

"All of it," Marino says. "He's the only one left. And we know the e-mail with the cut-off ear and maybe Emma Shubert in the jetboat was sent to you from Boston, from Logan. Where the hell was Luke yesterday at six-thirty p.m.?"

"How would Emma Shubert's disappearance relate to the pipeline being further delayed or blocked?" I ask him. "Explain how what you're suggesting makes sense at all or is anything more than wild theorizing. Because in my mind if it turns out that she's been murdered and it's connected to the pipeline, that will only outrage the detractors, the environmentalists more. It certainly can't improve public sentiment if the brutal death of a paleontologist is connected with it."

"Maybe that's the point," he says. "Like those investors who bet against the housing market and made a killing because it collapsed."

"Good God, Marino."

He is quiet for a moment.

"Look. I realize I've not always made the best choices in staff." I'll give him that, because it's beyond dispute, and I resist pointing out there are those who would say that my hiring him is a prime example. "I don't always have the best judgment about people closest to me." Including Pete Marino, but I will never say it to him.

When we first met more than two decades ago he was a homicide detective in Richmond, a recent transplant from the NYPD to the former Capital of the Confederacy, where I had been installed as Virginia's new chief medical examiner, the first woman ever appointed to that position. Marino went out of his way to be a bigoted ass at the onset of our working lives together, and there have been betrayals since. But I keep him and would choose no one over him because I'm loyal and I care and he's just as good as he is bad. We're an unlikely pair and probably always will be.

"I couldn't be more aware that whoever I choose impacts everyone," I add in the same calm voice, as I do my best to be patient with his insecurities and fears and to remind myself I'm far from perfect. "But please don't assume that if I know someone personally it somehow obviates any possibility of him being a good employee or even a civilized human being."

"That was something when the Bruins won the Stanley Cup." It's Marino's way of ending a conversation that no longer furthers his agenda. "Wonder if it will happen again in my lifetime."

The TD Garden, or the Garden, as the locals refer to the arena, looms ahead of us on the left, and on Commercial Street, the Coast Guard base is only minutes away.

"I've seen a couple of them around here out with their wives, walking their dogs. Really nice guys, not snooty or nothing," Marino says, and up ahead at the intersection a Boston cop is directing traffic.

"I think there's a funeral." I notice black hearses and orange traffic cones across from the ice-skating rink.

"Okay. We'll hang a right here and cut through on Hanover." He begins to do it as he says it. "I tweeted a couple of them, but they're not going to answer when you're anonymous and can't even use your own photo for your avatar."

"They might not do it, anyway, I'm sorry to tell you."

"Yeah, I guess when you got fifty thousand people following you. I only got one hundred and twenty-two," he says.

"That's quite a lot of friends to have."

"Hell, I don't got a clue who they are," he says. "They think I'm Jeff Bridges or whatever. You know, the movie. Tons of bowlers love that movie. Sort of a cult thing."

"So you're following strangers and they're following you."

"Yeah, I know how it sounds, and you're right. No question I'd have a lot more followers and more people would tweet me back if I could be myself instead of in disguise," he says.

"Why is it so important to you?" I look at him as he drives slowly past the Italian restaurants and bars of the North End, where the sidewalks are busy as this hour but very little is open except coffee and pastry shops.

"You know, Doc? You get to a point when you want to see where you fit in, that's all," he says. "Like the tree falling in the forest."

His big face is pensive, and in the sun shining hotly through the windshield I can see the brown spots on the tops of his muscular tan hands and the fine lines in his weathered cheeks and the heavy folds around his mouth and that his close-shaven beard is white like sand. I remember when he still had hair to comb over, when he was a star detective and was always showing up at dinnertime in his pickup truck. We've been together since it all began.

"Explain the tree and the forest," I say to him.

"If it fell, would there be anybody to hear it?" he ponders, as we bump over pavers along a side street as narrow as an alleyway.

At the end of it I can see Battery Wharf and the inner harbor, and on the other side of it, the distant brick buildings of East Boston.

"I believe the question is, if there were nobody to hear it, would it make a sound?" I tell him. "You always manage to make a lot of noise, Marino, and all of us hear it. I don't think you've got anything to worry about."

seven

THE WIND GUSTS SHARPLY OUT OF THE NORTHEAST,
pushing water in swells, and where the harbor is shallow it is
green, and farther out a dusky blue. From my seat to the left of
the pilot coxswain, who is chiseled and young, with ink-black
hair, I watch seagulls lift and dive around the pier while Marino continues to be ridiculous.

He is combative and loud, as if it makes any sense to declare
war on a five-point harness because its sub-strap and large rotary buckle of necessity must lodge snugly between one's legs.
The life vest he has on makes him look bigger than his more
than six-foot frame, and he seems to fill half the cabin as he
resists the assistance of a boatswain I know only as Kletty, having met this crew for the first time but a few moments ago.

"I can do it myself," Marino says rudely, and it isn't true that
he can do it himself.

He's been fussing with the straps, trying to defeat the buckle
as if it is a Chinese puzzle, making a lot of impatient clicking
and snapping noises as he turns the rotary and attempts to force
metal links into the wrong slots, and I can't help but wonder
what Bryce said, exactly, when he called the Coast Guard a
little while ago.

What persuasion of his resulted in the vessel we're on?

Typically a 900-horsepower 33-foot Defender with shock-mitigating seats that restrain us like fighter pilots isn't necessary for what we do. One doesn't need maneuverability or high rates of speed when there are no arrests or rescues, and then I recall snippets of what my chief of staff was describing over the phone, painting a morbid scenario about putrid human remains and hosing off the deck and double pouching. Better to be on a bigger boat with an enclosed cabin so we can rocket back to shore with our antisocial cargo, I suppose.

"It's tricky," says the boatswain named Kletty, as he finishes strapping Marino into the seat behind me.

"Don't need it."

"You do, sir."

"Sure as hell don't."

"Sorry, but we can't go anywhere if everyone's not strapped in."

Then the boatswain checks my harness, which is fastened correctly, the sub-strap and rotary buckle wedged where they belong.

"Looks like you've done this before," he says to me, and I sense he might be flirting, or maybe he simply is relieved that I'm not going to give him an argument about Homeland Security protocols.

"I'm all set," I reply, and he takes a seat next to the red-headed machinist mate, whose name I think is Sullivan, the three members of the crew friendly enough and quite compelling in navy blue fatigues and caps and blaze-orange life vests.

When so many young men I come across are very nice to look at, it reminds me I'm getting old or acting as if I'm getting old or feeling like a de facto mother, and I try to resist staring at the pilot, who looks like an Armani model. He notices me looking and flashes a smile as if we are on a leisurely cruise that involves nothing awful or dead.

"Sector one-one-niner-oh-seven under way. GAR score one-two," he radios the watch standard command center that the Green-Amber-Red risk assessment for this mission is at the moment low.

Visibility is good, the water relatively calm, the three-member team on board well qualified to transport a forensic radiologic pathologist and her grumpy lead investigator to a location amid islands and hazardous shoals in the south channel, where several hours ago a dead body and an almost extinct species of sea turtle were discovered intertwined in tangles of rope weighted down possibly by a conch pot.

"Coming up!"

A push of the throttle, and within minutes we are going thirty-six knots and climbing. The high-performance boat slices through the water, blue lights strobing, frothy white wake curling on either side of the bow, where a weapons post is lonely for its M240. Long guns and machine guns weren't part of the checklist, as interdictions and violent confrontations aren't anticipated. Other than the .40-caliber Sigs the crew members have strapped to their sides, there are no firearms on board that I'm aware of, unless Marino is packing a pistol in an ankle holster.

I glance at the cuffs of his khaki cargo pants, at his big booted feet, and see no hint of a weapon as he continues to complain, staring down at the hockey puck–looking buckle wedged snugly in his crotch.

"Leave it alone." I raise my voice above the loud rumble of outboard engines, turned in my seat so I can talk to him.

"But why does this thing have to be right here?" He places his hand protectively between the buckle and his "privates," as he calls them.

"The straps have to be routed so they restrain the body's hard points." I sound like a stuffy scientist making a sophomoric pun and am conscious of the handsome pilot, who was introduced as Giorgio Labella, and I can't forget a name when it belongs to someone who looks like that. I feel his large, dark eyes glancing at me as I talk. I feel them on the back of my neck as if a warm tongue has touched me there.

Technically, I've never cheated on my husband, Benton Wesley, to whom I've been devoted for the better part of twenty years. It doesn't count that I cheated with him when he was married to someone else, because that's different from cheating on him. It doesn't count that I was briefly involved with an ATF agent assigned to Interpol in France when Benton was in a federal witness protection program and presumed dead.

Any involvements before Benton or after I believed he was no longer alive are irrelevant, and I rarely think of those individuals, including a few I will never make confessions about, as the consequences would be unnecessarily damaging to all involved. I behave myself, but it doesn't mean I'm not interested. Being faithful to my commitments doesn't mean thoughts don't cross my mind or that I'm foolish enough to believe I'm not capable. As a somewhat isolated professional woman in a mostly male world, I've never lacked opportunities to cheat, even now that I'm not in my thirties anymore and could be someone's de facto mother.

To the young men I encounter in the line of duty I'm ripe fruit and cheese served on a formidable platter, I suppose. A cluster of red grapes and figs with a soft Taleggio on a plate featuring a distinguished coat of arms, perhaps, or a trophy, as Benton suggested. I am a chief. I am a director. I have a special reservist rank of colonel in the Air Force and am important to the Pentagon. Power is the forbidden appetizer the Labellas want to sample, if I'm honest with myself, and Benton says I'm not. A trophy, I think. A not-so-young trophy, attractive to attractive people because of who and what I am.

It isn't really about the way I look or my personality, although I'm diplomatic, even charming when needed, and not as shopworn as I probably deserve to be, blond and strong-featured, my Italian bones a sturdy scaffolding that continues to hold me up through decades of hard times and near misses. I don't deserve to be slender and toned, and I often joke that a life spent exposed to formalin in windowless rooms and walk-in coolers has preserved me well.

"I really am taking this thing off." Marino continues staring down at the heavy hunk of plastic as if it is a bomb or a giant leech.

"The pelvic bone, the clavicles, the sternum. Hard points of the body that can sustain several thousand pounds of force." I sound as if I'm delivering an anatomy lecture, and I sense the crewmen listening. "How many seat belt injuries have you seen? Thousands," I reply above thundering outboard engines as I check my e-mail again. "Especially when the lap belt ends up around the abdomen instead of low around the hips, and in a collision what happens? All that force is directed at soft tissue and internal organs. That's why we wear harnesses like this."

"What are we going to run into out here? A fucking whale?" Marino exclaims.

"I certainly hope not."

We speed through a light chop, past long fingers of wharfs and piers that date back to Paul Revere as a British Air 777 roars low overhead, inbound for Logan to the east, its runways surrounded by water and barely above sea level. Off our starboard side Boston's financial district sparkles against the bright blue sky, and behind us, rising above the Navy Yard in Charlestown, the Bunker Hill memorial looks like a stony version of the Washington Monument.

"Let's just see," I say to Marino. "We're what? Maybe a quarter of a mile from the terminals?"

"Not even." He sits tightly strapped in his chair, staring through water-splashed Plexiglas.

The airport is sprawled over thousands of acres that jut out into the water, the air traffic control tower's windowed floors supported by two concrete columns that remind me of stilts. Two intersecting runways extend far out into the harbor, their stony embankments remarkably close, not even a hundred feet to our left, I estimate.

"Depends on where the LAN is located, of course," I add, as I go into settings on my iPhone and turn on Wi-Fi. "But I know for sure I've been stuck in planes on the runway before and accessed Logan's wireless. Nothing out here, though," I observe over the noise of engines and the boat bottom thudding the water. "Logan's signal has dropped off. So if the person sent the e-mail from a boat, for example, I'm going to suspect it was practically right up on the rocks, right up next to the runway."

"Maybe someone sent it from a boat that has a router," Marino suggests.

"Lucy is absolutely sure it was sent from an iPhone. But I suppose it could have been synced with a router, making it easier to access an unsecured network," I consider, as we pass the curved glass building of the federal courthouse and its public park at Fan Pier.

I check my e-mail again. Nothing, and I write another note to Dan Steward, letting him know I'm en route to a death scene and will have to take care of what I suspect will be a complicated autopsy when I return to the office. *Please confirm whether I need to show up at two p.m. as planned*, and I continue to hope my presence won't be required after all. I hope it rather desperately.

It's absolutely absurd, my being subpoenaed by Channing Lott's attorney, nothing more than harassment and an attempt to intimidate and humiliate, and of course I don't say that to Steward. I'll never again say much at all in e-mails or any written communication, and I dread what I imagine will be tomorrow's headline:

MEDICAL EXAMINER SAYS LOTT'S WIFE TURNED INTO SOAP

Last March on a late Sunday night, Mildred Lott vanished from their oceanfront mansion in Gloucester, some thirty miles north of here. Footage from infrared security cameras shows her opening a door and emerging from the house into the backyard at almost ten o'clock at night. It was very dark out, and she was in a bathrobe and slippers, walking toward the seawall while apparently talking to someone, I've been told. The security recording shows that she did not return to the house, and the next morning when her driver appeared to take her to an appointment, she did not answer the door or her phone. Walking around back, he discovered a door wide open and that the alarm system wasn't set.

Deleted e-mails recovered by the police revealed a cyber-train that led directly to Channing Lott, whose wife isn't my case. Her body hasn't been found, and the sole reason for my being summoned to court today is an electronic communication, one I didn't think twice about last spring, when Dan Steward wanted to know if a body were dumped off the coast of Gloucester that time of year, how long would it take to completely decompose and what would happen to the bones.

I replied that for a while the coldness of the water would actually preserve the body, although fish and other marine life would do some damage. I said it could take as long as a year for saponification, for the body to form adipocere, which is caused by the anaerobic bacterial hydrolysis of fat in tissue. In other words, I made the mistake of saying in my e-mail that a body underwater for a long period of time *rather much turns into soap*, and it is this comment that Channing Lott's lawyer wants to confront me with in court today.

"If I end up having to appear at two, it probably is a good idea if you're with me. I agree," I say to Marino, because I already know what's going to happen—that I won't get out of it. "Maybe Bryce should be with us. I worry there will be a lot of media."

"What an idiot," Marino says. "With all his money and he stiffs the hit man?"

"That's not why I've been subpoenaed or my point," I reply, somewhat impatiently.

"Some dirtbag he hires off the Internet, Craigslist, whatever, and he wonders why he got caught," Marino says.

"The point I'm making is the abuse of the judicial system," I reply. "A perverting of fairness."

We are past the seaport and the massive stone fortification Fort Independence, which protected Boston from the British in the War of 1812, swerving away from Deer Island, where waste-treatment plant sludge digesters look like eggs. The gray sandy shoreline of Hull curves around a harbor packed with small boats, and a graceful white windmill rises from the hills. I let Marino know he should be careful that the same fate doesn't befall him that has befallen me.

"It's a sobering reminder of what can happen," I say to him.

The defense wants me in court because Channing Lott wants me there, for no reason other than to force me into something, which Lott legally has the right to do. Any report generated by any forensic expert no longer speaks for itself unless both sides agree that the forensic scientist, the medical examiner, the scene investigator doesn't need to appear in person. While I understand the logic of the Supreme Court's decision that a document can't be cross-examined, only a human being can, what has occurred in the wake of the ruling is that overworked, underpaid experts are being abused and run ragged.

Any time we generate a document that might end up in court, one side or the other can demand we take the witness stand, even if the written words are nothing more than a voice-recognition text message or a handwritten note on a Post-it. As a result, some key members of my staff have begun ducking cases. If they dodge a crime scene or an autopsy or don't offer their expert opinion or even a glib remark, there's no chance they'll be subpoenaed, which is yet another reason why I don't like the idea that Marino is allowing the death investigator on call to go home so he can sleep over at the CFC.

"If one isn't careful," I'm saying to him, "one might find he never has time to do his work anymore. I'm being dragged to court today because of an e-mail I sent to Steward when he asked my opinion and nothing more. My opinion and an admittedly careless comment in an e-mail and it's all discoverable, every keystroke. And you wonder why I don't involve myself personally in Twitter and things like that. Anything can and will be used against you."

That's all I intend to say to him while we're on a Coast Guard boat with a crew who can hear every word. When the timing is right, Marino and I will have a conversation about *ornamenting* and whatever else is going on in his life that has resulted in his turning the CFC's investigative division into a Motel 6 because he can't or won't go home.

"Coming up!" our pilot, Labella, lets us know as he monitors the depth sounder, and other vessels hail over the radio.

The water opens into a fan-shaped expanse that is bordered by the north and south channels and their many islands, and we pass green channel markers on our right, the boat rising and falling, its thrust pushing me back in my chair.

"It's going to be a cluster fuck," Marino says, when the fireboat comes into view, its emergency lights flashing red, a news helicopter hovering overhead. "Who the hell alerted the media?"

"Scanners," says Labella, without turning around in his chair. "Reporters monitor our freqs out here on the water just like they do on land."

He announces he's bringing back the speed as we approach the *James S. Damrell*, a seventy-foot FireStorm with a flat-planed red-and-white hull and raked forward windshields, and bow- and roof-mounted fire guns. Surrounding it are a shark-gray police Zodiac, fishing and pleasure boats, and a tall ship with red sails furled, the cops and the curious, or maybe it is both, and I don't look forward to what I must do, especially when there is an audience. I think of the indignity of being dumped like garbage or lost at sea and being gawked at.

A liquefied natural-gas tanker painted parakeet green moves at a glacier's pace, giving the flashing fireboat a wide berth, and Labella steers us closer and cuts the engines to idle as I recognize the marine biologist from the photograph Marino showed me. Pamela Quick and half a dozen marine animal rescuers crowd the lower deck and the dive platform, attending to what looks like a primitive cross between a reptile and a bird, some evolutionary manifestation from the dinosaur age, when life as we know it began to exist on earth.

The leatherback is at least nine, possibly ten, feet in length, his throat puffing out unhappily, his powerful front flippers pinned to his black leathery sides with a yellow harness that crisscrosses his carapace like a straitjacket. Lashed to the back of the platform and rocking on the water is an inflated float bag with a wooden ramp on top that I assume was used to pull the monstrous creature on board.

"This is insane." Marino stares in disbelief. "Holy fucking shit!" he exclaims, as I get out of my seat.

eight

ENGINES THROB IN IDLE AS WE EXIT THE CABIN TO THE
deafening thud-thud of a helicopter so low overhead I can easily make out the TV station's tail number and the pilot in the
right seat. Sunlight is bright on the water, the sky perfectly
clear, but off to the northeast cumulus clouds roll in like a vast
herd of sheep and I feel the dropping barometric pressure and
the wind blowing harder. Later today it will be much cooler and
rain.

"Fifteen feet! Ten feet!" Sullivan and Kletty tie off fenders
to handrails, yelling distances to Labella as he uses the wind to
ease in portside, and we tie off.

"Let me get on first, and you guys hand stuff over," Marino
says, and he climbs aboard the fireboat, reaching back for the
scene cases.

Labella places the flat of his hand protectively against my
back and tells me to watch my fingers so they don't get crushed
between fenders or rails and to be careful where I step. The
space between the two boats yawns wider and narrows as he
steadies me over one rail, then the next, and I walk across
the fireboat's swaying bow, where a heavy steel anchor chain
feeds from a storage locker on the nonskid gray deck, running

between two red fire guns in the front of the boat and dropping straight down into the ruffled blue water.

Marino sets the cases near an aluminum ladder leading up to the wheelhouse, and from its deck Lieutenant Bud Klemens waves and seems happy to see me. He motions for me to climb up as spectators circle the fireboat like shorebirds, and Marino scowls at the helicopter hovering not even five hundred feet directly over us.

"Asshole!" He rudely flaps his arms as if he has the power to direct air traffic. "Hey!" he yells to the Coast Guard boat, to Kletty, who is stacking drysuits and other equipment inside a Stokes basket. "Can't you radio them or something? Make their asses get the hell out of here?"

"What?" Kletty yells back.

"They got to be scaring the shit out of the turtle, and they're gonna blow the hell out of everything with their damn rotor-wash!" Marino bellows. "They're too fucking low!"

He opens the scene cases, and I climb up to have a word with Klemens, the commander of the marine unit, which is stationed at Burroughs Wharf, not far from the Coast Guard base and the New England Aquarium. At the top of the ladder a second firefighter whose name I can't recall offers me his hand and I steady myself on the upper deck as it dips and rises in the heaving bay.

"It's only going to get rougher, I'm afraid," says the fireman, thickly built, with white hair clipped close to his scalp, a tattoo of a bear on his bulging left calf. "The sooner we get this done the better."

Both men wear summer uniforms of navy cargo shorts and T-shirts, their portable radios slung over their shoulders. On a strap around Klemens's neck is a remote steering station, what looks like a high-tech PlayStation console, that he can use from any area of the boat to steer its four jet engines when they're running.

"I'm Jack." The fireman with the bear tattoo reminds me we've met before. "The *Sweet Marita*, the trawler that burned up near Devils Back last year? A bad one."

"Yes, it was." A liquefied petroleum gas leak caused an explosion, and three people died. "How's it going?" I ask Klemens.

"Too much of a carnival for my taste," he says, and I do my best to ignore the uncanny sense of familiarity he always makes me feel.

Tall and rawboned, with sharp features, vivid blue eyes, and a mop of sandy hair, he looks exactly the way I imagine my father would have, had he lived to see his forties. When Klemens and I work cases together, I have to resist openly staring at him as if the most dominant figure from my childhood has come back from the dead.

"I'm afraid we're attracting quite a crowd, Doc, and I know you don't like that." Klemens looks up, shielding his eyes with his hand. "Not a damn thing I can do about it, but at least this jerk's backing off, so maybe we can hear again."

We watch the helicopter ascend vertically, leveling off at about a thousand feet, and I wonder if the Coast Guard radioed the television news pilot and told him to gain altitude immediately. Or do we have the fire department to thank for it?

"Much better," I agree. "But I wish it would buzz off."

"It won't." The fireman named Jack scans the water with field glasses. "One hell of a story. Like capturing Nessie, and the media doesn't even know the half of it yet."

"What does the media know, exactly?" I ask him.

"Well, they know we're out here, obviously, and the sooner we get this big boy back in the water, the better."

"Should be releasing him in a few, which is damn good, for a lot of reasons," Klemens says to me. "You can see how low we are."

The dive platform is level with the bay because of the weight of the turtle and the rescuers attending to it, water rolling around them as the boat lifts and settles on swells.

"Rated for twenty-five hundred pounds and maxed out, never seen anything like the size of this one," Klemens says. "We run into entanglements and strandings all the time, and it's almost always too late, but this one's got a real good chance. What a monster."

Klemens balances himself against the tender, a rigid-inflatable rescue RIB with a gray tube hull and a 60-horse-power engine. I note that on the other side and still under its red tarp is the A-frame and hydraulic winch that can be used to retrieve people or other deadweight from the water, including a monster turtle. Obviously the winch isn't what got this creature on board, I remark to Klemens, and I'm not surprised. Whether it's an eight-hundred-pound gray seal or a huge loggerhead or dolphin, marine rescuers won't run the risk of causing further injury and typically refuse the help of a winch.

"Anything that might cause the slightest transfer of trace evidence or artifacts." I remind Klemens I need to know everything that's been done.

"Well, I don't think the turtle killed anyone," he says, with mock seriousness.

"Probably not, but all the same."

"No machinery was used," he confirms. "Of course, my feeling about it is if we can sling human beings on board without hurting them, we sure as hell can do a turtle. But they did it their usual way, pulled him in close, harnessed him, got a ramp under him, and inflated the float bag. Then it took all of them and us to pull him on the platform. That was after they got his flippers restrained, obviously. He gets going with those things, he could tear the damn boat apart and knock a few of us into last year."

I direct his attention to a yellow boat fender. Not far from the boat, it's attached to a buoy line, and I ask if that was what the turtle was entangled with. I notice that nothing has been cleated off.

"Nope," he says. "Some kind of fishing gear, possibly snoods from a longline or a trolling line that got wrapped around his left-front flipper."

"He wasn't entangled with the same line the body is attached to?" I don't understand.

"Not directly. What he got wrapped up in was about fifty feet of monofilament lines, three of them, and wire leaders with rusty hooks. I'm guessing the rig got free of its fisherman float at some point, drifted on the current, and got snagged up with that buoy line."

He points to the one attached to the yellow boat fender.

"And then the turtle got snagged in the fishing line. But like I said, that's just a guess," Klemens says. "We won't know until everything's recovered, and I'm assuming it will be you doing that?"

"Yes. When we're done here and he's safely back in the water and out of range."

"Seems like he's got very minor injuries, so they won't be trying to transport him, not that they could have," Klemens says. "You'd need a flatbed truck, and he probably wouldn't have survived rehab anyway. There's never been a leatherback from around here that did. All they know is the open ocean, swimming from continent to continent. You put them in a tank and they just keep swimming into the side of it until they beat themselves to death. Pelagic creatures don't understand what a wall is. Kind of like my sixteen-year-old son."

I watch the rescue team in green Windbreakers and latex gloves, the leatherback puffing out his throat and making ominous sounds, whistling and clucking, and I scan the bright choppy water. I think about what I need to do. There must be at least a dozen boats around us now, people attracted by the strobing red lights and the stunning creature on board, and no telling what's already hit the Internet.

I don't want an audience when I recover the body, and I sure as hell don't want it filmed by smartphones and the media. What terrible timing for me to retrieve a dead body from water, and I think uncomfortably of Mildred Lott and my idiotic comment about her turning into soap.

"The blond girl there." Klemens nods at Dr. Pamela Quick. "She says he's the biggest one they've ever seen, maybe even the biggest on record, close to ten feet long and more than a ton, and could be a hundred years old. Take a good look, Doc, because you're not likely to ever see something like this again. They don't survive long enough to get this big anymore because of boat strikes and entanglements and ingesting trash like plastic bags and party balloons they confuse with jellies. It's just one more example of us wrecking the planet."

Two transom steps lead from the dive platform up to the recovery deck under us, which is crowded with four marine biologists, and piles of towels and sheets, and tough plastic cases, ski bags, and other field kits containing emergency drugs and rescue and medical equipment. From where I'm standing, downwind of the leatherback, I detect his briny smell and hear him scraping the platform as he strains against his yellow harness, his every movement slow and heavy and suggestive of enormous physical power. The loud blasts of his breaths remind me of air moving through a scuba regulator, and then his throat expands again and he emits a deep guttural roar that makes me think of lions and dragons and King Kong.

"You hear that behind you on a dark beach, it would be a heart attack," Klemens says.

"What else have they done so far?" I ask.

"Cut the lines off of him."

"I hope they saved them."

"I'm not sure what you could tell from them."

"You never know until you look," I reply.

"PIT tagged him right before you got here, and I can tell you he doesn't like needles," he adds.

Pamela Quick works a spinal needle deep into the neck for a blood draw, while a second rescuer, a young man with brown shaggy hair, reads a digital thermometer and announces, "Temp's up two degrees. He's starting to overheat."

"Let's get him covered and wet him down," Dr. Quick decides, and she glances up at me and for a moment we are eye to eye.

They drape the ridged carapace with a wet white sheet, and I recall her tone to me on the phone earlier, her adamant way of telling me what she needed to do. It was my distinct impression that she didn't believe she required my permission and didn't want my involvement, and now she just looked at me resentfully it seemed, as if I have something personal with her that I know nothing about.

She squeezes ultrasound gel on the turtle's neck, moving around a handheld Doppler probe with a built-in loudspeaker to monitor the heart rate. The sound of the massive reptile's blood flowing is like the roaring of a river or a rushing wind.

"Normosol to replenish his electrolytes." She tears open the packet of a solution set, a twenty-gauge needle attached to an IV line. "Ten drops per one mil. He's stressed."

"Well, I would be, too. He's probably never been around humans before," Klemens observes, and I'm aware of the weird familiarity I feel that isn't about him.

A sad curiosity runs through me like a low-voltage current,

then is gone, and I imagine my father seeing such a marvel. Sometimes I wonder what he'd think of the person I've become.

"They say a turtle like this one's been on land only once in his life. Right after he was hatched on some beach halfway around the world and crawled across the sand and into the water. And he's been swimming ever since." Klemens talks expressively with his hands the way my father did until he was too weak from cancer to lift them from the bed. "So he's not happy resting on top of something, in this case, the platform. Not to be crude about it, but the only other time he's got something under him is when he mates. What do you want to do about her?"

He looks at the heaving water where the large yellow sausage fender bobs, which strikes me as quite odd, and I say so.

"You think it's attached to a conch pot or cinder blocks?" I point out. "Why?"

"When they were pulling the buoy line close with the grappler to cut the fishing line and get the turtle on board?" he says. "For a couple of minutes the body was at the surface. Her head was."

"Jesus. I hope we're not going to see that on TV." I look up at a second helicopter that has moved in, hovering directly over us, a white twin-engine, with what appears to be a gyrostabilized camera system mounted on the nose.

"I think all they're interested in is the turtle and got no clue what else is on the line." He follows my gaze up. "The first chopper got here just as we were pulling him on board, so I don't think they filmed the body or know about it. At least not yet."

"And what's gone out over the radio?" I ask.

"Not a distress call, for obvious reasons." He means any calls about the dead body didn't go out over the usual channels that might be monitored by mariners and the media.

"Did anybody touch it with the grappler or disturb it in any way?"

"Nobody got anywhere near it, and we recorded the whole thing with our onboard cameras, Doc. So you got that if you need proof in court."

"Perfect," I tell him.

"When the body was just at the surface you could barely

make out the shape of a wire mesh pot about four foot square, I'm guessing." He continues staring at the sausage buoy, as if he can still see the pot he's describing. "It's attached by maybe twenty, thirty feet of rope and obviously has something in it that's heavy as hell. Rocks, cinder blocks, I couldn't tell."

"And the body's tethered to this line? We're sure it still is? We're sure there's no way it got loose when they were pulling the turtle in and cutting him free?"

"I don't think it's possible that poor lady's going anywhere. Tied around the lower part, possibly the legs, the ankles." He stares at the yellow bumper moving brightly on the water and the yellow line dropping taut and straight below it, disappearing into the dark blue bay. "An older woman with white hair is what it looked like to me, and then when they got the turtle cut free, she dropped below the surface again, the weighted conch pot pulling her back down."

"She's tethered to the buoy line, which is tied around her legs, possibly? Yet she's upright?" I'm having a hard time envisioning what he's describing.

"Don't know."

"If her head appeared first, she's upright."

"Well, she definitely was headfirst," he says.

"If the conch pot, the body, and the buoy are all part of the same line or rig, I find that very curious," I insist. "It's contradictory. One is pulling her down while the other is pulling her up."

"I've got everything on video if you want to duck into the wheelhouse and take a look."

"If you could get me a copy, I'd really appreciate it," I reply. "What I need to do now is to take a look at the turtle."

It isn't mere curiosity on my part. From where we are on the upper deck I can see a wound near the leatherback's black-and-grayish-white mottled neck, on a ridge at the upper edge of its carapace, an area of bright pink abrasion that Pamela Quick is wiping with Betadine pads.

"I'll leave the body in the water until I'm ready to recover it and transport it to shore," I tell Klemens, as Marino climbs up the ladder with white Tyvek coveralls, boot covers, and gloves. "The longer it stays cold the better," I add. "I'm certainly no aficionado of fishing tackle," I then say, as I take off my down jacket, "but why would someone pick a boat bumper as opposed to fishing floats for a conch or lobster pot?"

"These watermen are like magpies and collect all sorts of things," Klemens says.

"We don't know that a waterman has anything to do with this," I remind him.

"Detergent and soda pop," he continues, "and Clorox bottles, Styrofoam, bumpers that come loose from docks, anything you can think of that will float and is easy to find, not to mention cheap or, better yet, free. But you're right. That's assuming this has anything to do with fishing."

"It doesn't have a damn thing to do with fishing," Marino says bluntly.

"More likely, the point was to use a line with a lot of weight and dump her overboard," Klemens agrees.

"You wouldn't use a float of any type if that's what you were up to." Marino has no doubt about it as we suit up in protective clothing. "You sure as hell wouldn't attach a big yellow bumper unless maybe you wanted her to be found damn fast."

"And hopefully she has been," I comment, because the better shape the body is in, the better chance I have of finding out what I need to know.

"Using a bumper or float at all? I agree. I think someone wants her found," asserts the firefighter named Jack. "And I bowled against you before," he says to Marino. "You're not half bad."

"Don't remember you, and I would if you were half decent."

"The Firing Pins. Right?"

"That's us. Oh, yeah, now I'm remembering. You're the Shootin' Blanks." Marino picks on him.

"Naw."

"Could've sworn it."

"You mind I ask why?" Klemens watches me pull on heavy-duty black nitrile gloves. "How come you're treating my fireboat like a crime scene?"

"He's part of one." I mean the turtle is, and that I intend to handle him like evidence.

nine

WORKING SHOE COVERS OVER MY BOOTS, I CLIMB DOWN the ladder while Marino and Jack continue to banter.

I pick my way around equipment and rescuers, the deck heaving slowly in the swelling surf, waves breaking over the edge of the dive platform and rushing around my feet. The beating of helicopter blades is distant but relentless, and I feel the coldness of the water through my Tyvek-covered boots as I move close to Pamela Quick, who is completely preoccupied and in no mood for my company.

In her mid- to late thirties, I estimate, she is pretty in an off-putting way, with wide gray eyes, a square chin, and hard-set mouth, her long pale blond hair tied back and under a cap. She's surprisingly small and delicate for the large creatures she routinely handles, and as steady as a professional surfer on the rocking platform, emptying a syringe into a green-top Vacutainer tube that has the additive heparin to prevent blood from clotting.

"I'm Dr. Scarpetta." I remind her we talked briefly on the phone earlier today. "I need to get some basic information and take a look, and then I'll be out of your way."

"I can't permit you to examine him." She is as brisk and chilly as the water and the wind. "He's stressed enough as is, and that's the number one danger right now. Stressing him."

She says it with emphasis, as if I might be the source of it. "These animals aren't used to being out of the water and touched by humans. Stress will kill them. I'll send you my report, and that should answer any questions you have."

"I understand, and later I'd certainly appreciate a copy of your report," I reply. "But it's important I know anything you can tell me now."

She withdraws the needle from the rubber top and says, "Water temp is fifty-one degrees Fahrenheit, the ambient temp fifty-seven."

"What can you tell me about him?" I have no choice but to be insistent.

"About him?" She glances up at me as if I have just offended her. "Not exactly relevant for your purposes."

"At the moment, I consider everything relevant. He may be part of a crime scene."

"He's a critically endangered turtle who almost died because of reckless, careless human beings."

"And I'm not one of those reckless, careless human beings." I understand her hostility. "I want him to thrive as much as you do."

She glances up at me condescendingly, angrily.

"Let's do this," I then say. "Tell me what you know."

She doesn't reply.

"I'm not the one wasting time," I add pointedly.

"HR thirty-six, RR is two. Both times by Doppler," she says. "Cloacal temp is seventy-four degrees." She drips blood into a white plastic i-STAT cartridge.

"Is it unusual that his body temperature is some twenty-five degrees higher than the water he was in?"

"Leatherbacks are gigantothermic."

"Meaning they can maintain a core temperature independently of the environmental temperature," I reply. "That's rather remarkable, and not what I'd expect."

"Like the dinosaurs, they can survive in waters as warm as the tropics or cold enough to kill a human in minutes."

"Certainly defies what I understand about reptiles." I squat near her as the boat sways back and forth and water laps.

"Reptilian physiology is unable to explain the biology of dinosaurs."

"You're not really calling this a dinosaur?" I'm baffled and strangely unsettled, considering how my day began.

"A gigantic reptile that has been here for more than sixty-five million years, the earth's last living dinosaur." She continues to act as if I'm to blame. "And like the dinosaur is about to become extinct."

She inserts the cartridge into a handheld blood analyzer while frigid water splashes over the platform and soaks the cuffs of my coveralls and begins to wick up the legs of my pants underneath.

"Fishing gear, ignorant people digging up their eggs, illegal poaching, speedboats, oil spills, and plastic pollution," she continues, with undisguised disgust. "At least one-third of all leatherbacks have plastic in their stomachs. And they don't do one damn thing to us. All they want to do is swim, eat jellies, and reproduce."

The leatherback slowly lifts his watermelon-sized head and looks directly at me as if to emphasize his caretaker's point. Nares flare as he exhales loudly, his protruding eyes dark pools on either side of a beaklike mouth that reminds me of a crooked jack-o'-lantern smile.

"I understand the way you feel better than you'll ever imagine, and I'm eager to get out of your way," I say to Pamela Quick. "But I have to know about his injuries before I can finish up here."

"Moderate abrasions circumferentially around the skin-carapace line of left distal shoulder extending about three centimeters on distal posterior margin of the left-front flipper," she describes with steely affect. "Associated with an abraded area of the distal leading edge." She reads the blood test results on the digital display.

"And his values?" I ask.

"Typical for entangled leatherbacks. Mild hypernatremia, but he should be fine. Until he encounters some other human detritus or a boat that kills him."

"I can understand how you feel about it. . . ."

"You really can't," she says.

"I need to ask if you saved the fishing gear."

"You can have it." She reaches inside a ski bag.

"Based on your expertise, can you reconstruct what happened?"

"Same thing that always does to these animals," she replies. "They run into a vertical line, freak out and start spinning around, and get wrapped up in it. The more they struggle, the worse it gets, and in his case, he was dragging a heavy pot and a body for God knows how far."

"And dragging the buoy."

"Yes. Dragging that, too." She hands me a transparent plastic bag that contains tangled monofilament, several leads, and rusty hooks.

"What makes you assume the body and pot were dragged? It seems you're assuming they weren't originally where they are now. Any reason to suppose he might have gotten entangled here, where he was found?" I label the bag with a permanent marker.

"Leatherbacks are in perpetual motion," she answers. "The monofilament probably was entangled with the buoy line. What we do know for a fact is he hit the fishing lines, and his left flipper got wound up, but he's programmed to keep swimming. The more he swam, the tighter the lines wrapped around him, it would seem. By the time we got to him, he could barely move his left flipper, and he was going under."

"Any estimate of distance based on how fast leatherbacks can swim?" I ask.

"We could have this conversation later." She barely looks up at me.

"Any information I can get now is really important," I say firmly. "It could help us determine where the body might have entered the water."

"That person is gone. He's not."

"This could be a homicide investigation. I don't think anyone wants to interfere with that."

"All I can tell you is the top speed for a leatherback is about twenty miles per hour," she replies flatly, "but no way he was going anything close to that dragging what was attached to him. It's not possible to say where he might have run into the line except that I'm thinking he didn't get very far after he did. Maybe a few miles at most, until he was running out of steam and getting pulled down by his load, barely able to keep his head above water."

"It's not likely he got entangled in the open ocean." I scan the horizon, the outer harbor separated from the open Atlantic Ocean by some sixty-five miles of bays, peninsulas, and islands. "It's too far from here."

"Absolutely no way," she agrees. "I'm estimating hours, not even a day, based on his injuries and what good shape he's in. There's nothing wrong with him that saltwater won't heal. Just moderate abrasions to this one flipper, a mild abrasion to the dorsal head, as you can see. Don't confuse the pink spot."

Her latex-gloved hand pats a pinkish splotch on the top of his dark mottled head, and she seems to have relaxed a little, to find me not quite as objectionable.

"Each leatherback has a unique fingerprint," she explains. "We actually can ID one of these by the spot on its head; not sure what it's for, but maybe a sensor of sorts that detects light or helps the animal determine its location in the ocean."

"Let me look at his injuries. And then I promise I'll get out of your way."

She pulls back the wet sheet from his neck, and I can smell his clean fishy smell as I get close to him, just inches from his restrained left flipper, which is at least six feet long. Then I smell the strong ammonia of urine.

"That's a good thing." She obviously smells it, too. "The more alert and active, the better. We want all-systems-go. Like I said, nothing all that serious. The worst offender is this. Part of a barnacle that's embedded in this ridge right here. I was about to extract it."

She shows me a fragment of what looks like white shell or white glass that she assumes was driven into the carapace close to his neck, where the leathery skin is inflamed and abraded.

"You're thinking he struck something that had barnacles on it," I infer.

"I'm thinking something with barnacles on it struck him," she replies, and already I'm not sure I agree with her, as I notice a scattering of clamlike barnacles that have colonized on the rubbery outer skin of the turtle's exposed carapace. "While he was entangled in the line and dragging all that weight, maybe a boat grazed him or he knocked into a channel buoy, a piling, a rock, who knows what. Something, at any rate, that has barnacles attached. Normally I would collect this and preserve it in formalin."

"It's better if I do it."

She seems reluctant and starts to protest.

"Really," I insist.

She falls silent, and I motion for Marino to bring a scene case to me, the Pelican 1620, I let him know, and I assure Pamela Quick I will collect the necessary evidence in a manner that does no harm to the turtle and do so as expeditiously as possible. I tear open a packet of disposable forceps and am surprised by the smooth, cool surface of the carapace, what feels like polished stone or an oily hard cured leather.

The dense texture of the flipper is unlike anything I've ever touched, maybe similar to ballistic gelatin, and I bend close, wearing a binocular magnifier, dual 3.5X acrylic lenses in a lightweight eyeglass frame so my hands are free. I feel the tension of life and struggle and hear the blasts of his breaths and am aware of his power, were he to break his restraints, his flippers as dangerous as whale flukes. His scissorlike jaws look capable of crushing or amputating a limb, were he to clamp hold of it.

In the magnification of the lenses, the protruding white shell is pearlescent and clam-shaped, with a dark muscular stalk that I gently clamp into the tips of the plastic forceps while I gently rest my right hand on top of the turtle's huge head. It is as cool and smooth as petrified bone, and I feel him slowly, heavily stir. I'm constantly aware of where his jaws are in relation to me, and I hear the blasts of his respiration and feel the softness of his pink-tinted neck against my leg as he puffs up and emits a loud groan followed by a low growl.

"Now, don't be such a grumpy old man," I say to him. "No one's hurting you, and you're going to be fine."

I'm careful not to break or damage the barnacle as I work it out of the leathery skin, and then it is free and I move out of the way so Pamela Quick can attend to the wound, which isn't what I'd expect if the turtle was struck by something covered with barnacles and stabbed or punctured by a glasslike shell. She swabs the shallow wound with Betadine, and I place the barnacle in my gloved palm. I can see a trace amount of a sub-

stance on it, what looks like a hint of bright yellowish green
paint on the plate farthest from the stalk, just a faint swipe on
an edge of shell that is broken.

I imagine an object covered with barnacles coming into contact with the leatherback, the force of the impact sufficient to
drive the tip of the shell into the hard leathery ridge and unseat
or pry the barnacle from whatever it was cemented to. But the
transfer of paint or what might be paint doesn't fit with such a
scenario, and I envision the natural-gas tanker that passed us
less than an hour ago. A number of them I've seen are painted
garish colors, chartreuse and teal green, neon blue or orange.

"Something painted yellowish green," I ponder out loud, as
I place the barnacle into a small plastic evidence container.
"Not likely a rock or a piling. More likely he struck a boat, a Jet
Ski, or something like that struck him."

"A rather insignificant glancing blow, if that's the case," she
puzzles. "Certainly not the usual thing we see in a boat strike.
When these animals surface for air and get hit by a speeding
boat or a tanker, usually the damage is profound. He must have
been barely bumped by something, or he barely bumped into
something."

"With bright green paint?"

"I got no idea," she says.

I label the evidence container and feel the boat heave from
side to side, the surf getting heavier. The temperature is dropping, and I'm chilled by cold saltwater flowing around my feet,
my pants soaked up to my knees underneath white Tyvek.

"Well, if whatever he ran into or ran into him is a boat, for
example, that's a little curious," I continue, "since most are protected with an antifouling paint, some type of coating to prevent barnacles or other organisms from attaching to the hull."

"Ones that are properly maintained. Yes." She is terse again
and wants me gone.

"I suspect the barnacle was attached to the turtle and not to
whatever struck him," I conclude. "And paint or something
greenish yellow was transferred to part of the shell."

"Maybe," she says distractedly, and I can tell she doesn't
think it matters and is eager for me to leave her alone.

"We'll get this analyzed in the labs and see what it is," I add.

Marino takes photographs while I look over the leatherback

a final time, placing a gloved hand under his head to keep his bony jaws from opening when I'm close to them. I peel the soaked sheet back from his massive body, which unlike other turtles has no lower flat bony shell, the leatherback barrel-shaped and disproportionately wide around the shoulders and tapering off to short rear flippers and a long tail. I see nothing else that might be of forensic interest, and I let Pamela Quick know I don't intend to interfere with her patient a moment longer.

"Just tell me how you want to go about things, because I've got to go into the water," I say to her. "What I don't want is to go in at the same time he does, and I certainly don't want him running right back into the same line and getting tangled up again."

"You're doing your recovery from here? Or over there?" She indicates the Coast Guard boat.

I stand up and steady myself as the fireboat rocks harder. The wind is biting, and saltwater has soaked through my shoe covers and is seeping inside my boots. Of course I have no intention of recovering a dead body from a boat crowded with marine animal rescuers.

"I'll tell you what," I decide. "Marino and I will get back on board the Coast Guard boat and pull the buoy line in close to it so we can take care of what we need to do. And the minute we're off this boat I suggest you get Lieutenant Klemens to move some distance from here so you can release our leatherback friend out of harm's way."

I climb back up the transom steps and retrieve my coat from the upper deck while Marino collects the scene cases. Then we return to the bow.

"Nice to look at, but she sure as hell doesn't win any personality awards," he says.

"She's just trying to do her job and wants no interference," I reply. "You can't blame her."

"Yeah, except she doesn't give a shit someone's dead. Not even interested."

Marino looks back in Pamela Quick's direction as we remove gloves, shoe covers, and Tyvek, stuffing them into a red biohazard bag.

"Some of these animal lovers are like that, though," he says.

"Fanatics. Certified whackos who will throw red paint on you or beat you up for wearing a fur collar or snakeskin boots. I got me a pair of rattlesnake-skin boots, and you think I don't get a lot of shit when I wear them?"

He hands the cases over the rail to Labella as the two boats plunge together and apart like an accordion.

"Tanned rattlesnake skins bought off eBay and custom-made," Marino continues to gripe.

"Sounds disgusting." I swing one leg over the first rail, and Labella reaches for me.

"Well, don't wear them in fucking Concord or Lincoln, in *Thoreau*ville"—Marino is right behind me—"where you go to jail for cutting down a damn tree," he adds at the top of his lungs.

ten

AN AIR HORN BLARES THREE TIMES, AND THE FIREBOAT
backs away from where it was anchored, pivoting on its stern,
nosing toward a lighthouse jutting up whitely on the horizon.
Jet engines gush and churn foamy water that dissipates into a
lacy wake as firefighters move the leatherback and its rescuers
toward the open sea, leaving us to take care of the rest of it.

The task I face is one I hope the media and the curious don't
know about, and I survey the water heaving in the sunlight,
looking for any sign that spectators and TV crews will move on
to witness the turtle's release. I want everyone gone. I want
whoever is dead recovered discreetly, respectfully, and at the
same time I feel very protective of the huge old turtle and furious at human selfishness and ignorance.

Leave him alone, for God's sake, I think, and I could easily
worry myself sick about it, imagining any number of awful
fates that might befall an almost extinct creature that lives simply to eat and swim and breed. I know the stories of people who
motor too close to great whales and other magnificent animals,
taking pictures, trying to touch or feed them, and inadvertently
maim or kill them. I'm dismayed, then outraged, as I watch
boaters pull up anchor and start their engines, the news helicopter already pursuing in a high hover.

"At least they're not going to hang around here," Labella says.

He's crouched next to the Stokes basket, checking the restraint straps and the harness, making sure everything is functioning properly. What we don't need is to have the body tumble out back into the water while we're trying to hoist it on board the boat.

"Which tells me they don't know the reason we're here," he adds.

"Maybe they don't, but what do you make of that?" I look up at the white twin-engine helicopter a thousand feet above us, I estimate. "It seems to be hanging around."

"Not a news chopper." He stares up, shielding his eyes. "Not MedFlight. Not Boston or state police or Homeland Security. Maybe a Sikorsky, something big, but for sure not one of ours, so I'm guessing it's private. Someone who's out flying and maybe wonders what's going on down here."

"It's got a camera mounted on it." I get an uneasy feeling as I watch the gleaming white machine hover steady as a rock, the nose pointed at us, the sun glaring on the windscreen.

"Maybe a TV camera. But it could also be a FLIR," Labella says. "I can't tell from here."

The only private pilot I know who might have a Forward Looking Infrared Radar system thermal imager mounted on his or her helicopter is my niece, Lucy. But I don't mention such a possibility, and it bothers me that I haven't seen her new ship, a twin-engine Bell that was delivered to her barely a month ago. Lucy wouldn't have a white helicopter, I reassure myself. Black or shark gray, but not white with red and blue stripes festooning the tail boom, and I don't recognize the tail number on this one, either. I wonder if Marino has seen her new helicopter, but he seems oblivious, is busy with Sullivan and not paying any attention to what's thudding overhead.

"Well, it's disgusting and shouldn't be permitted." I'm back to being upset about the turtle, about the ugliness of human nature, as I watch rubberneckers motoring after the fireboat. "People have no respect or common sense. If some goddamn idiot runs over that leatherback after all he's been through . . ."

"It's illegal to hunt, harass, or injure sea turtles." Labella gets up, a drysuit folded under his arm. "How about a hundred-thousand-dollar fine."

"How about jail."

"I wouldn't want to get on the wrong side of you."

"Not today."

"What we're going to do is start up the engines so we can get within reach of the buoy line," he tells me, while Kletty attaches an aluminum dive ladder to the transom and Marino opens the scene cases again, talking loudly with Sullivan about motorcycles and how bad the roads are up here in the Northeast. "But obviously we can't be running while you're in the water."

"Thank you. I'm not fond of close encounters with props," I reply.

"Yes, ma'am. Roger that." Labella smiles, and I try to forget what he looks like and how it makes me feel.

Orange-and-black nylon rustles as he unfolds the drysuit and hands it to me, asking if I need help getting into it. I tell him no, thank you, and sit down on a bench to take off my wet boots and socks, tempted to remove my wet cargo pants and long-sleeved shirt. What would make the most sense is to strip to my underwear and put on a liner, but no way I'm going to do that on a boat that has no head and is full of men, and I'm aware of how self-conscious I suddenly am. Modesty is a luxury in a profession where one works in the worst conditions imaginable, including outdoor scenes with no toilet and encounters with putrid body fluids and maggots. I've cleaned up in gas-station sinks before and dressed in the back of a car or van, not caring who was around.

I'm conditioned to be stoical. I know how to be indifferent and impervious. I'm damned accustomed to male colleagues looking at me and thinking tits and ass, and it doesn't bother me or it didn't used to because I was able to be oblivious, to be single-minded about my mission.

It's not like me to be so damned focused on myself, and I don't like it one damn bit as I think of things that have nothing to do with my responsibility or legal jurisdiction or what unpleasantness might await me underwater. I'm aware of the recent comments Benton made, aware of Marino's irritating bluster as he talks loudly with Kletty and Sullivan, about boats now, and what a good idea it would be for the CFC to have one, and what an experienced captain he is.

Insecurity, or maybe it's hurt and anger, have thinned my skin, and I mentally run through what needs to be done and how it should be done. I map out strategies precisely while anticipating what could be both useful and harmful in court because I must always assume everything ends there.

"What about a liner?" I decide.

"I was going to suggest it." Labella doesn't add what I can tell he's thinking, which is there is no place on board to change in private.

"Let's do it." I get up from the bench.

Inside the cabin he opens a diamond steel–plated locker and starts pulling out gray Polartec liners, checking the sizes until he finds the smallest.

"Are you sure you don't want one of us to go in with you?" He pauses in the doorway, his dark eyes on me. "I'm happy to suit up. Any of us are. Living people can stink just as bad as the dead."

"They probably can't."

"Trust me. We can handle it."

I close the lid of the storage locker and sit on top of it and tell him no. It's not a good idea legally. I explain that the death obviously is suspicious and I'm working it like a homicide, and every exposure alters the case, complicates and compromises and potentially ruins it. It doesn't take much for a jury to let the guilty go free these days, and he says he couldn't agree more. He's followed plenty of such travesties on the news and hears complaints all the time about crime scenes destroyed by TV drama–addicted citizens who collect the evidence and investigate on their own, saving the cops the trouble. The *CSI* effect, he says. Everyone's an expert.

Everyone is, I agree wryly, and I will dance this dance alone, and it will be a dance I've danced before, plunging into a dark coldness where I can scarcely see, moving with the currents and following tethers to bring home the dead. I tell Labella to make sure all of them don Tyvek and gloves, and to cover a portion of the aft deck with plasticized sheets and to spread open two body pouches inside the Stokes basket. Marino has sheets and pouches, new ones that aren't contaminated, of course. I want nothing coming in contact with the body that could transfer any type of evidence to it, I instruct.

"Now, if you'll just give me a few minutes," I say to Labella. "Then you can come back in here and start the boat."

When he is out of the cabin, back on the stern with Kletty, Sullivan, and Marino, I take off my cargo pants and shirt, undressing hastily with my back to the door, pulling on the soft absorbent liner. The drysuit is front-entry, and I work my bare feet through the neoprene ankle cuffs and pull up the legs. Sliding my arms into the sleeves, I ease my hands and head through the wrist and neck gaskets, finally pulling the metal-tooth zipper diagonally across my chest.

I emerge from the cabin as Labella returns to start the engines, and I look up at the big white helicopter. It's still thud-thudding directly overhead.

"I don't like it," I comment loudly to no one in particular. "I hope to hell someone isn't filming." I think of Lucy again, but it can't be her.

She's off in Pennsylvania, rounding up rogue pig farmers, no doubt, and I ask Kletty and Sullivan for Gore-Tex dry socks and booties, and cold-water gloves, a dive knife, a hood, and a scuba mask. Buckling on a low-profile life vest with a quick-release chest harness, I stretch out the thin rubber gasket around my neck to purge air from the drysuit, to burp it, so air bubbles don't build up in the lower legs and upend me in the water. Labella eases the boat close to the bobbing yellow fender, cuts the engines again, and drifts while Marino reaches a long-handled aluminum gaff and dips the hook in, snagging the nylon line before I can stop him.

"No, no, no." I shake my head. "Don't pull it. That's not how we're going to bring it in. Not from the boat."

"You don't want me to hook it? Probably a lot easier and safer than jumping in. Maybe you won't need to."

"No," I reiterate. "I need to see what we're dealing with. The body's not budging until I see what we've got."

"Okay, whatever you say." He releases the line.

"We want to make sure nothing comes in contact with the

body." I spit in my mask to prevent it from fogging as he stows the gaff back in its holder. "Whatever damage it has, it won't be caused by us."

Kletty attaches a line to the rescue buckle on the back of my suit, between my shoulder blades, to keep me tethered, and I lower the dive mask over my eyes and nose and climb down the ladder, my neoprene booties feeling their way on the metal rungs. When the surf is up to my hips, I push away from the back of the boat, the drysuit suctioned to me as if I'm shrink-wrapped, and I swim toward the yellow fender.

I grab the buoy line in a gloved hand, the life vest keeping me afloat and balanced, and I submerge my masked face into the cold salty water and am startled by the body just below my feet. The dead woman is fully clothed and vertical, her arms and long white hair floating up, fanning and moving like something alive as she slowly tilts and turns in the current. I surface for air and dive again, and the way she's rigged is grotesque and sinister.

A rope around her neck is tied to the yellow fender on the surface, while a second rope around her ankles drops tautly down and disappears in the darkness, attached to something heavy. A torture device that creates extreme tension by pulling, stretching, and dislocating the neck, the joints, ripping the person apart? Or is the purpose something else? And I suspect it is. She was tied this way for our benefit, and I look up again at the helicopter still hovering, then I hold my breath and drop below the waves.

Sunlight filters through the surface, the water green and clear just below, then turning darker shades of blue that become murkier and as black as coal. I don't know how deep the bay is here, but whatever the rope around her ankles is attached to most likely isn't resting on the bottom, which could be thirty feet or more below the surface. The rope runs straight down, as if there is plenty of tension in it, and I lift my face out of the water. I take a deep breath and motion for Marino to get ready with the gaff.

"I can't do anything with her right here," I shout. "We're going to have to somehow get the entire rig to the boat without causing a lot of damage to her."

"What entire rig?" Marino asks. "Just move her and the buoy line at the same time. Can't you do that?"

"No," I reply. "What we've got to do is pull her abeam the boat, right up to the side of it, so we can cut her free without losing anything and get her in the basket."

I float on the rough surface, the drysuit clinging tightly to me, and I can feel the chill of the water through it.

"The problem's going to be cutting the rope around her ankles," I explain. "I don't want to lose what she's attached to, the conch pot or whatever it is."

I want it. There's not a chance I'm going to let it settle out of sight to the bottom of the bay. I will recover every damn thing in this case, whether it is a barnacle or a pot, cage, container, or cinder blocks. I ask how deep the water is, and Labella tells me forty-two feet, and I'm aware of the helicopter beating overhead. Someone is watching our every move and probably filming it, dammit.

"So the line attached to the conch pot may not be that long." I blow water out of my mouth, the waves splashing up my neck and over my chin. "It's pulling her down while another line pulls her up."

"What other line?" Marino shouts. "It's just one line, right?"

"What we've got are two lines pulling her in two directions," I emphasize. "The one tied to the fender is a separate line."

"You mean she's entangled with something else?" Kletty puzzles.

"No. I mean she's been tied to two lines," I repeat slowly, loudly. "One around her neck that's attached to the fender, and the other around her ankles that leads down to whatever she's weighted with, a conch pot or who knows what." I spew out water as I talk.

The life vest keeps me on the surface like a cork, but the chop is getting stiffer, the wind gusting sharply. I work against the current so it doesn't carry me farther away from the boat.

"So if you pull too hard her head's going to pop off," Marino says, with his usual diplomacy.

"She'll come apart if we're not really, really careful," I reply, and by now I'm certain that whoever orchestrated the dumping of the body booby-trapped it.

I've no doubt it was deliberate. The person responsible wanted her discovered and intended for someone like me to be in for a gory shock when the body was pulled apart like a wishbone. I can't imagine any other reason to tie her up this way, and I envision tugging hard on the buoy line the way Marino was about to do a few moments ago and inadvertently decapitating her. We would have recovered only her head or, more likely, no part of her at all.

We'd be forced to call in a dive team or to put on scuba gear ourselves and search the bottom of the bay, finding what we could, maybe nothing, until whatever was left surfaced and washed ashore. The fact is she might never have been found. I can only imagine how such a grisly scenario would play out in court, especially if it were caught on film by a television crew hovering over us in a helicopter. Such a scenario is unthinkable.

A jury would be repulsed, as if what happened was due to callous carelessness or complete incompetence on our part. I'm not sure anybody would understand that some diabolical individual has all but assured that this dead woman will not be recovered intact or possibly ever. Some malignant murderer wanted us to get a close look at his handiwork before it vanished right before our eyes, maybe wanted to make sure we never know who she is, and we might not if we don't safely get her body out of the water.

What to do? My thoughts race through different possibilities, but there really is only one that seems workable, and nothing we try is foolproof. We need to be patient and careful, and we need to be lucky.

"What if we cut the line around her neck?" Kletty suggests, and I notice that all of them are in white Tyvek, and what a strange sight that must be from the air. "Cut her free from the fender so nothing's pulling on her neck?" he suggests.

"I can't," I answer. "I can't guarantee I could hold her up. I'm afraid whatever's attached to the line around her ankles will pull her down and out of reach. We've got to somehow secure the line that's tied around her neck without doing damage to her." I say this to Marino as I tread against the current.

"You and I are going to have to ease her to the boat, do it perfectly in sync, and hope she holds together," I continue. "I'll move her close enough so you can hook the line with the gaff and get hold of it, but don't pull it. The point is to pull me, not her, and I'll swim her in, keeping the line around her neck as slack as I can. Get the basket rigged and down, and gently pull me, not her," I repeat, and I feel tension increase on the line between my shoulder blades.

They lower the Stokes basket, the bottom of it covered by two spread-open black body pouches, and I help guide the hook of the gaff until Marino has the buoy line. He coaxes it closer to the boat, reaching down to grab it, and her pale fingers with their painted nails suddenly are visible just below the surface. Her white hair floats up, and for an instant her face appears in the trough of a wave.

eleven

"EASY!" I EXCLAIM TO MARINO. "HOLD IT! HOLD IT! DON'T pull." I push my mask up. "Just hold the line and let me do the rest."

I smell her odor, moldy and foul, and I reach down to grab her under the arms, turning my back to the boat. I hold her firmly from behind.

"Keep her rope as slack as you can," I call out, and I dip my right shoulder under the yellow buoy line, taking on some of its tension so it's not pulling hard on her neck. "Bring me in very, very slowly as I swim with her. Pull me, not her."

I feel the tug at my upper back and can feel the weight of whatever the line around her ankles is attached to. She is cold, at least as cold as the sea, her skin wizened and hard. Her arms are relatively limber, but the rest of her is stiff from the cold, as stiff as she will get. Rigor mortis bypassed her weeks, possibly months, ago while she languished somewhere in storage, a place very dry and frigid.

When she begins to warm up there will be no postmortem artifacts forming to give me the usual hints about when and where she died and exactly what position she was in, because it is much too late for that. Whatever is present right now is as much as I will see, and she will rapidly go from being cold and well preserved to putrid.

Parchmentlike tallow scalp shows through her wet white hair, her ears and the tip of her nose discolored brown, and there's the slightest frost of patchy white mold on her face and neck. She's been dead long enough to begin mummifying, was kept somewhere quite a long while before she ended up underwater. I move her very slowly, the crown of her head under my chin, and I worry about her holding together as I keep the buoy line on top of my shoulder and feel it hard and rough against the side of my jaw.

I do anything I can to keep the fender from pulling on her, and it bobs in front of us like a fat yellow fish in lazy pursuit, and then we reach the Stokes basket rocking against the side of the boat and I maneuver both of us around, facing the men. I tell Marino to hold his line steady, to keep the body close to the surface, and I ask Sullivan and Kletty to slacken the ropes attached to the basket's harness and the back of my drysuit.

"I need to get the basket under her. She's got to be on the surface as much as we can manage so I can push the basket down and slide it under her." I spit out water as waves slap my face and rush inside my mouth and nose. "But first we've got to get the conch pot up, got to free her from the ropes to prevent any further damage, and so I can manipulate her."

Taking a deep breath, I pull my mask down and duck back under the surface, pushing my way beneath the body and grabbing for the line that connects her to the weighty ballast that dangles at the bottom of the bay. A dark jacket and blouse blossom up from her waist, and her gray skirt billows out around her hips, revealing panties and bare legs that are pale and thin, moving as the water moves, fanning and swaying. The yellow line around her ankles is wrapped multiple times and drops straight down, vanishing in water that gets dark and impenetrable.

I tug the rope and feel what is attached to it move freely, which isn't an accurate indication of how heavy it is, because mass doesn't change underwater, but weight does, due to buoyancy. I'm able to run the rope over my shoulder and swim with it to the surface, where I take in gulps of air. I swim to the

Stokes basket, where Marino reaches down to assist, his big hand outstretched as he bends over the boat rail. Kletty holds the buoy line while Marino secures the one I just gave him, and I turn her over facedown in the water and move the basket so that it and the body are side by side.

Struggling with waves pushing and the current pulling, I roll her over into the basket so that she is on her back. Her shriveled face stares blindly through cloudy eyes that are dry and shrunken by dehydration.

"Hold everything tight!" I slide the dive knife out of the rubber sheath strapped around my lower left leg. "I'm cutting her loose. The buoy line first, then the other. Hold tight!"

I saw through both lines a good twelve inches above the knots at her neck and ankles, and I zip her up, double-pouching her.

"Make a note that the buoy line was around her neck, the conch-pot line was around her ankles," I call out, and the morbid black cargo is hoisted up. "We also need to label the cut ends." I swim around to the back of the boat. "Maybe someone could go ahead and do that, please, and we need to capture the GPS coordinates."

I climb up the ladder, and the basket is on top of a sheet near the big yellow sausage fender and its severed yellow rope, which someone has neatly coiled. I pull off my mask, hood, and gloves as Marino hauls in the second yellow line, and a square shape comes into view, silvery and foreshortened in the water, then bigger. It breaks the surface, water pouring through the wire-mesh sides of some type of cage. A snarl of manila rope and monofilament lines are snagged on a slide-locked door that is bowed out and impaled by a broken bamboo pole.

"I could use a hand!" Marino shouts, and Kletty and Sullivan rush to help him hoist up a heavy-gauge wire crate that looks fairly new and has a pan on the bottom stacked with green-and-black bags that are filled with something.

"What the fuck?" Marino exclaims, as they set down what appears to be a folding dog crate or kennel snarled with fishing tackle.

"Cat litter?" Marino says, incredulous.

"*World's Best Cat Litter*," he reads what's printed on the black-and-green bags. "Five thirty-four-pound bags of fucking clumping cat litter? Is this supposed to be some sicko joke?"

"I don't know what this is supposed to be." I recall what Lucy said in my office early this morning, what seems a lifetime ago.

Someone cunning but too smug to realize how much he doesn't know.

"Maybe using what was on hand to weigh her down?" Labella suggests. "Someone with pets? A lot easier than finding a conch pot, if you're not a commercial fisherman."

"Not to mention ubiquitous." I take a closer look. "Good luck tracing where a dog crate and cat litter were purchased unless whoever did it was kind enough to leave a price sticker for us. But maybe whoever did this didn't think we'd get this far. I'm not sure we were supposed to recover this or anything."

"I don't think we were," Marino agrees. "A friggin' miracle she didn't pop apart, and she would have if you hadn't gone in after her. If you hadn't done exactly what you did."

I look up at the helicopter still hovering over us, and then the big white bird noses around to the west and flies off toward Boston. I watch it get smaller in the distance, its noise diminishing, and I wait to see if it swoops toward Logan Airport, but it doesn't. It continues toward the city, headed toward the Charles River, and then I can't see it anymore.

"What about the rest of this?" I point out the mess of fishing tackle, leads and swivels and hooks, all of it brown with rust. "Do you think it's part of the same gear the turtle was entangled with?"

"Looks like it. Commercial longlining," Marino tells me.

He says that a longline literally is a long horizontal line attached by box swivels to vertical lines, possibly rigged for mackerel, based on the way the hooks are bent. The bamboo is a pole marker.

"See the piece of scrap iron tied to one end?" he explains. "That's what kept it upright in the water, and probably there was a bundle of corks attached at some point, and a flag."

All of it looks very old and could have come a long way from here. He guesses the turtle bumped into it, got wrapped in a couple of the lines, and dragged the gear, maybe for a while, before getting snagged in the buoy line.

"Could even be he was diving or coming up for air when the crate and the body was dumped in and all of it got tangled up together," he supposes.

I ask him to retrieve my magnifier from the Pelican case and hand me a pair of gloves, and I take a moment to survey every inch of the crate and the soggy bags of cat litter inside it. The bamboo pole is about five feet long, the top part of it snapped off rather recently, based on the appearance of the broken end, which isn't weathered the way the rest of it is. The bamboo impales the crate, spearing it at a thirty-degree angle through the top and out the slide-locked door, and I try to envision how that might have happened.

I imagine someone shoving the crate full of cat litter and the tethered dead body and the boat fender overboard. Instantly the crate would have sunk and the fender would have floated, submerging the body vertically very much the way I found her. How did the collision with the longline rig and bamboo pole occur and when?

Maybe Marino's right. The leatherback was dragging the fishing gear and could have been coming up to sound at the exact time the crate and body were dropped. I examine the exposed ends of the pole through acrylic binocular lenses that magnify what I'm looking at, and I see the same greenish-yellow paint. It's a faint swipe on the broken edge of the bamboo end that protrudes through the top of the crate.

I direct that we photograph the crate, the fender, and the tackle in situ. Then we'll protect all of it with large plastic bags and transport it to my office.

"Let's make sure Toby's waiting for us with the van," I say to Marino, as I unzip the drysuit and stretch the gaskets over my head and wrists. "We need to get her to the office as quickly as we can, because she's going to begin decomposing really fast now that she's out of the water. I don't know if she's been frozen, but she might have been."

"Frozen?" Labella frowns.

"I don't know," I reply. "Frozen or almost frozen. This lady's been dead for quite some time, and I suspect we were supposed to recover her just long enough to lose her. I suspect the goal was to really frustrate us. Rigged up like that and pushed overboard, and then she's decapitated, drawn and quartered, so to speak, as we try to get her into the basket. A dismembered body that slips away and is gone. Well, too bad, whoever you are," I say, and I'm not talking to the dead woman but to the person who did this. "We have her, and hopefully a lot more than someone anticipated."

Unzipping the body pouches, I leave them open just long enough for me to attach labeled tags to the severed end of each rope that binds her. I return to the cabin, grateful to be out of the wind and dropping temperature, and I don't bother putting my wet clothes back on but stay in the liner. It fits me like an oversized gray union suit.

I put on my jacket and buckle myself back into my seat, and I let Labella know I'm pinching their liner and promise to return it after I've cleaned it. Kletty pulls in the anchor, and Labella starts the engines, and Marino sits across the aisle from me, trying to figure out his five-point harness as I try to figure out the order of things.

I envision someone on a boat tying a large fender around the dead woman's neck, then tying a second line around her ankles and attaching the other end of it to a dog crate filled with bags of cat litter. I imagine all this being pushed overboard as a two-thousand-pound reptile appears, dragging fishing gear, bamboo, and monofilament lines that might have been little more than an irritant until he whacked into the crate, impaling it with the pole. Now he has hundreds of pounds dragging him down and tightening the fishing lines around his left flipper.

"What a strange world," I decide. "The one thing he for sure didn't anticipate."

I'm talking about the killer. I believe whoever dumped this woman's body is also responsible for her death. I will work this case as a homicide unless the facts prove me wrong.

"In my opinion?" Marino raises his voice above the thundering engines. "I think she was dumped overboard pretty close to where she was found."

"You might be right," I reply, as we speed back toward Boston's inner harbor. "The way the body was tethered, she couldn't have been dragged very far without being pulled apart."

"Five thirty-four-pound bags soaked with water, and when that shit gets wet it weighs even more and sticks together like concrete," Marino says. "So it's not like something that was going to dissolve and leach out of the bags anytime soon. Plus, the weight of the crate. We're talking at least one-sixty, maybe two hundred pounds, pulling on the body. A hell of a lot of stress on her neck."

"Any idea how long she's been in the water?" Labella turns around in his chair, the boat slapping up and down as we speed through the bay.

"Probably not long." I think about Channing Lott's trial, about the timing. "The big question's going to be where she died and where she's been since."

"It doesn't look like her," Marino says to me, and there's no need for him to elaborate.

I know what he's conveying, and the thought crossed my mind, too, at first, but only briefly, only long enough to be face-to-face with her. She isn't remotely familiar. I've studied photographs of Mildred Lott, a very young fifty, shapely and fit, with long blond hair and all the perfections her financial status could afford. I know about her every surgery, liposuction, and injection, having familiarized myself with records the police provided for me after she disappeared from her Gloucester home last March.

"I have no idea who she is, but it's not her," I inform Marino, the Boston skyline straight ahead. "I don't need to wait for DNA to tell us that."

"Someone's going to make a stink about it being her until we let everyone know otherwise," he predicts.

"We won't be letting anyone know anything until she's identified and it's safe to release information that's not going to help whoever did this."

"If she'd been torn into pieces and we couldn't recover her? Everyone would believe it's Mildred Lott." Marino is thinking about my appearing in court today. "People would be sure of it." He's saying a jury would. "They'd believe she turned up after all these months, and maybe that's the point of the way she was rigged. To also rig the trial, to booby-trap it so the case falls apart at the last minute."

He's referring to the notorious antics of Jill Donoghue, and as I understand it, I'm the last witness the defense is calling before resting a case that's been spectacularly highlighted in the news.

"You got to admit the timing's unusual. In fact, it's damn scary," he says. "I'm not sure it isn't deliberate."

"Channing Lott is in jail," I remind him. "He has been since April. And it's not his missing wife." I stress that. "It's someone else."

twelve

IT'S THREE MINUTES PAST ONE WHEN WE REACH THE
Longfellow Bridge connecting Boston to Cambridge.

On the other side, MIT's playing fields and buildings have
lost their charm, are squared shapes of dull grass, dark brick,
and washed-out limestone beneath a thick tarp of gray clouds.
Trees waiting for fall are suddenly skeletal, as if they've flung
their parched leaves in despair, and the Charles River is roughly
stirred by a blustery wind that matches my own agitation.

I read the text message again, wondering why I think it
might say something different this time:

*Just back in session after adjourning for lunch. Still on for
2. Sorry.—DS*

I refrain from answering Dan Steward, the assistant U.S.
attorney whose fault it partly or maybe mostly is that I'm being
dragged into court at what couldn't be a worse time or for a
more ridiculous reason.

From now on I'll communicate with him by phone or in
person. Not in writing again ever, I promise myself, and I can't
get over it. How awful. I'm thinking in headlines, and most of
all I'm worrying about the dead woman in the van behind us.
She deserves my complete attention right now and won't get it.
This is wrong.

"I've always lived over a microscope," I comment to Marino. "Now I live under one, every bit of minutiae open for examination and opinion. I don't know how we're going to do this." I tuck my phone back inside my jacket pocket.

"You and me both. I got no idea who to call first, and I'm sure as hell not doing what the Coast Guard said and bringing in the FBI right off the bat, just hand it over to them on a silver platter because Homeland Security says so." He is talking nonstop, and about something else. "A jurisdictional cluster fuck. Jesus Christ, could be half a dozen different departments claiming this one."

"Or not. That's the more likely story."

"A cluster fuck if I ever saw one."

Cluster fuck seems to be his favorite new expression, and I suspect it came from Lucy. But who knows where he got it.

"The FBI will want the case because it's going to be big news. No way this won't be high-profile, maybe a national headline. A rich old lady tied to a dog crate and dumped in the harbor. Assumed to be Mildred Lott. Then, when it turns out it's not, it will be an even bigger story."

" 'A rich old lady'?"

"You mind holding these?" He hands me his Ray-Bans. "Talk about the weather turning to crap. I got to go to the eye doctor, can't see worth shit anymore. Need a perscription instead of just using over-the-counter."

I've given up telling him the word is *prescription*.

"Now my distance vision sucks, too." He squints as he drives. "Pisses the hell out of me, everything blurry, can't remember what they call it. Presbyphobia."

"Presbyopia. Old eyes."

"Goddamn nothing focuses anymore, like Mister Magoo."

"You know she's rich for a fact? What makes you think that?" I place his sunglasses in my lap and adjust my vent, turning up the fan as we creep across the bridge in thick traffic. "And how do you know she's old?"

"She's got white hair."

"Or platinum blond. It could be dyed. I have to look at her."

"Nice clothes. And her jewelry. I didn't see it up close, but it looks like gold and a fancy watch. She's old," he insists. "At least seventy. Like she was out having lunch or shopping or something when she was grabbed."

"What she looks is very dehydrated and very dead. I don't know how old or how rich, but robbery doesn't appear to be the motive."

"Didn't say it was."

"I'm saying it probably wasn't. Assumptions are always dangerous," I remind him. "Especially in a case like this, where all we may have to go on are physical descriptions we put out there in hopes she's in a database. We say she's elderly with long white hair, when in fact she's in her forties with dyed blond hair, and we cause a big problem."

"Someone like that's probably been reported missing," Marino says.

"You would think so, but we don't know the circumstances."

"She would be reported for sure," he asserts. "These days people notice when your newspapers pile up or your mailbox overflows. Bills don't get paid and services get shut off. Appointments are missed, and finally someone calls the police to check on whoever it is."

"Often that's true."

"Not to mention her family complaining that Mom or Grandmom hasn't answered the phone in days or weeks."

"If there are family members who care," I reply. "What I will tell you with a fair degree of certainty is she's not an elderly shut-in with Alzheimer's who wandered off and got lost and didn't remember who she is or where she lives and somehow ended up in the bay tied to a boat fender and a dog crate."

"No kidding."

"She's a homicide, and her body was concealed for a period of time, then transported and dropped overboard," I add. "And obviously the way it was done is for some effect that isn't clear."

"Some sick fuck."

"It certainly seems malevolent."

"How long do you think she was kept?"

"It depends on the conditions. Weeks, at least. Possibly months," I reply. "It appears she was fully dressed when she died, and yes, I worry she was abducted. But it surprises me, if that's the case, that there's been nothing in the news. At least nothing I'm aware of. The police usually give us a heads-up."

"My point exactly. Unless she's not from Massachusetts."

"There is that possibility, of course."

"Kind of sounds like the dinosaur lady missing in Canada." He merges left onto Memorial Drive.

"There's no similarity I can see at a glance," I tell him. "But I don't know enough about Emma Shubert's physical description. Just that she had short graying brown hair and was forty-eight when she disappeared."

"Plus, this lady's still got both her ears," he considers.

"Assuming the photo of the ear sent to me is real and is Emma Shubert's. There are so many ifs."

Marino eyes the rearview mirror, making sure the van transporting the body is behind us. "Well, maybe this one's been reported missing and we'll get lucky."

I don't think anything about this is going to be lucky for us. I can't shake the feeling that nothing has been done since this woman vanished and died because no one close to her knows, not her neighbors, not her family or friends, and that's odd. I also find it odd and contradictory that while it's far from obvious who she is, the person responsible for disposing of her body didn't bother removing her personal effects. A victim's belongings can be quite useful to the police.

Why not get rid of her clothing and jewelry?

Why have her body found at all?

Of course, we might not have recovered her remains, I remind myself. I think of my shock when I first saw the way she was rigged underwater, one nylon rope around her neck, the other around her ankles. Had her tethers pulled her body apart, and I can't help but suspect that was the intention, we might not have found a trace of her.

Right this minute we might be on our way back to the CFC with nothing to show for our efforts except a yellow boat fender, rope, rusty fishing gear, and a fragment of barnacle and broken bamboo with a trace of something greenish on them. Questions and possibilities race through my mind and offer nothing useful, only more confusion and a growing sense of dread.

Some evil manipulation, I think. Someone toying with us. Some malignant game being played out with deliberateness, and I suspect there will be no DNA on file, no police report, nothing on record, because those who count don't know this lady has vanished from wherever she's supposed to be. Chilled to the marrow, I turn up the heat and aim vents at my face and neck.

"Really weird the way she was tied up." Marino hasn't stopped talking. "Maybe a different type of hog-tying. Then dump her and she gets tangled up with a dinosaur turtle. Geez, you're going to kill me from heat stroke."

He closes his vent and cracks open his window.

"Let's refrain from using the word *dinosaur*, please." I repeat what I've said several times.

"How come you're in such a shitty mood?"

"I'm sorry if I seem to be in a shitty mood."

"You seem it because you sure as hell are."

"I'm concerned and frustrated because I'm racing against the clock," I reply. "I need to start on her right now. What I don't need is to have this important window of time wasted by a court case where my appearance is simply frivolous. And good God, could the traffic be any slower?"

"It's always bad around here. Morning rush hour, lunchtime rush hour, late-afternoon rush hour. Between two and four a.m. is optimal," he says. "And just remember, the more pissed you get, the more you give them what they want."

How ironic that he of all people would be coaching me about the futility of allowing detractors to get me out of sorts.

"She's never going to be in better condition than she is right now," I remind him.

"There's some stuff we can do. Don't worry, Doc," he says.

My office is just ahead, silo-shaped, with the glass dome on top, like a missile, a dumdum bullet, or, as some bloggers call it, a *forensic erection*. Seven stories of ultramodern construction sided in titanium and reinforced with steel. The descriptions and quips, most of them irreverent and vulgar, are endless, and tomorrow's news likely will bristle with them.

Dr. Scarpetta returned to her forensic erection in Cambridge after testifying that Lott's wife turned into soap.

I glance at my watch and feel another wave of anger. It's exactly eight minutes past one, and I'm supposed to be in the witness stand in less than an hour. I can't possibly begin the autopsy now, and I'm certainly not going to let anyone else do it. The entire situation is outrageous.

"It's a leatherback, and that's what we need to call it." I pick up on my earlier point and try to sound less aggravated. "It's not helpful to the turtle or any of us if we continue referring to it as a dinosaur."

"Pam says leatherbacks are the last living dinosaur on earth." Marino takes the left turn that leads to our back parking lot.

"The problem is if you say things like that, some moron is going to set out in search of it as if it's Nessie or Bigfoot."

"I'd rather work with Jefferson at Boston P.D.," Marino then says, as if it's up to him to pick a homicide detective and sidestep what I have a feeling will end up being the FBI. "Technically, the outer harbor is Boston."

"I'm not sure of that at all," I reply. "It depends on the latitude and longitude, and I don't know enough about navigation to tell from the coordinates we got whether the water she was recovered from might be within the seaward boundary of Hull, Cohasset, or even Quincy. Add to that the question of where she went in and also where she died, where she was abducted from, assuming she was abducted. It probably will end up being FBI, no invitation needed."

"They'll sink their teeth into it like a damn pit bull and take over the investigation on prime time." He reaches up to the visor and presses the remote control that opens our gate. "I'm sure Benton will love getting his hands on this one," he adds, as if my FBI criminal intelligence analyst husband leads a sheltered life.

"Nobody wants something like this," I reply, as the gate slides open. "That's my bigger worry. That everyone will treat it like a hot potato. But more important than any of this is what we can do to establish her identity as quickly as possible. We need to enter a physical description of her and her personal effects into NamUs."

The National Missing and Unidentified Persons System is a relatively new central database for people who have vanished. It's a chance at least to connect the missing with the unidentified or unclaimed dead, but again, I have a strong feeling this woman's disappearance hasn't been reported.

"No matter what, we'll do that before the day's end. We'll

want to e-mail radiographs, her dental charts, any distinct body features." I continue going down the list as we drive into the back lot. "Put in a call to Ned or whoever might be available later this afternoon."

Ned Adams is one of several area dentists also certified in odontology and on call for us.

"We need to get some pictures before court." Marino parks the Tahoe in front of the bay.

"Absolutely." I reach down to pick up the trash bag of my wet field clothes.

"And her temp, since we didn't do that on the boat," he says. "Probably the same as the bay, fifty-one degrees. Maybe one or two degrees higher, because the Coast Guard boat and back of the van will be warmer than the water."

"Yes, we'll get it now, and then I need a few minutes to change back into my suit. I sure can't go like this." I climb out clad in the gray fleece liner, my orange down coat, and wet boots with no socks.

"Not unless you want everyone to think you're a whack job," Marino says, as the bay door begins to clatter up, the white windowless van stopping in front of it.

"We need photos, and most of all, swabs, because the quicker we can get her DNA profile in NamUs and especially NDIS, the better." I continue going through what needs to be done immediately.

"PERK her, clean up really fast, and get to court." I hold on to a thread of hope that law enforcement somewhere has entered this missing woman into the National DNA Index System.

"Tell Bryce to contact Dan and let him know we just got back from a difficult scene and I'm hurrying as fast as I can. Damn waste," I then mutter. "Ridiculous. Pure harassment. Unadulterated effort to interfere and create a spectacle."

"Yeah, you've only said it fifty times." Marino grabs the scene cases out of the back of the SUV, and I gather the evidence bags of the fishing gear Pamela Quick gave to me and the barnacle I extracted from the leatherback.

We walk into the bay, the van rumbling in behind us and parking. The driver's door swings open, and Toby hops out in his investigative uniform, a baseball cap pulled over his shaved head, a fad I'm sure Marino started, and it never fails to amaze me the influence he has without seeming to be aware of it. At least half of my male investigators now shave their heads as glossy smooth as cue balls and have got tattoos, including Toby, whose left arm is a solid sleeve of what reminds me of subway graffiti.

No one is immune to the Marino effect, as I've come to call the need his investigators have to emulate him for better or worse. I'm told that Sherry's gotten *Mortui vivos docent* tattooed on her back and has taken up boxing, and Barbara now rides a Harley.

"What's the plan?" Toby pulls on gloves and opens the tailgate. "You want her in decomp? I assume she's a homicide, probably dead first and dumped so she would sink, right? Really weird shit. Any idea who she is?"

"We need a few minutes with her before she goes into the cooler, and don't assume nothing," Marino says gruffly.

"You'll do her in the morning?"

"I'm definitely not waiting until the morning," I answer him. "As soon as I'm out of court I'm back here. She's going to be in bad shape very fast. Let's bring her straight into decomp, and we'll get a temperature and some photos. We can weigh and measure her later."

Toby unlocks the wheels of the stretcher with its black body bag that looks oversized and pitifully flat, as if what's zipped inside has shrunk in transit.

"What about the other stuff?" he asks.

In the back of the cargo area are the black plastic–covered shapes of what was recovered from the bay.

"All of it will go to trace, but not now," I tell him. "Let's get everything inside ID."

I instruct him to cover a table with disposable sheets and place all of the items inside, and to document them with photographs and lock the door. When I'm back from court I'll remove the wrappings, take a look and find out what interest or questions the police or FBI might have in the fishing gear, the boat fender, and all the rest. We'll submit all this to trace evidence first thing tomorrow morning, I tell Toby, and I ask him to give Ernie Koppel, the section chief, a heads-up about what's coming.

"Everything locked up tight and secured," I repeat. "Nobody's to touch anything without clearing it with me first."

They lift the stretcher out, slam shut the tailgate, and roll the body inside and toward the decomp room as the bay door begins to loudly crank back down. I stop by the security guard's window and check the sign-in log again, relieved that no other cases have come in since I last looked. The two motor-vehicle fatalities have been autopsied, their bodies picked up by funeral homes. That leaves the blunt-force trauma and possible drug overdose suicide to be released. Luke Zenner did those autopsies, I notice, and that's what I've come to expect. It's his nature to request the most complicated cases or assign them to himself because he wants experience and loves a challenge.

"Is there anything I need to know about?" I ask Ron through his open window.

"No, ma'am, Chief," he answers from inside his office, where security monitors mounted on three walls are split into quadrants, each showing exterior and interior areas of special interest for surveillance. "It's been real quiet. Just two pickups, with another on the way."

"We'll be in decomp for a few minutes, then I've got court," I let him know. "Hopefully they won't hold me up too long. Marino and I will be coming straight back here to take care of this post."

"You going to do her today?" he says, to my surprise.

I haven't mentioned or indicated to him or anyone in my building that the victim in this case is a woman. Only Marino and Toby know.

"Yes. No matter how late it is," I reply, as I fill in the log. "Since we don't know who she is, let's enter her as an unidentified white female found in the Massachusetts Bay."

He begins typing into fields of a software package that programs a Radio Frequency Identification, or RFID, chip embedded in a smart label. Checking scene notes for the GPS coordinates, I give those to him, too, as Toby reappears, pushing an empty gurney in a hurry and loudly shoving open the door that leads out of the autopsy floor and into the bay. A laser printer sounds, and Ron slides out a yellow silicone bracelet and the smart label embedded with the information I just gave him about our most recently accessioned case.

"What have you been hearing?" I question him casually, as

security cameras pick up Toby rolling the gurney toward the white transport van.

"Well, Toby said we have a Jane Doe coming in, that it could be the lady who's been missing, the one you're going to court about," Ron says. "I guess you also were filmed by some TV crews while you were out there."

"What makes you think it was TV crews, as in more than one?" I ask while I watch Toby from different angles on split screens.

He parks the gurney at the back of the van, points the key to unlock it, and I notice his lips are moving. It occurs to me he's probably listening to his iPod as usual and singing along. But that's not right, either. He appears to be talking emphatically. In fact, he looks agitated, as if he's arguing with someone.

"From what I saw, you were in different locations, on different boats, at different times," Ron describes. "The Coast Guard, the fireboat with a bunch of people from the aquarium. Some of it was filmed from the air. I do know that because you could hear the chopper in the background. But I'm not sure about all of it."

Toby is on the phone. He's wearing in-ear headphones that are connected to his iPhone, which is in a back pocket of his cargo pants. Maybe he's fighting with his girlfriend again, and he shouldn't be fighting with anyone or having any sort of personal conversation, period. He should be paying attention to his job, to his handling of evidence. It's one of my most common complaints that staff devote just as much time to their personal lives as they do to their work, as if it's perfectly fine to get paid for fighting with a partner or shopping online or chatting on Facebook or Twitter.

"You were doing something with what's for sure the biggest turtle I ever saw," Ron continues, and I'm barely listening. "Then you're in the water getting her out. An old lady, it looks like, tied up with yellow rope."

"You saw footage of me getting her out of the water?" I watch Toby cover the gurney with the sheet and open the tailgate, and he's scowling now, clearly unhappy with whatever someone is saying over the phone. "Do you happen to know which TV station it was?"

"No, ma'am, Chief. That I can't tell you for a fact," Ron says. "Because it's not just on the local stations. CNN, for sure, and a Yahoo headline on the Internet about a prehistoric monster turtle, and that's the exact words, and a dead body tied to a cage that the turtle got tangled up with. I think it's pretty much all over the Internet, pretty much everywhere."

thirteen

THE CFC'S SEVEN CORRIDORS ARE PAINTED WHITE, THEIR
recycled glass tiles glazed a grayish brown called truffle. Soft
reflective LEDs create a soothing cloud of light, and acoustical
drop ceilings conceal miles of wire while cameras and RFID
trackers monitor the passage of all who come here, the living
and the dead.

Our round headquarters was built by a bioresearch company
that went bankrupt late in construction, and with rare exception
the original design is ideal for what we do—in fact, a medical
examiner's dream. We can look out energy-efficient solar windows that no one can look in, and a high-performance HVAC
controls the environment so precisely we have our own custom-
ized weather. Boilers remove moisture from the air before
chillers cool it, preventing condensation and an inconvenient
phenomenon known as indoor rain, while robots and HEPA
filters suck in and scrub away pathogens, chemical vapors, and
accompanying awful odors.

The CFC is cleaner than most healthcare clinics, the tissue
recovery room I briskly walk past a hundred times more sterile
than a hospital OR. Patients declared brain-dead can be transported here while still on life support, ensuring that eyes, organs, skin, and bones are harvested without wasteful delays, the

dead helping the living and the living helping the dead. The
progress I've witnessed in my profession isn't the straight trajec-
tory I once imagined but a circle like the corridor I follow, passing ID now, then ducking inside large-scale x-ray to see if my
technician Anne is there.

Her chair is pushed back and turned around as if she just got
up, and glowing on flat video screens are 3-D images of a head
and thorax with bright white areas of fresh hemorrhage into
brain tissue and lungs, and the brighter white of bones, of a
basilar skull fracture that extends into the sinuses, and shattered scapulas, and ribs broken so badly they're detached from
chest walls. The blunt-force trauma case from this morning,
Howard Roth; I read the information on his CT scans. A forty-
two-year-old black male from Cambridge who allegedly fell
down his basement stairs, his body discovered late yesterday
afternoon.

I don't have time for this.

But I can't let it go, and I click through more images, view-
ing the body on different planes from the inside out, and the
gray shades of organs and muscles are vivid white where there
is bleeding and dark where air is trapped. Then brilliant star-
burst and streaking artifacts are at a high Hounsfield unit value
of almost 4000. Dense metal, possibly lead. Most likely old
bullet fragments in the soft tissue of the left hip, and more of
them in his right posterior thigh. A possible roadmap of the life
this man lived, but not what killed him, and the massive internal damage that did is grossly inconsistent with a tumble down
the stairs.

A flail chest is more common in the crushing injuries I associate with people pinned under machines or run over by trac-
tors or cars. Most people who fall on the back of their heads also
don't have a basilar fracture. They don't have broken cranial
bones at foramen magnum, the hole in the base of the skull. I
click through more images from the whole-body scan, finding
no fresh injuries to the arms, hands, pelvis, or lower extremities.

Beyond a leaded glass window, the silhouette of the large
bore CT scanner is indistinctly white in the near dark, no one
home, and I decide Anne probably stepped out for coffee or to
use the ladies' room. I jot her a note and place it on her key-

board, letting her know I plan to post the body from the Massachusetts Bay later in the day and will need to scan it first.

Should discuss Howard Roth, I add as a PS. *Confusing loc of fxx/injuries & lack of them. Need complete history & scene details. Do not want him released yet. Thx.—KS.*

I check the autopsy room next and find it quiet and shiny clean, the floor still damp from mopping, long rows of empty steel tables gleaming dully in natural light that filters in through the one-way glass of side windows and those facing the parking lot. Banks of high-intensity lamps in the thirty-two-foot ceiling are turned off, the observation windows in the upper walls opening onto teaching labs that are dim and empty.

Luke Zenner often lingers down here, enjoying the quiet to do paperwork, to check on pending projects, or to tidy up his station, number 2, right next to mine. But I don't see him or anyone else, my five other pathologists and team of investigators probably in their offices or taking care of various appointments or out on calls.

I enter my iPhone's password to send Luke a message and notice I have a new one from Benton.

We still on for 5 & you ok? Have seen the news.

I write him back that I will return directly to the CFC after court and probably work into the early evening. I can meet with him and the other agents as soon as I'm done with the post.

Will call when I get a breath, I text him. *Dinner? If really late, take-out here while we meet?*

My phone immediately chimes and he replies, *Will pick up Armando's.*

I answer, *Combos with xtra cheese, fresh tomato, peppers, onions. On 1 of them add spinach & artichoke hearts. Say they R for me.* I tell him I look forward to seeing him.

It will feel reassuring when Benton appears, when the rest of this afternoon is behind me, and I glance at my watch. It's twenty-eight minutes past one, and I text Luke about the Howard Roth case, letting him know we need to discuss it and not to release the body yet. *I should be back in a few hours,* I type, as I move on past the soiled room, the anteroom, the changing rooms and locker rooms, no sign of Luke or anyone, which is typical at this hour, unless we have an unusually heavy caseload.

Beyond anthropology the corridor bends around to the Bio4
containment lab, or what we informally refer to as decomp,
reserved for suspected infectious or contaminated or badly decomposed bodies. Pushing a hands-free button that automati-
cally opens a metal door, I walk into an air-locked vestibule and
hang up my coat. Grabbing protective clothing off shelves, I
push a second button that opens a second door and find Marino
covered from the neck down in white Tyvek, checking his camera equipment.

The stretcher bearing the black pouch is parked next to one of
three stainless-steel tables attached to wall sinks, and above
them observation windows are dark. A clock mounted next to the
walk-in cooler reminds me unpleasantly that it's now one-thirty.
I'm supposed to be in court in exactly half an hour, and I continue to hope, at this point rather ridiculously, that I'll be canceled at the last minute. Or perhaps the trial is running behind
schedule and the judge will understand that I am, too.

"Was afraid you got lost," Marino says, as he covers his bald
head with a designer surgical cap, this one a *medicine skull* that
he ties in back like a biker's do-rag.

"We've got a problem case maybe."

"Not another one."

"The man who supposedly fell down the stairs," I explain.
"It doesn't look like a fall to me, unless he went off a ten-story
building and hit a few things on the way down. Toby took that
call, I believe?"

"He went to the scene and said there was nothing to it."

I lean against a counter and pull shoe covers over my wet
boots.

"Do you know the details?" I ask.

"It's Machado's case."

"Did he attend the autopsy this morning?" I inquire.

"The Portuguese Man of War is always there for gore. Said
he was going to. I'll check with him when I get a minute or drop
by his house later and bang on the door."

Marino and Detective Sil Machado live on the same block
in their West Cambridge neighborhood and ride motorcycles
together. They're both into boxing and go to the same gym. It
seems they've become close friends.

"What Toby told me last night was pretty skimpy, not much

known at the time," Marino adds. "Victim's a chronic alcoholic. Appears he opened the wrong door on his way to the bathroom and fell down the basement stairs."

"Hopefully Luke got a STAT alcohol. Have you talked to Bryce or heard from him?" I cover my hair with a surgical cap.

"He left around eleven." Marino is looking me up and down. "You should suit up before walking in here," he says, as if I need him to remind me of protocols.

"What do you mean left? Left where? Here?"

"Apparently had to take his cat to the vet for what he claims is an emergency. He said he'd already let Steward know we're just getting back from a scene. Apparently he's cross-examining the witness who's right before you and it's going slow, and after that he's going to ask for a break." Marino picks up a six-inch plastic ruler and sticks a blank label on it. "But it's not smart to assume you'll be cut any slack for being late, not with that asshole's dream team."

He means Channing Lott's defense attorneys.

"There's no way around my being late," I reply. "Dan needs to let the judge know that matters are slightly out of my control at the moment."

"If we drove there right now you'd make it."

I imagine myself walking into the courtroom wearing wet boots and a drysuit liner so Channing Lott's attorneys can have fun with me.

"We got a case number?" Marino opens a drawer and finds several permanent markers.

I tell him what it is, and he writes it and the date on the ruler's label as I unfold a disposable lab coat. It rustles as I put it on over my gray liner, which I wish I didn't have to take off anytime soon. I'm still chilled, as if my blood is several degrees cooler than it should be.

"What's wrong with Bryce's cat?" I ask. "Nothing serious, I hope."

"Onions from chili they had last night; that's my story and I'm sticking to it, even though Bryce says they're really careful when they cook with onions. Never drops nothing on the floor or leaves a dirty bowl the cat might get into, right? Ethan and him. Mr. Slob and Mr. Clean."

"I'm curious how you know what they had for dinner last night." I pull examination gloves out of a box.

"Bryce brought me some leftover chili this morning, and I ate it for breakfast and tasted onions. Soon as I heard about the cat I said bingo, now you know what's wrong with it," Marino says. "Of course, he thinks it's some kind of flu bug it got from the groomer, vomiting and diarrhea."

"Ethan's with him?"

"Don't get me started." He bends down to open a cabinet and drags out a large plastic case. "Don't ask me why it took the both of them to transport that fleabag what's-its-name, *Indy Anna*? And they have to be together to rush it to the vet, it takes two of them?"

Clasps snap loudly as Marino opens the case and begins to remove a Xenon arc forensic light.

"That's not a very nice way to talk about the pet of someone who was thoughtful enough to bring you homemade chili at the crack of dawn. I'm not going to use the ALC."

There's not time for an alternate light source, and I wouldn't use one in this case, not on the body, at any rate.

"Well, Ethan could have just stuck it in one of those damn pet carriers and handled it himself." Marino sets the forensic light on the counter and plugs it in anyway. "Half the time he works out of the house. What's the big deal?"

"Am I to infer you mentioned your theory about the cat getting hold of onions?" I label a rack of blood tubes that I may not need.

"Yeah."

"Well, that certainly explains why they're treating it like a big deal." I lower a respirator particulate mask over my nose and mouth. "Eating onions or garlic can be toxic for dogs and cats, and most pet owners know that."

"Shit, it's like talking to Darth Vader." Marino stares at my mask. "Maybe you should wear that to court and see what happens."

"I'm sure if Bryce wasn't overwhelmed and beside himself before you got involved, he is now."

"When's he not overwhelmed and beside himself about something?" Marino continues in his same grumpy tone, but he doesn't dislike Bryce nearly as much as he pretends.

It seems to be one of the favorite sports at the CFC for the two of them to go at each other unmercifully, and five minutes later they're drinking coffee together or eating lunch, and at least once a month Marino is over at Bryce and Ethan's house for dinner or a cookout.

"He probably hasn't seen the news Ron just mentioned or is even aware of it." I unzip the first pouch. "Which is why we didn't know about it, either." I unzip the second one.

fourteen

INSIDE BLACK PLASTIC SHE'S PITIFULLY WIZENED, HER long white wet hair plastered over her leathery face. Her frail body seems to disappear inside a long gray skirt, a dark blouse that's either purple or burgundy, and a navy blue jacket with tarnished metal buttons. All of the clothing seems at least four sizes too big.

"What news are you talking about?" Marino pulls down his surgical mask.

"Apparently, video footage of my examining the leatherback and recovering the body is everywhere." I spread open the pouches and smell moldy old flesh. "Let's get photos in situ of the way she's bound. I'm going to need to remove the ligature around her ankles if I'm going to PERK her."

"A double fisherman's knot. And this is the backup knot. The knots on each rope are exactly the same," Marino observes.

He begins photographing the severed lengths of yellow nylon rope wrapped and knotted around the dead woman's ankles and neck.

"Which is exactly what it sounds like," he says. "You tie your primary knot, this one here, basically a double overhand knot. Then, for good measure, one of these."

He points a blue-gloved finger to show me.

"A backup, just to make sure everything's secure," he adds. "So what someone did was wrap two separate ropes around her ankles and neck, and tied two knots on each, leaving the longer ends to be tied to the dog crate and boat fender, and it will be interesting to see what those knots are. I'm betting they're the same."

He looks up at the clock and shakes his head.

"You're asking for it, Doc."

"Is there any particular reason to choose these types of knot, in your opinion?" I lock a new blade in a scalpel handle.

"No logical one. Usually a double overhand's what you use to join two separate fishing lines or if you're attaching two different ropes to each other, which isn't the case here. So there's no good reason, except it's probably what someone's used to. You're going to be late as hell, and this ain't a hair appointment."

"What someone's used to could tell us what sort of person is responsible."

"I think we've already figured whoever dumped her did it from a boat," he says. "I mean, she wasn't pushed out of a plane or a chopper."

"I don't know what she was pushed out of."

Moving clothing out of the way, I make a small incision in the upper-right abdomen.

"A fisherman, someone into boating," Marino says, as I insert a thermometer into the liver to get the core body temperature. "Someone who knows about ropes and knots. You don't just tie knots like this by accident."

Picking up a surgical knife from a cart, I cut through the yellow rope tightly looped three times around her ankles, and I tape the ends, labeling them, so I know which segment was attached to what. I measure the length and width of the rope, careful not to disturb the knots.

"Marks around her ankles are very superficial abrasions," I note. "No furrows or contusions, barely anything at all made by the ligature. Her neck will probably be the same, but we'll save that for later."

"She was tied up long after she was dead." He takes close-ups of the faint lines around her ankles.

"There's no question about it," I agree. "Toenails painted

pale pink and chipped. And she's got some sort of reddish staining on the bottom of her feet, which is strange."

"Like maybe she had on red socks or red shoes at some point, something that faded on her?" Marino bends down to photograph the bottoms of her feet, the camera's shutter clicking repeatedly.

"More likely she was barefoot and stepped in something." I look with a light and a lens, the dark reddish staining on the shrunken bottoms of her toes, the balls of her feet, and her heels. "Something that obviously doesn't wash off in water, something she might have stepped in. That's what it looks like to me. Whatever it is, it dyed her skin or is embedded in it, or both."

Using the scalpel, I lightly scrape some of the staining off the bottom of her left foot, wiping reddish flecks of skin off the blade and into an envelope as I resume relaying to Marino what Ron told me.

"It's on local TV stations but is also national news, fairly close-up video footage, some of which was taken from the air, but he's not sure all of it was," I explain. "We know there was a news chopper when we were on the fireboat, but what about when it was just the two of us with the Coast Guard? How about covering a table with sheets."

I peel the back off the smart label and stick it on the yellow silicone bracelet, which I fasten around her right wrist, and her skin is shriveled and tough like leather that is wet. Her fingernails are painted the same color as her toenails, a subtle peachy-pink, and they're broken, the polish peeling off, chipped and scratched, as if she were clawing at something or digging with her bare hands.

"Obviously the other helicopter did the filming if it shows you in the water." Marino shakes open a plasticized sheet.

"Unless someone was filming from a boat." On her right index finger is a ring, an 1862 three-cent silver coin set in a heavy yellow gold mounting. "There were a lot of boats around," I remind him.

"That big white chopper hovering over us the whole damn time you were getting her out of the water," Marino decides. "I should have noticed the tail number, dammit."

I try to wiggle the ring from side to side, puzzling over its size and that it fits snugly on her index finger when it shouldn't, and I wonder if she originally wore it on a smaller finger or if the ring is hers at all. If it fits her index finger now, it wouldn't have at death, because when a body begins to mummify, it becomes extremely dried out and literally shrinks the same way fruits, vegetables, and meats do inside a dehydrator. Jewelry, shoes, and clothing won't fit the way they did in life, and I imagine someone moving the body from wherever it was concealed and rearranging her jewelry or perhaps dressing her a certain way before she was tethered and dumped into the bay.

Why?

To make sure the ring was found? To make sure her personal effects were?

"I made a note of the tail number, wrote it down," I'm saying to Marino, as I'm pondering these other things. "We can have it checked out with the FAA database."

"It probably will come back to the bank financing it or some meaningless limited liability company; same thing Lucy does. So when the cops are behind one of her batmobiles or batcycles, they can't run her plate and figure out who she is, and air traffic controllers can't connect that sweet radio voice of hers with a name."

His Tyvek-covered feet make a slippery sound as he moves around.

"Almost none of these choppers, even news ones, come back to anything that's helpful," he says. "Especially if they're privately owned. When I started out as a cop, the world wasn't so friggin' anonymous. And you're going to be late as hell. No way you can make it by two unless you've got a jetpack."

"The white helicopter with red and blue stripes on the tail-boom struck me as private or corporate." I pick up her left hand, holding it in my two gloved ones, and I look at the watch fastened snugly around her wrist with a black silk strap. "Except for the camera mounted on it. Assuming it was a video camera and not a FLIR. But either is unusual for private or corporate aircraft."

"Pretty sure I've never seen that bird around here." Marino shakes open a second sheet. "Which is a little weird, because most of them end up flying right past us over the river on what's called the Fenway Route, in and out of Logan. Sure as hell got no idea what TV station it might be, if any, or how the hell they'd know we were out there and what we were doing. I know Judge Conry likes you, but you're pushing your luck."

"I am because I have to," I reply. "This lady can't wait."

"You'd better hope the judge sees it that way."

The watch appears to be Art Deco, in white gold or platinum, the bezel set with diamonds or some other clear gemstones, the movement mechanical. The time on the white oblong face is frozen at four minutes past six o'clock, and I can't know if that is a.m. or p.m. I can't know the date the watch stopped.

"Maybe some other type of filming," Marino then considers. "If they're filming a movie or commercial around here and whoever was flying just happened to see what we were doing and grabbed footage."

"It's obviously not Lucy's new bird."

"Haven't seen it yet," he says. "She's too busy going after pig farmers to give me a ride."

"We won't remove her jewelry now, but let's get photos, lots of photos. She's not going to look like this when we get back."

"Have got a shitload already, but I'll get more."

"More is better."

"Why would it be Lucy's?" Using the ruler as a scale, he places it next to the wrist wearing the watch. "She sure as hell wouldn't be moonlighting for some TV station or film crew, or posting videos of you all over the Internet."

"Of course not."

"You should give her the tail number and ask her to run it," he says. "I guarantee she'll figure out who it is and why they were spying on us."

"We don't know that whoever was in that white helicopter was spying. Maybe they were just curious. There also was a sailboat nearby," I recall. "A tall ship with red sails that were furled. It was sitting out there maybe a hundred yards from us when we were getting her and the gear out of the water, and it never moved. I'll e-mail the tail number to Lucy."

I dip swabs into distilled water.

"If we can find out where this lady died, we might find pieces of her fingernails," I decide. "No defensive injuries I can see so far, but she was doing something that broke all of her nails. Toenails, fingernails, every one of them."

I rub the cotton tips under each fingernail, and the swabs turn a reddish tint.

"The same reddish staining that's on her feet?" I wonder. "Whatever it is, I can't get all of it. It's way up in the quick."

I hold the red-tinted swabs under the surgical lamp and examine them with the magnifying lens.

"Something fibrous, maybe," I observe. "It reminds me of fiberglass insulation but more granular, like dust or dirt, and a darker color."

I cut her nails with a pair of small scissors, and pink-painted slivers make quiet clicking sounds as they drop into the bottom of a paper envelope I hold open.

"I'll take a look under the scope, then see what Ernie has to say," I add, and I'm mindful of seconds slipping away, of time running out for the dead woman and me.

I might get in trouble, it could happen, and I label nail clippings and swabs for trace and DNA, and arrange syringes with different-gauge needles on a surgical cart as the minute hand on the wall clock ticks closer to two p.m. My pulse picks up, but I can't stop, and inside a glass cabinet I collect ETDA blood tubes and FTA cards, although I know without a doubt that getting blood from her is going to be a challenge. It will have seeped out of vessel walls long ago, and I'll be lucky if I get enough to blot a card.

"You scribe and keep taking pictures, and we'll go at this really fast." I check the flexibility of the neck, the arms, and try to separate the legs, but they're stubborn. "Rigor's indeterminate," I dictate to Marino, and he writes it down as I remove the thermometer from the incision in her abdomen. "Temperature of her liver is forty-two degrees, and that's interesting. Are we sure about the water temperature of the bay? Pamela Quick said it was fifty-one degrees."

"The temp on the Coast Guard boat's GPS was fifty-one degrees," Marino confirms. "Of course, it would have been a little colder as the water got deeper."

"Nine degrees colder at the depth where she was held in place by the ropes?" I doubt it. "And she didn't get colder in water that is warmer than she was. What that means is she was colder than forty-two degrees when she first went in."

"Maybe she was kept in a freezer somewhere."

"There's no damage to her from fish and other sea creatures, which she likely was going to get if she was submerged for even a day or two. I seriously doubt she was in the water long enough to thaw," I decide. "Either she'd already begun to thaw when she went in or she was kept really, really cold somewhere but not frozen solid."

I begin to undress her, the clothing soaking wet, soiled, and gritty, and she smells more strongly of decomposition. The foul acrid stench crawls up my sinuses and coats my teeth, and soon it will be bad enough to make my eyes sting.

"Shit," Marino complains, and he swaps out his surgical mask for one with a filter.

I work silk-lined dark blue cashmere over her shoulders, pulling stubborn arms out of long, clingy sleeves, holding up her jacket to look at it front and back. I see no holes, no tears, no damage. But the three brownish metal buttons in front don't match and look very old.

"Possibly antique. Possibly military," I say to Marino. "Let's get close-ups. Like the ring with the old coin, these could be important because they're unusual."

I spread out the soaking-wet jacket on the sheet-covered table, noting the long curved back, the tapered waist, the tonal embroidery on the sides and sleeves.

"The label is *Tulle Clothing,* size six. Well, she's not a six now. More like a zero," I comment.

"How do you spell *Tulle*?"

I tell him, and he jots it down on a clothing diagram. "It's quite distinctive," I add. "Sort of a Tallulah style."

"Got no idea what that is." He begins taking photographs of the buttons.

"Retro-cut, with structured shoulders and wide lapels, and ornate embroidery stitched in thread the same color as the fabric," I explain. "Imagine Tallulah Bankhead."

"Someone with money trying to be glamorous," he says. "It doesn't make sense if no one knows she's missing."

"Someone knows. The person who dumped her in the bay does." I begin going over the buttons with a hand lens.

fifteen

TARNISHED BRASS WITH A HINT OF GILT, EACH BUTTON has some type of eagle design and an iron shank at the back that has been sewn onto the jacket's front with heavy dark thread.

"Civil War. The genuine article. Around the same date as the coin in her ring." Marino leans close, peering through his reading glasses. "Holy shit, these are something."

I return to the stretcher, and the putrid smell gets stronger as I begin unbuttoning the blouse. Decomposition is darkly swarming in like a plague of invisible insects as we work and time slips away, moving her closer to putrefaction as I move closer to being held in contempt of court.

"Probably not from a regular foot soldier. Probably officers' buttons." Marino reaches for a hand lens, judgment creeping into his tone. "Most people who collect old buttons don't sew them on clothes. No normal person would do that."

"It does seem a bit out of the ordinary," I remark. "Wearing antique or estate jewelry and so on is one thing, but sewing it on clothing would be another, I suppose."

"You got that right, and button collectors don't."

His voice is flinty with disapproval, as if he's made a sudden decision about the dead woman's character.

"They display them, put them in picture frames, swap them, sell them, maybe donate them to museums, depending on what they are," Marino says. "I've seen buttons like these go for hundreds, even thousands, of dollars."

He studies the three buttons closely with the lens, nudging each one with a gloved finger.

"If you look at them from the side"—he shows me—"they're not dented in at all, are in really great shape, which adds to the value. You'd never sew something like this on a jacket. Who the hell does that?"

"Well, she did, or someone did," I reply.

Removing her wet blouse, I decide it's purple, not burgundy. The tag at the back of the collar is *Audrey Marybeth,* size six.

"Maybe she was involved in antiques," I add. "Maybe she collected or was a dealer, or the buttons belonged to someone in her family."

The bra underneath is loose around her chest, the cups several sizes too big, and I estimate the body has lost at least twenty percent of its weight due to dehydration. She dried out while concealed someplace freezing or near-freezing, cold enough to prevent bacteria from colonizing and causing the decomposition that is beginning with a vengeance now. Minute by minute her odor is stronger, and I'm asking for trouble. I imagine Judge Conry calling lawyers to the bench, wanting to know where I am, discreet at first, and then demanding.

"Plenty of people collect in this part of the world." Marino has a hard look on his face, his mood turned sour. "You go in some of these junk shops and can buy vintage buttons, almost anything you can think of. Police, fire department, railroad, military. But you don't sew them on clothes, not even nickel-plated ones that go for five bucks apiece. Not even ones in really shitty shape you can buy in bulk."

"Since when are you an expert in vintage buttons?" I spread the blouse open next to the blazer.

"You really don't care." He's looking at the clock, and it's exactly two.

"What I care about most right this minute is getting what we need while there's still a chance."

Mostly I'm thinking about DNA. I've had cases where semen could still be recovered after a remarkably long time inside orifices, the stomach, the airway, deep inside the vaginal vault, and I'm not going to assume it's too late to get anything from this body, no matter how long she's been dead. The enemy of DNA is bacteria, and she's invisibly beginning to teem with it, and it literally will eat her to the bone.

I can gauge the breaking down of her tissue by the way she smells, insidiously foul at first and then much stronger and fast becoming a bristling stench from organisms that originated in her bowels but were dormant while she was kept dry and very cold or frozen. As she has warmed by degrees in the bay, in the boat and van, and now inside this room, the bacteria that cause putrefaction are having their way with her. They have begun a process I might be able to retard slightly by refrigeration but certainly can't stop. She's decomposing rapidly right before our eyes.

"Remember when I first got into metal detectors?" Marino is asking, and I really don't recall.

"Vaguely." I reach around to unzip her long gray skirt, discovering a bunched area of the waistband that has been cinched.

Three heavy-duty staples fasten inches of the material together. Stainless steel, no sign of rust.

"Why the hell do that?" Marino looks on.

"Like I said, she's not a size six anymore."

"If she ever was."

"When she was alive, she was bigger than this," I reply. "That much is a fact."

"But if the skirt slid off her because it was too big, it wouldn't have been lost because of the rope around her ankles and the dog crate," he says. "Why go to the trouble?"

"It depends on when it was done. All I can say with certainty is someone made the waistband smaller." I pull the skirt down over her wrinkled bare pale legs, surprised to find what's left of sheer pantyhose.

The stockings are in tatters, ripped off mid-thigh, and in my mind I see her alive. I see her terrified, locked up and trying to escape.

Clawing, pounding a door, breaking her nails. Frantically moving around shoeless on a surface covered with something dark red.

Then nothing; the picture blanks out. I can't imagine what

happened to her stockings except the legs weren't cut with anything sharp. The ultra-sheer nylon has runs all the way up
through the control top, and what is left around the thighs is
shredded, torn unevenly, like ragged transparent gauze loose
around her sallow dead skin. Did she rip off her hose mid-
thigh? If so, why?

Or did someone else do it?

The same person who stapled the skirt around the waist-
band and arranged jewelry so it wouldn't fall off the body and
be lost.

Like the jacket, the skirt is distinctive, quite stylish, con-
structed of two jersey layers that flow into a raw-edged handkerchief hem, *Peruvian Connection,* size six. I spread it on the
sheet to dry as Marino resumes reminiscing about our early
days together in Richmond, when apparently he became quite
the treasure hunter, using a metal detector he kept in the trunk
of his unmarked Ford to search crime scenes, primarily outdoor ones, for metal evidence, such as cartridge cases.

"Mainly when I was working evening shifts and had most
of the day off," he's saying, but the memory doesn't make him
cheerful and boisterous, the way he usually gets when he talks
about our past.

His voice has a hard, unforgiving ring that reminds me of a
shovel striking stone.

"I'd go out early in the morning to old battlefields, woods,
riverbanks, looking for coins, buttons, whatever I could find.
Got a belt buckle that cleaned up real good. You probably remember it."

I don't think I do, but I know better than to tell him.

"Brought it to your office and showed it to you," he says,
and he's always liked massive buckles, especially motorcycle
ones. "Oval-shaped, with U.S. stamped on cast brass in real big
letters."

I place nude panties and the pantyhose and the bra on a
sheet, and move the surgical light closer. I check her for lividity
as Marino again examines the antique buttons, leaning close,
shining a light on them.

"No sign of livor anteriorly," I note.

"What about when someone's been dead and maybe in a
cooler or freezer this long? Maybe they won't have it anymore."

"Unlike rigor, livor doesn't completely go away. It leaves a telltale sign." I look at her from head to toe, taking time I don't have, moving the overhead lamp as I search for the slightest hint of staining from when her circulation quit and blood settled due to gravity.

"I eventually sold it for five hundred bucks. Wish I hadn't now, because it sure as hell was worth more than that." Marino resumes talking about treasure hunting. "Also a two-piece CS buckle I found in Dinwiddie. Could have brought me a couple of grand if I hadn't needed quick bucks when Doris bailed, ran off leaving me with a shitload of debt. She's probably still with that douchebag car salesman, except I think he's selling Aflac now."

"Maybe you should find out."

"No way in hell. A real entrepreneur she's become," he says sarcastically. "Covers bricks with cloth and sells them as doorstops, no kidding, I mean, go figure. Like a symbol, huh? Something that gets in the way, an obstruction, a stumbling block, but not how she looks at it, of course."

"Maybe you should try to talk to her and find out from her how she looks at it."

"You can pull it up on the Internet," he says angrily. "Open Says Me. The name of her website. *I hold open your world to possibilities.* I can't believe it."

It figures he'd bring up his ex-wife when we don't have time to talk about her. I pull the body on its left side, and it's so light it feels hollow.

"There can be a lot of money in historic stuff like buttons, medals, old coins, but there's also such a thing as respect." He's back to that. "What you don't do is sew antique military buttons on a jacket or a coat to make a friggin' fashion statement."

"You can see it here. A livor pattern of hemolyzed blood." I press my fingers into different areas of the back. "No blanching, because the blood has seeped out the vessel walls. So after she died she was flat on her back for at least as long as it took for livor to set, probably twelve hours, possibly more. It could be that she was on her back the entire time since she died, stored somewhere until she was moved and dropped into the bay."

"You sure as hell don't send a jacket to the dry cleaner's if it's got a thousand dollars' worth of antique buttons on it." He won't stop talking about it. "But it's not the money."

"Moderate mummification, skin wet but hard and dried with faint remnants of patchy white mold on her face and neck," I dictate, and Marino scribes. "Eyes sunken and collapsed." I pry open her mouth. "Cheeks are sunken." I swab the inside of them. "No lip, tongue, or dental injuries," I say, as I check with a light. "Neck is free of any discrete discolorations." I look up at the clock.

It's eleven minutes past two. I move down and find more signs of moderate mummification but no injuries, and I open her legs. I ask Marino to bring me a Physical Evidence Recovery Kit, a PERK, or what a lot of cops call a rape kit, and I glance curiously at him as he walks to a cabinet, his face disgruntled and offended, as if there's something about this dead woman he takes personally.

"We'll definitely e-mail photos of the buttons and her jewelry to NamUs," I say. "These details seem unique enough to be significant. Especially if it's unusual to sew valuable antique buttons on clothing."

"It's damn disrespectful as hell."

He hands me a plastic speculum and opens the PERK's white cardboard box.

"When you find stuff like this, usually it's because the person got killed in battle and their body was left out there in a field or the woods."

He places bags, swabs, and a comb on a clean sheet.

"A hundred and fifty years later someone comes along with a metal detector and digs up their uniform buttons, their belt buckle, and when you find things like that you treat it like you've disturbed a grave, because you have."

I glance up at the clock again as I rehearse what I'll say to Dan Steward and Jill Donoghue when I see them, an apologetic explanation that I'll expect one or both of them to relay to the judge. My choice was to lose possibly critical evidence or be late for court, and I'll be very contrite.

"Even if the stuff comes from the attic," Marino says, "it's about respect, because it belonged to someone who made the ultimate sacrifice."

He begins filling out forms with what scant information we have, and he rants on and on.

"You don't sew buttons or shoulder epaulets on a jacket or put a dead soldier's cap box on your damn belt or wear his friggin' bloodstained socks. You don't cut up old uniforms that still have the soldiers' nametapes on them and make them into quilts."

He hands me envelopes for swabs.

"If you didn't go to Parris Island or OCS, then don't wear official U.S. Marine cammies, and for shit's sake don't make them into a purse. Jesus Christ, what kind of person does shit like that?"

"Don't see any evidence of sexual assault. Of course, that doesn't mean there wasn't one." I remove the speculum and toss it in the trash. "But it appears her legs were shaved not long before she died."

I look at a scattering of dark stubble that when magnified indicates a razor was used.

"Several days before she died, based on the new growth," I add. "Obviously the hair will seem a bit longer because of her dehydration. If she was kidnapped, she likely wasn't kept very long."

Marino's face is dark red, his eyes wide, as if he's reminded of something that really upsets him.

"What's the matter with you?" I insert an eighteen-gauge needle into the left femoral artery.

"Nothing." He talks the way he does when it's something.

I try the subclavian next, inserting a needle below the clavicle. No luck, and I try the notch to puncture the aorta, and manage to get a few drops. When I open her up later today, what I'll find is that her vessels are almost completely empty, the walls stained with hemoglobin, what looks like rust. For the most part, iron is all that's left.

I drip thick, dark blood on two sample areas of an FTA micro-card and place it under a chemical hood to air-dry.

"If you'll get her back inside the cooler, and this room stays locked. No one's to come in here," I tell Marino, as I pull off my lab coat. "Call DNA, let Gloria know they can collect the card within the hour. It should be dry by then, and we want a

DNA profile as fast as they can manage, and it needs to be entered into NamUs, NDIS, with as little delay as possible."

I toss the lab coat, shoe covers, and gloves into a bright red biohazard trash can and push open the door that leads into the air-locked vestibule, then the second door that leads into the corridor. It's twenty past two and I can't remember the last time I was this late for court or, better put, as late as I know I'm about to be. It will be at least two-forty-five, possibly as late as three-fifteen by the time Marino gets me to Fan Pier on Boston's waterfront, I calculate, and that's if traffic is reasonable.

Elevator doors slide open on my floor, and I jog along the corridor, not caring what a ridiculous sight I must be in a gray drysuit liner and tactical boots, carrying an orange jacket and a garbage bag. I scan my thumb to unlock my office, hurrying inside, as Bryce emerges from my bathroom, startling me. He's in his coat, his sunglasses parked on top of his head, and carrying the stainless-steel pitcher and demitasse cups Lucy and I drank café Cubano out of what seems light-years ago.

"I thought you were at the vet's." I drop my bag of wet clothes and jacket on the floor and stoop down to take off my boots. "I'm really, really late. Have you heard from Dan Steward? How's your cat?"

"Good God in heaven, what do you have on?" Bryce stares disapprovingly at the way I'm dressed. "Did you escape from the Ozarks? From a POW camp? Are you a biohazard? Kind of sexy, actually like a warm-fuzzy dive skin, but why gray? These are going into the dishwasher. Lucy must have cleaned up, am I right? Scummy milk film, and sticky enough to attract a flock of hummingbirds."

"I'm late for court, and you need to scoot so I can get ready. What are you doing in here, and does Dan understand what's going on?"

"Low on coffee and bottled water *avec gaz et sans*, completely out of trail mix, sugar-free granola, protein drinks, and those awful little crackers you like that supposedly are whole-grain or rice or particleboard. Dan's been dragging out cross-examining the witness who's right before you. . . ."

"Thank God." I pad barefoot to my desk and dig through files.

"But apparently the judge asked where you were and Dan

told him but said judges don't give a shit about excuses and to hurry and get there."

"Have you seen my Mildred Lott file?"

"So I stopped at Whole Foods and just got here a minute ago." He opens my closet door. "And of course noticed your little kitchenette in there is a mess just like it always is after Lucy helps herself. She needs to find a nice wife, because her domestic skills don't exist. It's right next to your microscope, where you left it. Under some histology reports?"

He retrieves my suit and blouse.

"I don't know what you did with your pantyhose. Figured you pitched them. I realize they don't have much of a shelf life."

I have no idea what I did with them. I probably tucked them in a desk drawer. I don't care.

He drapes my clothes over the conference table.

"I absolutely know Indy wasn't exposed to onions. Ethan was so happy I was finally back from being in Florida forever, and he made my favorite. His chili's really amazing, and of course Marino and everyone's blaming us as if we're irresponsible and don't care if we kill our cat." He looks at me and looks exhausted, fear crouched at the back of his eyes. "She's only ten weeks old, Dr. Scarpetta, and I've had cats before and know when something's really wrong."

"I'm sorry, Bryce." I set the file on the table and shut the door that leads into the corridor. "We'll talk about it when I'm back."

"I know it happened at the groomer," he continues from inside my closet, where he's now looking for something on the floor. "Well, your shoes are here but still no pantyhose. Just a week ago Saturday, her very first visit to get her claws clipped, and there she was with about twenty other animals, including a parrot that was making these strangling, hacking sounds like it had kennel cough. I realize it might have been imitating it, but what if it wasn't . . . ?"

"Bryce, I don't mean to sound insensitive, but I've got to get cleaned up."

He hands me my shoes.

"Do you have any idea how careful we are?" He's on the verge of tears.

"I promise we'll chat about this later. . . ."

"We're so paranoid about onions and poisonous things, like poinsettias, which we refuse to have in the house, and I don't eat raw onions anyway. . . ."

"I've got to get ready and can't with you standing here. . . ."

"So we always use onion powder, which is better all the way round, because there's no chance of the ittiest, bittiest piece escaping the counter and ending up on the floor." His eyes well up.

"You put onion powder in your chili?" I carry my suit and blouse into the bathroom and hang them on the shower door.

"Now's not the time to criticize our cooking." His voice shakes.

"I had a cat when I was in law school, and sometimes he refused to eat. . . ."

"They can be very sensitive. He was probably angry with you."

"A vet suggested I give him meat baby food, and apparently it had onion powder in it, which can cause toxicity, the same as raw onions, by oxidizing hemoglobin. . . ."

"Oh my God! Did he die?"

"No. It's just something to think about and mention to the vet. And you need to leave so I can change. Please."

"It's just terribly upsetting."

"Well, I guess I'll just change in here." I set my shoes on the toilet lid.

"You need to be aware the media's been ringing the phone off the hook."

His voice sounds loudly, tragically from the doorway that adjoins my office with his, and I unzip the gray liner and hurry out of it, leaving it in a pile on my bathroom floor.

"Calling my cell phone, too, at least those reporters who have my number. There's huge speculation that the old lady you just pulled out of the bay is Mildred Lott. . . ."

"No evidence of it." I run a washcloth under hot water and clean up as best I can, and of course a shower right now is impossible.

"You know? That someone obviously was holding her hostage all this time, or maybe her disappearance was faked back in the spring or how she's been hiding and finally drowned herself? You should hear the theories."

"There's nothing to make me think it's her." I pull on a new pair of pantyhose I retrieve from a cabinet.

"Meaning her husband, Channing Lott, couldn't have had anything to do with her death, since he's considered a flight risk and has been in jail without bond since April?" Bryce has the remarkable ability of talking nonstop without seeming to take a breath. "So how could he possibly have killed her or paid someone else to some six months after she supposedly vanished?"

I step into my pin-striped skirt and yank up the zipper in back. "I don't want you releasing any information at all, not one word about this case, please." I hurry into my blouse, fumbling with the buttons and tucking it in, disgusted by how quickly rumors can start and how difficult it is to disarm them. "Not even a hint of an opinion about whether the dead lady might be Mildred Lott or Emma Shubert or anyone. Understood?"

"Well, of course. I didn't just fall off the turnip truck. I know what the press does with the slightest nothing."

I turn on the vanity light, dismayed by my reflection in the mirror over the sink. Pale. Completely washed out. Hair flat from wearing a neoprene dive hood and submerging my head in cold salt water. I drip Visine into my eyes.

"I'm just warning you I've got no idea what might come up when you get on the stand, because they can ask you anything they want." Bryce is still talking.

I rub a dab of gel in my hair and muss it up to give it a little lift, and it still looks awful.

sixteen

TRAFFIC IS BAD IN BOSTON, AND AVAILABLE PARKING IS nowhere to be seen at the John Joseph Moakley U.S. Court-house, an architectural marvel of dark red brick and glass that embraces the harbor like graceful arms. I tell Marino to let me out.

"Park where you can or drive around and wait for me. I'll call you when I'm on my way down." I have my hand on the door.

"Hell, no."

"Right here is fine."

"No way. No telling what scumbag friends he's got hanging around." Marino means what scumbag friends Channing Lott might have.

"I'm perfectly safe."

Marino scouts the parking lot, where there's scarcely room for a bicycle, let alone a large SUV; then he stalks a Prius and curses when the driver gets out instead of pulling away.

"Piece-of-shit green-machine crap," he says, creeping off. "They should have reserved parking for expert witnesses."

"Please stop. Right here is perfect."

He targets the Barking Crab, with its yellow-and-red awning across the old iron swing bridge that spans Fort Point Channel.

"I can probably find something over there, since it's past lunchtime and too early for dinner." He heads in that direction.

"Stop." I mean it. "I'm getting out." I open my door. "Park anywhere you want. I'm so late I don't care."

"How about staying put if I'm not there before you're done? Don't wander off, assuming it's quick."

I hurry along the brick Harbor Walk, past The Daily Catch, to the waterfront, where there's a park with wooden benches and thick hedges of flowering *Justicia,* an evergreen shrub that can't have been selected by accident for a courthouse. Taking off my suit jacket, I push through a glass door that leads into a screening station where I'm greeted by court security officers, CSOs I know by name, retired cops now with the U.S. Marshals Service.

"There she is."

"We've been wondering when you're gonna turn up like a bad penny."

"On every TV channel. CNN, Fox, MSNBC, YouTube."

"I got a cousin in England who saw it on BBC, said the turtle you were working on was the size of a whale."

"Gentlemen? How are you?" I hand over my driver's license even though they are used to me.

"Couldn't be better if we lied."

"Last time I was this good I forgot about it."

Typical men of the dark blue cloth, they fire off quips that make less sense the more one thinks about them, and I smile despite it all. I surrender my iPhone, because no electronic devices are allowed inside, doesn't matter who you are, and my suit jacket is x-rayed as I walk through the scanner, everything by the book, doesn't matter how many times I've been here.

"I saw the fireboat go by earlier, Doc. Then the Coast Guard and choppers," says the CSO named Nate, solid gristle, with the flattened nose of a prizefighter. "That lady you pulled out of the water this morning. Somebody's mother."

"Or somebody's wife. You think it's her, Doc?"

"It's too early to say who it is," I reply.

"A terrible thing."

"Yes, it is." I put my jacket back on.

"Promise your phone will be right here when you leave. They just went into a recess," says the ruddy-faced CSO named Brian.

He nods toward the glass, drawing my attention to a well-dressed man and woman drinking coffee on the brick walkway.

"Those two out there?" he says. "Connected to him, to Mr. Lott. Maybe friends, relatives, bigwigs from his shipping company. Christ knows. He owns half the world. How come Marino's not with you?"

"He's investigating the crime of no parking."

"Good luck solving that one. Well, don't be wandering around here too much by your lonesome, you hear?"

The man and woman on the other side of the glass are huddled close, looking out at the water. They turn their backs to us as if they know we're interested, and I hurry up a stone stairway and take a marble-paneled elevator to the third floor. My heels click over polished granite as I rush past floor-to-ceiling windows that open onto the harbor and the outer reaches of the bay, the courtrooms on my right behind heavy double wooden doors numbered in brass. I weave through people waiting to testify and conferring and loitering, some of them attorneys I recognize, and Dan Steward walks out of courtroom 17 just as I reach it.

"I'm really sorry," I start to say, as he motions for me to follow him to an isolated area where the corridor ends beneath huge colorful panels of art.

"I managed to drag and stretch it out." He exaggerates a drawl, immensely proud of himself. "You're the last witness, and I probably won't need anything from you on cross, obviously."

"Both sides are resting their case for sure?" I can't stop thinking about the timing.

I really am the last witness the jury's going to hear, he says, and the timing is remarkable. It doesn't feel like a coincidence, no matter how much I reassure myself it must be one.

"After we start closing arguments," Steward says. "Hopefully we'll wind it up today and the jury will begin deliberations before we break for the night. The good news is you haven't delayed anything." He stares at my breasts. "I told the judge what's up, and I'm sure he'll give you a chance to explain. That doesn't mean he won't chew you out. But if it wasn't for me? Well, don't think Jill bothered to stick up for you, even though you're her witness."

He takes off his wire-rimmed glasses, wipes them with a handkerchief, his eyes riveted to my chest, where he has a habit of looking rather constantly. I've never thought he means anything by it. Dan Steward isn't the least bit lewd or crass, is a proper but awkward man of small stature in his thirties with a big head of dirty-blond hair and big teeth. He has terrible taste in suits, this one an ill-fitting tan corduroy with a cheap green paisley tie that's too long and unfashionably wide. He always seems frazzled and nervous, his demeanor grating to juries, I've been told, and I believe it.

"But she knows," I reply. "She understands why I'm late."

"Hell, yes. Your office was courteous enough to call her. . . ."

"My office?" I can't think whom he might mean.

"When we recessed a few minutes ago, she indicated she knew you were on your way."

Bryce let Dan Steward know I was running late, but I can't imagine which member of my staff might have left a message with Jill Donoghue, whose subpoena is the reason I'm here. I haven't spoken to her directly. I wouldn't in a situation like this, where there is nothing substantive I can offer to the case, only my physical presence so she can harass, manipulate, create high drama.

"And I told her not to make a big thing of it," Steward says, and Donoghue probably has earned the distinction of being the most hated human being on his planet.

"What is there to make of anything if I haven't caused a delay?"

"I'm sure you're aware of what's all over the news, Kay."

"The body I just recovered has nothing to do with this, and I certainly can't get into it, and I won't." I don't mean to sound impatient or entitled, but I'm weary of courtroom antics and what I've come to call magic tricks.

Maybe total disillusionment better describes what I feel, because it's simply stunning what defense attorneys manage to pull out of their hats these days. The more unbelievable and illogical the tactic, the more they seem to get away with it, and I'm not far from being entirely cynical about a process I used to believe in, at times unsure the jury system works anymore.

"Well, she just blasted a hole the size of the Grand Canyon in the Gloucester investigator, not Kefe, thank God, because he's dumb as dirt, but Lorey, who went away very unhappy. I feel kind of bad leaving him up there as long as I did during cross, but as a result technically nothing has been delayed," Steward says to my chest. "But what happens next isn't my call. And the judge happens to have a bit of a hard-on for her."

"I'm really sorry, Dan. But not even two hours ago I had on a drysuit and dive mask and was recovering a dead body that I'm in a very big hurry to get back to." I look out at the harbor, at a plane taking off from Logan and a red oil tanker gliding out to sea, and I can barely make out the Boston lighthouse jutting up in a volatile dark sky that threatens rain. "It was either be late for what truly is frivolous testimony or possibly lose evidence in what I'm fairly certain is a homicide."

"That's what I suspect Jill the cobra fully intends to spit into your eyes." Steward shuffles through a folder filled with notes he's made on sheets of yellow legal paper, and he seems rankled by my reference to frivolous testimony. "She hammered Lorey to a damn pulp about the obvious problem of there being no body in this case and the lack of scientific evidence, planting the usual doubts in the minds of the jurors, because no one seems to believe in circumstantial evidence anymore."

"As we've discussed, these types of cases are extremely difficult. . . ."

"I mean, come on. His wife is recorded on the security camera going out of the house at night because she hears something, is obviously talking to someone she knows outside in the pitch dark, and vanishes. Never to be seen again." He talks over me in his irritating reedy voice. "Evidence on her husband's laptop shows he'd been shopping around for someone to murder her for a hundred grand, and that's not enough to send him away for the rest of his life?"

"It's not my case, for the very reasons you're citing," I remind him. "Her body hasn't been found, and I've had nothing to do with the investigation beyond looking over medical records and your asking my opinion." I refrain from adding that I'm here right now against my will because of him, and he of all people should have known that if he asked me anything in writing and I replied in writing, it would be discoverable.

Especially if the opposing counsel is Jill Donoghue, who at this moment is heading in our direction, carrying a to-go cup of coffee, stunning in a fitted olive-green suit with wide lapels and a slim skirt, her long, dark hair softly curled with bangs. One of the most feared defense attorneys in Massachusetts, it doesn't help that she's quite beautiful, a graduate of Harvard Law School who last year was the president of the American College of Trial Lawyers.

She participates in workshops and seminars at the Federal Judicial Center, where I've run into her on a number of occasions, her expertise electronic discovery, which of course includes e-mails. I can't help but suspect that Steward deliberately set me up for exactly what I'm getting because he wants to sic me on his nemesis, as if I'm his pet pit bull when in fact what he's manipulated more likely has given Donoghue an advantage.

"Come on and tell me. No bullshit. Any chance that's Mildred Lott you just pulled out of the bay?" he says somberly, quietly, his narrow face tense, his gray eyes flat behind his glasses.

"I can't know anything with certainty at this time." I watch Donoghue head into the courtroom, and maybe it's my imagination, but she seems to be smiling.

"You can't say it's not her?" Steward asks. "It sure would be good if you could."

"I've barely looked at the body. I haven't autopsied it. At this time I have no idea who she is, but preliminarily and at a glance I didn't see scars from cosmetic procedures such as breast implants, liposuction, a face-lift, that we know she'd undergone. No physical similarities I saw so far under the circumstances." I stop short of saying what condition the body is in.

"What circumstances, exactly?" he asks.

"The circumstances of my having time only for a cursory exam before I rushed here."

"What about age, hair color?"

"Her hair isn't dyed platinum blond. It's naturally white," I answer.

"Are we sure Mildred Lott's hair was dyed?"

"I'm not sure of anything."

"The way she's dressed, any personal effects, such as wedding and engagement rings, an antique locket necklace Mildred Lott was known to wear and was believed to have on when she disappeared, that sort of thing?"

"I found nothing consistent with any of that."

"Any idea when this newest case, this lady, may have died and how?"

"I'm certainly not going to be compelled to testify about a dead body I've not even autopsied yet, Dan," I reply, with a trace of resistance that I can't seem to keep out of my voice.

"Hey. It's all about what Jill's buddy Judge Conry permits."

"Her *buddy*?"

"You know. Rumors. Not me who's going to repeat them." Steward glances at his watch. "I'd best get back in there."

I wait until everyone has gone inside, and I stand alone between inner and outer wooden doors, listening to the strong timbered voice of the clerk as he instructs everyone to rise for the judge. The sounds of people standing and resettling, and the gavel cracks, and court is back in session. Then a commanding woman's voice, what I call a radio voice, Jill Donoghue's voice, announces into a microphone that she's calling me as her next witness.

The door I face opens onto a vaulted arched ceiling hung with alabaster chandeliers, and tables occupied by attorneys and rows of crowded public seating leading to Judge Joseph Conry, robed in black and perched up high on a bench that's elevated like a throne before a backdrop of leather-bound law reviews. I feel his gravity from the far end of his courtroom as I follow gray carpet toward the witness stand, directly across from the jury box.

"Dr. Scarpetta." The judge halts me from what feels like miles away. "You were supposed to be here an hour and fifteen minutes ago."

"Yes, Your Honor," I reply, with appropriate humility, looking directly at him and avoiding Jill Donoghue standing at a lectern to my left. "And I deeply apologize."

"Why are you late?"

I know he knows why, but I reply, "I was at a scene several miles south of the city in the Massachusetts Bay, Your Honor. Where a woman's body was found."

"So you were working?"

"Yes, Your Honor." I feel eyes fastened to me like darts, the courtroom as still as an empty cathedral.

"Well, Dr. Scarpetta, I was here by nine o'clock this morning, as is required of me so I can do my job in this case." He is hard and unforgiving, not at all the man I know from swearing-ins and retirements, from the unveilings of judicial portraits and the countless Federal Bar Association receptions I've attended.

Joseph Conry, whose name is frequently confused with the English novelist Joseph Conrad, is strikingly handsome, tall, with jet-black hair and piercing blue eyes, *the black Irish judge with a heart of darkness*, as he has been described, a nononsense brilliant jurist who always has treated me kindly and with respect. I wouldn't call us personal friends. But I would say we are warmly acquainted, Conry always going out of his way to get me a drink and to chat about the latest in forensics or to ask my advice about his daughter in medical school.

"All of the lawyers and jurors were here by nine o'clock this morning, as required of them, so they can do their jobs in this case," he is saying in the same severe voice, as I listen with growing dismay. "And because you decided to put your job first, we've been forced to wait for you, implying you're obviously the most important person in this trial."

"I'm sorry, Your Honor. I never meant to imply that."

"You've wasted the court's precious time. Yes, I said *wasted*," he stuns me by saying. "Time *wasted* not just by you but also by Mr. Steward, because he doesn't fool me when he malingers with a witness to buy you time to get here because you're too busy or too important to obey an order of this court."

"I'm sorry, Your Honor. I hadn't thought of it as my intentionally defying anything. I've been consumed with—"

"Dr. Scarpetta, you were subpoenaed by the defense to testify in this courtroom at two p.m. today, right?"

"Yes, Your Honor." I can't believe he's doing this while the jury is seated.

"You're a doctor and a lawyer, are you not?"

"Yes, Your Honor." He should have asked the jury to leave before he started ripping into me.

"I assume you know what the term *subpoena* means."

"I do, Your Honor."

"Please tell the court what your understanding of a subpoena is."

"It's a writ by a government agency, Your Honor, that has

the authority to compel someone to testify under a penalty for failure to do so."

"A court order."

"Yes, Your Honor," I answer in disbelief I don't show.

He's going to make an example out of me, and I can feel Jill Donoghue's stare and can only imagine her immense satisfaction as she watches one of the most eminent judges in Boston dismantle me one piece at a time in front of the jury, in front of her client, Channing Lott.

"And you violated that court order because you put your work ahead of the court's, didn't you?" the judge asks in the same demanding tone.

"I guess that's right, Your Honor. I apologize." I meet his cold blue gaze from our impossible distance.

"Well, you're going to have to do more than apologize, Dr. Scarpetta. I'm going to fine you in an amount that will cover the hourly costs of everyone whose time you've wasted for the past hour and fifteen minutes. Actually, an hour and a half, if we include the time it's taking for me to handle this unnecessary and unfortunate matter. And more time will be added, because now we're going to run late, run past five and into the night. I'm going to guesstimate what you've cost the court is twenty-five hundred dollars. Now please take the witness stand so we can move forward."

The courtroom is deathly still as I climb wooden steps and settle into a black leather chair, and the clerk asks me to raise my right hand. I swear to tell the truth, the whole truth, and nothing but the truth as Jill Donoghue waits patiently at a lectern with a laptop and microphone in the midst of a vast space filled with wooden tables and Windsor benches, and so many flat video screens I'm reminded of a satellite's silvery solar panels.

I glance at the prosecution, three of them seated side by side and flipping through notes or writing them, and I can tell by the dazed expression on Dan Steward's face he wasn't expecting the blistering admonishment I just got. He's rapidly calculating the damage that's been done.

seventeen

RARELY AM I CALLED BY THE DEFENSE. IT'S ALMOST never necessary or even helpful to "the bad guys," as Marino unfairly calls attorneys who represent people indicted for murder.

If I'm a prosecution witness, and typically I am, the opposing counsel will question me anyway, while enjoying the advantage of stipulating that I'm an expert before the jury hears the laundry list of qualifications that might prove it. In fact, Jill Donoghue's modus operandi in every encounter I've had with her is to shut me up before I can so much as say where I went to medical school or if I did while addressing me as *Mrs. Scarpetta* and *ma'am,* to encourage those deciding her client's fate not to take me seriously.

I don't know what to expect right now, except I worry that Dan Steward won't be helpful. After the scolding he just witnessed, he's not likely to tamper with Judge Conry, whose presence I feel like a towering thunderhead, dark and ready to erupt again, the courtroom electrically charged the way the air is after lightning strikes.

I don't understand why he is so angry with me, as if what I did was personal and intentional, a slight or injury I can't fathom. I've been late to court before, not often, but it happens, and judges aren't nice about it. But I've never been threatened or reprimanded, much less fined. I've never been dressed down in front of a jury. Something is terribly off, and I can't think of a way to address it, as it's not possible to e-mail or call a federal judge and ask him what's wrong with our relationship.

Especially if the real reason is what Steward intimated. Jill's *buddy*, he'd said, and his reference to *rumors* was obvious.

"Good afternoon." Jill Donoghue smiles at me as if we are in for a pleasant time and are old friends, and only now, as we begin, will I look at her and to the left of her, between her lectern and the jury box, at the defense table. Channing Lott sits very straight, his hands clasped on top of a yellow legal pad with pages of notes folded back.

His jailwear has been traded for a double-breasted black suit with wide pinstripes that looks Versace, and a white shirt with gold cuff links, and a rusty red-and-brown silk tie that brings to mind Hermès. I've never met the billionaire industrialist or seen him in person, but he's instantly recognizable, handsome in a bohemian way, with long, snow-white hair he wears in a single braid, his eyes the pale blue of faded denim, his nose and cheekbones strong and proud like a Native American chief. For a second we are staring at each other, his gaze unflinching, as if he demands something and has no fear of me, and I turn away.

"For the benefit of the jury," Donoghue resumes in the same collegial tone, as if we work together, as if I'm on her team, "would you please state your name, occupation, and where you work?"

"My name is Kay Scarpetta."

"Do you have a middle name?"

"I don't."

"You were born Kay Scarpetta, with no middle name."

"I was."

"Named after your father, Kay Marcellus Scarpetta the Third, correct?"

"That's correct."

"A Miami grocer who died when you were a child."

"Yes."

"Do you have a married name?"

"I do not."

"But you're married. Actually, divorced and remarried."

"Yes."

"Currently you're married to Benton Wesley." As if I might be married to someone else a month from now.

"Yes, I am," I answer.

"But you didn't take your first husband's name. And you didn't take Benton Wesley's name when you finally got married to him."

"I did not," I say, as I look at men and women on the jury, who, if they are married, likely share a surname.

First box checked. Make me different so they can't relate to me and might disapprove.

"What is your occupation, and where do you work?" Jill Donoghue says, in the same friendly tone.

"I'm a forensic radiologic pathologist employed as the chief medical examiner and director of the Cambridge Forensic Center," I say to the jury, nine men and three women, two of them African American, five of them Asian, four of them possibly Hispanic, one white.

"When you refer to yourself as chief medical examiner and director of the Cambridge Forensic Center, which from this point on I will refer to as the CFC, does this also include other areas of Massachusetts?"

"Yes, it does. All medical-examiner cases and related scientific analysis in the Commonwealth of Massachusetts are managed by the CFC."

"Dr. Scarpetta . . . ," she starts to say, pausing, the flipping of pages amplified by the microphone. "And I call you *doctor* because you are in fact a medical doctor with a number of sub-specialties, isn't that right?"

She's giving me professional credibility before she takes it away.

"Yes."

"Dr. Scarpetta, am I correct in adding that you also serve in an official capacity with the Department of Defense?" she inquires.

Or maybe she just wants to portray me as a super-bitch.

"Yes, I am."

"Please tell us about that."

"In my capacity as a special reservist for the Department of

Defense, I assist the Armed Forces Medical Examiners as requested or needed by them."

"And what exactly are the Armed Forces Medical Examiners?"

"Basically, AFMEs are forensic pathologists with federal jurisdiction, similar to the FBI having federal jurisdiction in certain types of cases."

"So you're the FBI of medical examiners," she says.

"I'm saying that in some instances I have federal jurisdiction."

"An example?"

"An example would be if there were a fatal military aircraft crash in Massachusetts or near Massachusetts, the case might come to me instead of being transported to the port mortuary at Dover Air Force Base in Dover, Delaware."

"The *case* being a casualty or casualties. *Case* by your definition meaning a dead body or dead bodies, as opposed to actually working the crash itself. You wouldn't examine the crashed jet or helicopter."

Jill Donoghue is one of the few defense attorneys I know who dares to ask questions she doesn't know the answer to because she's that smart and sure of herself. But it's not without risks.

"It would not be my job to examine a crashed plane or helicopter for the purpose of determining mechanical or computer failure or pilot error," I reply. "Although I might be shown the wreckage and reports to see if the findings of the National Transportation Safety Board, for example, are consistent with what the body tells me."

"Do dead bodies speak to you, Dr. Scarpetta?"

"They don't literally speak to me."

"They don't speak the way you and I are talking."

"Not audibly," I answer. "No."

Check box two. Make me eccentric. Make me crazy.

"But inaudibly they speak to you?"

"In the language of diseases and wounds and many other nuances, they tell me their story."

A woman on the jury, African American, in a dark red suit, nods her head as if we're in church.

"And your area of expertise is the human body. Specifically, the dead human body," Jill Donoghue asks, and I can tell by her tone she doesn't like what I just said.

"Examining the dead is one area of my expertise." I will make it worse for her. "I examine every detail in order to reconstruct how someone died and how they lived, and offer everything I possibly can to those left behind who find the loss profoundly life-altering."

The juror in dark red nods deeply, as if I'm preaching salvation, and Donoghue changes the subject. "Dr. Scarpetta, what is your rank as an Air Force Reservist?"

"I'm a colonel," I answer, and a young male juror in a blue polo shirt scowls as if he doesn't approve or is confused.

"But you never actively served in the military."

"I'm not sure I understand the question."

"It wasn't a question, Dr. Scarpetta." She's not happy with me. "I'm stating that you were never active in the Air Force, didn't enlist, weren't deployed to Iraq, for example."

"When I was actively serving time in the military, we weren't at war with Iraq," I reply.

"You're saying no Air Force Reservists were deployed to Iraq?"

"I'm not saying that."

"Good, because that wouldn't be true, now, would it?" she says.

Check box three. Imply I have to be encouraged to tell the truth.

"It wouldn't be correct to say no Air Force Reservists were deployed to Iraq," I agree.

"I was using a deployment to Iraq as an example of what someone active in the military might be involved in." She winds up for her next spitball. "As opposed to someone who signs on with a branch of service simply to get his or her medical school education paid for by the government. Which is what you did, isn't it?"

Check box four. I'm entitled. I'm an elitist.

"After medical school I served on the staff of the Armed Forces Institute of Pathology, and my medical school tuition eventually was forgiven."

"So when you served your time you weren't actually de-ployed anywhere at all. You served as a forensic pathologist, mostly doing paperwork."

"Forensic pathologists do a lot of paperwork." I smile at the jurors, and several of them smile back.

"The AFME is part of the AFIP, correct?"

"It was," I answer. "The AFIP was disestablished several years ago."

"While it still existed and you were on its staff, were you involved in the Atomic Bomb Casualty Commission?"

"I was not."

Jesus Christ. Why the hell isn't Steward objecting? I resist looking back at him.

Don't look at anything or anyone but the jury.

"Well, some of your colleagues were on the Atomic Bomb Casualty Commission, were they not?"

"I believe a few of them had been involved in that," I reply. "A few of the senior forensic pathologists who were still at the AFIP when I was."

"Why weren't you involved with the Atomic Bomb Casualty Commission?" she asks.

Goddammit.

Why the hell is Steward letting her get away with this? I can't imagine the judge wouldn't sustain an objection that this line of questioning has nothing to do with this case or me. She's trying to inflame the Asian jurors, to prejudice them against me.

Like implying I might have had something to do with the holocaust in front of a jury of Jews.

"That was before my time with the AFIP." I keep my eyes on the jury.

I'm talking to them, not to Jill Donoghue.

"For a while the AFIP was studying autopsy specimens from Japanese people killed by the atomic bomb, correct?" She's not going to relent.

"That's correct."

"And this place where you served the time you owed the military for paying for your medical school education—the AFIP—was forced to return those ancestral autopsy materials to the Japanese because it was deemed disrespectful for the U.S. military to be a repository of Japanese human remains.

Especially since it was the U.S. military that killed these Japanese civilians by bombing the cities Hiroshima and Nagasaki."

You aren't going to say a damn thing, are you, you coward?

I resist glancing at Steward. I'm on my own.

"World War Two was before I was born, Ms. Donoghue. It ended some forty years before I was on the staff of the AFIP. I wasn't involved in any studies related to deaths caused by atomic bombs."

"Well, let me ask you this, Dr. Scarpetta. Were you ever a member of the American Society of Experimental Pathology?"

"No."

"No? You've never attended a meeting?"

"No."

"What about the American Society of Investigative Pathology? Have you ever attended one of their meetings?"

"Yes."

"The same group, isn't it?"

"Essentially."

"I see. So if the name changes, then your answer changes?"

"The American Society of Experimental Pathology no longer exists, and I never attended a meeting or was involved with it. It's now the American Society of Investigative Pathology."

"Are you a member of the American Society of Investigative Pathology, the ASIP, Dr. Scarpetta?"

"Yes."

"So whatever one might call this group, the fact is you're involved in experimental medicine?"

"The ASIP investigates the mechanisms of diseases."

Silence. I watch the faces of the jurors. They are alert but skeptical of me. An older man with short gray hair and a big belly looks intrigued but baffled. Jill Donoghue is squirting the ink of confusion into the water and lacing it with negativity, with insidious hints that I'm accustomed to getting a free ride that's financed by tax dollars and that I'm reckless and inhumane and a bigot and possibly don't like men.

One brushstroke at a time, she's painting the portrait of a female scientific sociopath, someone despicable, so when she gets to what's really important I won't be credible. I won't be liked. I might be hated.

"In what types of cases might an Armed Forces Medical

Examiner, an AFME, have jurisdiction, Dr. Scarpetta?" she then asks, and I've never felt this unprotected.

It's as if there is no prosecution, as if Dan Steward is watching me being marched up a hill to the gallows and has not the slightest protest.

"Any military death that occurs in theater," I say.

"'In theater'? Perhaps you could explain what you mean by *theater*?"

"A combat theater is an area of war operation, such as Afghanistan," I reply to the jury. "Other types of cases that are the jurisdiction of the AFMEs, the Armed Forces Medical Examiners, would include deaths on military bases, the death of the president of the United States or the vice president or members of cabinet, and also certain other individuals employed by the U.S. government, such as members of the CIA or our astronauts, should they die while on official duty."

"Quite a daunting responsibility." Donoghue sounds thoughtful.

One might even think she's impressed, and I continue looking directly at the jury and refuse to look at her.

"I can certainly see why you might assume your job is more important than mine or the members of the jury's or even the judge's," she says.

eighteen

SHE PAUSES DURING A SPATTER OF LAUGHTER FROM PEO-ple who are seated inside the courtroom, but the jurors aren't amused, not one of them.

"I don't assume any such thing," I answer.

"Well, you were an hour and fifteen minutes late today, Dr. Scarpetta. If you include the time it took for Judge Conry to reprimand you, an hour and a half, and this courtroom won't be adjourning before dark because of you."

"For which I continue to be apologetic, Ms. Donoghue. It was never my intention to disrespect the court. I was out in a boat at a death scene that demanded my attention."

"Suggesting that the dead are more important to you than the living?"

"It would be incorrect to assume that. Life always takes precedence over death."

"But you work with the dead, do you not? Your patients are dead people, are they not?"

"As a medical examiner," I reply slowly, calmly, as I anticipate where this is headed, "it's my job to investigate any sudden, unexpected, or violent death, and to determine the cause and manner of that death. In other words, what actually killed the person, and was it an accident, a suicide, a homicide, for example? So, yes, most people I examine are dead."

"Well, hopefully all of them are."

More laughter, but the jurors are somber and listening intently. A heavy woman in a purple pantsuit sitting in the middle of the front row leans forward in her chair. She hasn't taken her eyes off me, and on her left an older man dressed tidily in slacks and a pullover sweater has his head cocked to one side, as if trying to figure me out.

Jill Donoghue hasn't offered any surprises yet. She's trying to show me to be a cold-blooded peculiar woman who doesn't give a shit about living people. Meaning I wouldn't give a shit about her client Channing Lott.

"Not everyone I examine is dead." I'm speaking to the juror in purple, to the man next to her, and another juror in a blue suit. "At times I also examine living victims to determine if their injuries are consistent with information the police has been given."

"And where did you get the training to examine dead bodies and also the occasional living one? Where did you go to school? Let's start with college."

"I went to Cornell University, and after graduation attended Johns Hopkins Medical School, then I attended Georgetown Law and after that returned to Hopkins to complete my residency in pathology. This was followed by a year's forensic pathology fellowship at the Dade County Medical Examiner's Office in Miami, Florida."

It goes on. It is endless. For the better part of half an hour, Jill Donoghue interrogates me about every nuance of my education and training. Tedious questions about my time spent with the Armed Forces Institute of Pathology are followed by what I did while stationed at Walter Reed Army Medical Center in Washington, D.C., in the late eighties, before I was appointed chief medical examiner of Virginia and moved to Richmond. Then she digs into my more active involvement with the Department of Defense after 9-11, which ultimately led to my spending six months at Dover Air Force Base, where I learned computer tomography, or CT scans, to assist in autopsies.

Dan Steward doesn't stir until she brings up Benton in a confrontational way, wanting to know if it's true we met when

I was the new chief medical examiner of Virginia and he was the chief of what then was called the Behavioral Science Unit at the FBI Academy in Quantico. She asks if it's true that I was divorced at the time while he was married with three children.

"I object," Steward finally says.

I can't help myself. I turn to look. He's on his feet, his chair shoved back from the prosecution's table, directly to the right of the lectern, where I see Donoghue leaning quite comfortably, quite casually, quite confidently.

"Details about Dr. Scarpetta's personal life are beyond the scope of what qualifies her as an expert medical examiner," says Dan Steward, perhaps one of the most pathetic attorneys I've ever worked with, I decide.

"Your Honor," Donoghue addresses Judge Conry. "I respectfully offer that if it can be shown to the court that a witness has engaged in criminal or immoral or deceitful behavior, it absolutely is within the scope of what qualifies him or her to testify to alleged facts that could result in a defendant going to prison."

"Overruled. Ms. Donoghue, you may proceed."

It's now I know for a fact that this god who is judge has decided to consign me to his personal hell.

They're having an affair, or want to.

I refrain from looking in his direction.

"Isn't it true, Dr. Scarpetta, that you started an intimate relationship with Benton Wesley while he was still married to someone else?" Jill Donoghue asks, and I have no choice but to answer.

I am alone.

I look at the faces of the men and women on the jury and say, "If by intimate you mean we fell in love with each other. Yes, we did. We've been together the better part of twenty years now, and are married."

The woman juror in dark red nods, and Donoghue says, "So it would be fair to say that truth is whatever you decide it is."

"It would not be fair to say that."

"It would be fair to say that if someone is married, so what."

"That's your opinion, not mine," I reply, because Steward isn't going to do a damn thing.

"It would be fair to say you don't honor the law but do as you please."

"It most assuredly would not be fair to say that," I reply.

"But Benton Wesley was married."

"He was."

"And you took him from his wife and three daughters."

"He divorced his wife. I did not take him from her or anyone."

"Dr. Scarpetta? Would it be accurate to say that truth is what you decide it is?" She tries again.

"It would not be accurate to say that," I repeat.

"Was it accurate when you stated in an e-mail to Dan Steward that Channing Lott's wife has turned into a bar of soap?"

"That's not what I said."

"I'm sorry. Then what did you say?"

"On which occasion?"

"Well, let me produce the e-mail," she replies.

It appears on the flat screens around the room, the e-mail addresses in it blacked out, redacted, and she asks me if I recognize what I'm seeing, and I do, and then she reads it out loud:

Dan—

To answer your question in general and by no means specifically about Mildred Lott. If a body were dumped in the ocean near Gloucester in March and remained submerged in cold water for months, hydrolysis and hydrogenation of the fatty cells that compose subcutaneous fat tissues would result in the formation of bacterial-resistant adipocere, a postmortem artifact that basically turns a body into soap.

"Do you remember e-mailing that to Dan Steward, Dr. Scarpetta?"

"I don't remember those exact words."

"What do you remember, then?"

"I remember telling Mr. Steward that if a body remains submerged in cold water for a period of weeks or months, the result would be a process of decomposition known as saponification."

"Turning into soap," she emphasizes.

"In a manner of speaking."

"Not in a manner of speaking, Dr. Scarpetta. That's what you said in this e-mail, correct?"

"I believe I said 'basically turns into soap.'"

"Just to clarify, can a dead human body literally turn into soap under any circumstances?" she asks.

"Hydrolysis of fats and oils in the human body can indeed yield a crude soap. Also known as grave wax because of the way it looks."

"And the formation of this soap, or grave wax or adipocere, doesn't happen overnight, correct?" she asks.

"That's correct. It can take weeks or months, depending on the temperature and other conditions."

"Which leads me to what's been all over the news today." Of course she was going to get to that. "The body you recovered from the water almost in view of where we are sitting? Indeed, if you walk outside this courtroom and look through those huge windows you can almost see where you were on the Coast Guard boat but a few hours ago, correct?"

"That's correct."

"Do you know the identity of this dead woman whose body you pulled out of the water several hours ago?"

"At this time I don't," I answer, and of course Dan Steward is letting her get away with it.

"Do you know how old she is?"

"No."

"Can you estimate?"

"I haven't examined her yet."

"But you've obviously seen the body," Donoghue continues. "You must have an opinion."

"I haven't formed any opinions yet."

"The body is that of an adult female, correct?" She keeps going because Steward isn't stopping her.

"That's correct."

"Older than sixteen? Older than eighteen?"

"It's safe to say the body is that of a mature adult female," I reply.

"Possibly in her fifties?"

"I don't know her age at this time."

"I repeat the word *possible*. Is it possible she's in her late forties, in her fifties."

"It's possible."

"With long white or platinum-blond hair."

"That's correct."

"Dr. Scarpetta, are you aware that Mildred Lott is fifty and has long, very platinum-blond hair?"

Speaking of her in the present tense, as if she's not dead. If she's not dead, then her husband couldn't have had anything to do with murdering her.

"I'm vaguely aware of her age and that her hair has been described as platinum blond," I reply.

"With the court's permission, at this time I'd like to play footage from Fox News that shows Dr. Scarpetta pulling this body out of the Massachusetts Bay earlier today."

If the jurors even consider the body is Mildred Lott, they won't believe she could have been murdered more than six months ago.

"I'd like to access this Fox News footage on the Internet and play it on the flat screens in the courtroom so everybody can see what I'm talking about."

Dan Steward's case is cooked.

"Your Honor, I object," Steward says.

I glance back at him, and he is on his feet again and looks more bewildered than angry.

"On what grounds, Mr. Steward?" The judge's face is stony, and he sounds annoyed.

"On the grounds that playing such news footage is irrelevant and immaterial."

"Your Honor, quite to the contrary," Donoghue argues. "The footage absolutely is relevant."

"I'm also very much bothered by the fact that a segment of Fox News, or any televised news, is edited," Steward says to the judge. "And not edited by police but by a television network or show."

"And you know for a fact what Ms. Donoghue wants to show the court was edited?" the judge asks.

"My assumption is it would have to have been edited, Your Honor. News programs aren't in the habit of showing raw uncut footage. I'm asking that you prohibit this videotaped footage and any such footage during this trial."

Could you be any weaker? I think, with frustration.

"Generally, TV shows aren't admissible." The judge sounds bored. "What is your point, Ms. Donoghue?"

"My point is very simple, Your Honor. The footage edited or otherwise shows very clearly the dead body of what appears to be an older woman who had been submerged in cold water and certainly didn't, quote, turn into soap."

"Your Honor, this is ridiculous. This is a stunt," Steward protests in his irritating voice.

"May I continue, Your Honor?" Donoghue asks.

"If you must."

"So either Dr. Scarpetta's statement about what happens to a dead body after it's been submerged in cold water is incorrect or the dead body she just recovered from the bay earlier today is some older woman who hasn't been dead and submerged in the water for an extended period of time. Your Honor, let's just be blunt. How do we know this dead body that's just turned up isn't Mildred Lott? And if it might be Mildred Lott, then my client certainly couldn't have killed her, since he's been in jail for the last five months, held without bond, because Mr. Steward unfairly convinced the court that Channing Lott is a flight risk because of his wealth."

"Your Honor, she's turning this trial into a carnival!" Steward exclaims.

"The video clip is less than half a minute long, Your Honor. I'm only interested in showing a close-up of the dead body as Dr. Scarpetta is swimming with it to the Coast Guard boat."

"I'm going to overrule your objection, Mr. Steward," the judge says. "Let's watch the video and try to move on so we're not here until midnight."

nineteen

IT'S CLOSE TO SIX P.M. WHEN WE REACH THE LONGFELLOW Bridge in pouring rain and solid traffic, returning to Cambridge after one of the worst experiences I've ever had in court.

"I don't care what anybody says, there's something suspicious about why he let her get away with that," Marino hammers the same point, making me crazy with his speculations and theories of plots and plans and possible conspiracies. "It's one thing for the judge to be an ass because you pissed him off, and I warned you about being late."

I don't want to hear another word about it.

"As you've pointed out more than once? Since that Supreme Court ruling we're going to be jerked around more than ever, hauled into court all the time for nothing. But you can't just show up when you decide."

I'm in no mood to be lectured.

"But irregardless"—he uses a non-word of his that drives me mad—"the assistant U.S. attorney's supposed to be on your side." He turns up the windshield wipers full tilt, his reading glasses on the tip of his nose, as if they somehow will help him see in a downpour.

"I was a defense witness, not a prosecution witness," I remind him.

"And that's suspicious, too. Why didn't Steward subpoena you? He had to know you were a sitting duck because of that e-mail about Mildred Lott turning into soap, so he should have beaten Donoghue to the draw. Then you would have been his witness. He would have qualified you as an expert instead of her doing it, and you wouldn't have been put through the mill with all these personal questions that sure as hell didn't make you look good."

"No matter who ordered me to court, I was going to end up there, and Donoghue would have asked whatever she wanted."

"You're *her* witness and on *her* side, and still she does that to you?" he persists, and I can't stand it when he gets this way, defending me after it's too late, when he couldn't have changed anything to begin with.

"It's not about taking sides." My patience is almost shot.

"Oh, yeah, it is. Everything's about taking sides." Marino leans on the horn and yells, "Move, butt munch!" He honks again at the taxi in front of us, and the rude noise goes through my brain like a spike. "Like, whose side is Steward really on? You were the last defense witness, and he didn't bother to cross-examine you, just let that damn news clip hang in the air?"

"There really wasn't anything to ask me. I don't know the identity of the body we recovered from the bay, and that was made clear."

"Huh. Well, the way he handled you makes me wonder if maybe he's secretly in league with Donoghue, maybe getting paid under the table or has a promise of it if Channing Lott gets off. How do you know his billions of dollars aren't what's tipping the scales of justice in this case? Jesus! The asshole's tapping his brakes on purpose, wanting me to rear-end him! Move it, fuckwad!" Marino opens his window and gives the taxi driver the finger. "Yeah, go ahead and stop and come over here, see what I do to you, piece of dog shit!"

"For God's sake, can we do without the road rage?" I ask. "Let's just get there in one piece, please."

We're only halfway across the bridge, going ten miles an hour, the Boston skyline smudges of blurry light. Beacons on top of the Prudential Building are completely blotted out by heavy rain and dense low clouds that moil and churn.

"Why the hell didn't he object more?" Marino rolls up his

window and wipes his rain-spattered hand on his pants. "The one who got away with murder is Jill Donoghue."

"Maybe he's just a lousy lawyer." The high-speed dull thudding of the wipers is almost unbearable. "I don't guess you could turn those down?"

"As long as you don't care if I can't see."

"Never mind." I can't remember what I ate today, and then I realize the answer is nothing.

Cuban coffee and an empty stomach. No wonder my head hurts and I can barely think.

"Steward didn't try hard enough to get that Fox segment excluded, hardly tried at all."

I never got around to the granola and Greek yogurt that are still in my refrigerator.

"You ask me, he threw you and the case under the bus, and did it on purpose."

"Let's hope that wasn't his intention," I say, and what bothers me most isn't that a television news segment was ruled admissible and shown to the jury but that the video was filmed at all.

For several seconds the dead woman's gaunt leathery face was clearly visible as I was pulling her into the pouch-lined Stokes basket, and while it's possible she's no longer visually identifiable because of her severely dehydrated condition, I can't be sure of that. Someone who knew her well, perhaps family or close friends, might have realized who she is, and that's a terrible way to find out about a death. It should never happen.

"He'll get acquitted," Marino decides.

The wipers swipe and beat the glass, the hard, chilly rain drumming the roof and flooding the windshield as if we're inside a car wash, and Channing Lott might be acquitted, and maybe he should be. I have no idea. But if jurors witnessed what I did barely an hour ago, they must have been given a different picture of the formidable industrialist who seemed genuinely caught off guard by the video he watched in open court. He struck me as tragic and terrified, sincerely grief-stricken, as he seemed to anticipate what he was about to see. Afterward he shut his eyes, almost collapsing in his chair with what appeared to be immense relief.

If he realized the dead woman isn't his missing wife, then he shouldn't have felt he was just granted a reprieve, not if he's to blame for whatever's happened to her. Finding his wife's body right now would be the best thing for his case. It doesn't matter what I might testify as to how long she's been dead.

A jury would find such postmortem artifacts confusing, would be baffled by the idea of an intact body showing up in the Massachusetts Bay some six months after the person allegedly was a murder for hire. I also accept the distinct possibility that Channing Lott is a consummate sociopath, a poseur and manipulator who knew all eyes were on him during that pivotal moment when the news footage began to play. Maybe he intended to look sympathetic to whoever was watching, and he did.

"He may very well be acquitted, and if the jury has reasonable doubt, then that's the right verdict," I reply, and what I'd like to do this very minute is go home.

I want Advil, a long hot bath, and Scotch on the rocks, and I want to talk to Benton. I want to hear what he has to say about what just transpired in federal court. What are the rumors about Judge Joseph Conry that might help explain his anger toward me and unwillingness to sustain a single objection Dan Steward raised, few that there were? Then again, maybe I don't want to know. It won't change anything that's happened.

"Well, no way in hell the jury's going to convict him." Marino leans forward, squinting, trying to see through billowing sheets of water, the lights of oncoming traffic blinding. "All Donoghue had to do was introduce the suggestion that Mildred Lott's body just turned up now or might turn up later or maybe she's not even dead. Showing that news clip was something, a picture worth a thousand words, even though it's probably not her."

"It's not. Unless her medical records are fabricated and her height has shrunk."

"Well, it looks like everything else shrunk."

"Not her bones. Mildred Lott was supposed to be five-eleven, and this lady isn't close to that."

"You got to give her credit, though." Marino continues talking about Jill Donoghue, because he saw every second of what she did, having found a seat in the back of the courtroom without my being aware.

He was there for the entire ordeal, witnessing the judge's tirade and my punishment of a fine some five times stiffer than what's typical, not that I've ever been fined before. That judicial fireworks display was a perfect opening for what Donoghue did next, to build me up as a qualified expert before implying that I'm a feminist home wrecker, a medical experimenter guilty by association of snatching Japanese body parts and perhaps even indirectly to blame for atom bombs being dropped. Marino saw all of it and has chatted about nothing else as we've driven endlessly, slowly, miserably, through high winds and pounding rain that a few minutes ago was mixed with hail, the early evening unnaturally dark.

"She saved you for last, and that's what the jury goes away with—TV footage of a dead rich lady with long platinum-blond hair being pulled out of the water today."

"I don't think her hair's platinum blond. I'm pretty sure it's white." I can barely talk.

"Reasonable doubt." Marino wipes the inside of the glass with his jacket sleeve and turns up the defrost full blast. "If they didn't have doubt before, they got it now."

"Whether he's found guilty or not isn't my concern," I reply. "I have no opinion one way or the other about whether he had something to do with his wife's disappearance, and frankly, you shouldn't have an opinion, either."

"You know what they say. Everybody's got one."

At long last we are here, my metal-clad building an ominous tower in the storm, like the gray turret of a castle shrouded in fog, and I get an odd feeling that begins deep inside my gut, a chilly discomfort that moves up to my chest. The sensation reaches my brain as the black metal gate slides open along its tracks and Marino drives through, the Tahoe's headlights slashed by rain and illuminating vehicles that shouldn't be here. Benton's black Porsche SUV is next to three unmarked sedans, as if he and his FBI colleagues have shown up to meet with me anyway when there just isn't time, and it doesn't make sense.

I sent Benton a text message the instant I was out of court and said tonight was impossible, as I still had the autopsy to do and it likely would be a complicated one. I might not be finished until nine or ten.

"Who's here and why?" I puzzle, as Marino points a remote at the back of the building.

"That's Machado's Crown Vic. What the hell?"

The lights go on inside the bay, the heavy door cranking up, and in the widening space is the dark green low-slung hood of Lucy's Aston Martin backed in next to my SUV.

"Shit." Marino drives inside. "You expecting her?"

"I'm not expecting anyone."

We get out, the shutting of the Tahoe's doors echoing off concrete, and I scan my thumb in the biometric lock. Then we're inside the receiving area of the autopsy floor with no sign of the nighttime security guard, but I detect voices along the corridor. People talking, several of them, and as Marino and I approach ID, we find the door open wide. The yellow boat fender, dog crate, and other evidence are plainly visible inside on tables, and as we get closer to the large-scale x-ray room I can hear my technologist Anne. I hear Luke Zenner, and the security guard appears around the bend.

"Who unlocked ID?" I ask him. "Is everything all right, George?"

"You got company." He talks to me and won't look at Marino.

"So it seems."

"Mr. Wesley and some of his people are in there with Anne and Dr. Zenner. Don't know what it's about."

I don't believe he doesn't know, and he stares straight ahead as he walks off, jaw muscles clenching. The red light is illuminated over the door of the x-ray room, indicating the scanner is in use, and I'm not expecting my husband to be dressed the way he is, in running clothes, his silver hair wetly combed back. He's with Cambridge Police Detective Sil Machado and FBI Special Agent Douglas Burke and another woman I've never seen before, very short dark hair, maybe in her mid-thirties. I'm startled. I feel betrayed.

"For the most part, it's the opposite with CT," Anne is saying from her work station, Luke sitting next to her in a chair he's rolled up.

On the other side of the leaded glass, bare feet with shriveled toes and pink-painted clipped nails protrude from the bore of the eggshell-white Siemens SOMATOM Sensation scanner, and on video displays are images belonging to an *Unidentified white female from MA Bay,* I read. I can't understand why Anne and Luke have started without me. I made it clear I didn't want the body removed from the cooler. I gave a specific directive that the body wasn't to be touched, that the doors to the ID and decomp rooms were to remain locked until I returned from court.

"What's going on?" I meet Benton's eyes and see what's in them. "What's happened?"

He's in a crimson Harvard Medical School sweat suit and running shoes, a rain jacket draped over an arm, and I suspect he was at the gym when someone interrupted him. Probably Douglas Burke, it enters my mind, the tall brunette far too feminine and pretty for the names she goes by, Doug or Dougie, and it's not uncommon for her to vanish with Benton, to be unaccounted for. It could be any hour of the day or night or on a weekend or a holiday, and often I'm told nothing, and I know when not to ask, but now isn't one of those times.

When we have a moment alone I will demand that Benton tell me exactly what is going on, because I can tell by the hard set of his jaw and tension in his sharp-featured face that something is, and it occurs to me that he hasn't spoken to Marino or looked at him. Benton is completely avoiding Marino, as are Special Agent Burke and Machado and the woman I've never met. Only Anne and Luke are acting as if all is normal, oblivious to the real reason the FBI and police are here, which isn't because they want to watch a CT scan or an autopsy.

"How's everybody doing?" Marino asks, and only Anne replies that she's doing fine, and I can tell he senses something is off.

"I was just explaining that CT is pretty much the opposite of MR in some regards, blood showing up bright on CT, while it's dark on MR," Anne explains to Marino and me.

No one responds, and the tension gets thicker.

"But not so with other fluids—specifically, water—because water isn't dense," Anne explains to Machado and Burke, and to the woman I don't know, whom I suspect is FBI.

I hold Benton's gaze, waiting.

"These areas here and here?" Anne indicates the sinuses,

the lungs, the stomach displayed in 3-D on different computer screens. "If they were showing up really dark, pretty much black, it could indicate the presence of water, which would be typical in a drowning. CT is really great in drowning cases. Sometimes when you open up the body during autopsy, you lose the fluid before you can see it, especially if there's water in the stomach. But we scan first and don't miss anything."

"We wouldn't expect her to have water in her lungs, her stomach, not anywhere," I say to Anne, but my eyes are on Benton. "She's moderately mummified. She hardly has a drop of fluid in her entire body, barely enough to blot a card for DNA, and if she's a drowning, she didn't drown recently."

My mind keeps going back to the way Marino acted earlier today, as if the dead woman was personally offensive to him. His upset over the vintage buttons on her jacket was bizarre, and I have an incredible premonition, an awful one.

"She'd been dead quite a while by the time she was weighted down and dropped into the bay," I'm saying, "and I'm wondering who called this gathering?"

"We think we got an ID," Sil Machado says.

twenty

HE TURNS TO BENTON AND SPECIAL AGENT BURKE AND
the woman I don't know, as if it is up to them to continue, and
I know what that means.

The Portuguese Man of War, as Marino calls Sil Machado,
is a young hotshot, built like a bull, with dark hair and eyes and
preppy taste in clothes, and he's not a devotee of the FBI and
doesn't turn over a case to them without question and in some
instances without resistance. If he's deferring to them even as
we stand here, then the Feds already have taken over the investigation, and there has to be a justifiable cause for it.

"How come nobody let me know?" Marino glares at Luke.
"An ID based on what?" His tone is accusatory. "How's that
possible? It's not like we could have DNA this fast, and forget
a fingerprint match. That can't happen without rehydrating her
fingerpads, meaning we're probably going to have to remove
them first, which was what I planned to do—"

"Tell you what, Pete," Machado interrupts him. "Why don't
you come with me, and we'll let them talk while we go over a
few things?"

"What?" Marino instantly is paranoid.

"We'll go over everything."

"You don't want them talking in front of me?" Marino's voice gets loud. "What the fuck!"

"Come on, buddy." Machado winks at him.

"This is bullshit!"

"Come on, Pete. Don't be like that." Machado gets close to him, puts a hand on his arm, and Marino tries to shake him off, and Machado grips him harder. "Let's go take a load off, and I'll explain." He escorts Marino out into the corridor. "I know you got coffee in this place, course what I'd really like is a beer, but forget it."

"Let's back up a minute." I shut the door. "I thought I'd made it clear not to start this case without me." I address this to Anne, to Luke. "So if what I'm seeing is the result of the FBI coming in here and giving directives to speed things along, that's not how it works," I add, and I'm not nice about it.

"It's not like that," Luke says to me.

But it is like that.

"The ID room is wide open, and you've started the scan when that wasn't my instruction," I reply.

Luke turns his chair around so he's facing me, and there's no sign he's concerned about my displeasure or worried about why Marino was just removed from the room like a prisoner. Luke feels justified in what's unfolding, and in part this is due to inexperience, and it may be he's far more narcissistic than he seems, his well-mannered graciousness belying the ego I'd expect to accompany his blond good looks and gifted mind. My deputy chief is rather enamored of federal law enforcement agencies, the Secret Service and especially the FBI, which has managed to muscle him into rushing this case along, and I simply won't allow it.

"I wasn't going to start the autopsy without you," Luke explains, in his reasonable, pleasant British accent, dressed in scrubs, surgical clogs, and a lab coat with his name embroidered on it. "But we thought it might be expedient to go ahead and scan her while you were on your way back from court. Mainly because of the condition she's in, I doubted we'd find much on CT, anyway."

"And there's basically nothing." Anne's tone is subdued, unnerved by my reaction to what she and Luke have done, and she's probably upset about Marino, who flirts and kids with her, and for a while was giving her rides to work every day when she broke her foot. "No internal injuries," she says quietly, seriously, not looking at Luke or Benton, at anyone but me. "No evidence of what might tell us why she's dead. I mean, she's got some cardiac calcifications, some intracranial ones that are common. Punctate in the basal ganglia, plus arachnoid granulations, typical with aging, in people over forty."

"Hold on, now." Special Agent Burke is casual tonight in a brown sweater and black jeans, a leather shoulder bag likely concealing her gun. "Let's not talk about turning forty." She thinks she's funny.

"Evidence of atherosclerosis, calcification in some blood vessels." Anne isn't amused.

"You can tell hardening of the arteries from a CT scan?" Nothing Burke does is going to lighten the mood. "Seems like that's a good thing to find out before I eat another Whopper."

"Eat what you want; you don't look like you've got a worry," Luke says to her, and maybe he's flirting. "They've found atherosclerosis in Egyptian mummies four thousand years old, so it's not just a by-product of modern life. In fact, it's probably part of our genetic makeup to be predisposed to it," he adds, because he just doesn't get it, or maybe he doesn't care that Marino is in trouble.

"I suppose we have to consider she might have died from a heart attack or stroke, in other words, natural causes, and someone decided to conceal the body, then get rid of it." Burke's eyes are steady on mine.

"At this stage, it's wise to consider everything, to keep an open mind," I answer.

"Nothing else radio-opaque except dental restorations," Anne informs me. "And she has plenty of those. Crowns, implants, an expensive mouth."

"Ned's coming in to compare charts," Luke lets us know. "In fact, that's probably him now."

Car lights are white and glaring on a closed-circuit security screen, a small blue hatchback, Ned Adams's ancient Honda parking in the lot.

"Then we must already have premortem x-rays for comparison." I direct this to Benton.

"Records we got from a dentist in Florida," he says.

"Who do we think this lady is?" I ask him.

"It's looking like she's a forty-nine-year-old Cambridge resident named Peggy Lynn Stanton. She usually spends her summers at Lake Michigan, Kay," my FBI husband replies, as if we are amicable colleagues. "Much of her time is spent away from Massachusetts. It appears it was her habit to be here usually in the winter and fall only."

"It seems strange to spend winters here. That's usually when people leave," I remark.

"Sometimes she'd go to Florida," Burke says. "There's a lot to find out, obviously."

"Meaning friends, possibly her family, weren't always sure where she was?" I ask dubiously. "What about telephone calls, e-mail . . . ?"

"We sent agents to check," Burke says. "Well, why don't you pick up here?" She directs this to the woman I don't know. "Valerie Hahn's with our cyber squad."

"And for the record, everybody calls me Val." She smiles at me, and she shouldn't bother.

I don't feel friendly and am consumed by worry. What has Marino done?

"The bottom line is it certainly appears she never got to her cottage on the lake," Valerie Hahn says. "It's totally abandoned. No luggage. Nothing in the fridge. It's looking like she vanished into thin air around the first of May, possibly earlier, and Dr. Zenner mentioned that could be consistent with the condition of the body?"

"I'll know better when we autopsy her." It rankles me that Luke has told them anything.

"I don't know if you might have heard her mentioned?" Valerie Hahn says to me.

I open the door leading out into the corridor, where Ned Adams is headed toward us, carrying his old black leather medical bag.

"Why would I have heard her mentioned?" I ask bluntly.

"I'm just wondering if the name *Pretty Please* means anything to you, or perhaps anyone on your staff?" Hahn says.

"Hello, Ned." I hold open the door for him. "She's in the scanner. Help yourself."

"I can do it in there. Sure." He pushes back the hood of a long yellow raincoat that is dripping water on the floor. "Her films are up to date. Lots of crowns, implants, root canals, including a panoramic x-ray that's good of the sinuses. You got those?"

"I can put them up on the screens even as we speak." Anne starts typing. "You want a printout, too?"

"An old-fashioned guy like me still likes paper. She has lots of features, an embarrassment of riches, shouldn't take long. Are we hot?" He pauses at the door leading into the scanning room as if it's a military operations area that might be dangerous.

"The scanner's offline," I tell him. "You know how to slide out the table?"

"I do." He takes off his coat.

"Presumably because her initials are PLS," Douglas Burke explains. "One might suspect that's where *please* comes from."

"You're on Twitter, aren't you, Kay?" Valerie Hahn acts as if we're friends.

"Barely." I'm beginning to understand, or I think I do. "I don't use it to socialize or communicate."

"Well, I know you never tweeted Peggy Lynn Stanton, whose handle on Twitter is *Pretty Please*," Hahn says.

"I don't tweet anyone."

Marino, what have you done?

"It's easy enough to see that you two weren't tweeting each other." Hahn is quite sure of herself. "One doesn't even need admin privileges to see that."

"I don't think we need to get into this level of detail right now." Benton watches Ned Adams through glass.

"I think we do." I look at him until he looks at me.

"Suffice it to say that at least something useful came from all the television coverage." I can read Benton's reluctance in the flatness of his eyes. "Our office in Boston got phone calls, Cambridge got phone calls, Chicago and Florida got calls, at least a dozen people certain the dead woman is Peggy Stanton, whom these people said they haven't seen or heard from, apparently, since at least May, when she was supposed to be on her way to her Lake Michigan cottage or possibly Palm Beach. People here assumed she was in Illinois and people up there assumed she was still here. Some people assumed she was in Florida."

"People? As in friends?" It is all I can do to mask how much I don't like this.

"Various volunteer groups and churches." Benton knows exactly what I'm feeling, but it doesn't matter.

This is how we do our jobs. This is how we live.

"Apparently she was very involved in eldercare. Here, in Chicago, in Florida," he says.

"She has family and they haven't wondered where she is after all these months?" I think about what Marino said to me in the car this morning when we were on our way to the Coast Guard base.

"Her husband and two kids died thirteen years ago when their private plane crashed." Benton reports the information objectively, and he can sound so cold.

But that's not who he is.

"An investment broker with a hefty life insurance policy," he reports. "Left her fairly well off, not that she was poor to begin with."

"None of her vendors have complained that she's not paying her bills? No one noticed she wasn't answering e-mails or her phone?" I don't say what I'm thinking.

How simple it would be to hoodwink Marino in cyberspace, where he doesn't know how to navigate and his insecurity makes him vulnerable.

"She's been paying her bills all this time," Benton replies. "She was tweeting as recently as two weeks ago. She's made calls from her cell phone as recently as day before yesterday—"

"Not the person in there. She certainly didn't." Luke interrupts Benton while watching Ned Adams through the window.

"Someone's been doing it." Benton finishes what he was saying, but he doesn't say it to Luke.

Inside the scanner room, Ned Adams opens his black leather bag. He puts his glasses on. He squints up at a video screen displaying dental x-rays.

"She's been dead quite a lot longer than two days or two weeks," Luke volunteers, when he really should shut up. "She certainly hasn't been tweeting or writing checks or making phone calls for quite some time. Months, at least, I'd say. Would you agree, Dr. Scarpetta?"

"Her house is on Sixth Street," Benton says to me. "Very close to Cambridge P.D., which just makes this all the more curious. No one's been in it. The alarm is set, the car in the garage, police driving past it every day, and no one the wiser."

"A time capsule," Douglas Burke adds. "The fire department's at the ready to breach the back door as soon as we get there."

"I suggest you might want to go pick up those pizzas I asked you to order," I say to Benton in a way that communicates exactly what I want him to know.

This is my office. The CFC doesn't answer to the FBI. I will handle this case as I see fit.

"I'm posting her first. Her house can wait," I add, in the same tone. "It's waited half a year. It can wait two hours longer, but she can't."

"We were hoping Dr. Zenner could take care of the autopsy and you'd come with us and take a look," Burke suggests.

"Whatever you need me to do." Luke gets up from his chair as Anne walks into the scanner room and hands printouts to Ned Adams.

"What I need is for you to give us a chance to do our job here," I reply, as the x-ray room door opens, and now Lucy is here, looking at me from the corridor. "Searching a potential crime scene is much more meaningful if we know how the victim died and what we might be looking for."

"Could I see you for a minute?" Lucy doesn't step inside.

"If you'll excuse me. I think we're done for now," I say to the FBI.

"I noticed your car in the bay." I walk with Lucy back toward the receiving area, stopping where no one can overhear us. "I'm wondering why."

"And I'm wondering a lot of things." My niece is dressed the way she was when I saw her early this morning, all in black, and it's not like her to show up when the FBI is in the area. "I'm wondering why Marino and Machado are in the break room with the door shut. I can hear them arguing, that's how loud Marino is. And I'm wondering why a Sikorsky S-Seventy-six belonging to Channing Lott might have filmed you recovering that body from the water today?"

"His helicopter? That's stunning." I hardly know what to say.

With all that's gone on since, I haven't given the large white helicopter another thought since I e-mailed the tail number to Lucy while I was in the car with Marino, heading to court.

"That's really rather unbelievable," I add, as my thoughts dart through possibilities of what I should do.

Dan Steward needs to know before closing arguments. If Channing Lott somehow is behind his helicopter filming what we just watched in court, and I don't know how he couldn't be, then the jury should know before it begins to deliberate. But it may be too late for that.

"The Certificate of Airworthiness is registered in Delaware to his shipping company," Lucy informs me.

I can imagine how it would appear if I call Steward with this information and he's forced to say in open court or even to the judge who the source is. The information would be damaging to Jill Donoghue.

Stay out of it.

"His fleet of some hundred and fifty car carriers, container ships, the M V Cipriano Lines," my niece is telling me.

"I'm sorry." I try to focus on what she's saying.

"What the chopper's registered to," she says. "A shipping company named after his missing wife, Mildred Vivian Cipriano. Her name before they got married."

twenty-one

AROUND THE CFC, FORENSIC DENTIST NED ADAMS IS known as the tooth whisperer because of what the dead confide in him. Age, economic status, hygiene, and if that's not enough to tattle about, teeth snitch on diet, drink, drugs, and if the person were pregnant or had acne or an eating disorder.

In his late sixties, slightly stooped, with bad knees and a deeply wrinkled face that has smiled more than frowned, Ned can determine minutiae from a single tooth that the deceased's closest friends and family likely never knew or imagined. Peggy Lynn Stanton, he confirms, as we wheel her body along the corridor after weighing and measuring it in the receiving area, was victimized in life by a very bad dentist, who, as Ned puts it, cost her or someone "an arm and a leg."

"A Dr. Pulling; now, how's that for a name? Only he sure didn't live up to it in her case, as I'm about to tell you." Ned stiffly accompanies Luke and me toward the decomp cooler, his raincoat draped over his arm, a buoyant air about him, because his mission is successfully accomplished and he's in no hurry to go home to an empty house. "Some cosmetic dentist in Palm Beach, Florida, who didn't comply with the standard of care; not saying it was intentional. Maybe just incompetence."

"Yeah, right," Luke says sarcastically. "Where's the loot?"

"Tooth number eight, a maxillary central incisor with extensive internal root resorption coupled with a buccal fistula," Ned says. "You can't miss this big internal radiolucency in the middle of the pulp canal in her pre- and postmortem radiographs."

"This is under a crown?" I pull up the handle of the cooler door.

"Exactly. Trauma resulting in an infection and ongoing inflammation that went unchecked, and he slapped a porcelain crown on top of it anyway. I'm guessing this joker cost her about forty-K, all told, and a lot of pain and inconvenience. Her bite's messed up, I'm pretty sure, but can't prove it because I can't exactly ask her if she suffered chronic headaches. I wouldn't be surprised if she had TMJ, though. When you go to search her house, look for a night guard."

As if that's the most important thing I might find.

"The time frame for when the infection started?" I guide the gurney through frigid air stale with death, pushing past a silent sad audience of black-pouched mounds on steel trays, many of the patients stored here still unidentified.

"It's hard to pinpoint, but based on her charts?" Ned's breath fogs out. "I'd say it's related to a root canal two and a half years ago, which was followed by the porcelain crown this past March."

"So she was in Palm Beach as recently as March," I assume, as we exit through the rear cooler door that opens onto the decomp room.

"She must have been." Ned follows us in. "And it's impossible for me to believe that by then the resorption hadn't already progressed to involve the periodontal ligament space and the tooth. In other words, that damn tooth should have been extracted and not restored."

"Yet one more crook in the world," Luke says.

"Well, had she lived, she inevitably would have faced an extraction followed by an implant and another crown." Ned sets his black bag on a countertop and drapes his coat over a chair as if he plans to stay for a while. "Lots of root canals—eight, to be exact—likely from trauma caused by drilling down healthy teeth for crowns that I doubt she needed. Her rear molars, for example? Why bother putting porcelain on teeth no one's going to see? Use gold. Believe it or not, it's cheaper."

"Money, money, money." Luke hands me a mask and gloves, his blue eyes calmly on mine, as if he can explain everything that's happened, as if I should have no reason to be concerned about him.

"That and this same dentist was also doing facial injections," Ned lets us know, as Luke and I put on shoe covers and gowns. "The newest trend that I have serious qualms about? Dentists injecting patients with Perlane, Restylane, Juvéderm, and other facial fillers, and also Botox. Maybe I'm just old-fashioned, but I don't think dentists should be plumping up cheeks and smoothing out frown lines."

We slide the body from the gurney to an autopsy table, and she looks tragically small and wizened on cold stainless steel. Turning on an examination light, I move it along its overhead track as Luke labels specimen containers on a cart, and my feelings about him are mixed and confusing. They're ambivalent and scary, and I try not to think about the outrageous accusations Marino made in the car this morning. I don't want to admit they might have merit.

"So this Dr. Pulling, who saw her in March, also injected her with fillers or Botox during that appointment?" I direct six thousand foot-candles of light at the anterior upper arms.

"Lip augmentation. One CC of Restylane," Ned says. "It's in her chart. At least the guy kept pretty good records."

"Four small contusions." I direct Luke's attention to them. "With another one here."

"A thumb bruise?" He reaches for the light's handle, his arm lightly touching me.

"Possibly. On the opposite side. Very possibly a thumb bruise. Yes." I show him, and he leans against me.

"Fingertip bruises from gripping her," he describes. "Gripping her upper arm, four fingers there and the thumb here."

"Thank you, Ned." It's my way of letting him know I've got what I need.

"At least it's not one of these situations that I see all too often." He picks up his black medical bag, worn and scuffed, a wedding gift from his wife, who's dead. "All sorts of things charted that were never done so the dentist could submit claims to the insurance company or disguise noncovered services as those that are covered. Not to mention just plain shoddy work."

"It's really difficult to see, in her condition." Luke uses a hand lens to examine the subtle contusions I've pointed out, and I'm aware of the whisper of his white gown moving as he moves, the intense light shining on his pale blond hair.

"It helps to illuminate areas at different angles, getting an overview before doing a close visual exam of a particular feature or features," I suggest to him, as I feel the heat of him and the heat of the lamp. "The same way you enter a crime scene. The big picture first. Then narrow it down. Don't fixate so much on one thing that you miss all of it."

"I certainly wouldn't want to be so fixated I miss all of it." Luke adjusts the light again.

"Had a case not all that long ago that I was called in to consult on." Ned collects his raincoat from the chair. "In New Hampshire, several patients with broken dental tools in their teeth."

"Thanks so much, Ned." I look up at him. "You saved the day, as always, and I'm grateful, the FBI is grateful, everybody's grateful."

He lingers by the door. "That particular dentist is up to his eyeballs in more than a hundred civil malpractice suits."

"Benton ran out to pick up pizza, and I'm guessing he's back by now," I let Ned know.

"He'll probably be going to prison for a few years and could be deported back to Iran."

"Maybe check on the seventh floor?" I suggest. "I'm sure they'd love your company, if you're not in a hurry to get home."

"Maybe a few here as well?" Luke points out more brown spots, small and almost perfectly round, his arm touching mine, and I feel its firmness through the Tyvek sleeve. "If a grip was intermittent? Like we see when someone is being forcibly held, and the grip tightens and relaxes, tightens and relaxes. Would you expect fingertip bruises through her layers of clothing?"

I pick up a camera and the six-inch scale Marino labeled earlier today.

"Would you expect her to bruise like this through a blouse and a wool jacket?" Luke asks, and I begin to take photographs, because Marino isn't here.

While I don't know exactly what is happening, I've gathered

he's still upstairs, being questioned by Machado and the FBI, their interest related to Twitter, to the woman Lucy told me about. Someone Marino met on the Internet and recently *unfollowed in more ways than one*, my niece said early this morning, when she informed me that he'd been sleeping over at the CFC on an AeroBed.

Twat was the crude word Marino used while we were driving to the Coast Guard base, and whatever foolishness he got involved in, it's simply not possible he recently was tweeting *Pretty Please,* or whatever name Peggy Lynn Stanton went by on the Internet. Marino may have been tweeting someone with that handle days and weeks ago, but it wasn't this lady on the autopsy table. She was dead long before he began tweeting whoever he assumed she was, dead before he even got his Twitter account, possibly dead and in cold storage since the spring, and my mind sorts through information nonstop, my blood pounding.

My thoughts race to connections and possibilities, my pulse rushing hard. I try to distract myself from what I'm feeling as Luke touches me, as he brushes against me and I don't stop it.

"I really didn't mean to step over you," he says, now that Ned is gone. "I sincerely apologize. I thought I was helping."

I incise the brownish marks on the upper right arm to see if they are well defined beneath the epidermis. I look for staining left by hemorrhage that extends into the dermis or the deeper layer of the skin, and it does.

"The question, of course, is when she might have gotten these bruises." I grab the lamp by its handle, shining it down her arms to the shriveled tips of her fingers, with their chipped polished nails that are clipped to the quick.

I check the undersides of her wrists and the tops of her hands.

"It's very difficult, if not impossible, to age these contusions, because of her condition," I add.

The light paints over the leathery upper chest, the wasted breasts, illuminating the wrinkled abdomen.

"But depending on the degree of force used by the person gripping her, she could have been bruised through layers of clothing," I answer Luke's question.

"Important to know if she was clothed or not, it seems to me," he says. "I realize this is more Benton's department. I'm not a profiler."

"The FBI can be very persuasive." I illuminate her hips, her upper thighs. "And I'm sure they were all the more convincing to you because Benton showed up with them. But we don't work for law enforcement, Luke."

"Of course not."

"It's our duty to objectively answer questions raised by the evidence." I direct the light at her knees. "And we must vigorously adhere to chain of custody, meaning we don't open up our evidence room for the FBI or allow them to whip us into a frenzy of activity, no matter their reason or sense of urgency."

"He's your husband, so I assumed—"

"Assumed that our being married changes how he does his job or how I do mine?"

"I apologize," Luke says again. "But after his annoyance when we were in Vienna . . ."

He doesn't finish. He doesn't need to spell out that the last thing he'd want to do after Benton's blatant display of jealousy last week is to anger him further. Luke knows he can. He knows why he can, and I'm not going to discuss my marriage with him or the truth about why he might be a threat to Benton.

I'm not about to openly admit to Luke Zenner that my husband and I have had our share of friction of late, episodes of uncertainty and distrust that aren't as baseless and irrational as I've let on. If what we've fought about was truly groundless, Luke and I wouldn't be dancing this dance of touching, of leaning, of lingering, of speaking the subtle language of heated attraction, and it's only when it happens that I'm honest with myself.

"What I can't help but wonder is if she might have been stripped of her clothing at some point," Luke says, as I reposition the plastic ruler, the scale, for each photograph I take. "I offer that only because the contusions look quite distinct. Here and here."

He moves closer, his forearm touching mine, his shoulder brushing against me as he bends into what he's examining, and I don't want to feel what I'm feeling.

"You can see where it appears someone's fingertips pressed with considerable force, and I'm wondering if there were layers of fabric in the way."

He leans forward, leans into me and stays there.

"Would the contusions look exactly like this, were that the case?" he asks.

"We can't know for a fact whether she was bruised through clothing or not," I reply.

"Would it be worthwhile to try the ALS?" He indicates the alternate light source still on the countertop, where Marino plugged it in hours earlier.

"It's not going to help."

"So that's a no." He meets my eyes.

"If you want to scan her in the very off chance you might visualize any faint or nonvisible bruises we're missing, assuming we're missing any brown patterns that are contusions?" I offer in a way that discourages him, because I must.

"It's probably ridiculous."

"It's not ridiculous, just illogical," I reply.

"I agree. I mean, what are the chances?" he says.

"The chances of finding the usual evidence the ALS can be most helpful with are next to none." But that's really not what I'm discouraging him from, and it's not really what we're talking about.

I won't have an affair with him unless I decide I don't care if I completely destroy my life. It's not about whether he has a chance with me but about how crazy it is that I'm even thinking these thoughts.

"Body fluids, fibers, gunshot residue, latent prints, deep tissue bruises?" I'm still talking about the ALS and what it might find under different circumstances, and I'm letting him know I understand what it's like to want what you can't have.

"Right. Forget it," he agrees.

"That's what I recommend. Not that I don't understand being tempted to try."

"She's been in the water," he says. "A waste of time."

"And then it has to be explained," I add. "Everything we do has to be explained."

"Should I unplug it?" He reaches for the ALS power cord.

"Please," I reply. "I'm really not interested in putting on goggles and spending an hour scanning the body from head to toe with the Crime-lite just so I can say we did. It might be worth going over her clothing, but that can wait."

"We don't know if she had on the clothing when she got these bruises." Luke returns to that thought as he returns to the table. "Knowing whether she was dressed or not when someone grabbed her upper arms would be an important fact, wouldn't it? Stripping a prisoner is more about submission than anything else, isn't it?"

"Depends on who is doing it to whom and why."

"The logic of torture, a terrible thing to consider, but there is a logic to it. Humiliation, intimidation, controlling your prisoner by stripping him, hooding him. Or her," he says. "I'm assuming she could have been bound at some point with some type of ligature that was soft and wouldn't necessarily leave marks on her skin."

"It's possible."

"I imagine him coming up behind her like this." He holds up his hands to grip imaginary arms, orienting his fingertips and thumbs the way they would be if he grabbed someone by the upper arms from behind. "Maybe to forcibly move her from one place to another, such as if he forced her into a room or dragged her, were she unconscious. Or if she were tied up in a chair and he's trying to make her give him information so he could steal her identity, for example. Her PIN, her passwords."

I shine the lamp down her lower legs, brightly illuminating the tops and sides of her ankles and feet, and I find more brownish marks, only these are darker and drier and indistinct in their shape. Picking up the scalpel to make small incisions, I find the darkened areas of skin have lost elasticity, are extremely hard, with no evidence of hemorrhage to the underlying tissue. Not contusions but patterns caused by something else, and I find more of them on the tops of her bare feet and areas of her ankles.

We pull her on her side so I can check her back, and there are two more indistinct hard brown areas on the underside of her right elbow and forearm.

"I've got no idea," I puzzle. "Absolutely none."

"Some type of postmortem artifact?"

"Unlike any I've ever seen before." I excise a small section of the hard brown skin for histology. "It's like cutting through stiff leather. I can't imagine what might cause that, swaths of skin as much as four by three inches."

"Like freezer burn, perhaps?"

"No. She'd have it all over if she was in a freezer and it caused that."

"But what about if certain parts of the body came in contact with metal inside a freezer?" he suggests.

"Then the skin would stick."

I insert the tip of the scalpel blade into leathery flesh just below the left clavicle and incise down and to the right, and then do the same on the left and cut straight down to the navel, detouring around it to the pubic bone. It's like making a Y-incision in wet slippery leather, and I reflect back tissue, cutting through ribs, removing the breastplate of them. I make an incision beneath the jaw to remove the neck organs and tongue.

"Her hyoid's intact." I make notes on a body diagram as I work, the odor of decomposition overpowering now. "No sign of injury to the strap muscles, to soft tissue. No airway obstruction or aroma of chemical asphyxia, such as due to cyanide. No injury to the tongue."

Luke peels back the scalp, and the air vibrates with the loud whining and grinding of the oscillating saw, and bone dust is suspended in the bright white light. I open the major blood vessels, the inferior vena cava, the aorta, finding what I expect, that they are empty, with dry diffuse hemolytic staining. I see no evidence of blockage or injury or disease, just a moderate amount of calcification, certainly not enough to kill her.

"The brain's too soft to section," Luke reports. "But I'm not seeing anything to suggest cerebral injury. Dura's intact and free of staining." He writes it down.

Her organs are decomposed. Her lungs are collapsed, reddish-purple and very soft, the airways devoid of water, froth, sand, or foreign material, the gallbladder dry and wrinkled, with no residual bile. With each minute we work it becomes abundantly clear that this is an autopsy of exclusion, of ruling out possible causes of death and leaving little doubt that she either asphyxiated or was poisoned. But it will be a while—days, at least—before we have a complete ethanol and drug screen of liver tissue.

"No petechiae I can find." Luke opens each eye. "No irregular areas of hemorrhage to the sclera or the conjunctiva. Of course, that doesn't rule out asphyxia by smothering or strangulation," he adds, and he's right.

While there are no abrasions or contusions, no injuries I might associate with smothering or strangulation, the absence of facial or scleral pinpoint hemorrhages called petechiae doesn't mean that someone didn't place a plastic bag over her head or tie a gag around her nose and mouth or ram a cloth down her throat that obstructed her breathing.

Her gastric contents are granular and dry like animal feed. I adjust the light and use a lens, moving the material around with forceps.

"Dried out, desiccated meat," I observe. "If I can see it grossly, it wasn't very digested when she died."

"There's very little in her small intestine," Luke lets me know. "Almost nothing in her large intestine. It usually takes what? A good ten hours for food to completely clear?"

"It depends on a lot of things. How much she ate, whether she exercised, her hydration. Digestion varies considerably with individuals."

"So if she ate and the food hardly had begun to digest before she died," he supposes, "chances are we're talking only a couple of hours after her last meal?"

"Maybe. Maybe not."

I tell him to weigh the gastric contents and place some of it in formalin so we can process it histologically.

"An iodine test for starch, napthol for sugar, Oil Red O for lipids. Hopefully we can pick out identifiable food particles on the stereomicroscope." I explain the special stains I'll want used.

We are working side by side, our backs to the door.

"So I'm going to make evidence rounds to tox, to histology, to trace, with special instructions." Luke goes down the list. "What about SEM?"

"Maybe for botanicals." I'm vaguely aware of a shift in the air behind me. "For stomatal comparisons. For example, is it napa cabbage? Is it Chinese broccoli? Is it bok choy? Is there any evidence of arthropods such as shrimp? Are there cellular structures that might be oats? Are there cereal grains that might be wheat?"

Luke turns around, and then I do.

"I'm wondering how much longer," Benton says, from the open door he holds.

"Didn't hear you come in," Luke replies, as if making a point.

"We're actually finishing up now." I meet Benton's eyes, and his are wary.

"Find anything helpful?" He stands in the doorway.

"The long answer is undetermined for now, pending toxicology and further studies." I untie my gown in back. "The short answer is I don't know."

"Not even a guess?" Benton stares at what's on the table, and the reason he doesn't come closer isn't because of the odor or the ugliness.

He isn't bothered by such things. He's bothered by something else.

"I'm not going to guess about what killed her." I toss my gloves and shoe covers into a biohazard can. "But I can give you a long list of what didn't."

twenty-two

HEAVY RAINS HAVE TURNED TORRENTIAL, THE VIOLENT storm unseasonable for fall, with high winds stripping trees of any leaves left and thunder cracking like a war going on. Water sprays the undercarriage of the SUV and splashes the glass, and Benton seems miles from me as I drive through the dark puddled streets of mid-Cambridge.

"It's common sense that he can't be involved," he says from the passenger's seat, where he's alert to his surroundings and not looking at me.

"Whose common sense?" I try not to sound tense.

"Do you want him leaving his DNA inside her house?"

"Hopefully he wouldn't, but of course not." I try to sound reasonable.

Benton's phone glows in the dark, and he types something on it.

"After he's possibly already transferred his DNA to her personal effects, to her clothing?" He returns the phone to his lap. "Because I'm betting he handled all sorts of things."

Wipers thud and the defrost blasts.

"I don't care what protective shit he had on," Benton then says. "These days you can get DNA from air."

"Not quite," I reply. "But he shouldn't search her house." I agree with that. "Although there's no proof he knew her, ever met her, or had a clue someone stole her identity on Twitter. There's no shred of evidence he's done anything wrong."

"It doesn't look good."

"It looks like what it is." My anger glints. "Someone intended to implicate him."

"We shouldn't do anything to make it look worse."

"So I lose my chief investigator because he got set up and made a fool of by whoever's involved?" I'm frustrated, on the verge of furious, that the FBI suddenly assumes it has a say in how I run my office.

I'm angered by the suggestion that investigators I train leave their DNA everywhere.

"He was set up because he was an intended target," I add.

"He needs to stay out of this case. He needs to stay away from the CFC for a while."

"That's what you think or what your colleagues think?" Lightning flashes and the sky looks bruised.

"It's not for me to decide how Marino should be handled. It's not appropriate for me to decide, in light of personal connections. In light of our history." Benton doesn't look at me, and I know when he's wounded.

"It seems if anyone should decide, it's the one who knows him best."

"Yes, I know him," he says.

"You certainly do. And your colleagues don't."

"Not the way I know him. You're right about that. And maybe you should think about what you know."

"I should think about what you know of Marino's flaws." It's obvious what he's alluding to, and I can't stop this from where it's going.

"Flaws. Christ," he says.

"Don't do this, Benton."

"Yes, flaws," he says.

"Goddammit, stop."

"What a way to put it," he says, in the voice of anger, of hurt.

"You're finally paying him back?" I ask.

"Nothing more than a flaw or two."

"You're going to pay him back at last for a night when he

was drunk and on medication?" I go ahead and say it. "When he was out of his mind?"

"The oldest excuse in the history of the world. Blame it on pills. Blame it on booze."

"This isn't helpful."

"Plead insanity when you sexually assault someone."

"Please don't tell me what happened then has a bearing on decisions you're making now," I say to him. "I know you wouldn't throw him to the wolves for a mistake he made years ago. One he couldn't be sorrier for."

"Marino throws himself to the wolves. He's his own wolf."

I drive past a construction site where bulldozers parked in muddy rivers of rainwater remind me of prehistoric creatures stranded, of floods, of life swept away. My every thought is dark and morbid and honed by the fear that Benton stood silently inside the doorway of the decomp room to send me a message. I fear the flaws he's really talking about aren't Marino's. They're mine.

"Please don't punish him because of me," I say quietly. "He's not a predator. He's not a rapist."

Benton doesn't respond.

"He's certainly not a murderer."

Benton is silent.

"Marino's been framed; if nothing else he's been discredited, been humiliated by Peggy Stanton's killer." I look at Benton as he stares straight ahead. "Please don't use it as an opportunity to punish." I mean as an opportunity to punish me.

The SUV splashes through water that has pooled in low-lying areas, broken branches littering the street, as neither of us speaks, and the silence convinces me of what I suspect. The space between us is vast and empty, as rain billows in sheets and dead leaves dart and swarm in the dark like bats.

"He was set up, yes. That much I believe," Benton finally says, almost wearily. "God knows why anyone would bother. He's perfectly capable of setting himself up. He doesn't fucking need help."

"Where is he? I hope he's not alone right now."

"With Lucy. He's managed to make his compromised position much worse because of his rude defensive behavior."

I glance in the mirrors, my eyes watering in glaring headlights as cars go past.

"Acting like a defiant, uncooperative total jerk," Benton continues, and his tone has changed, as if he let me know what he wants me to know, and it's enough.

"I'm not surprised he's beside himself," I hear myself say, as I'm realizing something else entirely.

The observation windows that overlook the autopsy rooms didn't enter my mind at the time.

"I can only imagine his embarrassment and anger," I add, but that's not what's got my attention.

I didn't think of the teaching labs. It never occurred to me that anybody might be in them with the lights turned off.

"He certainly can be his own worst enemy." I keep talking while my thoughts course along a different track.

Benton was up there watching, and during certain moments it couldn't have been more obvious. I didn't move away. I didn't try to stop it, because I couldn't, because I wanted it. I desired him in the midst of what was dead and horrible, when the urgency to feel alive can override what is logical.

"His rages, his insults; he was completely uncooperative," Benton is saying, and I'm barely listening.

Luke asked me and I thought about it, wondered where and when as I entertained fleeting plans about how to get away with it. I said no and felt yes, what Benton accused me of in Vienna true.

"I had to leave the room at one point so I didn't lose it with him." What I hear Benton saying is he left the conference room upstairs.

He's making sure I know what he did, checking on us from behind the darkened glass of a teaching lab.

"All because he had to start a relationship with a complete stranger in cyberspace, for Christ's sake," Benton says.

"Welcome to modern life," I reply bleakly. "People do it every day."

"No one I know."

"Marino's been as voraciously lonely and as empty as a black hole ever since Doris left, and that was almost longer ago than they were married. He's had nothing but meaningless encounters ever since, most of them with women who hurt him, take advantage, are a horror show."

"He's certainly had his turn at being the horror show, the one doing the hurting," Benton says, and I don't argue with him.

I can't possibly.

"No one I work with meets people on the goddamn Internet." He makes that point again.

"That's rather difficult for me to believe."

"No one I work with is that stupid," he says. "The Internet's the new mafia. It's what the FBI infiltrates undercover and spies on. We don't go there for our fucking personal lives."

"Well, Marino can be that stupid," I reply. "He's that lonely and misses his wife and misses being a cop and fears getting old and has no insight about any of it."

I drive slowly along 6th Street, the Cambridge Police Department's headquarters shrouded by rain, Art Deco lights glowing blue in the fog.

"What I don't understand is how someone might think anything's accomplished by making it appear he was tweeting a woman who clearly couldn't have been alive while it was going on," I then say.

"How long she's been dead isn't going to be clear to everyone."

"You saw her body. What's left of it."

"It all depends on the interpretation." He makes his point in a way that's disturbing, as if it might be one that's been made before.

"The 'interpretation'?" I repeat rather indignantly. "It's clear she's been dead for months."

"Clear to me, but I'm not most people," Benton says. "It depends on what TV shows they watch. They hear the word *mummified* and expect she was wrapped in bindings and found in a pyramid."

I can barely make out the charter school and biotech buildings we pass, the lighting in most parts of Cambridge notoriously bad.

"It doesn't help matters that he was at Logan around the same time you got the anonymous e-mail relating to Emma

Shubert's disappearance." He gets to that, and nothing would surprise me.

"He's never been to Alberta, Canada, and wouldn't know the first thing about anonymizing software or proxy servers, Benton."

"As far as anyone knows."

"What possible motivation could he have, even if he were able to?" I ask.

"I'm not the one who thinks he might."

"Others think he could have something to do with Emma Shubert." I want him to spell it out.

"Or have something to do with what was e-mailed to you. It's all part of the same discussion," he says, and it's ridiculous, and I tell him that, but I've seen ridiculous things before, the wildest of goose chases.

I know better than to dismiss any notion investigators might get into their heads.

"I'm worried it's someone who knows him, Kay."

"These days anybody can know anybody, Benton."

"A paleontologist has vanished and is presumed dead, and you're sent a photo of a severed ear," he says. "Mildred Lott has vanished, her husband on trial for her murder, and then his helicopter films you while you're getting Peggy Stanton's body out of the bay just hours before you're supposed to testify. I'm worried whoever's doing this—"

"Whoever? As in one person?"

"Connections. There are too many. I don't believe it's coincidental."

"You think it's one person doing all of it?" I ask.

"If you want to get away with something, do it by yourself. And I worry this person knows Marino, knows you. Maybe knows all of us."

"It doesn't have to be someone who knows him or any of us," I disagree. "If you search Peter Rocco Marino on Twitter you can find him. You can find so much about any of us on the Internet it's rather terrifying."

"Why would this person look for him on Twitter to begin with? Unless there's a personal reason to get him into serious trouble?"

"Lucy set him up on Twitter in early July. When he moved

into his new house," I recall. "When did he and *Pretty Please* start tweeting each other?"

"He claims she tweeted him first. He says this was late August, close to Labor Day, maybe the weekend before. That she said she was, quote, 'a fan.'"

"A fan of Jeff Bridges' or of Marino's?"

"Exactly. Because he's such an idiot," Benton says. "Using the avatar of a character from some bowling movie, calling himself *The Dude*. From which Marino instantly concluded that she must be a bowling enthusiast, meaning they have something in common."

I slow to a stop in Peggy Lynn Stanton's neighborhood, the headlights shining through rain, illuminating the dark street and the cars lining both sides of it.

"I'll go through all the tweets, his e-mails, his phone records, whatever it takes," Benton says. "Because I'm the one who will get him out of this mess he's made, isn't that the irony?"

Houses are old but not historic or expensive for Cambridge, single-family and occupied, charming and pristinely kept, and so close together it would be difficult for a person to walk between them.

"He assumed she bowls, or she said she did?" I ask.

Yards are small or nonexistent, parking coveted. Neighbors would be keenly aware of vehicles that don't belong here.

"I don't know in detail what was tweeted back and forth between them, but he seems to have the impression she's an avid bowler. Or was."

I try to imagine forcing a woman from her house, and I can't see it. I can't imagine someone screaming or causing any sort of disturbance that wouldn't be witnessed. We sit in silence in the drumming rain, distant lightning like a flash going off as thunder rolls. I don't believe Benton thinks Peggy Lynn Stanton was killed in her house or abducted from it, and I ask him that.

"The fact is we don't know," he says. "Doug has her own opinion, but it's not necessarily mine."

"Tell me yours."

"I'll tell you who."

"Do you have a suspect in mind?"

"I know who he is, in his late twenties at least but probably older." Benton scans where we are on the dark rainy street.

"Intelligent, accomplished, blends in but is isolated emotionally. Doesn't get close. Those who think they know him don't."

" 'Him'?"

"Yes." Benton looks at cars; he looks at houses. "Familiar with boating. Likely has a boat or access to one."

I think about Marino's obsession with the CFC getting a boat, and I wonder who else he's said this to.

"Needs no help operating it, is skillful enough to pilot it alone."

Benton rolls down his window and stares out at the dark.

"A smooth talker, glib, completely confident he can convince anyone of anything, including police, the Coast Guard."

He's unmindful of the rain blowing in.

"If his boat broke down or he got stopped while he had a dead body on board, he would be certain he could charm and convince and no one would know. Someone fearless. Someone with financial means."

Marino has a captain's license issued by the Coast Guard.

"A narcissistic sociopath," Benton says, to the rain and the night. "A sexual sadist whose arousal comes from causing fear, from tormenting, from degrading, from controlling."

"So far I've found no evidence of sexual assault," I let him know.

"He doesn't sexually assault them. He has a physical aversion to his victims because they're beneath him. He makes sure they know how beneath him they are. Your description of a booby trap is correct, the more I think about it."

"A booby trap intended to pull her apart, to decapitate her, and maybe some or all of the body is lost. Why?" I ask. "Because he doesn't want her identified?"

"Because killing her wasn't enough. He could kill her every day and it wouldn't be enough to fill the void in him that was left by some terrible devastation he suffered earlier in life."

"A devastation you know about?"

"I know because they're all different and the same. A monster no one recognizes. Goes about his normal business while he keeps a dead body in a refrigerator or a freezer because he can't let it go, can't let go of the fantasy. He has to relive what he did to her constantly. And even when he finally decided to dispose of her, he had to destroy her one last time. He wanted her ripped apart and wanted it witnessed, and intended whoever witnessed it to be shocked and made a fool of. Someone who mocks."

Benton rolls his window up.

"Did he know her?" I ask.

He wipes rainwater off his face with his hands.

"He knows who he was killing," he answers. "Peggy Stanton was just the stand-in. All of his victims are stand-ins. He's killed before, and he'll kill again or possibly already has, and he'll play his games with those involved because it gives him pleasure."

Wipers sweep water off the glass as I slowly move forward toward the unmarked cars parked just ahead.

"The same victim each time. A woman." Benton zips up his coat. "Most likely an older woman, older than himself. An established, accomplished mature woman. It could be his mother or some other woman who played an overwhelmingly powerful role in his life."

"What you're describing certainly isn't an impulse crime." I notice curtains moving in the houses we pass.

Neighbors are aware of our SUV stopping and then creeping slowly on their street.

"You don't abduct someone or get into a struggle or do much of anything around here without being seen," I say. "You don't carry a dead or unconscious body out of the house and load it into a car, doesn't matter how dark it is. The risk would be enormous."

"What happened to her was calculated."

"Meticulously," I agree.

"There was an encounter, maybe more than one. But they didn't know each other," Benton says. "Or at least she didn't know him."

twenty-three

THE TWO-STORY WHITE COLONIAL IS TUCKED IN ON
three sides by homes almost on top of it, the narrow yard in
front overgrown with shrubs that obscure first-floor windows
and crowd a brick driveway leading to the detached garage.
Rain pelts our faces and soaks our hair as we follow a slate
walk slick with dead leaves and overgrown with weeds.

"The yard work certainly hasn't been done in recent memory." I raise my voice over the smacking rain. "I'm surprised if
nobody complained, and it's important to determine which
lights have been on all this time and those that haven't," I add,
because many of the windows are dark.

We hurry up steps to a covered front porch illuminated by a
pair of ceiling-mounted glass lanterns, and we take off our
dripping coats as the door opens wide. Douglas Burke looks
monastic in white hooded coveralls, as if she's part of some
higher order, and she lets us into a small but elegant entryway,
a dining room and living room on either side, a staircase curving up to the second floor.

An antique gold pendant chandelier that looks French is
lighted over a Persian rug protected by heavy clear plastic, and
on top are the suede lace-ups that Burke had on earlier and

oxfords that I assume are Machado's, and boxes and stacks of protective clothing. The air is stagnant and tastes like dust.

"If someone grabbed her from this place or killed her here, they didn't leave any sign of it that I can see." Burke hands out towels. "But I'm not that kind of expert."

The way she says it catches my attention.

"Did you turn the porch lights on?" Benton dries his face, his hair.

"Everything on we turned on. When we got here the house was in a complete blackout. A lot of burned-out bulbs. What a night." She closes the door. "Hope Noah's building another ark."

Drying off my crime scene case, I set it down next to a box of boot covers with PVC soles that one can wear without shoes, and I towel off my dripping hair. I feel clammy and wilted and vaguely self-conscious, sensing something I can't define that I don't trust.

"Nothing was on when you got here?" Benton is making sure.

"The only thing *on* is me. On Sudafed, and it's hardly putting a dent. Just the kind of place to make my allergies go wild." Her eyes are watery, and she sounds congested.

"And the neighbors didn't notice and wonder why her house would be pitch dark?" Benton asks.

"Lights burn out gradually and not at the same time? Maybe the neighbors mind their own business or weren't into minding hers?" Burke supposes, and she's talking fast, hyped up.

"We got a lot of neighbors to interview, but I'm guessing the assumption was she'd left town like she often did. One of these people typical for around here, doesn't have to work for a living, dabbles in volunteer work and intellectual pursuits. You know the type," she says to Benton, as if he's that type, and it's hard to tell if she's teasing or flirting or means nothing by it.

"Most people leave at least a few lights on." He continues assessing how much Peggy Stanton kept to herself or encouraged her neighbors to mind their own business, or if she might have been liked or resented or avoided.

Predators pick their victims for a reason.

"We've been through every room," Burke lets us know.

"Sil's still roaming around in the basement, says he wants to point out something electrical to you." She directs this to Benton. "Don't ask me. I can barely plug in a toaster. Nothing interesting so far, except it's obvious the place has been empty for several weeks at least."

Several weeks.

I don't like the impression I'm getting.

"We've requested records from the alarm company, which probably will be the best indication of when she was here last," Burke adds, and I don't agree.

"An indication of when someone was here last doesn't mean that person was Peggy Stanton," I remind her. "It could have been someone else who was here."

I take off my tactical boots, not the same ones I had on earlier today, having insisted on a shower and a change of clothing before I was going anywhere.

"And I can tell you with reasonable certainty that she wasn't here in recent weeks, because she was dead by then. What about a housekeeper?" I ask.

"One hasn't been here for weeks; that's obvious."

Weeks, I think, and I don't like where this is headed already. Burke is going to question any conclusion I make about facts she decides are debatable, and Benton isn't going to intervene.

"Do we know if she has a housekeeper?" I inquire. "Or if, perhaps, she might have cleaned her house herself?"

"We don't know yet. The yard man hasn't been around, you probably noticed," she says to me, and my regard for her hasn't changed over the several years I've known her rather distantly.

A former prosecutor, reasonably bright and aggressive, Special Agent Douglas Burke has always been appropriately attentive to the wife of the man she works with most closely and in secret. I like her and I don't. I've never been sure what she honestly thinks of me or feels about my husband, her emotions and interests covert, and right now what I'm starting to sense is strong.

"People tend to notice things like that in Cambridge." Benton wipes down his coat, his shoes with the towel. "If the yard, the maintenance of the property are neglected long enough, inevitably someone calls the city and complains."

"We're getting that information, too." Burke hands us coveralls. "We have found out she stopped the newspaper delivery May third."

"Or somebody did." Benton neatly places his coat and shoes on the plastic-covered safe area. "You can do it online. You abduct someone and don't want it discovered anytime soon that the person is missing, go online and suspend the newspaper delivery. Make sure you place occasional calls on their cell phone to directory assistance, wherever you'll get a recording. Or call people from the contact list at weird hours and hang up or don't leave a message."

"It was her habit to suspend delivery every spring or early summer," Burke informs us. "Specifically, the *Boston Globe,* whenever she was leaving Cambridge, and it doesn't seem she spent summers here after her family was killed in the plane crash. I can't imagine going through something like that. I can't even think about it. Losing everybody at once."

"It would have reshaped her. She wouldn't have been the same person after that, for better or worse." Benton continues assessing who Peggy Stanton may have become.

"If she was at her Lake Michigan cottage, she'd have the *Chicago Tribune* delivered, but that was never started up this summer." Burke gives us gloves, and I notice her hands are shaking, probably from the Sudafed, or maybe she's excited by the hunt.

You want to hunt me, go ahead.

"As I've indicated, all signs so far point to her never getting to Illinois." She stares at me and I stare back.

"The rug underneath?" I indicate what's under the plastic as I walk across it in booties.

"Nothing's been done." She knows what I'm asking.

Any areas of flooring near entrances are important. If a perpetrator was in and out of the house, most likely this person used a door. I would hope Burke and Machado wouldn't walk on the entrance rug, dripping rainwater and tracking dirt on it. I would hope they wouldn't cover it with plastic without checking for evidence first. For hairs, fibers, soil, botanical debris, for anything.

"You've done nothing at all?" I step onto the uncovered floor, noticing the iron umbrella stand in the corner to the right of the door.

In raised letters on its bottom tray is *A la Ménagerie du Jardin des Plantes*, the name of the Paris zoo. Wedged underneath the stand, between the back of it and the wall, is a twisted dark blue plastic ring.

"We've been here all of an hour. The plan is for us to do the walk-through with you before anything's disturbed," Burke explains, as if I'm the one who requested this tour, which really isn't a tour.

It's a hunt.

"Then Sil will collect evidence if there is any," she says. "He'll lift prints if we find them. But I don't think anyone of interest was in here. I don't think this is a crime scene. Hard to know at this point who's been in and out and how recently, and we'll certainly get those answers, but it's doubtful they'll be relevant."

It's obvious she's convinced of that by now, and probably was convinced of it before she got here.

"There's no sign of a struggle, of violence, but you're the expert," she says to me the way a defense attorney might. "Nothing seems to be missing in terms of possible robbery. Some rather expensive jewelry in her bedroom, in a dresser drawer, nothing looks rifled through or disturbed. Her car's locked up in the garage."

"We'll want to look," Benton says. "We'll want to check gauges, check how much gas, check the GPS, if she's got one."

"Sil's called for a truck," Burke says.

"Good, because the car shouldn't be examined here," I answer. "It should go to the labs, to the evidence bay."

She asked me here as an expert, and I will be one. I could walk back out the door, but I won't.

"The battery's probably dead," Benton comments.

"Shit." Burke dabs her nose with a tissue. "I'm going to claw my eyes out with this goddamn dust."

"What about the car key?" he asks.

"On that table there in the bowl, probably where she usually left it."

"A pocketbook, a wallet?" His sharply handsome face is framed in white polypropylene.

"No sign of either," Burke says. "It's looking like she went somewhere and then whatever happened happened. Of course, we don't know if she's a homicide. We don't know for a fact she met up with foul play, do we, Kay?"

She isn't asking. She's testing.

"How do you suppose she managed to vanish if she didn't drive," I ask pointedly. "She physically left this house at some point. Yet her car key is here? Her car is here?"

"The thing is"—Burke watches me crouch near the umbrella stand, looking at the twisted plastic ring without touching it—"we don't know for a fact that she vanished from Cambridge or even from Massachusetts."

"Except Massachusetts is where her body was found." I get back up.

"She could have been abducted in Florida, in Illinois, who knows where." She poses it as a hypothetical, and I don't buy that's what she thinks.

"You're right. We don't have all the facts," I reply. "But her body ended up here. That's beyond dispute."

"Even so, we just don't know where she vanished from." If nothing else, Burke is reminding me why the FBI is involved, reminding me of the Bureau's jurisdiction when crimes cross state lines, reminding me why it's justified for me to feel intruded upon and confronted. "She might have left town of her own volition, been in and out, ended up in the area. Maybe she was with someone and died of natural causes and the priority became to dispose of the body for some reason."

"Nothing indicates she died of natural causes," I assert.

"And nothing indicates otherwise," she pushes back.

"Someone likely held her hostage and kept her body in cold storage for months. And then tethered it in such a way that it would be pulled apart when we tried to recover her from the bay. I'd say that's an indication she didn't die of natural causes," I remark.

"But you don't know what killed her, as I understand it?" She lets that same question hang in the air.

"At this time I don't."

"You don't have a guess."

"I don't guess."

"Then you don't know."

"I don't know for a fact at this point."

"Isn't that unusual, when the body is in relatively good

shape?" Burke hasn't taken her eyes off me, and it occurs to me she might think I'm lying.

"Yes," I answer. "I find this case extremely complicated and unusual. It's probably going to be a tox case or asphyxia. It may take a while to sort through it."

"Then we'll look for anything in here that could point in the direction of an overdose, a poisoning, or asphyxia," she says. "Drugs, meds, something like a plastic dry-cleaning bag that could have been used to smother her."

"Then what?" I remind her. "Someone carried her body out of here without anybody seeing it and dumped her into the bay?"

"I'm hoping you'll tell me. Cold storage or heat?" Her questions are beginning to feel like an interrogation, as Benton looks around and doesn't look at us.

"Where she was kept was cold," I reply. "Very cold and dry."

"We just don't have the facts," Burke says dismissively, as my boot covers make plastic sounds on heart pine flooring.

"Are you allergic to cats?" I ask.

"As a matter of fact, horribly. And I thought Benton was the psychic."

"The plastic ring on the floor." I indicate what's behind the umbrella stand. "A cat toy."

"No sign, but appears there was one."

"As in recently?" Benton is interested.

"There's a litter box in the master bath," Burke says. "Water and food bowls are on the kitchen floor."

"But no cat alive or dead?" Benton is caught up in what it might mean.

"Not so far."

"Where is her car key now?" I inspect the entryway table, crafted of old distressed wood with hammered copper accents, the bowl high opalescent glass with a pattern of bluebirds.

I pick it up and read the back. Lalique, another expensive antique, and I wonder if Peggy Stanton spent much time in France.

"Sil has it. Swabbed it and the keychain for DNA, checking them for possible prints, for anything, before he unlocks her car, assuming the car is locked," Burke says. "But when the fire guys got us inside, the key was right there in that bowl you're looking at, what appears to be a key to her 1995 Mercedes. The keychain has an old compass on it, maybe an old Boy Scout compass? Where you'd expect keys to be when someone's walking into the house. A typical place to put them, just inside the door."

"Except if she's coming in from the garage she's not likely to walk all the way around to the front, up the steps, and onto the porch, especially if she's carrying groceries," I reply. "There's a path that leads from the garage to a side door that I'm guessing is the kitchen door."

"Anything else on the keychain besides a car key and a compass?" Benton asks. "A house key, garage key?"

"No."

"What about mail?" He looks through doorways, but he doesn't walk inside the rooms. "I noticed a mailbox in front."

"Empty."

"Was she having her mail forwarded to another address?" I set down the bowl on the smooth top of the hand-built table and don't believe for a minute that Peggy Stanton kept her car key or any keys in the entryway. "If her mail wasn't forwarded, the mailbox should be overflowing."

"Nothing in it but a couple of circulars, junk mail," Burke replies. "So it appears someone was taking it for some reason."

"The same person paying her bills and impersonating her," Benton says, as if he knows. "What I'd like to do first is check out the garage, walk the property with Machado, then walk through the house while giving Kay room for what she needs. Doug, maybe you can show her around in here."

What he's doing is giving me space, but he knows I can't be alone. I convince myself he's simply following protocol because I don't want to believe he's delivered me to this place and to Douglas Burke so she can casually and spontaneously continue an inquisition I can't afford to abort.

Looping the camera strap around my neck and picking up my scene case, I tell her for the record that I intend to go through certain areas of the house very thoroughly and it's important she's with me the entire time. I won't open drawers or look inside medicine cabinets or closets unless what I do is witnessed, and I won't collect any evidence myself unless it directly relates to the body, I explain.

Biological materials, medications, for example, I say to her.

But I will look at whatever I'm allowed to look at, assuming my opinion is helpful, I make myself clear.

"Sure, it's all helpful," she says. "I'm curious if you usually do your own photography."

"Generally, no."

"So if Marino's not available, you wouldn't bring one of the other investigators. You have what? About six of them?"

"I wouldn't bring Marino or anyone here," I answer her. "Not under the circumstances."

twenty-four

OFF THE ENTRYWAY TO THE LEFT IS THE DINING ROOM, small, with Wedgwood-blue walls and white molding and trim, the mahogany table in front of the fireplace set with six antique chairs upholstered in dark red velvet.

A built-in hutch displays royal-blue dishes trimmed in gold, French Saxon china that is old, and sterling flatware in cabinets, also French and antique, is stored in wooden chests, a patina of tarnish on all of the pieces. White candles on the table and the mantel have never been lit, and potted plants by the curtained window are long dead, everything covered in dust that hasn't been disturbed in many months, I estimate. I flip a wall switch and nothing happens, the bulbs of the chandelier and sconces burned out.

"It doesn't appear they're on timers." I scan wall switches and outlets, looking for any sign of power strips or other devices that might have allowed Peggy Stanton to program certain lights to turn on and off. "Were these switches in the on position when you got here?"

"Yes." Burke is interested in her cell phone.

"And you left them in the on position?" I ask because it's important.

"Any lights that are burned out, it's because they were left on by whoever was in the house last." She's scrolling through e-mails.

"It's probably safe to assume that either she left the dining room lights on the last time she was in her house or someone else did."

"The window in here faces the street." She's reading e-mails and wiping her nose with a tissue. "Maybe she was in the habit of leaving the lights on in the dining room so it looked like someone was home."

"Most people wouldn't leave on a crystal chandelier and crystal sconces when they go out, especially if they were leaving town. It's a real pain to replace the bulbs." I've seen what I need to see in here, and Burke is barely listening.

I walk out of the dining room and across the entryway, waiting for what's next as I wonder how much of what's happening was masterminded by Benton. How much is he allowing? Burke is walking me through this house because she intends to walk me through something else.

"If it was her habit to come and go in her car, it might have made more sense to leave lights on that illuminate the garage." I tell her my thoughts anyway, feeling uncannily the way I did earlier today when Jill Donoghue played her games with me in court.

I stop by the floral upholstered couch in the formal living room and look around at more European antiques, probably French, everything immaculate and dusty. I notice a canvas bag on the floor next to a wing chair, and inside are skeins of wool and knitting needles, and a navy blue scarf that looks about halfway done. If she'd left town for the summer, would she have neglected to take with her a project she'd begun? The fireplace is fitted with a gas insert that's supposed to look like birch logs, a remote on top of the mantel.

"The fireplace works; I checked," Burke says.

"Most people shut off the pilot light in the summer and turn it back on in the fall. Is her house heated with natural gas? It's warm in here." I find the thermostat. "The heat is on and set to seventy degrees."

"Not sure if it's natural gas."

"Most likely it is. Pilot lights burn gas, too. You leave one on for five or six months and chances are good the gas will run out. So she's been getting fuel deliveries."

"Someone collecting her mail, paying her bills, making sure gas deliveries don't stop, and suspending her newspaper." She doesn't indicate what that makes her think or even if she finds it noteworthy. "I don't mean to tell you how to do your job."

"That's good, because you couldn't possibly."

"I don't mean to question you."

"Of course you do. But go right ahead." I look at flowers on the coffee table that are so wilted it's difficult to tell what they once were.

"You're sure she didn't die in the bay?"

"She didn't." Possibly tulips and lilies, which I associate with spring, an empty plastic card holder stuck in the vase.

"No way she was tied up, thrown overboard, and drowned?"

"There's no way," I reply. "She was already dead when she was tied up. If she were leaving town for the summer, would she leave a fresh flower arrangement on a table? Why not throw it out?"

"And she was in the water how long?" Burke isn't interested in the flowers.

"I'd estimate her body hadn't been in the water even twenty-four hours by the time she was found."

"Estimate based on what? If you don't mind my asking."

"I don't mind," I answer, because it doesn't matter if I do, and I'm certain she will ask whatever she wants, and I wonder if she's slept with my husband.

I wonder how much of this is competitive and personal.

"My estimate is based on there being no evidence of significant immersion changes or marine depredation, for example," I explain.

"'Marine depredation'?"

"Fish, crabs. Nothing had started eating her."

"Right. So she died somewhere else."

"Yes, she did."

"Your thoughts based on the autopsy?"

"I think she likely was held hostage someplace she attempted to escape from," I reply. "Her postmortem findings indicate she's been dead for months."

"Any chance she's not been dead as long as you think?" Burke studies me as if I'm a puzzle she can take apart and reconstruct.

"I'm not sure how long she's been dead," I reply. "Not down to the week or day or hour, if that's the answer you want. But based on what I'm seeing so far, it appears to me she hasn't been home since it was still cool enough to keep the heat on. Around here, that would be last March or April. I assume there was no card in this floral arrangement?"

"I didn't touch it, and Sil wouldn't have. So apparently not." She pinches her nose together with the tissue and looks miserable and irritable.

"Do we know when these flowers were delivered or by whom?"

"We'll be checking area florists to see if there's a record of a delivery," she says. "And we'll check her credit card bills to see if she might have bought the flowers herself."

"I wonder if someone was paying those, too."

"Someone who had access to her bank account. Someone who had her checks," Burke says. "Wouldn't be anyone in her family. Her family's dead."

"Most people don't remove the card from the arrangement and throw it away. Not if the flowers came from someone who's significant to them."

"I haven't checked the trash yet."

"To answer your question as definitively as I can?" I look through magazines on the coffee table. "Based on the condition of her body, I'm estimating she's been dead for many months."

Antiques & Collecting, Antique Trader, Smithsonian from December through April.

"Knowing for a fact how long is really important," Burke says, and that's what she wants from me and intends to dispute because she has her mind made up about what she's looking for and what she believes she can prove.

Some theory that at the moment I can't fathom, but I have no doubt I wasn't asked to do a walk-through of this house for the reasons I assumed. I'm not here to check for evidence of violence, for asphyxia or a drug overdose. I'm here because of Marino.

He is what Burke wants to ask about, and I have a leaden

feeling of inevitability, a sense of something dark and heavy spreading over me that I can't escape, don't even dare to run from, because it will only be worse if I do. I know what she's walking me deeper into, and Benton saw it coming. He warned me in his own way while we were driving here. Burke is aware of details about Marino's past that aren't found in searchable records.

"Months? Two, three, five months? How does this work when you look at a dead body and calculate?" she asks, and I do the best I can to explain what isn't simple as I walk into a kitchen dominated by an antique oak table and handmade iron chandelier.

Double porcelain sinks are empty and dry, the bistro coffeemaker unplugged and clean, and blinds are shut in windows on either side of the door that leads out to the garage. She follows me, lets me lead the way, scarcely attending to what I say as she continues to check her phone and probe, carrying on with what feels like a chipping away of who and what I am. I can't help but feel betrayed. I can't help but feel Benton chose the side he's on and it isn't my side, and at the same time I completely understand and would expect nothing less from him.

The FBI is doing its job the same way I do mine, and Burke can ask anything she wants without Mirandizing me because I'm not in police custody. I'm not a suspect in a crime or even a person of interest. Marino is. I could stop Douglas Burke at any time, but that would only further galvanize her suspicions about him.

"It's impossible to precisely determine how rapidly a body desiccates unless you know the conditions." I explain mummification as she continues to question whatever I say about it. "How hot?" "How cold?" "How humid?" The name Stanton isn't French." I look around. "Antiques and certain other items in this house are French and quite fine and somewhat unique. What was her family name?"

"Margaret Lynette Bernard. Peggy Lynn. Born on January twelfth, 1963, in New York. Father was a French antiques dealer with shops in New York, Paris, London. She grew up in the city, was working on her master's degree in social work at Columbia but didn't finish, presumably because she got married and started a family."

She's been doing research, digging into records, covering a lifetime of history in the blink of an eye or in the keystrokes of a cyber-expert like Valerie Hahn, who is conspicuously absent, it crosses my mind. E-mails seem to be landing nonstop on Burke's phone.

"All that sacrifice. Look what she gave up for him, and the guy decides to fly in bad conditions." She stands in one spot, her watery eyes on me. "Pilot error." She sneezes, and I think of the irony.

The FBI's DNA, not Marino's, will be all over the house.

"That's the NTSB's conclusion or yours?" I inquire.

"Took off in an overloaded aircraft, failed to maintain airspeed, possible the nine-year-old daughter, Sally, might have been at the controls—"

"A nine-year-old child was flying the plane?"

"She'd been taking lessons, apparently was quite skilled, a lot of media attention about the latest little Amelia Earhart."

Live feeds from headquarters, I think. Search engines chugging through the news and downloading it to Burke so she can ambush me while she's got the chance. I could walk out, leave.

"Anyway, the plane went into a stall after taking off from Nantucket. One hundred percent pilot error. One hundred percent parental error." Burke says it judgmentally.

"That's very sad. I'm sure a father would never mean to make such an error," I reply. "And what did Peggy Lynn do in life after her entire family was gone?"

"It appears she received a few public-service awards that made the news," Burke says. "Volunteer work with the elderly, teaching them hobbies, arts and crafts. Exactly how long do you think she's been dead?" she asks, as if I've yet to answer that.

The black granite countertop is neat and mostly bare, a pad of paper and a pen next to the phone, and I notice a six-ounce pouch of salmon-flavored cat treats that has been torn open and resealed.

"I think this should be collected." I nudge the cat treats with my gloved finger, and the space beneath it is free of dust.

Burke stares at the bag on the counter without stepping closer, a blank expression on her splotchy face.

"The cat appears to be missing," I remind her. "And it appears someone gave it treats, which suggests the cat wasn't missing while the house was still occupied."

"She would have taken the cat with her wherever she went when she left here." Her voice is nasal. "And she obviously left here, and I would say willingly as opposed to having been abducted. And it's obvious that when she left this house she wasn't coming back for a while." She fires this off at me as if I'm trying her patience and have about used it up.

"So she left with her cat but without her car, possibly for Illinois or Florida, and along the way something happened that ended with her being dumped in the bay," I summarize what is illogical.

"We can't assume she wasn't meeting up with someone." She pulls a fresh tissue out of her Tyvek sleeve. "Someone who perhaps picked her up, which is why her car's still here. That maybe she got involved with the wrong person, someone she met on the Internet, for example."

The cat bowls are on a mat on the floor near the door leading outside, and one is empty, and the other has a hard residue, what's left of wet food.

"You've known Pete Marino a long time," Burke says.

"I would collect it," I repeat my suggestion about the cat treats. "It strikes me as out of place. Nothing else is left out and opened. It should go to the labs to be checked for fingerprints, for DNA. It's best you don't touch it."

She's wiping her nose and sneezing. Her gloves aren't clean.

"Benton's told me a little bit about him." She intends to ignore me about the cat, and I won't let her.

"One dish is empty because the water would have evaporated," I continue. "The other dish had food in it and wasn't washed. Sometimes it's the one little thing that doesn't seem to matter."

"A troubled volatile marriage. Abusive to his wife."

"I'm not aware he was abusive to Doris. Not physically," I say, and I can't imagine Doris's shock if she picked up the phone or opened her door and the FBI was there to question her about Marino.

"A son who was involved in organized crime and was murdered in Poland." Burke is looking at her phone.

I can take care of the bag myself, but I prefer not to because it's not related to the body, it's not biological, and I open my scene case. Burke has left me no choice. I collect the cat treats and label the bag and initial it.

"You shouldn't dismiss the possibility that whoever might be responsible for what happened to her has been inside this house after the fact." I continue thinking about the missing house keys and pocketbook. I think about a car key left in an expensive antique Lalique bowl where someone fastidious about her belongings would never keep keys or any items that might break or scratch delicate glass or polished old wood.

"The case in Virginia about nine years ago, by which time Marino was working for you." Burke is relentless, not the least bit subtle about it anymore. "You returned to Richmond, were called in as a consultant on the unsolved death of a little girl named Gilly Paulsson."

So now the search engines have found that, I think.

"While you and Marino were there he had a problem," she says.

That wouldn't be on the Internet, and it's unlikely Marino told her. Maybe Benton did. It's also possible Gilly Paulsson's mother has been questioned already, I suppose. Lucy knows what Marino was accused of, but she would never talk to Douglas Burke or give her the time of day.

"A charge that was proven to be completely unfounded." I try not to be too adamant or show my anticipation of what I'm certain is next.

"No report was ever filed with the police." Burke types another e-mail.

"There was no report because it was a groundless accusation made by a disturbed individual who Marino was unwise enough to get involved with," I tell her.

"It seems he's done his share of unwise things."

"If you look at most people's relationships, they include a lot of unwise things."

"I don't think his list is exactly typical."

"No, it probably isn't." I open the refrigerator door.

twenty-five

THERE IS NOTHING INSIDE BUT CONDIMENTS AND SUG-
arless fruit preserves. No juice or milk or food with an expira-
tion date that might be helpful, and either Peggy Stanton
cleaned out her refrigerator because she was leaving town or
someone else did for another reason, a malignant one. I feel
Burke watching my every move, my every facial expression.

She's dissecting me, picking at every part of me, and I'm
allowing it. Like any determined investigator, she'll go as far as I
let her, and she has other motives, and maybe pseudoephedrine
is having its way with her, is making her overly aggressive.

"You've known him about half your life, haven't you, Kay."

I step on the metal trash bin's foot pedal and find nothing
inside but an empty bag. I open a cabinet under the sink and
pull out an open box of kitchen trash bags and set it on the
counter.

"Maybe someone emptied the trash," I explain. "Maybe
someone other than her. Maybe someone who came in here to
do a number of things."

"He has quite the temper, has been through rehab, and in
recent months started drinking again." Burke isn't looking at
anything except me as she stands near the door, her arms folded
across her chest.

"This should be checked for prints, for DNA. If you don't want to collect it, I will." I retrieve a paper bag from my case and collect the evidence myself.

"He started drinking again about the time he started tweeting Peggy Stanton."

"She was dead by Labor Day." Next I collect the empty bag lining the trash can. "She was dead long before then."

"When did you become aware that Marino had started drinking again?"

"I don't know for a fact if and when Marino started drinking again."

"She was dead long before Labor Day? You're absolutely sure of that?"

I tell her I am.

"And how you arrived at what you seem to believe is gospel I simply find confusing." She's typing on her phone again. "In fact, it's about as subjective as three blind people describing an elephant."

"Time of death is dependent on many factors, and it's complicated." I won't give her the satisfaction of making me defensive.

"Tell me why you're so sure this lady's been dead since the spring. Tell me why, based on information other than dates on magazines and how wilted the flowers are or how many burned-out lights there are or how overgrown the yard is."

I check the gas burners on the stovetop, and they flame up.

"The lack of insect damage, the mold on her face and neck, and decomposition of organs, and her core body temperature are indications that she was stored in a closed structure where the air was dry and very cold," I tell her again. "Possibly she was frozen."

"According to articles I've looked at, complete mummification can occur in as little as two weeks. So it really is rather up for grabs how long this lady's been dead."

"It really isn't."

"You say months. Someone else says weeks."

I open the pantry and find nothing that wouldn't keep. The usual canned goods, all of them sodium-free, and whole-grain cereals, rice, and pasta.

"It requires more than surfing the Internet to have an informed opinion." I let her know someone is doing just that, probably whoever is sending the e-mails.

"I'm sure I could find experts with your level of training who might have opinions very different from yours." I've made her angry.

"I'm sure you could." I feel her eyes on my back. "That doesn't mean those opinions would be correct."

It appears Peggy Stanton ate a lot of salads. A shelf is filled with bottles of fat-free Italian dressing, what must be two dozen bottles that were on special at Whole Foods. I shut the pantry door.

A lady who was cautious and took good care of herself and her cat. She was frugal. She tightly controlled the world she had left.

"Two weeks." I consider what Burke said earlier. "Cases of a body completely mummifying in two weeks? That's very interesting."

"It's in the literature." She's openly argumentative, and it's better that way.

It's easier. Let her skim through whatever lands in her inbox and hammer away.

"And where might this have been? Where human remains were completely desiccated after only two weeks?" I walk out of the kitchen.

"I certainly can't tell you exactly where. Only that it's possible."

"If you're talking about the Sahara Desert, I suppose." I head upstairs. "The hottest desert on the planet, and a body in those conditions will have some seventy percent loss of volume through dehydration in no time at all. It will be as dried out as beef jerky."

Burke is right behind me.

"A hundred-and-forty-pound person who becomes completely mummified will weigh maybe forty pounds, will be leather over bones, hard dried-out skin that splits," I let her know. "That's what extreme heat and aridness does. It's not something you find around here."

"People are creative. Especially if they're experts, if it's what they do professionally." Of course she means Marino. "Experts in death investigation and all associated forensic evidence."

A guest room is on the left of the landing, and straight ahead through an open door is the master bedroom. I ignore what she's so blatant about.

"You were quoted all over the news for saying in court today that it would have taken months for Mildred Lott's body to turn to soap." Burke brings this in, and I'm not surprised, and I wonder if that's been e-mailed to her, too. "You said one of the requirements is submersion in cold water."

The queen-sized bed is canopied, the black-and-white damask duvet smooth and neatly tucked under three pillows. The one nearest the bedside table where the phone is plugged in has been plumped but is wrinkled, the way pillows look when they've been slept on.

"But they've also found this same soaplike condition when bodies have been sealed in watertight coffins and vaults, isn't that correct?" Burke isn't going to quit, and she should. "Bodies forming adipocere when there's no water."

"*Watertight* isn't always as advertised," I reply.

"You seem to believe you're infallible."

"Nobody is infallible. But a lot of people are misinformed."

I pull back the duvet, and the sheets and pillows underneath are perfectly smooth on one side of the bed and wrinkled on the side near the phone. I notice cat fur that looks short and grayish-white.

"The linens weren't changed after whoever slept in here last." I continue taking photographs of everything I look at. "Someone slept or lay down on the right side of the bed next to the phone. It appears the cat was in the bed at some point. I'd like to check the bedside drawer."

A night guard in a blue plastic container is labeled with the name and address of the West Palm Beach dentist who caused Peggy Stanton so much damage and unnecessary expense. I set two prescription bottles on the table and photograph them, then place them in separate plastic evidence bags.

"Muscle relaxers prescribed by her dentist, Dr. Pulling," I let Burke know. "Any meds should go in to the labs. And I'd like to collect the night guards. Dr. Adams might want to take a look at them."

"What I'm getting at, Kay, and what I need you to objectively comment on—" she starts to say, and I cut her off.

"Why would you assume I might be anything other than objective?" I open the closet door.

"I'm sure you can imagine why I might be concerned." Her tone is no longer accusing or hostile, but sympathetic, as if she can well understand why I would cover for Marino, why I might slant or even falsify autopsy findings for him.

I run my gloved hands through the clothing on hangers, a lot of pantsuits and slacks and blouses that are prim and old-fashioned, with hanging cedar planks spaced along the rod. I don't see a dress or a skirt, and no blazers or jackets have antique military buttons or even distinctive ones.

"You care about him," Burke says, as if it's a good thing.

Peggy Stanton lost her family and never moved beyond it, everything old and the same, the future she looked forward to crashing with that plane. Her existence was rigidly maintained and obsessively protected, and it's hard for me to imagine she was on Twitter.

"I'm wondering if you've come across a computer?" I ask.

"Not yet."

Photographs displayed on tables and dressers are of an era when Peggy Stanton had people in her life she loved, her husband a pleasant-looking man with mischievous dark eyes and a lock of dark hair falling over his brow, the two girls into horses and swimming, one of them into airplanes. None of the photographs is recent. Peggy Stanton isn't in any of them.

"If she has no computer, how was she on Twitter?" I ask.

"Maybe a laptop she took with her. Maybe her phone, her iPad, whatever she had with her when she left here."

"I see nothing to suggest she was interested in technology," I reply. "In fact, quite to the contrary, if you look at the old TV in here, at the princess phone."

I open another closet, where button-up sweaters are folded on shelves with cedar blocks tucked between them, and shoes arranged on a rack on the floor are crepe-soled and low-heeled, made for comfort, not style. I'm not surprised that Peggy Stanton's hair was prematurely white and that she didn't bother to dye or style it or that her nail polish was an understated pale pink, almost flesh-colored. I see nothing to indicate she made any effort to be alluring or attractive beyond what the dentist did to her, and I suspect she was talked into those procedures.

"No Tulle or Audrey Marybeth or Peruvian Connection, not a single label like that." I look at a men's outback hat box, thick with dust, on the closet floor, PHOTOGRAPHS printed in neat block letters on the lid. "Most of her clothing is size eight or ten, not size six. I'd like to open this."

Inside are framed photographs that I look through, all of them of her, a pretty woman with jet-black hair and dark sparkling eyes, vibrant and not at all the way I have imagined her after examining her dead body and now her belongings. In riding clothes, and hiking and kayaking, and a picture of her in Paris when she must have been in her twenties, someone adventuresome and full of life before her world stopped.

"I seriously doubt she was looking for a romantic relationship or was the sort to connect with a stranger on the Internet who called himself *The Dude*," I remark. "There's not the slightest suggestion she was an avid bowler, no bowling shoes or balls or trophies, I assume? And no clothing or jewelry I've seen in photographs is remotely similar to what the body had on. It doesn't appear to be the right size. It would have been too small for her, at least when she was alive and not mummified."

"What I'm just wondering is if the conditions necessary for a body to mummify rapidly might be manufactured," Burke says.

"Whatever she had on when she was abducted or vanished," I add, "isn't what she was wearing in the bay. She was dressed. She was staged. Someone did it for a reason."

For his pleasure. I think of what Benton said. The killer choreographs what makes him feel important and powerful. Whatever it is, he plays it out with victims who have nothing to do with him. They aren't who he's kidnapping and killing.

"Might mummification be induced artificially?" Burke says, and I know what she wants.

"You mean if the body were placed inside a very hot, dry space, for example"—I give her the pitch she's waiting for— "and left to dehydrate?"

I walk into the bathroom, black-and-white subway tile and a claw-foot tub with brass cross-handled faucets.

"Which would require having access to such a place and feeling confident what you're doing wouldn't be discovered." I lead her down the path she's already on.

"Isn't it true that mummification in a closed structure that's hot and dry could occur in as few as eleven days?" She lets me know what I've by now deduced is her theory. "What if the person installed a sauna in his basement? Couldn't that work?"

"You mean the way Marino did?"

"Yes," she says. "The way he did when he bought his house this past summer."

"You mean the sauna he built from a kit that can fit one person sitting up on a bench not much wider than a toilet seat?"

The shower stall is the same tile, and bars of soap are dried out, and nothing looks recently used. I open the mirrored medicine cabinet door over the marble shell pedestal sink, the handles and fittings malachite and bronze.

"That rather horrible little sweatbox that looks like a Porta-John?" I ask.

She has more night guards, each from the same West Palm Beach dentist.

"A sauna that's on a sixty-minute timer so one is constantly having to reset it?" I continue, and Burke is silent in the doorway.

I pick up prescription bottles, more muscle relaxers, Flexeril, Norflex, and the anti-inflammatory drugs Vioxx and Celebrex. She was taking the antidepressant nortriptyline, all of the medications prescribed by this dentist, Dr. Pulling, and consistent with treatments for the temporomandibular joint and muscle disorder known as TMJ.

She had a bad case of it. She would have suffered chronic pain. She was in a vortex of getting dental work done to relieve a wretched condition that can cause the jaw to lock or dislocate and the ears to ring and a constant ache that radiates down the neck and shoulders and debilitates.

"So I guess he dehydrated her slowly, running downstairs on the hour to reset the infrared heater, including last week, when he was out of town, in Florida?" I'm careful not to sound sarcastic. "And by the way, that kit he bought because he thought it would help him lose weight would mean the body was propped up in a sitting position."

I walk out of the bedroom.

"She would have desiccated, dried out in that position." I keep talking as I go down the stairs and Burke is behind me. "And if the body was straightened, such as by weights or floats pulling on it when it was tethered in the water? Tension at the joints and the skin's going to split. She has no skin splitting, and her core body temperature was colder than the bay, which isn't possible unless the body was refrigerated, possibly frozen."

We are back in the entryway. I stop near the table with the glass bowl, where I'm sure Peggy Stanton never kept her car key, and Burke and I face each other, hooded and in white, with no pretenses or cordiality.

"He assaulted you five years ago in Charleston, South Carolina." She fires the shot she's saved. "He came to your house late at night and tried to rape you, and you never reported it to the police."

There's a note of triumph in her voice, and I'm sure I'm not imagining it.

"Why would you tell us anything now that might get him into trouble if you refused to do it then, after what he did?" she says.

"You don't know the facts." I hear footsteps on the front porch.

"I'm asking you for them."

I don't answer, because I won't.

"Are you aware of what the statute of limitations for sexual assault is in South Carolina?"

"I'm not."

"You haven't exceeded it," she says.

"It's not relevant."

"So you're still protecting him."

"You don't have the facts," I repeat.

"Here's a fact. He used to be into treasure hunting. Yet something else you know about him," Burke says, and it's what she's been waiting to do.

It's why I'm here inside this house with you.

"And Peggy Stanton had Civil War buttons on her jacket.

Did Marino bother to mention to you that he'd been tweeting a woman who collected antique buttons?"

"I've seen no evidence of an antique-button collection in this house," I answer, with no emotion she can detect.

"You're not going to talk to me about what he did to you."

"I'm not."

"Do you understand the problem I'm having? And it's not as if I enjoy bringing this up. I'm sorry—" Douglas Burke starts to say, as the front door opens wide and rain blows in.

Benton is carrying something wrapped in a towel.

"If he'd really attempted to rape me, I can assure you he would have succeeded." I don't care who hears. "Pete Marino is a very big man, and at the time this occurred, he was armed. So if he'd intended to physically overpower me or put a gun to my head to make me do what he wanted, he could have. But he didn't. He stopped what should never have started. But he stopped."

Benton and Machado drip on the plastic-covered rug beneath the French chandelier, and the towel is dirty and wet, and I notice gray fur peeking out.

"A broken-out window with no screen," Machado says, and what he just overheard seems etched in the air. "You know, near the ground, and the garage doesn't have an alarm, maybe the cat somehow pushed it open and pushed out the screen. So I guess it's been in and out of the garage all this time, made a bed in a box in there. Probably plenty to eat around here, or maybe people were feeding it."

I take the cat from Benton, short-haired gray-and-white, with gold eyes and flat ears, a Scottish Fold that looks like an owl, the flea collar around its neck faded and old.

"No tag," Benton says, and the look he gives Burke is piercing.

"Obviously an indoor cat. A girl. What's your name?" I wrap her in a clean towel, and she doesn't resist me. "I see. You're not going to say."

She's thin and dirty but seems in relatively good shape, her claws very long and curled and needle-sharp.

"Well, it didn't get out of the house on its own." Benton looks at me, and he knows what just happened. "And she certainly wouldn't have abandoned it."

Peggy Stanton wouldn't have put her cat outdoors and then left town, and his rage is simmering.

"So who let her cat out?" He pulls off his white hood and runs his fingers through his hair. "Someone who has no regard for human life but wouldn't hurt an animal." He bends over to take off his boot covers. "Had it been left in the house, it would have starved to death. So he came back. He let himself in. He knew her alarm code. And he had her keys."

"There was an open bag of treats on the counter." The cat has tucked its head under my chin and is purring. "Treats to lure her so he could let her out, perhaps?"

"Where are these treats?" Machado takes off his boot covers, and they are wet and dirty from walking outside.

I indicate the bags of evidence I've set on the entryway table.

"If he needed to lure the cat, then he wasn't someone familiar," Benton says.

"Did she run from you?" I ask.

"Came right up to us when we were inside the garage."

"Well, she seems very friendly but maybe wasn't with him. Maybe she sensed something that made her wary," I reply, as I wonder what I'm going to do with her.

I'm not leaving her here.

"It looks like the electrical panel was recently modified." Benton says this to me and ignores Douglas Burke, and I know when he's seething. "A subpanel that doesn't meet code. In the basement."

"Hooked up to what?" The cat rubs against my ear, purring.

"To nothing. No slots left in the main panel. It looks like she had someone come in, maybe a handyman, maybe an electrician, but what was done is substandard. It appears she intended to install something that would need to be connected to a breaker." Benton won't look at Burke, practically has his back to her. "A new cable runs from the subpanel along the wall to a new outlet."

"Work that's recent; how recent?" Burke asks, and it's Machado who answers, but he doesn't answer her.

He explains to me that there is a work area in the basement, a large table with paintbrushes, cookie cutters, wooden utensils, and a rolling pin.

"Like she was going to do baking down there," she says, and he describes a portable sink on casters, and I don't know what he means.

"A portable sink?" I puzzle. "Connected to a faucet? Why would she bake in the basement? Why not use her kitchen?"

"More like a plastic basin on a stand with wheels. I can show you if you want," Machado says.

"Yes, before I take all this off." I mean the protective clothing. "She doesn't seem to mind my holding her, so I don't think she'll mind if we look. There's a basement door that leads outside?"

"What the firefighters came in."

"We can go down and then out from there."

"The sink or basin looks pretty new, right there in the area where the new outlet is." He puts on clean boot covers. "Lots of pieces of cut wire scattered around. Black, white, green, number-six wire like you'd hook up to a pole circuit, to the neutral and ground bars," he explains. "But whatever she planned to hook up, she didn't get around to it. I'm thinking maybe she was going to put in an oven, but I agree it's a strange place to bake cookies or whatever. We need to find who did that electrical work."

twenty-six

THE RAIN HAS STOPPED, THE NIGHT COLD AND FLOODED, as I drive home alone, just the cat with me.

Benton asked Burke to give him a lift to the CFC so he could get his car, but I don't believe that's the real reason. They will have words. He will let her know what he thinks of her being on pseudoephedrine, on speed, and laying into me aggressively, and the hell with her allergies. What she did was out of line. I don't give a damn about the reason, and neither will he, and he's enraged by what he overheard, and he should be.

It's not that I don't understand why Burke needs to know about Marino, but I wouldn't have pushed the way she did, were I the investigator. It was wrong. It was badgering. It was bullying. There can be only one answer to how she knew what to confront me with, and I imagine her talking to Benton and have no doubt what he felt compelled to reveal. He couldn't lie or evade, of course not. I tell myself I can't blame him for being honest, and he couldn't truthfully say Marino has never shown a potential for violence—specifically, sexual violence—because he has.

But Burke didn't need the gory details, questioning me as if she wanted to envision it, as if she intended to humiliate and overpower, to do exactly what Marino did, and that's what troubles me. I worry what her motive is, and I'm amazed by the way events recede so far into the past that they round a bend and end up in front of us again. What Marino did five years ago is directly in my face, so close I can touch it, I can hear it, I can smell it like a posttraumatic flashback. Nerves that were numb have come alive, tingling and smarting as I drive, and I will get past it, but I won't forgive Douglas Burke. I blame her for willfully inflicting injury when it wasn't called for, wasn't warranted, certainly wasn't needed to prove her goddamn point.

I follow Massachusetts Avenue through Harvard Square, the cat curled up in the towel on my lap, and it bothers me that I don't know her name. The need to know it obsesses me, because she's had her name for quite some time, likely since she was a kitten, and I don't want to call her something different, something wrong. She's been through enough.

Out in the weather and God knows what traumas she's sustained and how lonely and hungry and uncomfortable she's been, and I imagine Peggy Stanton putting food and water into bowls in the kitchen. I imagine her collecting her pocketbook and keys, going out somewhere and fully intending to return home. But the next time the door opened, it wasn't her coming in.

A stranger using her house key, and he probably entered through the kitchen door so he wouldn't be seen by the neighbors or by anyone on the street. This person who somehow abducted and killed her entered her alarm code and walked from room to room, leaving lights on in some of them, and I continue to be suspicious about the flowers and who they were from. I'm bothered by the car key found in the Lalique bowl, where I feel this person deliberately left it.

Left it for whom?

Flowers with no card. Fresh flowers that were never thrown away. Food and any perishables in the kitchen were cleaned out, but not the flowers, and I keep going back to that as I think of the key placed in the entryway near a door I doubt the killer used.

Who were these things left for, really?

I unlock my phone and call Sil Machado because I can't call Marino.

"It's Dr. Scarpetta."

"What a coincidence."

"Why a coincidence?"

"What's going on, Doc?"

"I'm pondering her car being inside the garage." I head north to Porter Square.

"Already delivered safe and sound to your bay. Why? What's up?"

"The key you found inside the house," I say. "For sure it's her car key?"

"Yeah. I unlocked the driver's door with it just to take a quick look but didn't touch anything or try to start it."

"That's good. And what about the keychain?"

"I got the key, the keychain. Yeah."

"I'd like to see them at some point."

"Just a key and the pull-apart chain and an old black compass I'm thinking may have belonged to one of the little girls," he says. "A Girl Scout compass. Maybe her little girls were Girl Scouts. Or Brownies, I guess. How old's a girl got to be to go from a Brownie to a Girl Scout?"

"We don't know that her daughters were Brownies or Girl Scouts."

"The compass. Definitely a Girl Scout compass."

"I think it's possible he drove her car to her house, returned it to her garage, and left the key where he did because he didn't know where she usually kept keys," I tell him. "Because he probably didn't know her. But more important, maybe he left the key there for a reason, possibly a symbolic one."

"That's interesting."

"He may never have been inside her house before and walked around inside it after she was dead," I continue. "But we need to be careful not to let that be known. I wanted to make sure I said that to you because I have a strong feeling he might not realize anyone would figure it out."

"You mean that he went back in her house."

"I mean that he went in there at all. Even if it was only once."

"Interesting you'd say that, because I just got the alarm log. Other than the firefighters prying open the basement door with the hooligan?" He means a Halligan tool. "Last time the alarm system was disarmed was April twenty-ninth, a Sunday, at eleven-fifty p.m. Someone was inside the house for approximately one hour and then reset the alarm. Obviously this person left and never went back. There's been no alarm activity since until tonight, like I said."

"Not even false alarms?"

"All she's got is door contacts. No motion sensors or glass breaks, none of the usual shit that goes off."

"And before April twenty-ninth?"

"That previous Friday, the twenty-seventh," he says. "A couple ins and outs, and then someone left around six p.m., reset the alarm, and it wasn't disarmed again until Sunday the twenty-ninth at the time I just told you. At almost midnight."

"Possibly on that Friday night it was she who went out. She went somewhere, possibly in her car. And the person who came back late on Sunday was someone else."

"I'm with you so far."

"Did you happen to notice if her garbage cans had anything in them?" I ask.

"Totally empty," he says.

"Trash collection's on Mondays," I reply. "I'm wondering if this person emptied her refrigerator of perishables, took out the garbage, and rolled her super-can curbside."

"Then rolled it back under the side porch?"

"Yes. Possibly when this same person cleaned out her mailbox and suspended her newspaper delivery."

"Jesus. Who does that? Not some stranger."

"She might not have been a stranger to him. But that doesn't mean he wasn't a stranger to her. I'm not saying their paths didn't cross, but that doesn't mean she was personal with him or even aware of him." I think of everything Benton said about who we're looking for. "What I'd like to do is get trace and latent prints started on her car first thing in the morning. In other words, a full-court press. Not just checking mileage and the GPS but checking everything. Can you come in?"

"With bells on."

"And if you happen upon paperwork such as vet records or bills? Maybe something will have the cat's name on it?"

"She could have one of those chips."

"I'll have her scanned at the vet's office," I reply. "Maybe Bryce can take her in tomorrow. We'll see if there's an ID number we can check with the National Pet Registry."

I get off the phone, turning right on White Street, and feel terrible that I don't know what to call her.

"I'm really sorry, but I can't just call you 'the cat,'" I say to her, and she purrs loudly. "If you could talk you could tell me who put you out of the house, what bad person did that. Not just a person who isn't nice but an evil one, and I suspect you were scared of him because you sensed what he really is. A man nobody thinks twice about. But he's cruel. And you picked up on it, didn't you, when he let himself inside your house? You wouldn't come up to him until he tricked you with those treats I saw on the counter?"

I stroke her flat-eared head, and she rubs her face against my palm.

"Or maybe you ran out the door. Maybe you fled. I'll buy you a bag of treats. The same thing, salmon Greenies, because I know that's what your mother bought for you, lots and lots of bags of them in a cupboard. And grain-free turkey and salmon, which I also saw in the kitchen, plenty of it. She made sure you were well fed, had lots of healthy things to eat, didn't she? You don't seem to have fleas, but I'll give you a bath and get you cleaned up, so you're probably going to be angry with me."

It's almost midnight as I pull into the Shaw's supermarket parking lot, illuminated with tall light standards and bordered by bare trees moving in a wind that has died down considerably.

"I guess I could call you Shaw, since this is our first outing together." I park near the brick columned entrance. "I apologize I don't know who you are exactly, and I don't want you to worry, but I'm going to have to leave you in the car for a few minutes because I don't have anything at home for a cat. Only things for a dog, his very boring fish diet and sweet-potato treats. An old greyhound named Sock who is very shy and probably will be afraid of you."

I leave her wrapped in the towel in the driver's seat, shut the door, and am pointing the remote to lock it when headlights blind me as another car turns in. For an instant I can't see, and then a window rolls down and Sil Machado is grinning at me.

"Hey, what's doing, Doc?"

"Cat shopping." I walk over to his Crown Vic. "You following me?"

"We sure it's really her cat?" He shifts the car into park and props an arm on the door frame. "And yeah. I'm following you. Somebody's got to."

"Logic would tell you it's her cat. But I don't know it for a fact. She certainly seems lost and homeless." I look around at the almost empty lot, at someone rolling a shopping cart at the far end of it. "Are you coming inside?"

"Don't need anything at the store," he replies. "Just making sure you get home okay."

It seems a strange thing for him to say.

"I know you're used to riding around all over the place at all hours. But I'm just making sure," he repeats.

"Do you know something I don't?" I notice bags of evidence in the dark backseat, including those I collected.

"Someone who's familiar with Cambridge, right?"

"Someone who's familiar with her house, her neighborhood. Someone who made himself familiar, anyway." I step back to look through the driver's window of my SUV, making sure the cat's okay.

She's sitting up on the towel.

"Getting her mail out of the box, right? Maybe emptying her garbage and rolling out her can?" Machado looks at me, and he's as serious and unyielding as granite. "So I'm thinking this guy's way too comfortable around here. Knows when to get mail out of her box, probably at least once a week? Knows when garbage collection is. I hate what happened back there. I mean, Burke was out of bounds."

"I don't know how much mail she got." I'm not going to discuss what he's just brought up.

"Me and Marino ride Harleys together. Which is how we got in tight." Machado stares past me. "He drops by with pizza, to have coffee, sometimes we meet up at the gym, a real good guy and respects the hell out of you. I had no idea. I mean, I don't know what to say except I know what he feels about you. I know he'd take a bullet."

"I'm assuming this person was getting her mail once a week or a couple times a month at an hour when he's not likely to be seen. The obvious point would be he didn't want to raise suspicions and have people looking for her while he still had her body, storing it wherever he did for months." I'm not going to talk about Marino with him. "Do you have that keychain with you?"

"Okay, sure." He reaches over the back of the seat and finds the brown paper bag.

He opens it and pulls out a smaller bag that has the car key inside it, and he hands it out the window to me.

"Never had a case where someone's this brazen. Well, it's not normal, Doc."

"When is murder normal?" I hold the transparent bag up and illuminate it with the light from my phone.

"So you think it's some sicko who lives in a sick fantasy world, but he looks like the average man on the street."

"What do you think?" The car key is infrared, with a battery, the compass attached to it by a quick-key-release chain with a split ring at either end.

"Yeah, no doubt about it. Someone who blends. Someone no one thinks twice about."

"A pull-apart key holder that looks fairly new." I hand the bag back to him. "Connecting the key of an eighteen-year-old Mercedes to a compass that's vintage."

"Vintage meaning what? Like as old as the car?" He returns the plastic bag to the brown paper one.

"Meaning I think you're going to find Girl Scouts haven't used compasses like this one in recent memory. I'm going to guess at least fifty years."

"You kidding me? So maybe it was Peggy Stanton's."

"She was forty-nine, so it was before her time, too, and it depends on where she got the compass or where someone did." I check on the cat again. "An old compass, an old coin ring, and antique buttons sewn on the jacket she had on? Someone into history and collectibles, but who?"

"You go on in," Machado says. "I'm going to wait and follow you home, just to make sure. I'd feel better."

I head to the green awning over the entrance and go inside, rolling a cart to the aisle for pet supplies, where I find a litter box and scoop, and clumping litter, Wellness food and treats, and several toys. I find soothing oatmeal and flea shampoos and a nail trimmer, and when I return to my SUV and open the back door, Shaw is sitting on the backseat with her hind legs straight out, the way Scottish Folds sit, which is unlike the way any other cats sit.

"Come on." I pick her up, conscious of Machado parked nearby with his headlights burning. "Let's get you back in the towel and in my lap, okay?"

She doesn't fight or resist me in the slightest as I drive home with Machado right behind me, and I wonder what he's worried about. I can't help but suspect he knows something he's not saying, and maybe it's related to Marino, but it seems impossible that Machado could think for even a minute that Marino has anything to do with Peggy Stanton's death or a missing paleontologist. But it depends on what Machado's been told, especially if Burke's the one doing the telling.

I drive south, cutting over to Garfield, to Oxford, working my way toward Harvard's divinity school, to Norton's Woods, where the American Academy of Arts and Sciences is dark on its densely wooded acres. The pavement hisses wetly beneath my tires, Machado right behind me as I turn off Kirkland and onto Irving Street. Our three-story Federal-style house is white, with black shutters and a slate roof, and I can't tell if Benton is home. I pull into our narrow brick driveway and park to one side of the detached garage, and Machado stops on the street and waits as I get groceries and Shaw out of my car.

I unlock the door of the glassed-in porch, and the alarm begins to beep. Entering the code, I step inside and shove the door shut with my hip as Sock's nails click over hardwood from the direction of the living room. Benton isn't here. I can feel Shaw tense up inside the towel as Sock appears along the hallway, and I can't properly greet him.

"We have a visitor." I talk to our rescue brindle greyhound, who has a graying muzzle and is never in a hurry. "And you two are going to be friends."

I turn on lights as I pass through rooms, and inside my kitchen of cherry cabinets and stainless-steel appliances I set down shopping bags and shut Shaw inside the pantry so she doesn't wander off or hide. I take Sock out to the backyard, where my rose garden has lost its last blooms and the stained-glass window in the stairwell is backlit and vibrant. I apologize to Sock for getting home so late, and I know from e-mails that the housekeeper last let him out at five and gave him several treats. But he hasn't been fed, unless Benton took care of it, and I feel like a negligent mother.

Sock is a lean, long-legged silhouette sniffing his pointed nose, moving like a shadow through the yard with its stone wall that neighborhood children like to climb over, and he has his favorite spots where there are no motion-sensor lights. Then he follows me back inside, and I feed him and pet him and begin to fill a sink with warm water as I gather towels and wonder where Benton is.

"I haven't had a cat in a while." I talk to her as I retrieve her from the pantry and she purrs. "And I know you aren't going to be happy, but try to think of it as a spa."

I pull a chair out from the kitchen table and place her in my lap and clip her claws.

"Well, it seems you've had that done before, but maybe not a bath. Cats hate water, or that's what we're told, but tigers like to swim, so who knows what's true."

I put on rubber gloves and lower her into the warm water, lathering her with flea shampoo and finishing with oatmeal, and she looks at me with her big, round eyes and I start to cry.

I don't know why.

"You're quite the sport." I rub her with a big, soft towel. "I've never seen a cat that's such a good sport."

I wipe my eyes.

"You're more like a dog." I look at Sock, who is in his bed near the door. "Both of you orphaned rather much the same way."

I cry some more.

"The people you were with aren't around anymore, and then I bring you home with me and I realize it's not the same."

I can't begin to imagine what animals remember or know, but Shaw may have been Peggy Stanton's best friend and saw who killed her and can't tell me. She can't tell anyone. Now this mute witness is inside my house, sprawled out on her back on top of a towel, in a position no dignified cat would ever be in. I close the pocket doors and look in the freezer for what I might warm up, and I'm not interested in any of it. I open a bottle of Valpolicella and pour a glass, and decide on fresh pasta with a simple tomato sauce, and I return to the pantry. Shaw is by my feet.

I retrieve cans of whole peeled tomatoes and melt salted butter in a saucepan and add an onion sliced in half. She rubs against my legs, purring.

"If Benton were here we might grill Italian sausage outside," I say to the cat. "Yes, it's cold and wet, but that wouldn't stop me. Don't look worried. I won't. Not out there in the dark all alone."

It enters my mind that Machado hopefully has left, and I remember to reset the alarm, and I boil salted water. I set the coffee table in the living room and turn on the fire, and I drink more wine and try Benton several more times. His phone instantly goes to voicemail. It's now close to one a.m. I could call Machado, but I don't want to ask him where my husband is. I could call Douglas Burke, but hell would have to freeze over first, and I turn off the stove. I sit in front of the gas fire with Shaw in my lap and Sock snuggled next to me, both of them sleeping, and I drink, and when I've drunk enough I call my niece.

"Are you awake?" I ask, when Lucy answers.

"No."

"No?"

"This is voicemail. How can I help you?" she says.

"I know it's late." I hear someone in the background, or I think I do. "Is that your TV?"

"What's going on, Aunt Kay?" She's not alone, and she's not going to tell me.

twenty-seven

I WAKE UP WITHOUT THE ALARM AND FOR AN INSTANT don't know where I am or who's in bed with me. Moving my hand under the covers, I feel Benton's warm slender wrist and tapered fingers, and I go hollow inside as I feel what I was feeling in my dream. It was Luke I was with.

A dream so vivid, sensations linger where his hands and mouth had been, nerves alive and wanting, and I slide close to Benton and stroke the lean muscles of his bare chest and belly, and when I have roused him we do what we want and we don't talk.

When nothing is left we shower and start again, hot water coming down hard, and he is hard, almost angry, our lust the way it was when we cheated and lied, desperate to satisfy what raged beneath our outward calm, and relief never lasted long. We could not stay away from each other and could not get enough, and I want it back.

"Where have you been?" I say into his mouth, and he moves me against the wet tile wall, and water is loud, and I ask him again.

He tells me he's here without saying it, and I'm here and belong to him and there can be no denying it. We make love the way we did when it was wrong, when he had a wife he was unhappy with and daughters who had little use for him, and then for a long time he was gone.

He was nowhere and back, with me but not, and Marino made it worse, and touching felt different after that. Nothing was the same until betrayal and jealousy reset us like a bone mending badly that needed to be broken again. We had to hurt.

"Stay this time," I say into his mouth, steamy water pouring over us. "Stay this time, Benton."

When we are dressing he asks me what I was dreaming.

"What makes you think I dreamed anything?" I go through suits hanging in my closet, and it reminds me of looking through Peggy Stanton's clothes.

"Doesn't matter." He stands in front of the full-length mirror, tying his tie.

"It matters or you wouldn't ask."

"Dreams are dreams unless they become something else." He watches my reflection as I decide on unstylish pants and a sweater and practical ankle boots that are warm.

It will be a long day, hopefully not as long as yesterday, but I'm going to be comfortable in corduroys and a cable-knit cardigan, and it's very cold, the temperature below freezing.

Ice has formed on bare trees and evergreens, as if they've been varnished or glazed with sugar, and as I move the shade to see the street below and imagine what driving might be like, Benton walks across hardwood and the rug and puts his arms around me and kisses my neck.

His hands rediscover what was all his moments ago, and he pushes under everything I've just put on.

"Don't forget," he says.

"I've never forgotten."

"Lately you've forgotten. Yesterday you did."

"Go ahead and say it." I want him to say what he saw, to just go ahead and say it.

His hands are where he wants them.

"Did you?" he asks.

"Did I what?" I'm not going to make it easy for him. "You need to ask me what you want to know."

"Did you tell him you would? Did you let him think you would?"

"I told him I wouldn't."

"He was touching you," Benton says, as he touches me. "He thought you would. That you wanted it."

"I told him I wouldn't, and that's the end of it," I reply, and he moves me back to the bed.

"Is it really all there is? Has there been anything more?"

"There is nothing more than that." I unbuckle his belt.

"Because if there's more, I might kill him. I will, in fact, and get away with it."

"You won't." I unzip his pants. "And you can't get away with it."

"I wanted to kill him in Vienna because I knew it then."

"There's nothing to know. There's nothing more than you already know," I reply, and I ask about her. "You're going to wrinkle your shirt." I ask about Douglas Burke. "I'm going to wrinkle it. I'm going to ruin it."

White cotton and dark silk are smooth against my bare skin, and I ask him again, and then I don't ask him anything else until we are in the kitchen and I'm feeding the dog and the cat.

"Shaw certainly seems to have made herself at home." I spoon her food on a plate and set it on a mat near the pantry door. "It's as if she's always lived here, but I think it's a good idea to shut her in the guest room, in a confined space, until she's really familiar with the house. Although I have a feeling Bryce is going to want her. He'll take one look at her and that will be that."

"She should be checked by the vet." Benton pours coffee, and he's tall and straight in a dark suit, his silver hair damp and combed straight back.

He doesn't answer me about Douglas Burke.

"I'll send Bryce to get her at some point today, get her checked from stem to stern." I open a can of dog food. "Are you coming by my office to see what we find with the car?"

"I have to deal with the Marino problem."

"You'll talk to him?"

"Talking to him doesn't help anything. He's been talked to enough, and there's nothing else. And nothing happened, Kay," Benton then says, and he's referring to something else entirely. "Nothing happened, but not because of her. But because of me."

He lets me know that Douglas Burke is attracted to him and has tried to do something about it. She might be in love with him, and when he says that, I know she is. I know she has it bad.

"That could be part of the problem." He sips coffee and looks at me as I set Sock's bowl on his mat, which is a safe distance from Shaw's mat, although the two of them seem at peace with each other, as if they know what they've been through and wouldn't deny any creature the courtesy of rescue.

"What do you mean, '*could* be'?"

"When we first started working together I really thought she was gay. So it's been very confusing." He hands me a coffee.

"How did you suddenly become so obtuse? What is it you do for a living? Suddenly you're a blockhead?"

He smiles. "Not so astute when it comes to myself, maybe. I'm always the last to know."

"Bullshit, Benton."

"Maybe I didn't want to know."

"That's the more likely story."

"I would have bet you money she was gay."

"Whatever she is, she shouldn't have done what she did last night."

"She knows that, Kay. And as bad as it was for you, it's pretty terrible to be an FBI agent and lose control like that. She's lost control. She has. Badly. And it will have to be addressed beyond my giving her hell about it."

"You don't want her." I give him another chance to confess.

"I don't want her like that, and in fact I was sure she wanted Lucy. She'd get unbelievably flustered around Lucy," he says.

"Lucy could fluster Mother Teresa."

"No, I mean it." Benton opens the refrigerator and retrieves a jug of blood-orange juice and pours each of us a glass. "I'm trying to think of the last time when it was so obvious I was almost embarrassed. Doug was dropping me off at Hanscom, where Lucy was meeting me. She'd just shut down the helicopter and was walking across the tarmac, and Doug was so distracted I thought she might hit a parked plane."

"When Lucy flew you to New York this past June, right before my birthday," I recall. "That recently you didn't get what was going on?"

"Her face was flushed, her hands were shaking, agitated, and she stared holes in her."

"Sounds like Sudafed, or whatever else she's on."

"Now I'm wondering," he says. "Now I'm really wondering."

"It could be Lucy, too. She might have been reacting to Lucy," I consider, as I get eggs from the refrigerator and begin cracking them in a bowl. "People aren't always one thing. Almost never, if they're honest about it. I'm not aware they really know each other, beyond Lucy making a point to avoid her and every other FBI agent if possible."

"Could be something conflicted there." Benton refills his cup and checks mine. "She's asked me about her."

"She's asked you about Lucy?"

"She's curious about Lucy's FBI past. Why she left the Bureau. Why she left ATF."

"What did you tell her?" I turn on the stovetop.

"Nothing."

"She's just curious, or are her questions an attempt to be critical? Maybe she wants to find out information that might make her feel superior to Lucy."

"Doug's competitive."

"You probably don't know the half of it." I open a cabinet, deciding on cookware.

"I don't talk about us, don't confide in her, never have and wouldn't."

"I'm not surprised. You barely confide in me."

"I know Doug takes all sorts of stuff, has real problems with allergies, but I'd never really given it a second thought."

"Have you seen symptoms and behavior like this from the beginning?" I whisk eggs and melt butter in a saucepan. "What about when you first started working with her closely?"

"On and off and then on. These past few months? On all the time. Revved up like an overspeeding engine." He drops English muffins in the toaster. "I thought it was her mood, her problem."

"Her problem with you. There should be chopped asparagus and fresh basil on the top shelf. Refrigerator one. Fig preserves are in the door of refrigerator two." I am overly diligent about having plenty of food in the house.

If I have a compulsion, it's making sure I don't run out of anything I might need for cooking, especially if the weather is taking a turn for the worse.

"When I finally realized what she felt, by then it was pretty bad, and I attributed it to her being anxious, stressed, when she was around me." He sets the jar of preserves, the basil, and the asparagus on the counter near me. "Cheese?"

"Parmesan is already grated. And you're in charge of the preserves." I slide the jar back in his direction. "It will be good on the muffins."

I need to get to the store today. There probably won't be time. I uncover Parmigiano-Reggiano I grated late last night and asparagus I chopped while I was waiting for Benton to come home. I whisk the eggs, adding salt and pepper.

"Pseudoephedrine is structurally similar to amphetamine and has been used for performance enhancement." I tear the basil leaves and mix them in. "It's commonly abused by athletes, for example, causing euphoria, boundless energy, and people can get dependent, taking it three or four times a day or even more. Some use it to lose weight because it's an appetite suppressant."

"She certainly doesn't need to lose weight."

"Maybe that's why."

"I'm suggesting she request a transfer to a different field office."

"You suggested it or you're going to suggest it?" I turn the heat down very low. "And how did the moment of enlightenment happen after you'd gone all this time supposedly assuming she's gay?"

"When we went to Quantico together in August." He checks the muffins and presses the levers back down. "She wanted to come into my room, and it became quite apparent what her interest was, and I made it very clear it wasn't going to happen."

"And last night?" I open the oven door to make sure the broiler is heating up. "When she dropped you off to pick up your car and you didn't get home until some two hours later? By which time I'd gone through half a bottle of wine by myself and dinner was ruined."

"We sat in your parking lot talking," he says, and I believe him. "She can't get over it."

"She can't get over you."

"I guess not. No."

"I guess even an FBI agent can have a personality disorder.

Narcissist? Borderline? Sociopath, or a little dash or all three? What is she? Because I know you know."

"I don't expect you to feel sorry for her, Kay."

"Good." I grab potholders. "Because I don't."

I lift the stainless-steel saucepan off the induction stovetop and place it inside the oven on the top shelf.

"This will take all of ten seconds, and I'm quite sure the muffins must be done," I say. "She tries to seduce my husband, wants Marino to go to jail and basically accuses me of being a liar and resorts to interrogation methods reminiscent of rubber hoses."

"She probably needs a leave of absence."

"It was her intention to degrade if not annihilate the competition."

"She probably needs to see someone." He pops up the muffins and quickly drops them on a plate and butters them. "She needs to be away from Boston and, quite frankly, away from me. I need her away from me."

Lightly brown on top, the frittata is done, and I slide it out of the saucepan and onto a platter and slice it like pizza while Benton continues telling me his concerns about Douglas Burke.

"The problem is, you seek counseling, especially if you need to be on meds, it's not just your own private business." He carries our coffees and silverware to the breakfast table by the window. "With the Bureau, nothing is just your own private business. So she doesn't want help even though she needs it."

"Are you worried she might be a danger to herself?"

"I don't know."

"If you don't know, that's the same as saying yes." I pull out a chair, and the morning beyond the window is getting light and a car going by on the street is moving slowly, carefully, because of ice. "If you don't know if she's safe for herself or maybe others, then you have to assume she isn't. What do you do about that?"

"I'm afraid I'm going to have to talk to Jim."

Jim Demar is the special agent in charge of the Boston Field Office.

"Unfortunately, it will give a life to something." He spreads fig preserves on half a muffin, which he offers to me. "She could be put on administrative leave with pay, which wouldn't be the worst thing if it gives her time to get her head straight, maybe get her moved and let her start fresh."

"Where?"

"I'm going to recommend Louisville, Kentucky, where she's from. A new office there, a great facility and lots of opportunity. Maybe the Joint Terrorism Task Force or the Intelligence Fusion Center or foreign counterintelligence or public corruption."

"Whatever gets her mind off of you," I reply.

"I'm sure she'll be fine. It's just not a good fit for her around here."

I think about that as I drive back to the CFC, *not a good fit*, and yet Douglas Burke's problem has nothing to do with Boston and everything to do with Benton. He's being naïve, and it concerns me, and I contemplate how strange it might seem to almost anyone that my husband the profiler can be thick, downright dense. I've never been in this exact predicament. I've never had to deal with someone obsessed with my husband quite to this degree, and he doesn't see it the way I do. Douglas Burke is dangerous to herself and I'm not sure to whom else.

twenty-eight

I PULL IN BEHIND MY BUILDING AND CAN DETERMINE BY the cars in the lot the key people who are here, the ones I will need. Luke and Anne, and Ernie, George and Cybil, and I notice Toby's pickup truck. He's on call tonight and is supposed to be off today. His red Tacoma is parked in an Investigation space next to the white Tahoe I was in yesterday, and I think of what Lucy said when we talked at one a.m.

She told me the reason she was still up at that hour, as if it required an explanation, is that she and Marino had been arguing rather fiercely. He refused to stay in her house and she refused to drive him to the CFC to get his car, and she wouldn't drive him to his home in Cambridge, either. From that I inferred he'd been drinking or wasn't to be trusted for one reason or another, and as she was telling me this I could hear someone in the background who wasn't him.

The person was speaking in a low, quiet voice I couldn't make out while Lucy went on to say that Marino finally agreed to stay in the stable, an outbuilding that really isn't a stable anymore because she's converted it into a washing and detailing bay with an underground firing range. Upstairs on the second floor is a guest quarters, an efficiency apartment, and she was moving about as she described this, and I couldn't hear the other person anymore, and that probably was deliberate.

It's been a while since I've been invited to Lucy's country home, as she calls her sixty-some acres on the Sudbury River west of Boston, a horse farm she's spent the past year renovating and retrofitting to handle her collection of gravity-defying machines, the barn converted into a monster garage, the paddock now a concrete helipad. Marino is *reasonably okay,* and I shouldn't be worried, Lucy informed me, and the last time I knew she was dating anyone was in early summer, a person she rendezvoused with in Provincetown more than once.

Of course Marino's upset. He's angry, Lucy explained, and I couldn't stop thinking of the gold signet ring she had on yesterday. I didn't question her. I know when not to, but she seemed so uneasy and guarded, and it occurred to me that whatever she and Marino were fighting about may have nothing to do with the mess he's in. Maybe he moved into the stable because of who she's with, someone she doesn't want to talk about, someone Marino doesn't approve of, and he's never hesitated to give Lucy his opinion about choices she's made.

The CFC seems lonely, Marino's absence a void that is palpable, and I enter my building through the bay. I don't see Lucy's car, whatever she's decided to drive today, but by now she's on her way here to help me with what I've asked. How to track an imposter on Twitter, and is it possible the person who sent me the video clip and image of a severed ear also pretended to be Peggy Stanton and tweeted Marino? It would seem unlikely, were it not for the timing, everything horrid happening all at once.

I unlock the door to the autopsy floor, pausing at the security desk to check the log. Five cases have come in since late last night, two possible drug ODs, a gunshot homicide, a sudden unexpected death in a parking lot, a pedestrian hit-and-run, the autopsies already under way. I told Luke to start without me and to make sure we discuss Howard Roth at some point. I want to review scene photographs, to examine his clothing and take a look at his body before it's released. I want as much history as we can find because I don't believe he got a flail chest from falling down his basement steps.

Through another door I go down a ramp, the evidence bay a walled-off windowless space where my staff are working, all of them in white Tyvek and face shields. They are covered from their scalps to the soles of their feet by the same water- and bacteria-proof flashspun polyethylene barrier used to wrap houses and commercial buildings and boats and cars and mail. Faces behind plastic and cocooned in a sheen of white, scarcely recognizable as people I know, barely people at all, making synthetic crinkly sounds as they move around.

They are setting up cyanoacrylate evaporators with fans and humidifiers around the 1995 pale yellow Mercedes sedan, its doors and trunk open wide, in an area of the bay where the lights have been dimmed. Trace evidence examiner Ernie Koppel has on orange goggles and is using the ALS on the driver's seat, and I suit up and put on gloves. I ask him what's been done so far.

"I wanted to go through it with a fine-toothed comb before we fume it," he says, and while the hood covers his baldness it plumps up his already plump cheeks, his teeth and nose seeming unnaturally large. "You might want to put these on if you're going to look." He hands me goggles the same way he always does, as if I don't know to put them on when using wavelengths that require filters.

Crouching by the open driver's door, he moves the guide, what looks like a cone-shaped lamp attached to a black cord. He paints ultraviolet light over brown carpet that is stained and worn, and I wonder out loud if there might have been mats and someone removed them. Maybe the killer did when he returned the car to her garage, and I'm not the least bit hesitant about referring to a murderer even though I don't know why Peggy Stanton is dead. I've already decided if toxicology turns up negative I will sign her out as a homicide with a cause of death that's undetermined.

"There were no mats front or back when the car was brought in," Ernie says. "I can't answer if there ever were any, but I have a feeling maybe not based on what I'm seeing." He directs the light to show me. "Mostly in this area." He means the driver's side of the front seat.

Fibers look like snippets of wire fluorescing white, orange, neon green, and rainbow blends as the UV light passes over them. Ernie reaches in with adhesive carbon tape stubs that he gives to me as he finishes with each one. I place them inside screw-cap vials, sealing them in bags I label with the location they were recovered from and other information Ernie gives to me.

"I already went over the back and the passenger's side." His coveralls and booties make plastic sounds, and intermittently his voice is muffled when he's inside the car. "First with white light, then blue, just in case there's fine blood spatter or gunshot residue. I tried green for latents. UV for semen, saliva, urine. There's no evidence thus far that anything bad happened in this car. It's dusty and lonely, if a car can be lonely, like an old person's car."

"She wasn't old, but I think she lived like it."

"I found what looks like some cat fur, grayish-white," he says. "On the carpet in back where you might expect someone to put a pet carrier."

"I'm reasonably sure she had a cat." I need to talk to Bryce about that, about taking Shaw to the vet.

"It may have been her only passenger," Ernie supposes. "Typical for what I see in a vehicle usually driven by one person, especially an older person. There's a high concentration of fibers, hair, other debris transferred to the driver's area and tracked in and ground into the carpet, which I could cut out, but I'd rather collect what's obvious first. What I am noticing and what you'll be most interested in is this stuff here."

His gloved hand holds out another stub to me.

"You'll need a lens to see what I'm talking about," he says. "It doesn't fluoresce because it's absorbing the UV and looks black, pretty much like blood does, but it's not blood. In normal light and under a lens it's dark red. There's a fair amount of it in the carpet near the brake and the accelerator, like someone had it on his shoes."

I step away from the car and take off my goggles. Retrieving a magnifier from a cart, I examine the stub and agree with Ernie that blood wouldn't look like this. The woody material is familiar.

"I'm thinking the stuff could be mulch," he says.

"Do you know what kind of wood?"

"The chemical spectra for that may take a day or two.

Assuming you want to know if all of it came from the same localized area, from the same tree, for example?"

George and Cybil from trace want to know when they can begin to set up the tent. It will completely enclose the car so no one is inhaling superglue fumes or is exposed to them. I tell them not quite yet.

"To determine that degree of specificity? Well, it depends on the uptake from soil, various elements in it; we are what we eat. It's true of everything, even trees," Ernie is saying from inside the Mercedes, and I know he's thinking about what I recovered from Peggy Stanton's body.

The fibrous red material on the bottom of her feet and under her nails looks identical to what he's finding inside her car.

"If you want that level of detail, I might have to send a sample to a lab where they specialize in wood analysis." He continues painting UV inside the Mercedes. "It goes without saying in trace amounts like this you can't exactly count the rings."

"I'd settle for type of tree. Pine, redwood, cypress, cedar. It does look a lot like mulch."

Soft-sided carrying cases are set down close to me, scientists unpacking the cyanoacrylate monomer and cabling.

"Hardwood shredded mulch as opposed to mulch made from bark," I specify.

"There's no bark I can see," Ernie tells me.

"Sort of like shredded wheat," I describe, as I look at it. "Fibrous, hairy. Almost like cotton. Not milled like wood that's sawed or cut with machines. But extremely fine. Without magnification it almost looks like soil, like dirt, like fine coffee grounds. Only dark red."

"No, it's not milled. It's totally irregular. A red-colored mulch, and usually mulch is made from scrap pallets and other wood that's chip-ground." His head is ducked in the driver's side. "Not popular with a lot of people, because it bleeds in the rain and the dye masks treated lumber, which you don't want in your yard, certainly not near your vegetable garden. Recycled CCA, chromated copper arsenate, and whatever this stuff is, it doesn't have a trace of CCA, that much I can say. Assuming it's the same stuff you found on the body. I did find iron oxide, which could be from a dye or from good ole dirt."

I tell him it would be very helpful if he could examine what he's finding inside her car, to do it as quickly as possible. It might be quite important, I add, and he promises when he gets back to his lab he'll take a look with the stereomicroscope, the polarized light scope, the Raman spectrometer.

He's confident he's going to find the same chemical fingerprint, he explains, the same interference colors and same birefringence he saw when he took a look at the reddish material I collected from Peggy Stanton's body.

"Red-stained wood but not stained all the way through." I study another stub he hands to me. "If it were ground up and sprayed with dye, would it look like this?"

"Maybe. I do know when I examined what Dr. Zenner submitted to me yesterday, I noted that some of the fibers are charred," Ernie says. "And that I don't necessarily expect to find in mulch. But it completely depends on what it's made from. Scrap wood from a torn-down building where there may have been a fire, for example? I also found charcoal and a lot of minerals mixed in."

"The question is whether the charcoal, the minerals are indigenous to this mulchlike material or are from dirt on a floor or carpet."

"That's exactly the question." Ernie stands up and straightens his back as if it's stiff. "You start looking at the world through a microscope and you see salt, silica, iron, arsenic, insect pieces and parts, skin cells, hair, fibers, a holy horror."

"It certainly appears he drove her car." I feel sure of it. "Wherever he took her must have this reddish debris on the floor, on the ground."

"Maybe a landscaping business or an area where a lot of red-colored mulch is used. Golf courses, apartment complexes, a park. Or maybe a place they manufacture mulch. Did you see anything like this around her house?"

"No. She stepped in it wherever he took her, and he did, too, and he tracked it into her car. This splintery material would work its way into clothing, carpet, skin, hair, and stick to everything like Velcro."

"Some synthetic fibers on the leather seats," he lets me know as he looks. "Probably from clothing, and a fair amount of white hair everywhere."

"Her hair was white. Long. Shoulder length."

"A little bit of these same wooden fibers." He finds more of them. "Possibly transferred from clothing. Hers or some other person's." He turns a knob on the ALS's panel, changing wavelengths, and the light turns green-blue.

I put my goggles back on, the orange filter blocking light not absorbed by the evidence, and I return to the car. Ernie is painting the steering wheel, the dash, the console, and the seat belt's metal buckle and tongue, areas that will be swabbed for DNA next. Some smudges light up, nothing discernible, no latent prints we can do anything with, and I'm not surprised.

Maybe we'll get lucky when the car is fumed inside and out with cyanoacrylate, better known as superglue, but I don't want to get my hopes up. I can't imagine a killer driving Peggy Stanton's Mercedes or exploring her house and not wearing gloves or covering his hands or wiping things down after the fact, but I also know better than to project what I think onto someone else. Bad people can be incredibly stupid, especially arrogant ones who have never been caught and aren't in a database.

"I always feel like the abominable snowman in this damn stuff," Sil Machado complains, as he walks up. "Or maybe the Pillsbury Doughboy."

Ernie explains what we've found as another text message lands on my phone. A third one from Lucy, who wants to see me upstairs.

"I saw nothing like that anywhere inside her house," Machado lets Ernie know. "Not in the basement. Not in the garage. Not in her yard. No red mulch. Not even old mulch. You got a minute?" he says to me. "Actually, I'm going to need more than one."

"I was just heading up to take care of a few things," I reply. "Come on."

twenty-nine

HE SAYS HE WOULD HAVE GOT HERE SOONER, BUT LUKE called him earlier this morning, asking questions about Howard Roth. Apparently, Luke told Sil Machado it was urgent.

"Did he explain why?" I walk us through the evidence bay.

"Yeah, he said you don't think Howie fell down the stairs."

"Howie?"

"What people called him," Machado replies.

"I'm not suggesting he didn't go down the stairs. I'm suggesting he might have had some help," I clarify. "His injuries aren't consistent with a typical fall."

"Dr. Zenner said you think maybe somebody beat the shit out of him."

I hope Luke didn't say it like that, and I take off the Tyvek and drop it in the trash.

"So I shot right back over to his place." Machado yanks off his coveralls, booties, and gloves, as if he hates them. "And I admit I didn't look through things the first time thinking homicide. But if ever there was an obvious scenario I've seen? A known drunk has an accident and there's blood on the steps he fell down, I'm telling you, Doc, I don't make assumptions. But this was straightforward. I'm still blown away you're thinking he might be a homicide."

"Who found him?"

"A buddy, a guy who works maintenance at Fayth House just a few blocks away. Said he had the day off, dropped by for a beer. Apparently, Howie did some odd jobs over there. General labor, when he was sober enough."

Machado hands me a transparent plastic bag that has a check inside it. I again press the button for the elevator, which seems to be stuck on my floor.

"This was in his toolbox. I didn't look the first time because he's an alcoholic who fell down the stairs into the basement, right? I mean, that's where his body was found. He was in his underwear like he'd been in bed. And he's got scratches, a gash on his head, broke ribs, is banged up like he went down the steps, and like I said, there's blood on them and at the bottom of them."

Peggy Stanton's choice of a design for her personal checks is folk art reminiscent of Charles Wysocki Americana, a brick house with a white picket fence, a horse and buggy going past.

"Every indication is he took a fall so there was no reason for me to go rooting around inside an old toolbox," Machado says. "Not unless I was looking for something in particular, which I wasn't at first."

"He may have gone down the stairs, but he may have been injured first," I reiterate, and now I'm more convinced of it because of the check.

It's handwritten in black ink, made out to Howard Roth for one hundred dollars.

"I don't think it's likely the fall is what killed him," I add. "He died from hemorrhage and possibly respiratory distress caused by blunt trauma so severe segments of his rib cage separated from his chest wall with as many as two to four fractures per rib. He has severe underlying lung injury."

The check's memo blank has been filled in with "home repairs."

"He has blunt-force trauma to the back of his head. Do we know how he really got that?" I ask.

"Couldn't hitting concrete steps do all of it?"

"I'm very concerned," I tell Machado, as we wait for the

elevator to budge from the top floor. "More so now that there's a connection between Peggy Stanton and him."

"Easy to imagine. The basement door right next to the bathroom." He's not going to stop defending his initial belief that Howard Roth is an alcohol-related accident. "I figure he gets up in the middle of the night? Drunk. Opens the wrong door, and one small step for man, one huge tumble."

Printed in the check's upper-left corner is the bank account holder's name, *Mrs. Victor R. Stanton.*

"Where was the toolbox?" I ask.

There's no address or telephone number on the check, and I continue looking at it. I can't take my eyes off it.

"Oh, geez, Doc. You got to picture it in your head, okay? This old run-down place, really small, a real shit can."

"I'm going to need to review the scene photographs."

Her signature is *Peggy Stanton,* and it's not a good forgery.

"A dark pit, a dump," Machado is saying. "One naked lightbulb and six concrete steps leading down, with a rope for a railing. The toolbox was down there. I guess he carried the check around with him in his toolbox."

"He's making the rounds in Cambridge. Maybe stopping by her place because he wanted his money. Obviously he never cashed the check." I tap-tap the button for the elevator, which hasn't moved, someone holding open the door, no doubt.

My impatience reminds me of Marino.

"Fayth House is a residential nursing home," I then say. "It might be worth checking on whether Peggy Stanton did any volunteer work there. It could be how she connected with him and why she would have trusted him to do an occasional job for her. A hundred dollars isn't insignificant. I'd say he did more than rake her yard or unclog a drain."

I think of the substandard wiring that was recently done in her basement as the elevator takes forever to descend.

"What else do we know about him?" I ask.

"Apparently, he was a mechanic in the Army. Served in Iraq when we first went over there, and didn't do so good after the fact. Came home with a traumatic brain injury, a TBI from an explosive blast. Was discharged, moved back into his Cambridge house, couldn't hold a job, wife left him seven years ago. A lot of drinking."

"His STAT alcohol was point-one-six," I repeat what Luke told me over the phone earlier, our discussion about his problematic case quite brief and frustrating.

Neither Machado nor Luke took the case as seriously as I wish they had, because it seemed so obvious.

"His level of intoxication would have made him more vulnerable to anyone who wanted to hurt him," I add. "If he's cirrhotic, he's also going to bleed excessively. I've not gone over his autopsy findings in detail yet. But I will."

"He pretty much drank up his pension every month and made money any way he could," Machado says. "All these garbage bags in his house, nothing much else, just bag after bag like a hoarder. Filled with cans, bottles that he obviously was turning in for money, probably digging through trash cans, taking them out of peoples' recycling bins that they leave curbside."

The check is dated this past June first, and I tell Machado I seriously doubt Peggy Stanton was still alive then.

"If she was," I add, "she wasn't in her own house, since it appears the last time it was accessed was April twenty-ninth, according to the alarm log."

"Obviously someone was able to get enough of her information to impersonate her. Must have stolen some of her blank checks, got her PIN number for the ATM because there are some cash withdrawals, nothing abnormal but enough so you think she's alive and well. He got the code to her alarm, who knows what all? Any signs of torture?" he asks, as the elevator doors finally slide open.

"She has some strange brownish areas that I'm not sure about." I describe them. "No obvious injuries or marks I'd immediately associate with torture. But not everything leaves a mark."

"Probably just scared the shit out of her and she told him whatever he wanted, believing he wouldn't hurt her."

"Did you talk to Howard Roth's wife?" We ride up in what Marino calls "the slowest boat in China."

"Yesterday. She came down here and ID'd a photograph, and I talked to her for a while and then called her back as I was driving here. Apparently, he's a regular in Cambridge. In fact, I think I've seen him walking around, and a couple of guys I work with know about him. Doing the odd job, a pretty decent handyman, and honest, harmless, according to the ex. But she couldn't stay with a drunk," Machado says. "No car. Driver's license is expired. A real sad case."

I return the envelope to him, and he verifies that personal checks and checkbooks he found inside Peggy Stanton's house are like this one, exactly like it, he says.

"That's the other thing I find really interesting," he adds. "She had all her bank statements in a file drawer, you know, with all her canceled checks? Years' worth of them, but only through this past April."

"Because someone began intercepting her mail." We get out on the seventh floor, where Toby seems to be having difficulty pushing a cart loaded with boxes. "Are you considering that Howard Roth killed her?"

"It's always smart to consider everything. But it wouldn't make sense to think he had anything to do with it."

"He had something to do with it even if he wasn't aware of it," I reply, as we follow the corridor toward the computer lab. "Are you the one holding the elevator door open forever?" I say to Toby, when we get to him.

"Sorry about that. I'm having trouble with a stuck wheel, then it turned over when I was pushing it out."

"I thought you were off today."

"Well, with Marino not here, I thought it was good to come in." He's not looking me in the eye and I notice the boxes are computer supplies.

Machado and I walk off, and I comment, "It says a lot that she continued using her husband's name when he's been dead thirteen years."

Toby pushes the cart behind us, stopping every few steps to straighten out the wheel.

"Maybe she didn't want people to know she lived alone," Machado supposes. "My girlfriend's like that, doesn't have her address or phone numbers on her checks. Doesn't want her information out there so someone can just show up at her door, doesn't want strangers calling. Of course, being with me and hearing all my stories about what goes on has made her a little paranoid."

"Why do you think he didn't cash the check? Based on your description, he could use every penny he got."

"I'm betting he tried and couldn't," Machado says. "A handyman who basically would go around Cambridge collecting bottles and cans, doing anything anybody might hire him for. I seriously doubt people paid him with checks."

We walk through Lucy's open door, and she's at her desk, surrounded by large flat-screen monitors, and Toby pushes the cart in after us. He begins stacking the boxes against the wall.

"You want these anyplace special?" he asks her.

"Just leave them." She says it like an order, staring at him.

"Raking leaves, yard work, home repairs, even electrical, and he's not licensed in anything, according to his ex-wife. Probably paid in cash," Machado is saying to me.

"He probably wasn't mailing invoices to people," I point out.

"No sign of anything like that in his house."

"Then why did she owe Howard Roth money? Why didn't she pay him at the time he did the work? Maybe it was for a job he hadn't finished?" I suggest.

"I'm thinking what you are," Machado says. "The work in the basement. Nothing hooked up yet. Maybe he drops by a couple times to finish and no one's answering the door. Maybe he leaves a note in her mailbox."

"Maybe."

"And whoever is impersonating her sends him a check. The perp had to have his address." Machado's talking to me and looking at Lucy.

"Howard Roth, forty-two years old, died over the weekend at his central Cambridge home." She reads what she's just pulled up. "Bateman Street. You can Google it."

"So maybe that's how, and he gets the check in the mail," Machado says. "He has no account at Peggy Stanton's bank and nothing that might inspire a teller to hand over a hundred bucks to him."

"Her bank would have her signature card on file, and it's not a great forgery." I sit next to Lucy.

"I agree with you there."

Machado pulls up a chair and unzips his briefcase.

"If you put her signature and this one side by side?"

He slides out two plastic bags, and Toby is taking his time.

"So maybe some teller pulled up her signature card and got a bad feeling, wouldn't cash it for him, plus his driver's license isn't valid, like I said. And that might be what the bank was calling about," Machado says. "There are a couple messages on her answering machine from Wells Fargo, asking her to call. First one in early June, about the time the check was mailed to Howie."

"How do you know it was mailed?" Lucy scans information scrolling by on every screen, what I recognize as files her search engines are finding.

I can't tell what they are. I can't decipher what I'm seeing, and that's deliberate, because I'm not alone.

"What's called the power of deduction." Machado continues looking at my niece as if she might not be a waste of his time.

She's in faded jeans, a long-sleeved white T-shirt that is tight and could use ironing, and tactical boots. I'm aware of the big ring on her index finger as she moves the wireless mouse. I smell her cologne, and I can tell when she wants people to leave us alone because she has something important on her mind.

"If someone stole her identity," Machado is saying, "then this person wasn't going to show up at Howie's house and hand him a check, right? Safest thing would be to mail it. My guess is it's the same thing this person was doing with her other bills. Forging checks and mailing them, and the bank probably wasn't going to question checks made out to the gas, electric, and telephone companies. But they might pull up her signature card when someone walks in and looks like a homeless person."

"It's not a good forgery, hardly a serious attempt at it," Lucy says.

I have two transparent plastic bags side by side, the check Howard Roth never cashed, and an earlier canceled one that Machado found in a file of bank statements inside Peggy Stanton's house.

"Not signed but written or basically drawn." She moves close to me, her eyes locked on Toby as he finally leaves.

"I didn't realize she was a handwriting expert," Machado says, and now he's openly flirting with my niece.

"I don't have to be an expert." She gets up and shuts her door, and Machado watches her as if she's a tartar. "Somebody lousy."

"Maybe he got better at it," I reply. "June first was early on."

Lucy sits back down. "Since when is Toby in charge of mail?"

"I sent Bryce on an errand," I reply. "He's taking Shaw to the vet. In fact, I'm hoping he'll fall in love with her and decide Indy needs a sister."

"The shaft of the letter *P*?" Lucy slides the plastic bags closer.

She isn't going to talk about Toby in front of Machado. She's got something to tell me.

"Slants differently, and you can see where the person hesitated," she says. "Thinking it instead of doing it, and the line is slightly crooked, the shaft is. Plus, her *t* has a high cross bar and the other doesn't. Her *a* is well formed, and the other's not. Her *n* looks more like a *w,* and the tops are pointed, and the other's rounded." She shows us as she describes it, adding, "Just my thoughts. I'm not an expert."

"You ever testify in court about this stuff?" Machado can't take his eyes off her.

"I never testify in court about anything."

"I don't get it. You'd be great in court."

"They can't stipulate me."

"Why not?"

She doesn't answer. Lucy was fired by law enforcement. She's a hacker. A shrewd attorney would destroy her on the witness stand.

"What's going on?" I say to her, since she's the one who has been texting, saying she needs to see me.

"When you're done?" It's her way of telling me that Sil Machado needs to leave.

thirty

LUCY EXPLAINS THAT PEGGY STANTON IS CONNECTED TO the paleontologist missing in Alberta, Canada.

The fake Twitter page used to dupe Marino was set up by the same person who e-mailed the video clip of the jetboat on the Wapiti River, my niece says. The footage was recorded on Emma Shubert's iPhone around the time she vanished thousands of miles northwest of here.

"The Twitter account with the handle *Pretty Please* was opened August twenty-fifth, and Twitter verified it by e-mail sent to *BLiDedwood*." Lucy spells the username. "The avatar is a photo of Yvette Vickers when she was in her heyday in the fifties."

I reply I don't know who that is, as I look around the space my niece is in.

"A B-list actress Marino wouldn't be familiar with. I wasn't, either. I had to use facial-recognition software to figure it out," Lucy says. "She's believed to have died of natural causes in 2010, was dead the better part of a year before her body was discovered in her run-down Los Angeles home. She was mummified."

"It's probably not a coincidence that she was picked for the avatar." I think of what Benton said.

A serial killer. Someone older. He targets mature women who represent someone powerful he's obsessed with destroying.

"All Marino's going to see when he gets the first tweet from Peggy Lynn Stanton is a picture of a beautiful sexy woman," Lucy is saying. "Someone who describes herself as *into things old with character* and she *doesn't mind keeping score because hers is impressive.*"

"The Twitter account was opened two days after Emma Shubert disappeared from the campsite in Grande Prairie." I make that observation as I'm making other ones.

Lucy's office is Spartan, brightly lit, with silvery electronic equipment that does what she directs, and thick hanks of bundled cables, docks for charging various devices, routers, scanners, and very little paper. There are no photographs, nothing personal, as if she has no life, and I know better. She has something, and I'm constantly aware of the large signet ring on her index finger, a rose-gold ring that I don't believe is hers. I've never known her to wear another person's ring, and I'm going to find out.

"Two days was enough time for someone to abduct and kill Emma Shubert and get back to this area," Lucy speculates. "But what the hell's the connection? Why was he up there in the land of dinosaurs and tar sands, and what does it have to do with a victim in Cambridge?"

"You're absolutely sure it's Emma Shubert's phone?" I ask. "That he's got her iPhone?"

"Yes, and I'm going to explain it."

"The Canadian police, the FBI . . . ?" A serial killer, I again think, and those who count don't know the details Lucy is telling me.

"I can't tell them for a fact that Emma Shubert and Peggy Stanton are linked," Lucy replies, and I understand it, but I'll have to do something, and she knows I will.

She can't tell police or the Feds unless she explains how she came to her conclusions.

"Of course, we don't know what happened to Emma Shubert, but I'm guessing nothing good," Lucy says, and she's somber and hard, her determination unyielding.

"Well, she's either a victim or involved in all this," I comment.

"Since it appears no one has heard from her for two months, I'd say it's one or the other. She's either not innocent or she's dead."

"Marino *wouldn't* be familiar with the actress's photo used in the avatar, or he *wasn't*?" I want to know what Lucy has told him.

"He doesn't know, didn't know," she says. "He tweeted *Pretty Please* twenty-seven times thinking it was a hot young woman named Peggy Stanton. He's enraged about it. We were having it out last night because it's made him feel stupid. At this point it's lost him his job. He's fucking crazed, ready to kill someone."

"He never tried to look her up? He never tried to find her address, her phone number, to verify who she is? Jesus, what kind of detective, what kind of investigator, is he?" I can't help but feel frustrated and angered by his carelessness.

"He wasn't being an investigator when he was tweeting," Lucy says. "He was being lonely."

What kind of world do we live in? I think.

"A lot of people on these social networking sites don't research whoever they're tweeting or direct-messaging or making comments to. They arrange to meet and haven't a clue. Unbelievable how trusting people are."

"*Desperate* is what comes to mind."

"Stupid," she says. "Really stupid. And I told him."

"Marino should know better." *Damn him.*

"Nothing in Peggy Stanton's profile suggests she's local or from Massachusetts." Lucy indicates what's on a computer screen. "I'm not sure Marino was doing much more than cyber-flirting."

"Cyber-flirting? You could be flirting with a damn serial killer or a terrorist."

"Obviously, that's why he's in this trouble," she says. "I'm not sure he was serious about actually meeting her or dating her. They never arranged anything that might have worked. It was all talk. He thought it was safe."

"He told you they never arranged anything, or you can tell from the tweets?"

"Twenty-seven from him," she repeats. "Eleven from her, from whoever was impersonating her. There's nothing to suggest they ever got together, although he bragged to her he was going to Tampa and maybe she'd want to, quote, *'drop by for some fun and sun.'*"

"Did he say when he was going?" I think of the timing again. "When he was arriving and departing?"

The video clip was e-mailed to me not even an hour after Marino's plane landed in Boston this past Sunday after he'd been in Tampa for a week.

"You got it," Lucy says. "He gave the info in a tweet and she never answered. Like I said, it was all talk. But you can see why it's a problem for the police, for the FBI."

"It still is?"

"I don't know. He never called her, never met her. But he needs to stay in his foxhole right now."

"He's still at your house?"

"He needs to stay there. Nobody's going to bother him without our seeing it coming."

I'm not sure what she means by that or who might see it coming.

"The problem is, he wants to go home, and I can't exactly keep him against his will. The account's gone now." She means the *BLiDedwood* e-mail account is. "The bad guy"—that's what she calls whoever it is—"created it, then deleted it, right before he e-mailed the video clip to you."

"I'm confused," I admit. "I thought it was created two months ago, at the end of August. Yet I just got the video clip, the e-mail from *BLiDedwood,* on Sunday."

"I know it seems complicated," she says. "But it's really not, and I'll give you the broad strokes because I know what happened, am absolutely clear about it. The bad guy creates an account with the username *BLiDedwood* on August twenty-fifth. The Internet service provider, the IP, dead-ends at a proxy server, this one in Berlin."

A proxy server Lucy has hacked into. "Sent from where?" I ask. "Obviously not from Germany."

"Logan Airport. Same as later. That's what he does. He captures their wireless."

"Then he wasn't setting up the account in Alberta, Canada, on August twenty-fifth."

"Definitely not," Lucy says. "He was back in this area and close enough to the airport to pick up the wireless signal."

A boat, I'm reminded, and I send Ernie Koppel an e-mail about the swipe of what looks like garish green paint.

Anything at all from the barnacle, the broken piece of bamboo? I write to him.

"This person then creates Peggy Stanton's Twitter account that same day, on August twenty-fifth," Lucy continues to explain, "and submits the e-mail username *BLiDedwood* so Twitter can contact that address, making sure it exists, before verifying the account."

Something old, something new, Ernie writes back almost instantly.

"Then very recently the bad guy deletes that e-mail account, *BLiDedwood*, and uses a different application to create a new anonymous account with the same name but a different extension, this one *stealthmail*," Lucy says, as another message from Ernie lands on my phone.

If we ever find the boat, we can definitely match it. Will call when back in the lab.

"So he waits twenty-nine minutes and sends the video file and jpg to you and then the account is gone like a bridge blown out," Lucy says. "Again, he was physically close enough to Logan Airport to send the e-mail to you from their wireless network."

"Which also is in the area where Peggy Stanton's body was found in the bay, maybe dumped there, possibly around the same time that e-mail was sent to me, about the same time Marino's flight from Tampa arrived," I reply. "I don't understand the motive."

"Games." Lucy is calmly quiet, like stagnant weather before a violent storm. "We don't know what his fantasies are, but he's getting off on all of this."

Someone who mocks.

"Whatever he does to his victims, it's part of a much bigger picture," she says, in the same tone. "The prelude, the aftermath are obsessions. It isn't just the capturing and the killing. You don't have to be a profiler to know that."

He's killed before and will kill again, or maybe already has.

"An attempt to frame Marino?" I ask.

"To fuck him up, anyway. It must be fun to cause so much trouble," she says angrily. "I've let Benton know he probably should get down here."

"Does he know about Emma Shubert's phone?"

"I've suggested it's a possibility they might want to check out, that it might connect everything to her. I've not stated anything as a fact."

A mature accomplished woman, a paleontologist who takes boats to dig sites and works outdoors and is skilled in labs, I contemplate. She's described by her colleagues as driven, indefatigable, passionate about dinosaurs, and a proactive environmentalist.

"The MAC address, the Machine Access Code, is the same for e-mails she sent, for any apps and data she downloaded before she vanished, and I didn't tell Benton that." Lucy continues to describe what she knows but can't relay in detail to the FBI. "It's the same MAC for the video file and jpg of the severed ear sent to you. The same MAC for this Twitter account." She means Peggy Stanton's fake account.

"Let's talk about Twitter." It's my way of asking but not wanting details I'm better off not having.

"It's pretty simple, really," Lucy says. "Hypothetically?"

When my niece says *hypothetically*, it usually means it's what she did, and I leave it alone. I don't question.

"Find someone who works for Twitter, Facebook, Google Plus, any of these social networks," she says. "There are employee lists, people who work in various capacities, and their titles and even detailed descriptions of their level of importance. Getting employee info isn't hard, and I work my way up the chain of people a certain employee follows and is followed by, and I send a link to click on and when they do it gives me their password unbeknownst to them. And then I log on as that person."

She tells me she leapfrogs from one impersonation to the next, and it's hard for me to listen to what she thinks is perfectly acceptable behavior.

"And finally the system admin believes it's a high-level colleague sending her something important she needs to look at," she admits. "Click. And now I'm in her computer, which has all sorts of proprietary, sensitive information. Next I'm in the server."

"Does the FBI have any of this same information? Any of it at all?" I'm thinking of Valerie Hahn, and then I'm reminded of Douglas Burke, and she is something dark and ugly spreading over my mood.

"Don't know," Lucy says. "Court orders are a little slower than what I do."

I'm not going to respond to that.

"But Marino's tweets and the fake person's tweets? All you've got to do is go on their pages. The tweets are there for the world to see," she says. "It's just I know where they came from. Real garbage, whoever it is. Unfortunately, someone smart. But arrogant. And arrogance will always get you in the end."

I move my chair closer to read the tweets she's rolling through on the screen, and they make me sad. Peggy Stanton's impersonator wrote Marino the first time on August twenty-fifth at almost midnight, saying she was a fan.

Bowled over by U, she tweeted. *I strike and leave nothing to spare, an honest gal whose only game is right up UR alley.*

Six tweets later she said she was into antiques, collected vintage military buttons and wore them proudly, and this deteriorated into comments that Marino found offensive, if not appalling.

I've got buttons I know U want to push, she tweeted to him toward the end of their exchanges. *Dead soldiers all over my enviable chest.*

Marino unfollowed her on October tenth.

"Why?" I try to imagine the point of it, and I try to imagine who.

"We've got a problem with Toby, but he's too damn stupid," Lucy then says, and I figured she would get to him, based on her demeanor when he appeared at her door with a cartload of boxes.

"No way he's doing it," she adds.

"Obviously he's doing something." I wait for her to tell me what as I wonder why it's so difficult to find people to trust.

"You need to be careful about anything you say in front of him or anything he might overhear or see." Lucy says she started getting suspicious of Toby over recent weeks, about the time Channing Lott's trial began.

She would run into Toby in areas of the building where he generally doesn't need to be. The mailroom, for example, where he started picking up packages that gave him an excuse to stop by the computer lab, various offices, and intake, the autopsy rooms, conference rooms, locker rooms, the break room. Often he was going through the log at the security desk, she describes, as if he was intensely curious about bodies going out and coming in, especially if they were unidentified, in cases that occurred when he wasn't working.

"It wasn't typical," Lucy says. "At first I thought it's because of Marino, because of him not bothering with the electronic calendar anymore, staying over, ornamenting, and maybe Toby saw an opportunity. But truth is, he was trumping up reasons to walk in and out of rooms where meetings were going on, where people were talking, where information was out in plain view."

She tells me that after I got the disturbing e-mail on Sunday night she decided to look into Toby, who can't access anything at the CFC, including Investigations, without his key card ID, which has an RFID chip embedded in it. We also have satellite tracking on all our vehicles, she says, but Toby just didn't think she'd look.

"I guess it never dawned on him I'd start rolling back the tape and checking what's been recorded by the cameras and the vehicle GPS locators," she says, and I recall watching Toby on the security monitors yesterday, when he was inside the bay.

He seemed to be arguing with someone on the phone. Something had struck me about it, bothered me. It didn't seem normal.

"He's been entering all sorts of areas where he has no business," Lucy continues. "Your office. Luke's office."

"He can't unlock my office." It's not accessible by key card, and I don't wear such an ID on a lanyard around my neck.

I can unlock any door in the building by scanning my thumb, and Lucy, Bryce, and I are the only staff who have what I call the skeleton key, a biometric one.

"And your door is usually wide open if you're in the building, or Bryce's door is wide open," Lucy points out. "He's always leaving his door open and also the door connecting your office to his. So Toby finds reasons to deliver things, check on this or that, or asks a question or passes on information or volunteers to take orders for take-out food. Or he simply wanders in and out if he thinks no one's looking."

I get up from my chair and reach for the phone as Lucy lets me know the jury is out. For an instant I think she's talking about Toby, that she's saying it's up in the air what to do with him. Then I realize she means something else.

"It's all over the Internet," she says, as I dial the extension for the autopsy room. "The jury's left the courtroom, and the pundits are predicting they'll find him not guilty."

I get hold of Luke and ask him to place Howard Roth's clothing in ID and to e-mail all photographs to me, that I'm coming down now.

"Perhaps Toby? He's right here. Maybe he can . . . ?" Luke is busy.

"No. I want you to do it personally and lock the door. I don't want anybody near the clothing and whatever else came in with him."

"Shorts, socks, a T-shirt, his meds. The police have any other personal effects, his wallet, his house keys, not sure what all." Luke's in the middle of an autopsy and doesn't want to be interrupted, but that's too bad.

"Thanks. I'll take a look."

"I mean, they didn't even have to think about it. Not guilty," Lucy says, when we're in the corridor, and she shuts her door, making sure it's locked.

"Is what you suspect about Toby why you were looking around my office yesterday morning? Is he why you were acting as if someone might be spying on me?" I ask.

"Let's take the stairs." She heads us to a lighted exit sign. "Someone is spying but not by using surveillance devices. I've been checking." She opens the metal door. "Toby's not sophisticated enough to plant covert devices, certainly not ones that I'd have a hard time finding, but I've been looking. And he's been spying."

"Why?"

"How do you think Channing Lott's helicopter ended up filming you while you were getting the body out of the water yesterday?" she asks.

"Toby was the only person who knew what Marino and I were headed out to do," I remember. "Except for Bryce. Possibly Luke, if Marino said something when they ran into each other in the parking lot."

We go down the stairs, and our voices seem loud, bouncing off concrete.

"I'm pretty sure I didn't give details to Luke." I'm trying to recall exactly what I said.

I was about to walk into the bay and was startled by him suddenly standing so close we were almost touching, and he asked me where I was going. I told him I was on my way to recover a body from the harbor, and he said he'd be happy to help, reminding me he's a certified diver. I didn't say the body was a woman's. I'm pretty sure I didn't, but I was distracted by him, the way I've been distracted for a while, a way I don't intend to be distracted by him again.

"Toby was aware hours in advance that you were heading to the Coast Guard base," Lucy states. "He knew he was going to meet you with the van so he could transport the body. A woman's body entangled with a turtle."

"And he somehow contacted Channing Lott's pilots?" That I don't believe.

"He contacted Jill Donoghue, who contacted the pilots."

"You know that for a fact?"

"Are you aware he's applied for a job at her ritzy law firm and that he's driven company vehicles to her building, to the Prudential Center?" Lucy asks. "Guess he's forgotten I can look at GPS maps of where everyone goes, and I can look at everybody's e-mail if they're dumb enough to use their CFC account for personal communications. I don't even have to hack."

"Jesus."

"Exactly." She unlocks the door to the lower level.

thirty-one

TOBY IS IN THE CORRIDOR, CARRYING BRIGHT RED BAGS of biohazard trash destined for the autoclave, and I tell Lucy I'll meet her in ID. He offers right away that he just left the evidence bay, and I know a guilty conscience when I see one.

"I guess you're aware of what just happened in court," I say to him, and no one is around to hear us, Ron the security guard behind glass some distance away.

"In court?" Toby is in scrubs and nitrile gloves, and his tattoos and shaved head might make him sinister, were it not for what's in his eyes.

"Yes, an acquittal that is cause for concern about breaches of security here," I say, and his reply is to play dumb. "I'm sure you realize that communications on the CFC server aren't private, and if deleted still exist."

"Like what?" He looks around, looks everywhere but in my eyes. "What communications?"

"In other words, CFC e-mails neither vanish nor are considered *purely personal*. Therefore they aren't an employee's private business, not if these e-mails could be evidence in a disciplinary investigation that involves the misuse of government resources or the violation of confidentiality and CFC policy." I look directly at him, and he won't look at me. "In such instances, personal communications are subject to disclosure under the Public Records Law."

"I don't know what you're talking about." But he does, and his face is red.

"Why?" I ask him, and he knows what I'm really asking.

"Why that rich guy got off?" He frowns and is frightened and pretends he doesn't understand.

"I would have given you a good recommendation, Toby. I'm not the sort to hold someone back. All you needed to do was tell me if you weren't happy here or felt you weren't appreciated or wanted to pursue what you viewed as a better opportunity."

It's not lost on him that I'm speaking of his job in the past tense. He shifts the red bags to a different hand, his eyes darting.

"But at least Ms. Donoghue knows exactly what she's getting," I add. "Although I'll point out the rather obvious fact that if you'll do this to me, you'll do it to her. Or at least the thought will cross her mind, and my guess is it already has."

"It's not like I've been sleeping on the job because I can't drive home." He takes a shot at Marino, and it's the last shot he'll take.

"No, you've been sleeping with the enemy, and that's worse," I reply. "I wish you well in your next venture, whatever it is. It's best you pack up your things immediately."

"Sure." He's not going to argue.

He might even be relieved.

"I need your key card." I hold out my hand, and he removes the lanyard around his neck.

"While this matter is being investigated, obviously you can't be here." I make sure he's clear on that.

"I was going to quit, anyway."

I walk him to the receiving area and ask Ron for his assistance.

"Yes, ma'am, Chief." He gets up from his desk and steps out into the corridor, and I can tell from the look on his face he knows what's happened, and maybe he's been aware of the same behavior that Lucy has discovered.

"Toby's no longer with the CFC," I let Ron know. "If you

could make sure he turns in any equipment and meets with Bryce for an exit interview. He'll take care of the usual details. You know the routine."

I give him the key card and ask him to accompany Toby into the waste disposal room so he can leave biohazard bags at the autoclave, and I walk away, texting Bryce, letting him know what just occurred, as I wonder the same thing I always do when someone behaves this way: *What might I have done to inspire such massive disloyalty, such disrespect?*

Toby was a physician's assistant with no training in medico-legal death investigation, which was his dream, as he described it to me when I interviewed him for the job several years ago. I took a chance on him. I sent him to basic and advanced forensic training academies in New York and Baltimore, and I personally instructed him at death scenes and spent time explaining autopsies and teaching him to assist.

"Money and myopia," Lucy says, when I walk into the ante-room, where she's swathed in white and senses my mood. "People are assholes."

"It always seems like it's more than just being assholes." I collect clothing from shelves. "It feels like it's something I didn't do right."

"It's not personal, Aunt Kay."

"Then why does it feel like it?"

"To you, everything that happens with everyone here feels personal." Lucy isn't gifted at cushioning her convictions. "But what you feel is never reciprocated, never has been."

"Well, that's damn depressing if what you're suggesting is everybody who works for me now or in the past doesn't care about anything other than their own ambitions, their own selves."

"It's never as personal to them as it is to you, because most people are out for what they want and don't give a shit about anybody else."

"I don't believe everybody is like that."

"I didn't say everybody. I'm not."

"You're certainly not. I don't even pay you." I find gloves, a mask.

"You couldn't afford me."

"No one could."

"There's a limit to what Toby can earn in the public sector compared to what he might get as an investigator for the Jill Donoghues of the world," Lucy says, and of course she's right. "He's about to get married, wants kids, and has overextended himself buying his truck. I think that's what started his troubles. He's been complaining about it a lot, apparently owes more than it's worth. Not to mention what he's spent on tattoos."

"How depressing. Betray the world for tattoos and a pickup truck."

"The American dream. Buy everything on credit and drive off into the sunset with body art and piercings you'll live to regret."

"There's no excuse for what he did." I unlock the door to the evidence room. "And shame on Jill Donoghue."

"It's really rather brilliant." Lucy follows me in.

"Luke should have e-mailed photos, and I'm expecting ones from Machado. Can you check?" I don't want to hear how brilliant Donoghue is.

"All is fair. A shrewd defense attorney using whatever resources happen to be available." Lucy's blue gloved hands type on a biosafe keyboard as she goes into my e-mail. "Her client happens to have his own pilots and a helicopter that can do aerial filming."

"I'm just sorry Judge Conry doesn't know what she's done."

"Why would he care?"

It's a good question. Literally, the judge allowed television news footage to be played in court. He didn't allow footage from the defendant's helicopter, which the judge would have deemed inadmissible. But the source of the news footage wasn't known or questioned at the time, and it's too late now.

"Nothing illegal about it," Lucy says. "Not even improper from a legal standpoint."

"You sound as if you're applauding it."

"Maybe I would have done the same thing."

"I have no doubt you would have," I comment, and I don't want to get into what she does or might do.

Howard Roth's clothing looks dirty and shapeless and seems forlorn on waterproof white paper, a large black T-shirt, a pair of woven cotton boxer shorts in a red plaid pattern, and white tube socks speckled with blood that is dark, almost black. On another table against the far wall are the dog crate and soggy bags of clumping litter, the yellow rope and old fishing gear, and the yellow boat fender that I realize is slightly scuffed, a detail I didn't notice when it was wet.

"Nothing wrong with her letting Toby know that whatever he overhears at work might be helpful." Lucy is playing out what she thinks happened. "And certainly he'd want justice to be done, and by the way, how does he like working for the CFC, and does he ever think about his future?"

She continues describing what she imagines Donoghue's line to Toby must have been, and I look for a measuring tape.

"So she's with her client right before court's in session yesterday morning, or maybe already sitting at the defense table with him, and gets an electronic communication from Toby. A woman's body has just been discovered in the bay. Maybe she even gets the details that the body has fingernail polish, has long white or blond hair. A fucking gift."

"Are you guessing that's what happened, or do you know it?" I open a drawer and find what I'm looking for, a pocket rod, the type of tape measure we carry in our scene cases.

"I know what the Sikorsky pilots said to ATC," Lucy answers. "I'd just taken off from Hanscom and was monitoring Logan on comm-two when the S-Seventy-six that I later found out was Channing Lott's helicopter contacted Approach, radioing that they were out of Beverly and had a request. They wanted to do some filming in the outer harbor."

I wipe down the rigid metal tape with a spray-on disinfectant, making sure it's clean.

"Wow, he's got quite a gash on the back of his head," Lucy says. "It's really apparent after his hair's been shaved."

"What time did you hear the pilots on the radio?" I take a look at autopsy photos on her computer screen.

"Approximately two hours after you got the call about the body in the bay," she says.

"Definitely blunt force, not sharp force," I observe. "You can see where the tissue's torn, and in the depths of the wound is bridging." I point out nerves, blood vessels, and other soft tissue extending like threads across the gaping gash. "His head impacted with a surface that has no discrete edge."

"So it wasn't caused by the edge of a concrete step catching him at the base of his skull."

"I seriously doubt it."

"I don't see how that part of your head could hit the floor?" Lucy feels the back of her head, where her skull connects with the hollow of her neck.

"It's troubling," I agree.

I lean over her, clicking through other autopsy photographs.

"An open slightly depressed comminuted fracture," I note. "Intracranial and intracerebral bleeding."

I look through more, resting my hand on Lucy's shoulder, and I'm always startled by how strong she is.

"A subdural hematoma overlying contusions, hemorrhages. A significant blow to the back of the head but with very little swelling. He didn't live long." I return to the boat fender and begin to measure it. "Does Marino know what Toby's done?"

"It's probably best their paths don't cross for the next hundred years."

The fender is heavy-duty vinyl, fifty-eight inches by eighteen, and I ask Lucy if the size is significant, and keys click as she checks the Internet.

"In the marine world, that's extra-large," she says. "Fenders associated with yachts."

"And it's not inflatable," I point out. "So if extra-large fenders were being stored on a boat as opposed to off-site, it had to be a really big one. At first I just assumed whoever did this bought it new. Like the dog crate, the bags of litter. I assumed this person shopped for new items that couldn't be traced."

I clean the measuring tape and return it to a drawer, and I change my gloves.

"But you can see this fender's rubbed up against something, suggesting it's not new," I explain. "It's used. Possibly it was removed from a large boat."

"Someone with money," Lucy says. "Channing Lott has a hundred-and-fifty-footer he docks in Boston. Some of the time it's in Gloucester, a very well-known yacht."

"Why the airport in Beverly?" I ask if there's a special reason to keep a helicopter there.

"He has a hangar in Beverly, has hangars in a lot of places,"

Lucy says. "Beverly's convenient to Gloucester, where his ocean-front mansion is, where his wife disappeared from."

I open a large black plastic case and get out a handheld crime light and goggles, and Lucy dims the lights in the room. I start with the wavelength for blue, painting it over the black shirt, and a galaxy of fibers and debris fluoresce in different colors and intensities. What look like orange-hot coils and multicolored ones are probably synthetics, and those that are coarse I associate with carpet. The clothing front and back is dirty with construction dust and debris, bits of paint and glass, and animal and human hair, much of it from contact with flooring, I suspect.

I feel the thick stiffness of dried blood I can barely see on the black fabric, dark voids where blood likely dripped from Howard Roth's lacerated head, and I ask Lucy to turn the lights back on. Most of the blood is concentrated on the back of the collar and shoulders, as if he bled from the back of his head while he was lying faceup and blood seeped under him. I can imagine why Luke assumed the injury was caused when the body came to rest on the basement floor at the foot of the stairs, but I don't believe it.

"I'm sure it's crossed your mind that what happened to his wife is similar to the other ones." Lucy continues talking about Channing Lott.

"I need scene pictures of Roth's body as it was found. Check to see if Machado has sent them yet."

"His missing wife is in the same general age group, distinguished for one reason or another, a formidable woman." Lucy returns to the computer. "She certainly wouldn't appear to be in a high-risk category, and in fact quite the opposite. Scene pics have landed. Opening them now."

"Is he on his back, his side, facedown?" I open a cabinet, looking for three-percent hydrogen peroxide.

"On his back and left hip, kind of twisted in a heap," she replies.

I go to the computer and take a look. Howard Roth's body is turned to one side on the basement floor at the bottom on the steps. He stares straight up, his knees drawn, his arms bent by his sides, and blood is coagulated and drying under the back of his neck, spreading to a stain that disappears under his shoulders. Once he landed in this position, I'm fairly sure he didn't move.

"It bothers me that it seems the sole reason Channing Lott became a suspect is an e-mail exchange between him and whoever he allegedly was attempting to hire," Lucy says. "You're aware of it, I assume?"

"Not specifically." I return to the cabinet and find jars of sodium acetate and 5-sulfosalicylic acid.

"I'll pull it up from online news," she says, as she does it. "So this past March fourth, a Sunday? An e-mail was sent to Channing Lott's personal account from a user he later claimed he didn't recognize but assumed it was someone from one of his shipping offices. He said in direct testimony that he can't possibly know the names of everyone who works for him around the world."

Lucy reads what's quoted in the story.

I realize it's inappropriate for me to contact you directly through e-mail, but I must have verification of the partnership and the subsequent exchange before I proceed with the solution.

"And what did Channing Lott reply?" I dissolve the sulfosalicylic acid into hydrogen peroxide.

"He wrote, 'Are we still committed to an award of one hundred thousand dollars?' "

"Certainly sounds incriminating." I check the reagent Leuco Crystal Violet, LCV, making sure it hasn't turned yellow, that it's white and fresh.

"He claims he assumed the e-mail exchange was about a monetary prize his shipping company offers," she reports. "That he often partners with other marine transport companies in rewarding scientists for coming up with viable solutions for reducing greenhouse gas emissions."

I pour in the LCV, a cationic triarylmethane dye, and mix with a magnetic stirrer.

"The amount of the award was in fact one hundred thousand dollars," Lucy says.

"Sounds like an argument Jill Donoghue would come up with." I transfer some of the solution into a spray bottle.

"Except the Mildred Vivian Cipriano Award has existed for more than a decade," Lucy says. "So it wasn't just trumped up for his defense to explain away the e-mails. And since whoever initiated them has never been arrested or even identified, I conclude the e-mail sent to Lott wasn't traceable. Sounds familiar, doesn't it?"

"If you could go into that cabinet and get the D-Seventy." I tell her which lens I want. "We're going to try infrared to see if there are any bloody impressions we can enhance that aren't going to show up any other way on black cotton."

We begin taking photographs using different filters and shutter speeds and distances. First we try without chemical enhancement, and on the front and back of the T-shirt and on the plaid boxer shorts are indistinct areas where a bloody residue was transferred to the fabric by something coming in contact with it. Then I spray the LCV and it reacts to the hemoglobin in blood, and I get discernible shapes, startling ones.

Footwear images, the outsole, a heel, a toe, glow a vivid violet, the bloody shapes overlaying one another as someone repeatedly stomped and kicked Howard Roth's chest, his sides, his abdomen, his groin, while he was on his back, probably while he was already down on the basement floor. He bled from a gash on his head, and he bled from his nose and mouth, frothy blood from shattered ribs puncturing lungs, and I try to imagine it.

A man drunk and barely dressed, and I don't believe he was in bed when his killer showed up. Most people don't wear socks to bed, especially in warm weather, and I go through the scene and autopsy photographs again, and I'm not satisfied.

I call Sil Machado.

"Free as a bird" are the first words out of his mouth. "And Donoghue's giving you all the credit."

"Wonderful."

"She says you reminded the jury, and *rightly so,* that it can't be proven that Mildred Lott is dead, much less that her husband did it."

"Where are you now?"

"What do you need?"

I ask him to meet me at Howard Roth's house as I pull off protective clothing in the anteroom, and the door leading into the corridor opens. Benton is here.

"Give me about twenty minutes," I tell Machado. "If you get

there first it would be helpful if you wait outside." I meet Benton's eyes. "It appears Howard Roth had a visitor right before he died. The check you found in the toolbox? Have you submitted it?"

"Latents has it," Machado says. "And by the way, when they fumed the car they got a print from the rearview mirror. And it isn't Peggy Stanton's."

thirty-two

BENTON DRIVES MY SUV WEST ALONG THE CHARLES, PAST the Art Deco former headquarters of Polaroid and the patinated copper-roofed DeWolfe Boathouse. It's noon, and patchy ice has melted, sunlight sparkling on water and bright on the old Shell sign. We head toward Central Square while I return Ernie's call.

"Marine paint," he says right off. "No big surprise, since the turtle obviously was in the water when he bumped into something or something bumped into him. An antifouling paint loaded with copper to retard the growth of barnacles, mussels, and so on. Also zinc, which would be consistent with primer."

"And consistent with the color," I reply. "That yellowish-green brings to mind a zinc-based primer."

"Microscopically, you got more than one color," he says. "In fact, you got three."

We cross Massachusetts Avenue, City Hall up ahead, Romanesque, with a bell tower and stone walls trimmed in granite, and Ernie explains that the traces of paint transferred to the barnacle and also to the broken end of the bamboo pole came from the bottom of a boat. Possibly the prop or an anchor or anchor chain that at one time, he says, probably a number of years ago, was painted black.

"Often whatever is used to paint the bottom of a boat is also used on other areas that remain submerged when the boat is moored," he adds.

"A quick-and-dirty way of doing it," I reply, as Benton turns at the YMCA. "Use the same paint on everything."

"Quick-and-dirty is what a lot of people do, and then there are those who don't give a damn and are really sloppy and irresponsible," Ernie says. "Whoever painted the boat you're looking for falls into that category."

It doesn't fit with what I think of him, a killer tidy and meticulous, who plots and plans in his malignant fantasyland.

"The zinc-based primer went on top of the old paint, which wasn't sanded off; someone couldn't be bothered." Ernie continues to describe what he found on a swipe of color almost invisible to the unaided eye.

A boat this person uses for his evil but not for his leisure, not for his pleasure.

"And over that a deep red coating with copper or cuprous oxide, which is usually used on wood," he says. "I have a feeling the boat you're looking for has a lot of chipped, peeled, or damaged red topcoat, some areas of exposed primer. In other words, something not well maintained at all."

An old boat in ill repair that probably isn't registered in his name or docked where he lives or even near there.

"If it were a prop, wouldn't you have expected more damage to the turtle?" I ask.

"If the prop was turning, yes. But maybe it wasn't. Maybe the person cut the engine while he did what he did."

Did what he did.

Which was stopping the boat and shutting down the engine so he could push the dog crate, the boat fender, and the body overboard. I try to envision it and can't imagine hoisting a crate containing more than a hundred and fifty pounds of cat litter, dropping it and a body over a high side rail. A dive platform, a boat with an open transom, I consider. The cut-down transom of lobster boats around here that make it easier to launch pots and buoys, boats that are ubiquitous at all hours and in all types of weather, attracting no attention, and I try to reconstruct it.

The open transom of an old wooden boat that's been repainted, and the crate, the fender, the body pushed into the water at the same moment a gigantic leatherback became entangled with fishing tackle, with an old bamboo pole, is there. I see the strike, the encounter, I almost can. The turtle surfacing for air, dragging the fishing gear wound around him, and running into the bottom of a boat, perhaps glancing off its prop, and now he's dangerously trussed up in yellow nylon buoy line, weighted down, slowing down, pulling his burden until it almost pulls him under.

It's quite likely the killer wasn't aware of the leatherback, knew nothing of what occurred. For one thing, I suspect it was dark, and I imagine the boat near Logan, where the e-mail was sent from Emma Shubert's iPhone on Sunday at six-twenty-nine p.m., and then this person waited, possibly for hours, until he was sure no one would see him.

"What makes you say *a number of years ago*?" I ask Ernie. "You're able to date when the hull originally was painted black?"

"Traces of TBT," he says.

The paint contains tributyltin oxide, he explains, an anti-fouling biocide that has decimated marine life—shellfish, in particular—killing them off, causing them to mutate. TBT is one of the most toxic chemicals ever deliberately released into the world's water and has been illegal in high-traffic areas such as harbors and bays since the late 1980s. But the ban unfortunately doesn't include oil tankers and military vessels.

"So unless the boat in question is military or a tanker, and I seriously doubt it, then the boat you're looking for could be at least twenty years old," he adds, as Benton looks for parking on the street near Machado's Crown Vic.

Howard Roth has no driveway, his small frame house overtaken by trees and shrubs behind an abandoned factory on Bigelow Street in an area that's a mixture of historic homes and Harvard apartments and affordable housing. While I can't see it from where we are, I know that Fayth House is but a few blocks west on Lee Street, an easy walk from here. I continue to wonder if Peggy Stanton might have volunteered there.

"The important point for your purposes?" Ernie says in my wireless earpiece, as I get out of the SUV. "Whoever repainted the boat to be in compliance didn't give a shit that there's a reason for the ban."

I get scene cases out of the back.

"Apparently, the person just slapped coats of primer and red paint on top of original black paint, which doesn't stop the TBT from continuing to leach out and into the water," Ernie adds, and I think about what Lucy just told me.

Channing Lott's shipping company offers a hundred-thousand-dollar award for solutions that help preserve the environment. I can't imagine any of his tankers painted with a dangerous biocide or that any boat he might have would be, certainly not his yacht that he sometimes moors in the Boston Harbor.

"It could be anything," Benton says, after I tell him, and we're climbing the weathered wooden front steps of Howard Roth's three-room frame house, which doesn't look as uncared for as it simply looks poor. "Any type of vessel or marine object originally painted with the antifouling stuff, from a buoy to a piling to a submarine. Then repainted."

"I doubt a submarine would be repainted red." I notice a coiled garden hose connected to an outside faucet and wonder what Howard Roth used it for.

There's no grass, nothing to water, and he didn't own a car.

"More likely we're talking about a boat bottom and maybe its prop that were repainted with primer, and then a red antifouling paint that's environmentally safe and legal." We put on gloves and shoe covers, and I open a rusting screen door.

Sil Machado is waiting on a porch crowded with open black garbage bags overflowing with cans and bottles. Shopping carts are filled with bags, and more of them are stacked in the seats of a metal slat porch glider. I wonder how Howard Roth got his recyclables to a redemption center, and I ask Machado if he knows.

"Nearest one's on Webster Ave." He unlocks the front door with a single key attached to an evidence tag. "I think his buddy from Fayth House used to give him rides. Jerry, the maintenance guy who found him."

He lets us in and stays outside because I intend to spray for blood if I don't find any that's visible, and there's very little room inside. Machado explains through the open door that Roth's friend, maybe his only friend, got a DUI and his license was suspended.

"He told me on Sunday afternoon when I responded to the

call that as soon as he got his license back he was going to help Howie haul all this in," Machado says.

"When might that have been?" Benton asks, and we're just inside the door, covering our clothes. "When was he going to get his license reinstated and give him a ride?"

"It was his first offense, so his license was revoked only for a year," Machado says. "He has three months to go. He said he told Howie to stop collecting before the floor caved in, to hold off until he could drive him. But he went out every day, digging through trash anyway. Not sure what you get for this stuff. Maybe a couple bucks a bag, total? Enough for one quart of the shit he drank."

I crouch by an open scene case, getting out the spray bottle of LCV and the camera, scanning my surroundings before I do anything. The living room and kitchen are one open area separated by a Formica countertop, an old TV against one wall, a brown vinyl recliner parked in front of it, and that's about the only place someone could sit.

Bags of metal cans and glass and plastic bottles are piled on a sofa, on a small table and on its chairs, and I can understand Machado's attitude when he first got here after the body was found. I know all too well what it's like to walk into a death scene that is so overwhelmed by what obsessive unwell people collect or hoard or don't bother throwing out that it's like sifting through a landfill.

"This isn't just about the money." Benton stands by the kitchen counter, looking, taking in every detail.

"It's sad," I agree. "Maybe he started out collecting all this for whatever petty cash he could get, but then it became a compulsion."

"Another addiction."

"Addicted to digging through trash," I reply, noticing all of the window shades are down, the shapes of bottles and cans showing behind the yellowed fabric as the light shines through.

I ask Machado if the shades were just like this when he came here the first time. Were they down in every window and he tells me through the open door that they were, and I ask him about lamps or overhead lights. He replies that the only light on was the single lightbulb in the basement, and it's probably still on, he adds, unless it's burned out.

"When you're done," he says, "I'm going to dust all the switches, swab them, if need be. I'll go over anything someone might have touched."

"A good idea," I reply, and I ask if it would be all right to open the shades, to get a little light in here.

"Help yourself, Doc. I've got photographs of the way everything was," he says. "So no problem if you need to change or move something."

The windowsills are lined with vintage bottles and pop-top cans that are collectibles, Coca-Cola, Sun Drop, Dr Pepper, and a mucilage glue and jar of paste that I remember from my childhood. Items tossed when someone cleaned out the attic, and I imagine Howard Roth rescuing them from the trash and placing them on display in his house like trophies, like treasure.

"What about the TV? On or off when his body was found?" Benton stares into the carpeted hall that leads to the back of the house.

"It was off when I got here," Machado says, and I'm interested in the two forty-ounce Steel Reserve 211 malt liquor bottles and three screw caps on the floor by the recliner.

I wonder how long they've been there.

"What about when his friend got here? What's his name? Jerry?" Benton opens the bathroom door.

"According to his version of things? The front door was unlocked, and when Howie didn't answer, he walked in and called out to him. Says it was about four in the afternoon."

"Sunday afternoon?" Benton steps into the doorway that leads to the basement.

"Right. And I got here about four-fifteen."

"Did this guy Jerry have a reason to hurt anyone? Maybe they're drinking cheap malt liquor together, maybe arguing, maybe something got out of control?"

"Can't imagine it," Machado says from the front doorway. "But I got his prints, swabbed him for DNA. He couldn't have been more cooperative, says Howie never locked his door. Jerry says he was used to just walking in."

The remote is on top of the TV, neatly placed exactly in the middle, and I suggest to Machado we might want to collect it. He sounds dubious but says that's fine, and I package the remote as evidence and hand it through the doorway to him.

"I'm just curious why you might think someone touched it," he says, and Benton has walked down the hallway to the bedroom.

"He may have been drinking beer in the recliner, in his underwear and socks, possibly with the TV on, and he fell asleep there." I notice that one of the garbage bags tucked under the counter is twisted shut with a tie but none of the others are. "I'd like to look inside the kitchen cabinets, if you don't have a problem with it."

Under the sink are nine boxes of commercial can liners, a hundred to a carton, heavy-grade and not inexpensive, and I wonder where Roth got them.

"I don't think he bought these." I reach inside for an open box and pull out green plastic ties exactly like the one twisted around the bag under the counter.

I suggest to Machado he may want to check with Fayth House and see what brand of industrial waste-can liners they stock. I tell him that a carton this size with bags of this quality can cost thirty or forty dollars, which is considerably more than what Roth was going to get for the recyclables he placed inside them.

Maybe his buddy Jerry who works maintenance at the nursing home was keeping Roth well stocked, or maybe Roth was taking the bags when he was in and out, still working the occasional odd job there. I remind Machado that we must find out if Peggy Stanton volunteered at Fayth House.

"A careful, cautious woman who had an alarm system and didn't want her address and phone number on her checks wasn't going to let just anybody in her home." I collect the open carton of liners. "She must have had some connection with him; she must have felt safe with him if she let him do any sort of work inside her house or even on her property."

"Unless whoever killed this guy planted the check in his toolbox as an alibi." Machado takes another evidence bag from me.

"Why?" I wander back to the TV.

"We find it and assume Howie killed her. Case solved. Sort of like the way he set up Marino, right? It's what this son of a bitch does, right?"

I don't believe he's right at all, but I listen to him spin his theory as I let him know I'm untying the garbage bag under the counter because it's peculiar that it's the only one closed. All the other ones are open, and maybe Howard Roth left them that way because he rinsed out all the bottles and cans and jars and left the bags open so everything would dry.

I point out to Machado that there's a garden hose outside, and most redemption facilities require recyclables to be emptied and rinsed, and I also haven't noticed any odors. I tell him that if he doesn't object I'm going to see what's in this one bag and then I'm going to look for blood.

"Thing is, we find the check and bingo." Machado continues to describe what I don't think is possible. "Some lowlife who killed Peggy Stanton. Her handyman did it and then died in a drunken accident. The killer sets that up and we think case closed."

"And where does the killer think we'll assume Roth kept the body after he supposedly murdered her?" I inquire, as I untwist the tie. "Where might he have kept it long enough for it to begin to mummify? Certainly not in this house over the summer, and are we supposed to believe Howard Roth had a boat or access to one?"

"Maybe the killer assumed she wouldn't look mummified," Machado says. "Maybe he thought she wouldn't look dehydrated after she was in the water for a while."

"Mummified remains don't reconstitute like freeze-dried fruit. You can't add moisture back to a dead body."

I open the bag, and the bottle is right on top of other bottles and cans and jars. It's right there where the monster placed it.

"But would the average person know that a dried-out body wouldn't rehydrate?" Machado asks.

The forty-ounce Steel Reserve 211 bottle is the same as the two empties by the recliner, each with a price sticker from a Shop Quik.

"I'm not going to do anything with this here," I say to Machado, as I hold up the bottle in my gloved hands, turning it in sunlight shining through a window. "I see ridge detail, and I see blood."

thirty-three

I DON'T UNDERSTAND WHY A KILLER WHO HAS ELABO-rate fantasies and premeditates and seems meticulous makes so little effort to hide evidence that matters. In fact, I'm baffled, I tell Benton.

"You've got to focus on his priorities," he says, as he drives us through mid-Cambridge. "You have to get inside his head and know what he values. Neatness, tidiness, everything exactly the way he likes it. Restoring order after he kills. Showing he's a nice guy, a decent guy, someone civilized. I'm suspicious the flowers in Peggy Stanton's house were from him. When he returned her car and entered her house he left flowers to show what a sterling fellow he is."

"Any luck finding a record of a delivery?"

"Not any of the florists in the area. It's been checked." He glances at his phone, and he's been glancing at it a lot. "I think there was no card because there never was one, that he walked in with a spring arrangement like a thoughtful son stopping by to see his mother. It's very important to this person that what he believes about himself is reasserted after he's killed. A great guy. A gentleman. Someone capable of meaningful rela-tionships."

"What he did to Howard Roth wasn't exactly gentlemanly, and he certainly didn't leave him flowers."

"Howard Roth had no value." Benton glances at another text message, and I wonder if it is Douglas Burke who is writing to him every other minute. "He was an object no better than the trash he dug through, and the killer assumed you wouldn't value him, either. He assumed it would be a case that wouldn't merit your attention."

"Me specifically?"

"What it tells me is whoever he is, he doesn't know you personally. I retract what I said earlier about my worrying he knows you, knows Marino. He knows about you, about your office, but he doesn't know you," Benton says, as if there can be no doubt about it. "He's getting it wrong. He's making mistakes. Maybe you could text Bryce to let them know we'll be there in fifteen minutes."

It's almost three p.m., and we're going to be late for a meeting Benton scheduled in my TelePresence conference room, and I'm not happy that Douglas Burke has been included. I thought Benton made it perfectly clear that they couldn't work together anymore.

"He stages his crimes in a premeditated and precise way, he's obsessed with games that include framing people, and then is careless about fingerprints and blood?" I worry again that something might have gone on with Benton and Burke.

"He has reason to believe such evidence isn't incriminating to him," he says, as we go back to the CFC the way we came, following the river, and the water is dusky, the sky a pale blue haze. "For one thing, he probably assumed it wouldn't be found. He didn't think you'd look. That's the important part, Kay. He didn't assume you'd bother with anything you've bothered with. He doesn't know you, not in the least," he says that again.

Douglas Burke will be waiting in my conference room, and I'm not sure what I'll do when I see her.

"There's ridge detail all over the bottle," I reply. "I didn't even need dusting powder or an ALS to see that there's enough minutiae for an identification."

"But we don't know whose identification." Benton glances at his phone in his lap, at whatever's just landed. "Could be

Roth's prints on there. Most likely he bought the malt liquor and drank it."

"The important point is the killer didn't even bother wiping off the bottle, which is really careless," I repeat. "The smartest thing would have been to take it with him and toss it somewhere it would never be found."

"Disposing of the weapon in a bag full of bottles and cans that Roth collected shows the killer's complete disregard for his victim, his utter indifference." Benton glances down at his phone again. "Roth was nothing to him, nothing more than an inconvenience, and the killer assumes everybody would feel that way because he doesn't know how to feel any other way. He can't project values onto you or anyone that he doesn't have."

"Onto me specifically?"

"Yes, onto you, Kay. He doesn't know you." Benton drums that in. "He can't imagine what you'll do or how you feel because he's incapable of empathy. Therefore, he reads people wrong."

"We'll see about the print on Peggy Stanton's rearview mirror, if it matches anything on the bottle." I think out loud as I worry, and I don't want to worry.

I want to trust Benton. I want to believe every word he's told me.

"Maybe he left a print on her mirror but no hit in AFIS." Benton scrolls through messages. "He's not in the system. He's someone no one would suspect. He's never been arrested and has no reason for his prints to be in a database. He's quite comfortable he'll never be a suspect, and you've caused a problem he's not expected. The question is whether he knows it by now."

"I wish you wouldn't look at that thing when you drive." I take his phone from him. "If you do it when I'm with you, what do you do when I'm not?"

"Nobody you need to worry about, Kay." He holds out his hand. "I don't do anything when you're not with me that you need to worry about."

"I thought you talked to her." I return his phone.

"She's not leaving Marino alone. Probably the biggest reason to have this meeting."

"But she'll lay off him when she hears what we know," I assume, because Burke certainly should.

"It's ridiculous," he says. "Marino's prints, like yours, like mine, are on file for exclusionary purposes, and it's not his fingerprint on Peggy Stanton's rearview mirror. And he sure as hell didn't murder Howard Roth. Marino was in Tampa when Roth was killed. The meeting will put an end to it."

"He probably still thinks we believe it was an accident." I'm not thinking about Marino but the person Burke should be looking for.

I'm thinking about the killer.

"Unless he's been following us," I add. "In that case, he might know what we do. If he's cruising around, watching us."

"I doubt it."

"Why?"

"He's not nervous," Benton says. "This person is confident and never imagines he's making mistakes. He never imagined you'd spray everything with chemicals, that you'd find blood he didn't bother to clean up."

"He couldn't have cleaned it up," I reply. "Not all of it."

It wasn't apparent to the unaided eye, a medium-velocity impact spatter I associate with blunt force. Varying sizes of elongated drops were on the left side of the recliner, on the brown vinyl armrest, and on the dark brown paneled wall left of where I believe Howard Roth's head was when he was struck hard enough to lacerate his scalp and fracture his skull.

The bloodstain pattern that glowed violet for me told the heartless story of him asleep or passed out drunk in front of the TV when a murderer walked in a door that apparently was never locked. Roth was struck once in the back of the head with a malt liquor bottle that the killer placed inside a trash bag he closed with a twist tie.

Bloody streaks and swipes on dirty stained dark carpet and bloody drag marks soaked into the pile led from the living room to the basement door, and then blood was plainly visible where one would expect it to be if he were an accidental death. Drips and smears were on the six concrete steps leading to the basement, his unconscious body pushed down the stairs and then kicked and stomped where it landed. The killer made sure Roth wouldn't survive and assumed no one would entertain the possibility he was a homicide, that it would never enter our minds.

"He did make some effort to disguise what he's done," Benton points out, as we pass the boathouse, the old Polaroid building again. "He could have just showed up late at night and shot him, stabbed him, strangled him, but that would have been obvious. He got some of it right but not the rest of it, because he's unable to anticipate what normal people do."

"He can't imagine any of us caring."

"That's right. Someone empty, hollow. He's probably seen him around here."

Benton suspects the killer has noticed Roth in Cambridge, has been aware of him for months, observing the handyman wandering about looking for work and digging through trash cans and recycle bins, sometimes pushing a grocery cart. This killer is aware of everyone when he's stalking his next victim, Benton says. He prowls, cruises, researches, observing patterns and calculating. He does dry runs, feeding his cruel fantasies.

But that doesn't mean he knew who Howard Roth was by name. The killer forged a hundred-dollar check that he likely sent in the mail as he continued to pay Peggy Stanton's bills long after she was dead. But that doesn't mean he had a clue that the Howard Roth whose check he wrote was the homeless-looking man he saw rooting through the trash in Cambridge.

"What I'm sure of is he killed Roth when he did for a reason," Benton says. "This was an expedient homicide devoid of emotion."

"Stomping and kicking him seems rather emotional."

"It wasn't personal," Benton replies. "He felt nothing."

"It could be construed as angry. In most stomping cases, there's rage," I reply.

"He felt he needed to get it done. Like killing a bug. I'm wondering if he'd been to her house recently, if Roth had." Benton's looking down at his phone again. "Maybe wanting his money, and it was bad timing."

"If the killer happened to be stealing Peggy Stanton's mail when Roth appeared, that would be bad timing, couldn't be worse timing." My building is in sight. "But I wouldn't expect him to do that during daylight."

"We don't know that Roth only went out during daylight.

There are all-night markets all around where Peggy Stanton lived, a lot of them on Cambridge Street, a Shop Quik that's open twenty-four-seven just around the corner from her," Benton says. "He was going to go out no matter the hour if he ran out of beer, and he might have frequented her neighborhood because he wanted his money."

"After dark on a poorly lit street?" I reply. "Chances are Roth wouldn't have gotten a good look at him, even if they were face-to-face."

"He felt he had reason, a need to play it safe." Benton says the killer did. "He had reason enough to take the risk of following him home with the intention of murdering him."

We turn off Memorial Drive, and I imagine Howard Roth on his way to or from the Shop Quik. If he'd seen someone getting mail out of Peggy Stanton's box he might have spoken to this person, inquired where she is or when she might be home and even explain why he was asking. A disabled vet, an alcoholic who goes through trash cans and recyclables, a part-time handyman described as harmless. Even if he looked the killer in the face, why was murdering Roth a chance worth taking?

I wonder if the killer had some other reason for being familiar with Howard Roth, if they'd seen each other before. They may not have known each other by name but by sight, by context.

"And the rest was easy," Benton is saying, as we stop at the CFC gate, and my phone begins to ring.

Bryce.

"Follow a drunk home who doesn't lock his door." Benton reaches up to press the remote clipped to the visor.

What does Bryce want that can't wait until I'm inside? He knows I'm here. He can see us in the monitor on his desk, in almost any monitor in any area of the building, and I press *answer.*

"Watch and wait." Benton drives in. "Let him go through a few quarts and pass out in his chair. He probably never knew what hit him."

"I'm pulling in now," I say to my chief of staff.

"Oh my God, have I got news." He's so keyed up I have to turn my volume down.

"There should be people waiting for us—" I start to say.

"You were expecting them? Oh, Lord. I made them wait in the lobby."

"You what?"

"Love, love the cat. Little Shaw's in perfect cat health." He says *purrfect*. "Okay, hold on, I'm calling Ron now, gonna get him on his cell, sure am sorry. It would be helpful if you'd let me know things like this, for God's sake. Ron? You can escort them up immediately. I didn't know they were expected; no one tells me anything.

"I certainly apologize, but if you would just inform me? I had no idea?" Bryce is back to me, and I can't get in a word. "Well, Shaw almost got all A-pluses. A touch of dry skin, a little anemic, vet says it's best she's not left alone all the time, since she used to be with someone rather constantly until the bad thing happened, not to mention she's been traumatized. And Ethan works out of his home office three days a week, and I think we should keep her, especially after the scare with Indy, who's fine, thanks for asking—"

"Bryce!" I interrupt him for the third time.

"What!"

"Why would you make the FBI wait in our lobby," I ask. "Or have them escorted up by security?"

"No. Oh, no, the two women agents? Not them. Oh, Lord, I didn't realize . . . They're in the war room and not who I meant, oh, shit." He sounds shocked. "Hold on, hold on, let me catch him. Ron! Don't escort them up. You're with them now? Oh, shit," he says.

thirty-four

I FAULT HIM FOR NOT MAKING AN APPOINTMENT AND then showing up unannounced at the CFC, but I can't say he has no right to talk to me. I decide that Channing Lott and his companions are to be brought upstairs.

"Just give me a minute to get settled," I instruct Bryce over my cell phone. "Take them into the break room, get them water, coffee. I can see them for a few minutes only. Please explain I'm late for a meeting. I'll text you when I'm ready, and you can bring them to my office."

I push the elevator button for the seventh floor and know what Benton is going to insist on, but it's out of the question.

"Kay, I should be with you—" he begins, and I don't let him finish.

I shake my head. "It's no more appropriate for you to sit in on whatever he wants to discuss than it would be if he were any family member, any other loved one of the deceased. He's the husband of someone whose case is mine."

"Her body's not been found. She's not your case."

"I've been consulted about her, and he knows it. I've testified about her in his trial, and in his mind she's my case. She has to be somebody's case, for God's sake, because it's highly improbable she's still alive. Let's face it, she's no more alive than Emma Shubert is."

"You can't make that connection based on fact." The way he says it is revealing.

"I know when people aren't going to walk through a door ever again, Benton." I study him carefully. "Those women are dead."

He says nothing because he believes it, too. He knows more than he's saying. I think of the meeting I'm about to be quite late for, but whatever is happening will have to wait.

"What if Channing Lott really didn't have anything to do with his wife's disappearance and people like me won't talk to him?" I ask.

"People like you?"

"I have to, Benton."

"This is dangerous, Kay."

"We're obliged to respect that he's been acquitted of her murder for hire, and what's dangerous is to assume he's not grieving, not distraught, not devastated." I'm firm. It's not negotiable. "I won't have the FBI sitting in. In fact, the FBI has interfered with my office enough."

"I'm not trying to interfere. I'm trying to protect you."

"I know you are." I look at him and can see how unhappy he is. "And I can't allow it."

He realizes when arguing will be fruitless, and while I always listen to his opinions and what he warns me about, I have to handle my responsibilities the way I know is right. If I weren't his wife he'd never make the suggestion he just did. Inside the CFC there are no suspects, no innocent or guilty, only people dead or desolate. Channing Lott is the bereft, and to ignore him would be a violation of what I'm sworn to do.

"He's not going to hurt me," I say to Benton. "He's not going to attack me inside my own building."

"I'm not worried about what he's going to do," he says. "I'm worried about what he wants."

"I'll meet you and your colleagues in a few minutes. I'll be fine."

We get off on my floor, and I watch Benton walk away, tall and lank in his dark suit, his hair thick and silver, his stride purposeful and confident, the way he always walks, but I feel his reluctance. He heads toward the TelePresence conference room, which is referred to as the war room, and I go the other way.

I follow the curved corridor to my office and unlock the door, taking a moment to inspect myself in the mirror over the bathroom sink, to wash my face, brush my hair and teeth, and put on lipstick. Of all days to wear a pair of shapeless old corduroys and what looks like a fisherman's cable-knit sweater, and plain black ankle boots.

It's not what I would have picked, had I known I was meeting this notoriously powerful man who many still believe orchestrated the murder of his wife, and for an instant I consider changing into investigative field clothes, cargo pants, a shirt with the CFC crest. But that's silly, and there isn't time.

I text Bryce and ask him to please remind our uninvited guests it will have to be quick, that I'm late for another meeting. I don't mind making the FBI wait, truth be told, especially making Douglas Burke wait; I wouldn't mind making her wait for a hundred years. But I want an out if I need it. I don't know what Channing Lott has planned or why he's brought people with him.

I hear Bryce in the corridor being his usual hyperfluent self, and he can't help it. His need to talk is like his need for air. He opens my door as he's knocking on it, and Channing Lott is there in a dove-gray suit and gray shirt with no tie. He is quite striking, with his long white hair braided in back, and he shakes my hand warmly and looks me in the eye, and for an instant I think he's going to hug me. It takes a moment to regain my composure and recognize the man and woman accompanying him.

"We can sit here." I show them to the brushed-steel table. "I see Bryce made sure you have something to drink."

"This is Shelly Duke, my chief financial officer, and Albert Galbraith, my chief of operations," Lott says, and I remember the two of them huddled close and looking at the harbor outside the courthouse when I was going through security yesterday afternoon.

Attractive, well-paid executives finely dressed, in their late thirties, early forties, I would guess, neither of them as warm or friendly as their boss, whose blue eyes are intense, his face vibrant as he gives me his complete attention. When we are seated, I ask him what I might help him with.

"First and most important, I want to thank you, Dr. Scarpetta." Lott says what I was afraid he might. "What you were put through couldn't have been a good time." He means what happened in court, and I'm reminded unpleasantly of being fined by the judge and Lott's own attorney attempting to impeach me on every front.

"There is nothing to thank me for, Mr. Lott," I reply, as I think of his helicopter filming me. "I'm a public servant doing my job."

"Without prejudice," he says. "You did it without preconception or prejudice. You simply stated what was true, and you didn't have to."

"It's not my job to take sides or have an opinion unless it's about why someone has died."

"That's not my wife," he says, and Peggy Stanton's identity hasn't yet been released. "When they played the TV footage in court, I knew it wasn't her. I knew it instantly, and I wanted to tell you myself in the event there's been a question."

I wonder if Toby leaked the identity to Jill Donoghue and if she knows her client is here.

"As grim as the condition of the body seemed to be, I could tell without hesitation it's not Millie." Lott removes the cap from a bottle of water. "She couldn't possibly look like that, and if you've been through her medical records or been given details of her physical description, you'll realize what I'm saying is correct."

I have little doubt he knows I've been through those records and am aware that Mildred Lott is or was almost six feet tall. Peggy Stanton, whose murder Channing Lott shouldn't know about unless he had something to do with it or his lawyer's been told, was barely five-foot-three. When she was visible on TV as I was getting her body into the Stokes basket, it was obvious she wasn't tall. I know from examining her that her hair was white, not dyed blond, and that she had no scars from recent cosmetic surgeries, an abdominoplasty, a rhytidectomy.

"It was the first thing all of us thought when it hit the news." Al Galbraith reaches for his coffee, and he seems disquieted, as if the subject is a distasteful one. "No matter the condition, someone doesn't get shorter," he says awkwardly, as if he feels compelled to say something about his boss's missing wife.

"Postmortem changes, changes after death, don't make someone shorter," I agree.

"An imposing woman," Galbraith says, and it flickers in my mind he didn't like her. "I think anybody who met Mrs. Lott was struck by how statuesque she was."

"Exactly," Shelly Duke agrees, and it occurs to me that they don't want to be here. "A stunning, overwhelming woman. She filled a room, just dominated it when she walked in, and I mean it in the best way," she adds, with sadness that is unconvincing.

Lott has made them come. They are as unsettled as one might expect them to be inside a forensic facility, sitting down with me and discussing someone I sense they had ambivalence about. I wonder if Jill Donoghue has masterminded this unscheduled meeting, but I can't imagine a motive. She has boldly stated that there will be no double jeopardy in this case, that her client won't be tried again for the same charge or anything similar.

This nightmare is over but not the worst one, Donoghue has been telling the media since the acquittal was announced this morning. Now Channing Lott gets to deal with his own victimization, because he's the real victim here, she's been saying, jailed for a crime he didn't commit, as if the tragic loss of his wife wasn't horrific enough.

"Dr. Scarpetta, might I ask you a question?" He is completely focused on me, sitting very straight and turned in a way that tells me why his two chief executive officers are with him.

He gives them his back and doesn't look to either one for anything. They are witnesses, not trusted friends. Lott didn't achieve what he has in life by being naïve or stupid. Even as I worry about his intentions, he's ensuring I won't be the one causing trouble.

"I can't promise I'll be able to answer, but go ahead." I recall what the Gloucester detectives Lorey and Kefe said when they met with me after Mildred Lott vanished.

"You know the details, I assume. Millie was home alone in our Gloucester place on March eleventh, a Sunday," Lott says, as if he's making an opening statement.

A vain woman who courted the rich and famous and had visited the White House more than once and had even met the Queen, the detectives described to me, and when I asked if they knew of anyone who might have wanted something bad to happen to Mildred Lott, they said to get out the phone book and point.

Point to any page, they said. Could be anyone she'd ever stepped on, overworked, or underpaid, or had treated like *the help*, they claimed, and I remember thinking at the time how common it is that victims aren't likable. No one deserves to be abducted, raped, murdered, robbed, or maimed, but that doesn't mean the person didn't deserve something.

"She'd just relocated us back to Gloucester. We keep the house closed during the bleakest months of winter," Lott repeats what he obviously has said many times before. "And I'd spoken to her at what was morning for me and about nine p.m. for her, and of course she was very upset. I was away on business in Asia and in fact had decided to cut short my trip because of the dog. Millie was a wreck."

"She may not know about Jasmine," Shelly Duke prompts him. "Their dog," she says to me.

"Our shar-pei vanished on March eighth," Lott explains. "The landscapers left the gate open again. It had happened before and Jasmine got out. Last time she was found frantic and lost, the police spotted her. The local police know her and an officer picked her up and brought her back to us. Then we weren't so fortunate, it seemed at first. Police suspected someone stole her, a rare purebred, a miniature and not inexpensive, and Millie was beside herself. There aren't words to describe how upset she was." Channing Lott blinks back tears.

"Your dog vanished three days before your wife did," I say to him.

"Yes." He clears his throat.

"Did Jasmine ever show up?"

"Two days after Millie disappeared, Jasmine was found wandering several miles north of our house, close to the Annisquam River," he says, and I think of Peggy Stanton's cat. "In an off-leash walking area with a lot of brush and boulders above Wheeler Street. Some people out with their dog found her."

"Do you think she'd been loose the entire time she was missing?" I ask.

"Couldn't have been, not for the better part of a week in the rainy raw weather, down in the low forties at night, without food or water. She was in too good of shape to have been out that entire time. I think whoever took her changed his mind. Jasmine can be aggressive, unpredictable, isn't fond of strangers."

Someone who has no regard for human life but wouldn't harm an animal.

"The Ransom of Red Chief." Channing Lott's laughter is hollow, and what is significant to me is the chronology.

Most likely Peggy Stanton's cat got out or was put out after her owner had disappeared and possibly already was dead, yet Mildred Lott's dog vanished before any crime had occurred.

"It's been suggested that my wife might have drowned accidentally." He gets around to asking my opinion about that, and I can't possibly have an answer. "Or maybe took her own life."

He goes on to describe the theories, which have been endless and far-fetched, some of them recited by Donoghue in court. Mildred Lott was drunk or on drugs and wandered outside and fell into the ocean or deliberately went into the frigid water to drown herself. She was having an affair and ran off with whoever it was because she feared her husband's wrath. She'd been stashing millions of dollars in offshore accounts and is now living under an assumed identity in the Caribbean, on the Mediterranean, in the South of France, in Marrakech. Alleged sightings of her have been all over the Internet.

"I'm interested in your opinion." He presses me for one. "A person drowns either accidentally or is murdered or commits suicide? Wouldn't the body turn up eventually?"

"Bodies in water aren't always found," I reply. "People lost at sea, people who go overboard from ships or get pulled under or swept away by strong currents, for example. Depending on whether the body gets hung up on something—"

"Eventually there would be absolutely nothing left?"

"Whatever is left has to be found, and it isn't always."

"But if my wife fell into the ocean, perhaps stumbled over rocks or fell off our dock, wouldn't you expect her to show up?" He persists bravely and not easily.

His eyes are bright with sorrow that seems real.

"In a case like that, generally, yes," I answer.

"Al, if you would?" Lott says, without looking at him.

Al Galbraith opens his briefcase and withdraws a manila envelope he pushes across the table to me, and I don't open it. I don't touch it. I won't until I know exactly what it is and whether it is something I should see.

"A copy of the security camera recording," Lott explains. "The same thing the Gloucester detectives, the FBI, the lawyers have. What the jury saw. Twenty-six seconds. Not much but it's the last images of her, the last thing Millie did before she vanished in thin air. She's opening a back door of our house at exactly thirteen minutes before midnight on that Sunday, March eleventh. She's dressed for bed, and there's no damn reason for her to go out into the backyard at that hour. Certainly she wasn't letting Jasmine out. Jasmine was still missing. It was cold, quite overcast and windy, and Millie walked out of the house not at all dressed for the weather and seemed to be a bit panicked."

At this point, he turns to look at his colleagues.

"It's still not the right choice of words. A word I've struggled with, trying to precisely describe the look on her face, her body language." He seems sincerely at a loss and genuinely pained. "How would you describe it?" he asks his chief executives. "Urgent, distressed, alarmed?"

"I don't get that when I watch it," Galbraith says, as if he's said it before.

It sounds flat. It sounds rehearsed.

"Only that she appears to have a purpose," Lott's chief of operations says. "She emerges from the house as if she has a reason, is directed. I wouldn't think of the word *panic* when I look at the video, but it's very quick and not all that clear, except she's saying something to someone."

"I'd describe the look as urgent, yes." Shelly Duke nods. "But not upset and definitely not panicked." She directs this to Lott. "I don't think she looks frightened the way someone might if they're worried a bad person is lurking around or trying to break in."

"If she'd been frightened and worried someone was trying to break in," Lott replies, and I detect annoyance and impatience beneath his charm, "she wouldn't have turned off the alarm and gone out into the dark at that hour. Not when she was there alone."

He's the type to get frustrated with people not as smart and determined as he, and that would be almost everyone.

"Millie was very security-conscious," Lott says to me. "She absolutely didn't go out of the house that night because she heard a noise, was scared of someone or something. Most assuredly not. That was the last thing she would have done. When she was scared, she called the police. She certainly didn't hesitate to call nine-one-one. I'm sure you've talked to the Gloucester police and are aware they were quite familiar with her and our property. In fact, several officers had been to the house just days before when Jasmine disappeared."

I tell Channing Lott I'm very sorry but I have people waiting for me. I'll be happy to review the security footage, although it's unlikely I'll have anything to add that hasn't already been observed by others who have viewed it. I push back my chair because I feel he's making a case for his innocence and I don't intend to be manipulated.

"It just nags at me." He makes no move to leave. "Who was it? Who could she have been talking to? You see the prevailing theory, and one that the prosecution continued to beat like a drum, is she was talking to me. She's come out into the yard and is saying something to me."

"A theory based on what?" I ask him, and I probably shouldn't be asking him anything further. "Is there audio on the security video?"

"There isn't, and you can see her only from the side. You can't really make out how her lips are moving, not clearly. So to more precisely answer you, Dr. Scarpetta, the theory, like all of the theories about me, is based on nothing but the prosecution's, the government's, determination to win their case."

He looks angry. He looks wronged, and it's not lost on me he won't refer to Dan Steward by name.

"I'm sure you saw all over the news that the prosecution suggested I wasn't really traveling," he says. "That my being in Tokyo the night Millie disappeared was a ruse somehow, that I actually was back here and in collusion with whoever I supposedly hired to murder her. The point the prosecution made relentlessly is my wife would never have left the house late at night unless the person she heard was someone she completely trusted."

"Exactly right, she wouldn't if she didn't know who it was," Shelly Duke agrees.

"Yes, that we all knew about Mrs. Lott," Al Galbraith says. "Considering the position she had in life, she was keenly aware of the risks. I don't want to use the word *paranoid*."

"Kidnapping for ransom," Lott says to me. "Which was her first thought about what happened to our dog."

"That someone grabbed Jasmine and soon enough would demand ransom," Shelly Duke, his chief financial officer, says. "Kidnapping is a billion-dollar industry, and it's a depressing reality that certain individuals, particularly those who travel internationally, should have appropriate insurance coverage. Millie asked me on a number of occasions if one could get the same insurance for Jasmine."

"She worried someone might pull a boat up to our dock in the middle of the night." Lott has a way of talking over people without interrupting them. "After those Somali pirates abducted that British couple from their yacht? Well, that was upsetting enough to Millie, and then when bandits murdered a tourist and kidnapped his wife from that luxury resort in Kenya, she became quite concerned. Obsessively concerned. Our property is fenced in and gated, but she worried about vulnerability from the deep-water dock, was sufficiently worried to ask me to get rid of it, which I certainly didn't want to do, as on occasion I moor the *Cipriano* there."

"Your yacht?" I ask, because I can't help it.

If he in fact is charged with some other crime, I've just ensured I will be a witness, possibly for the defense again.

"Was your yacht docked there the night she vanished?" I then ask, because I don't care about Jill Donoghue.

I care about the truth.

"It wasn't," he answers. "It was spending the winter in Saint-Tropez. I usually don't have it brought back to this area until May."

I open the door adjoining my office to Bryce's and give him the envelope, telling him to e-mail copies of the security video to Lucy and me. I let him know that he can show our guests out, and Channing Lott gives me a card, engraved on creamy paper of heavy stock. He's written his private telephone numbers on it.

"Millie wouldn't go with anyone, even if a gun was pointed at her head." He pauses in the corridor, his eyes intensely locked on mine. "If someone tried to grab her in our backyard, she would have fought like hell. He'd have to shoot her on the spot right then and there."

thirty-five

TOXICOLOGY IN PEGGY STANTON'S CASE IS LIKE SEARCH-
ing for a needle in a haystack when the needle may not be a
needle and the hay may not be hay. I can't grab at straws and
wildly guess. I can't demand every special drug screen imaginable without running out of samples and Phillis Jobe running
out of patience.

"An ordeal, I admit," I say to my chief toxicologist over the
phone. "I'm asking a lot and offering very little, I know."

Frozen sections of liver, kidney, and brain are in poor condition that will only worsen and be consumed with each test we
run. I don't have urine or vitreous fluid. I don't have a single
tube of blood.

"It's like pulling a sword from a stone, but I believe it can
be done." I'm at my desk inside my office, where the doors are
shut as I explore possibilities with confidence I didn't feel before. "I believe we've got a chance if we try a very practical
approach."

New insights about Mildred Lott combined with what I
know about Peggy Stanton lead in a more obvious direction,
which I suspect strongly is the same direction for each victim,
whether it is two or three or, God forbid, more. If what Benton has projected is true and the killer is murdering the same

woman every time, perhaps his mother or some other powerful female figure, then he likely picks the same type of woman, at least symbolically, and chooses the same way of overpowering her.

"No possible injection sites you found when you posted her?" Phillis gets to that.

"None we could see," I reply. "Her skin wasn't in great condition, but we went over her very carefully with injection sites in mind, with any injury in mind. What seems probable if not evident at this point is she was last home on the early Friday evening of April twenty-seventh, fed her cat, unset and reset her alarm system at about six p.m., when she headed out with her pocketbook and keys. Most likely she drove off in her Mercedes and had an encounter that ended in a place where she was held hostage and killed. Possibly the same place where her body was frozen or kept in cold storage until she was weighted down and dumped in the bay as recently as yesterday or the night before."

"If the same person killed Mildred Lott, I wonder why her body's not been found," Phillis says.

"Not found *yet*." I know what Benton's opinion is, that the killer keeps the bodies because he doesn't want to give them up. "Part of the fantasy may be the aftermath, not letting them go, continuing some bizarre relationship he has with them," I explain.

"Necrophilia?"

"No evidence with Peggy Stanton, but I can't absolutely rule it out. Although I doubt it, to be honest. But if Mildred Lott was his first victim, his attachment to whatever she symbolized, his fantasy, in her case likely is stronger. She may be more personal to him, but that doesn't mean his interest is overtly sexual. Benton thinks it's about degrading, about power, about destruction."

"She disappeared about six weeks before this one did." Before Peggy Stanton did, Phillis means. "Any other missing women we know of who might be even earlier?"

"There are always missing people. But no similar case comes to mind. If Mildred Lott was his first, he likely has stronger feelings and fantasies about her," I repeat emphatically, because I believe she is the key. "She might represent something different to him, a bigger prize."

"A billionaire's socialite wife is a pretty big prize."

"That might not be why she would be a bigger prize to him. Her status and wealth may have nothing to do with why he targeted her. More likely it has to do with what she represented and what that triggered in him," I answer, and I should be concerned about the FBI in my conference room and how late I'm going to be.

But I have other troubling matters on my mind. Murdering Howard Roth may have been *expedient*, as Benton described. But it also was poor judgment. It was impulsive. It probably wasn't necessary, and I fear it is a harbinger of things to come. If someone crosses the killer's path, that person may be next.

"But if Mildred Lott was his first victim, I can't help but feel that she's important to him, that he has a stronger attachment to her," I say. "Which might be why her body hasn't been found. He may still have it."

"Possibly a drug he slipped into their food or drink," Phillis considers. "Saying she met her killer in a restaurant or some public place." She's talking about Peggy Stanton. "Maybe someone she met on the Internet, on Craigslist, Facebook, Google Plus. On one of those dating sites, what I'm constantly telling my kids not to do, for God's sake."

"I really doubt it," I reply. "I can't imagine Peggy Stanton, or Mildred Lott, for that matter, hooking up with strangers on the Internet, and there's no evidence they did. But to be safe we should screen for Rohypnol, gamma-hydroxybutyrate, ketamine hydrochloride." I go through the list of date-rape drugs, despite my conviction that the killer has an MO, a method of operation, that he repeats, and it doesn't include having a date or even a social encounter with whoever is on his violent radar.

Mildred Lott was a dominant, assertive, yet extremely cautious woman who was quite tall and worked out diligently in the gym. She would not have made it easy for someone to take her anywhere she did not want to go, and her husband was adamant that if anyone tried to harm her, she would resist.

After listening to what he said about his wife and knowing what I do about Peggy Stanton, I'm convinced the killer finds a way to incapacitate his victims and likely uses the same method each time. I don't think these women went anywhere willingly with him. I think they were ambushed and abducted.

"Poppers, snappers, whippets, fumes people sniff and huff or inhale from bags." I suggest volatiles typically abused in cases we see. "Aromatic and aliphatic hydrocarbons, solvents found in Magic Markers, adhesives, glues, paint thinners, propane, butane, or alkyl halides in cleaning fluids. But hard to use any of these as a means to subdue someone for purposes of abduction, I should think."

"There are any number of volatile organic compounds that could render someone unconscious," my chief toxicologist says. "Toluene, carbon tetrachloride, one-one-one-trichloroethane, tetrachloroethylene, trichloroethylene, provided you use high enough levels."

"Almost anything can be a poison or render someone unconscious if administered the wrong way, in a deliberately harmful way." I ponder what she's describing. "But it's a matter of what's practical and accessible, and what might occur to a perpetrator and what he might be comfortable with."

"Basically, what can be used as a weapon."

"Exactly," I reply. "And I'm not sure you'd douse a cloth with paint thinner or dry-cleaning fluid and clamp it over someone's nose and mouth, for example, if your intention is to incapacitate that person instantly. And you certainly wouldn't try it if you're not sure it would work."

"Diethyl ether, nitrous oxide, and chloroform." She names the three earliest known general anesthetics. "Chloroform is easily acquired if one is involved in an industry or works in a lab where it's used as a solvent. Unfortunately, as the whole world now knows, it's also possible to make it at home. All you need are chlorine bleach powder and acetone, the recipe available on the Internet."

She's alluding to what was sensational news not long ago, the highly publicized trial in Florida when Casey Anthony was acquitted for the murder of her two-year-old daughter, Caylee. Televised testimony claimed the Anthony home computer was used for Internet searches on how to make chloroform and that traces of it were detected in Casey Anthony's car trunk. While none of this resulted in a conviction, it could have planted a diabolical idea into a demented person's head. One can shop at the hardware store and find instructions online to mix up chloroform in the garage or kitchen or workplace and use it to incapacitate or kill.

"Maybe he knocks them out." Phillis continues to offer possibilities. "Drives off with them in his car trunk so if they come to in transit, they can't pose a problem, can't struggle with him."

"He may use a boat," I reply, recalling what was said to me.

Mildred Lott was so afraid of a kidnapper or someone else with criminal intentions mooring a boat behind the Gloucester mansion that she inquired about insurance and asked that the deep-water dock be removed, a request her husband denied because of his yacht. Who, in addition to him and key members of his staff, knew she was consumed by this worry? It would be a dangerous suggestion to make to the wrong person.

Don't announce what you fear could happen or someone evil might make it come true.

"Brain's going to be your best bet. Chloroform binds to proteins and lipids. It infiltrates neurons," I say to Phillis, as I get up from my desk and notice the two SUVs that were picked up on security cameras moments ago as they waited for the gate to open.

The black Yukon driven by Channing Lott turns east on the street below, perhaps returning to his headquarters in Boston's Marine Industrial Park. It interests me that he is alone with his young, attractive CFO, while Galbraith, in a silver Jeep with a mesh grille, heads the opposite way toward Harvard.

"Assuming the victim wasn't kept alive long after it was used," Phillis Jobe lets me know. "Two or three hours, maybe four. After that, we might not find it."

Kept alive for what? An assault of some type that may not be physical, and I think of Peggy Stanton's undigested food. I imagine her eating dinner somewhere that April night and being grabbed or knocked out as she was returning to wherever she was parked, then driven someplace, possibly in her own car. What I'm certain of is at some point she was conscious long enough to break her nails and step in red-stained wooden fibers that got embedded in the bottoms of her feet, and I recall the inside of her closets and dresser.

I envision the neatly folded clothes hanging and on shelves

and in drawers, slacks and pantsuits, sweaters and blouses, old and unstylish, and not a single pair of nylon stockings, yet her dead body had on torn pantyhose. I imagine her waking up in a nightmare, inside the place he held her, a place where he had no fear of discovery and could completely control her.

I wonder if he had dressed her in hose, a skirt, a jacket with antique buttons by then, if she regained consciousness in clothing that didn't fit and wasn't hers. Or did he force her to dress herself in a costume that means something to him, perhaps garments that once belonged to the original source of whom and what he hates?

Peggy Stanton had a cluster of contusions on her upper right arm, what appear to be fingertip bruises, and I think of Luke's speculation that they weren't inflicted through clothing but rather by someone gripping her bare skin. He theorized that the killer terrorized and humiliated her by stripping her nude the same way prisoners of war are tortured, and I don't think that's it.

I don't believe the killer wanted her naked. I think he wanted her dressed for the role he sadistically cast her in, and months after she was dead and desiccated he adjusted the wardrobe, the jewelry, so it didn't fall off her mummified body when he pushed it overboard into the bay. I explain all this to Ernie Koppel as I continue making evidence rounds by phone.

"I need to rule out that she was dressed this way when she left her house," I say to him. "If at all possible, I'd like to answer that. This is a bad one, Ernie."

"I know."

"And I'm pushing everyone."

"Imagine that," he says sportingly.

I ask him about fibers he recovered from inside Peggy Stanton's Mercedes, explaining that I saw no clothing inside her house remotely similar to what she had on when I recovered her body from the water.

"I don't know if you've had a chance to take a look," I then say, and it's my way of acknowledging I'm persistent and always in a hurry. "Any chance the fibers you collected from her car could have come from the clothing she had on? If she was dressed that way for some unusual reason when she went out last, most likely this past April twenty-seventh?"

Specifically, I want to know if fibers recovered from the floor, the seats, and the trunk might have come from the dark blue wool Tallulah jacket, the gray wool skirt, the purple silk blouse, and Ernie says no.

"Carpet fibers, synthetics," he says, and then he gets to the wood fibers he thought were mulch.

"They're not," he lets me know. "I'm not saying I know what this stuff is used for, but it wasn't made by feeding wood or bark through a tub grinder and spraying it with a dye."

He says he used gas chromatography–mass spectrometry, GC–MS, to analyze what he recovered from the driver's area of the Mercedes, and the red-stained wood debris has a specific cyclic polyalcohol profile consistent with American oak.

"Characterized by a richness in deoxyinositols, especially proto-Quercitol," he explains. "A very interesting way of identifying the botanical origin of natural woods used in aging wine and spirits, obviously to guarantee authenticity. You know, some winemaker or distributor claims a red wine was aged in French oak barrels and GC–MS says nope, it wasn't. It was aged in American oak barrels, so there's no way what you're about to pay a fortune for is a Premier Grand Cru Bordeaux. Quite a science to it, and you can imagine why. If a distributor is trying to sell you a young wine they're passing off as a fine one?"

"Bordeaux?" I ask. "What's this got to do with wine?"

"The wood fibers from her car," he replies.

"You think they're from wine barrels?" I can't imagine what that might mean.

"Common oak, white oak used in cooperage to make barrels, and also a secondary source of tannic acid, or the tannins you find in red wine," he says. "In your case we're talking American oak stained a red-wine color, with trace elements of burned wood, most likely from what's known as toasting or charring the inside of the barrel, and sugar crystals and other derivatives such as vanillin, lactones."

"A woody debris that looks like mulch but isn't. Wineries or some place that makes use of wine barrels," I think out loud. "But not where the barrels themselves are made, because new barrels wouldn't be stained."

"They wouldn't be."

"Then what?"

"It's frustrating as hell," he says. "I can tell you the origin of this stuff likely is wine barrels, but I can't tell you why it's shredded, absolutely pulverized, or what it was used for."

He mentions that it is a common practice for people to cut old wine barrels into pieces, char them, and toss them into whiskey they're aging.

"But this stuff's way too fine for that, fine like dirt," he says. "Doesn't look like it was from planing or sanding, either, but I suppose the debris could be from someplace where old wine barrels are being recycled or reused for something."

I'm aware that barrels no longer suitable for aging wine can be handcrafted into furniture, and I recall some of the unusual pieces inside Peggy Stanton's house, the table in the entryway, where her car key was found, the oak table in the kitchen. Everything I saw was antique and certainly not recycled from used barrels, and there was no evidence she collected wines or even drank them.

"What about the woody fibers from the bottom of her feet and under her nails?" I inquire. "Same thing?"

"American oak stained red, some of it charred," he answers. "Although I didn't find sugar crystals and some of these same derivatives."

"They would have dissolved in the water. It's probably safe to assume what was on her body and tracked into her car came from the same source," I decide. "Or better put, possibly the origin of the debris likely is the same location."

"You can assume that," he agrees. "I was thinking of checking with some wineries around here to see if they know what this wine barrel debris might be—"

"Around here?" I interrupt him. "I wouldn't."

thirty-six

IT IS ALMOST FOUR P.M. WHEN I WALK INTO THE WAR room, as it's called, where experts and investigators, including scientists and doctors from the military, convene face-to-face both in person and remotely. Here behind closed doors we wage battle against the enemy using high-definition video and CD-quality audio, and I recognize who is speaking.

I hear General John Briggs's deep commanding voice saying something about transport on an Air Force plane in Washington state. A C-130, he says, and he's talking about someone I know.

"He just took off from McChord, will land in about an hour." The chief of the Armed Forces Medical Examiners, my boss, fills integrated LCDs around the geometrically shaped computer conference table.

"He won't supervise, of course. He'll be there to observe," Briggs says, and displayed on the deep blue acoustical uphol-stered walls are scene photographs that are unfamiliar to me, a skull, scattered bones, and human hair.

I take a chair next to Benton and across from Val Hahn, who is in a khaki suit and a serious mood, and she nods at me. Next to her is Douglas Burke, in black, and she doesn't give me so much as a glance. Turning on the HD display in front of me, I look at Briggs's rugged face on my monitor as he explains what the Office of the Chief Medical Examiner in Edmonton, Alberta, is doing as a courtesy because we don't have jurisdiction.

"We could argue it, but we won't." Briggs has a way of assuming authority and making people believe it. "We're not going to have a pissing match in a case where it's an ally capable of conducting a competent forensic investigation. This isn't Jonestown or American missionaries murdered in Sudan. It will be a fully coordinated effort with our Canadian friends."

I can tell from the military coin and memorial flag displays on the shelves behind him that he's sitting at his desk inside his port mortuary office at Dover Air Force Base. He's in scrubs because his work isn't done, a planeload of flag-draped transfer cases scheduled to arrive by the end of the day, I know from the news. A chopper shot down. Another one.

"His role is to observe, to be a conduit between them and us," Briggs is saying, about the AFME's consulting forensic pathologist in Seattle.

"I'm sorry I'm late." I speak to my monitor, and Briggs is looking at me and he's looking at everyone.

"Let me fill you in, Kay." He informs me that Emma Shubert is dead.

Her decomposing remains have been found not even five miles from the Pipestone Creek campground where she was last seen by her colleagues on the night of August 23. Dr. Ramon Lopez is being flown to Edmonton, and the AFME consultant, the retired chief of Seattle, a friend of mine, will be in touch with me as soon as he has information.

"Some kids looking for dinosaur bones." Briggs describes for me what he's already explained to everyone else. "Apparently, they were exploring a wooded area off Highway Forty-three and noticed several small bones. They thought at first they'd discovered another bone bed, and they had, in a sense. Only these bones weren't petrified or old. Small human bones of the hands and feet, most likely scattered by animals. Then a human skull near a pile of rocks accompanied by a foul odor."

"When was this?" I again apologize for what he has to repeat.

"Yesterday late afternoon. Most of the body was under

rocks that someone obviously piled on top. So she's not completely skeletonized, as you can see."

Briggs clicks through an array of photos that are large and graphic on the wall-mounted flat screens. Small human bones, carpals, metacarpals, and phalanges, what look like white and gray stones in a dry creek bed overwhelmed by trees, and a skull wedged under a shrub as if it rolled there or perhaps an animal nudged it.

A pelt of matted grayish-brown hair at the edge of piled rocks, and then the shallow grave is exposed, revealing the remains in situ, a body in a blue coat and gray pants curled up on its side. Areas not protected by clothing, the head, the hands, the feet, likely were preyed on and gnawed on by insects and wildlife, and were disarticulated and scattered.

"What about boots or shoes?" I inquire.

"Not on the clothing inventory I've received." Briggs types on a keyboard I can't see and puts on his glasses. "One blue rain jacket, one pair of gray pants, a bra, a pair of panties, a silver metal watch on a blue Velcro band that believe it or not is still ticking."

"No shoes or socks," I comment. "Interesting, because at some point before she died, Peggy Stanton was barefoot."

"Psychological hobbling," Benton says, and I wonder how long he's known. "Rendering the victim submissive and dominated."

"And also making it harder to run," Douglas Burke says to him and no one else.

Her wide-eyed stare brings to mind a wild animal, a rabid one.

"It was a cool and rainy summer in northwest Alberta." The most powerful forensic pathologist in the United States resumes briefing me. "And of course it's been quite cold during the month of October. So two months out and most of the body is reasonably intact because of temperatures that almost mimic refrigerated conditions, and also clothing and rocks protected it somewhat. If she's a stabbing, a shooting, blunt force, possibly even strangulation, there may be enough soft tissue for us to tell. ID by dental charts has been confirmed, and we're awaiting DNA, but there doesn't seem to be a doubt it's her."

"Any apparent injuries?" I ask.

"Not that I'm aware of," he says. "We know she wasn't shot in the head. No skull fractures." He's looking at a computer on his desk, obviously scrolling through an electronic file. "No projectiles, no fractures on x-ray. They haven't autopsied her yet, are waiting for Dr. Lopez."

"The Canadian authorities understand we believe she's not an isolated case," Benton says to me, and when we were on the elevator earlier and I mentioned that Emma Shubert is dead, he knew it was true.

He knew it for a fact. It was he who instigated this meeting.

"They understand she's linked to at least one homicide here, possibly two, possibly more," Benton fills me in, and I have no doubt the Grande Prairie detectives and Royal Canadian Mounted Police working Emma Shubert's disappearance would have contacted the FBI the instant they realized the remains were hers.

She was an American citizen. A disturbing jpg image and video file possibly relating to her were anonymously e-mailed to me two days ago, and the local police and RCMP are aware of that. I suspect Benton was notified and got in touch with General Briggs, who contacted the OCME in Edmonton and also Dr. Lopez. The AFME would want to know about the Emma Shubert case because ultimately the Department of Defense would want to know. If my office is in the middle of a serial murder investigation that is federal jurisdiction and linked to a homicide in Canada, General John Briggs has to be informed. He will demand every detail and constant updates.

"The timing. Am I the only one who finds the timing as in-our-face as a billboard?" Burke says, and her eyes are glassy.

Pseudoephedrine, or she's excited by something far more dangerous, dressed in a suit with a very short skirt and a red scoop-neck sweater that's so tight it seems airbrushed on. Directly across from Benton, she arranges herself in such a way as to give him an eyeful and give me one, too, and possibly Briggs, depending on the angle of her camera and what is displayed on his desktop screen.

"Both bodies are found on the same day?" She is emphatic with Briggs, almost argumentative. "Peggy Stanton's body turns up here in the Massachusetts Bay the same day Emma Shubert turns up in Canada? Isn't that a little too coincidental, John?"

"Exactly that, a coincidence," Briggs states, in his calm, unflappable way, and her feminine attributes wouldn't be lost on him as much as they would be completely dismissed. "It stands to reason whoever piled rocks on top of her out in the middle of the woods had no control over the timing of when kids searching for fossils, for dino bones, would happen upon it."

"It's different," Benton says, but he's not saying it to Burke. "The killer wanted Peggy Stanton's body found when it was and intended to shock whoever attempted to recover it from the bay, possibly intended exactly what he got, which was the thrill of a highly publicized spectacle. His handiwork was all over the news. In contrast, when he murdered Emma Shubert he did not intend to shock whoever found her remains, because he didn't intend for them to be found at all. He carried or dragged her body probably from the highway and into the woods and covered it with rocks."

It's at this point I mention Mildred Lott. I describe the parallel of missing pets that later turn up, and her fear of being kidnapped and her husband's assertion that it would be extremely difficult for someone to pull that off. She would rather be shot on the spot than comply with an attacker, according to him, and those who knew her found her condescending and overbearing, I explain.

She didn't treat all people kindly or fairly, and Peggy Stanton seemed to have withdrawn into the confined space of her own private grieving, not venturing out much unless it was to perform acts of charity. Emma Shubert had a singular focus, impassioned by hard, cold remnants of a prehistoric past, with very little evidence she connected with anyone.

"All three of these women are unlikely candidates for abduction and murder," I suggest. "They were going about their business, on their own property, or carrying out their usual routines when they vanished. They were formidable and not necessarily accessible or sociable, and they weren't quick to trust. In fact, I get the impression they weren't trusting at all."

"You're pretty certain it's one perpetrator, Kay," Briggs doesn't ask but states.

"I think that's what we're going to discover and need to keep in mind."

"It's one person," Benton agrees. "And Emma Shubert was

a victim of opportunity. I don't think he planned her well in advance, or at least that what happened to her was premeditated to the degree the other two were. I suspect he was out of his normal habitat, was in the Grande Prairie area for a reason."

"Something that ties him to northwest Alberta and also to Cambridge," Burke asserts, as if she's answering a question that's not been asked.

"Maybe they met. Maybe they didn't. But they encountered each other somehow," Benton tells Briggs as if it's fact, because there's no other way it could have happened.

Emma Shubert came to the killer's attention, became a target, and she probably had no awareness of it. He may have stalked her, followed her, and likely was waiting for her in the remote wooded campground where she was last seen alive.

"There's no lighting. Just the ambient glow of small trailers widely spaced in the woods," Benton says. "And it was solid overcast and raining that night."

thirty-seven

VAL HAHN OF THE FBI'S CYBER SQUAD DESCRIBES SUM-
mer days in Grande Prairie as endless, with dawn coming early
and darkness descending as late as ten p.m. due to the region's
northern latitude.

"The night of August twenty-third," she tells the image of
General Briggs streaming live to us, "it was pouring rain and
cold enough to see your breath. By the time Emma was returning to her trailer from the chow hall after having dinner with
her colleagues, it was pitch dark in the campground."

The mosquitoes were bad, and there were warnings about
bears, she adds, and the paleontologists were reminded in an
e-mailed memo not to let the wet miserable weather deter them
from hauling garbage to the Dumpsters.

"'*Hungry bears don't care if they get wet*,' the e-mail read."
Hahn continues to set the scene for us. "And the night before,
a bear had gotten into bags of trash left on a picnic table and
had tried to break into a trailer. According to Emma's colleagues, she was afraid of bears. She listened for any noise and
looked for any movement, anything at all that might be a bear.
She would not have approached her trailer or even continued
walking toward it had she heard or noticed anything out of the
ordinary."

"Obviously someone stealthy." Douglas Burke says it as if she has a certain suspect in mind. "Stealthy as a ghost. Someone with the skill sets of a paid assassin."

"The campground and the weather that night," Benton says, as if Burke said nothing. "Ideal for a violent offender who wants to be invisible and silent and completely unanticipated. One might expect a bear but not a human predator."

"Assuming he knows about the place." Briggs has his glasses on again and is looking down at his desk. "It's off the beaten track if you're from out of town. Unless you're into camping, seems to me."

"One has to assume he knew. Yes, sir, I agree," Hahn replies. "When the paleontologists are subjected to the worst weather, they work and eat late. So did the perpetrator know that? I'm thinking he did. I'm thinking he had to be aware of their habits."

She continues to give us a snapshot of Emma Shubert's daily life when she spent her summers in Alberta's Peace Region, a name that couldn't seem more ironic now. During downpours or high winds, she and her colleagues typically would stay in the campground trailers, what those working the bone beds think of as temporary barracks, cramped, sparsely furnished, with electricity supplied by gasoline-powered generators. Early mornings the scientists would meet in the chow hall for breakfast, then cross a footbridge over Pipestone Creek and slog through woods and mud to the pachyrhinosaurus site.

It can be a monsoon, Hahn says, and the scientists are going to dig as long as they are physically able to access an excavation site, and they could always access the local one. Muddy and as slippery as hell, but it's not a sheer riverbank or hillside that requires a long drive or jetboat ride and rock-climbing gear. They're going to dig somewhere, going to scrape away sedimentary mud and chip away shale, unearthing what appears to the untrained eye to be nothing but rocks, in a part of the world where the months one can work outside are limited because it's not possible once the ground freezes. Late fall, winter, and early spring, the paleontologists are in the labs. They teach, and like Emma Shubert, many of them return to where they're from.

"According to interviews made available to us and other research I've done," Hahn says, "on August twenty-third the paleontologists had been digging in a sea of mud at the Pipestone

Creek site, a pachyrhinosaurus bone bed discovered twenty-something years ago, what's believed to be a mass grave where hundreds of the dinosaurs drowned, were wiped out by some natural disaster. The rain made it impossible to access the hilly slope of the Wapiti site where Emma usually excavated. Even on a good day you need ropes to get up there, so in a downpour, forget it."

"Which was where she wanted to be," Benton says. "A relatively new site, one she'd staked out as her territory. The Pipestone Creek site has been around much longer, as Val has said."

"It was picked over, or at least this was how Emma thought of it, based on interviews with her colleagues," Hahn says, and Briggs is looking at something else, possibly e-mail.

"What's important," Benton adds, "is the weather dictated Emma's routine. If she traveled by jetboat or car an hour each way to the Wapiti bone bed, then she didn't typically stay in the campground. The trailers she and some of the other visiting paleontologists used were mainly for the convenience of staying near the Pipestone Creek bone bed if that's where they were working, which was an easy walk from the campground. The Wapiti bone bed, where Emma made the important discovery of a pachyrhino tooth two days before she disappeared, is some twenty miles north of Grande Prairie. And often after she'd worked there Emma would stay in town, in a studio apartment she rented in College Park."

"Meaning if it hadn't rained," Briggs comments, "she might have gone up the river to her usual site and stayed in town and maybe she'd still be alive."

"If it hadn't rained, she would have excavated her usual bone bed," Benton confirms. "It might have saved her life, but it's hard to say. Maybe impossible to say."

"Sounds to me like she was being stalked." Briggs is looking down at his desk again, and while I can't see what's on it, I know him.

He's multitasking. If the FBI is willing to go over the details of their investigation, he'll listen. He'll listen to the most obscure minutiae as long as he's taking care of whatever's in front of him, which is always something.

"Watching her at any rate, yes," Benton is saying. "Enough

for the killer to know her routines, unless he was just damn lucky she happened to be staying in the pitch-black mud hole of a campground the night he decided to grab her."

"It makes me wonder if it's not someone local." Briggs reaches for something.

"Or has been in and out of the area." Burke has her own theory.

I can look at her and know she has something to prove, probably to prove to Benton, who wants her transferred to another field office, maybe one in Kentucky. I don't know if he's told her yet, but I suspect he has, based on her demeanor, stony and stubborn and seductive. I can feel her anger smoldering as she continues to flaunt her opinions and herself.

"Someone who knew the area," she says, "and had reason to know details about Emma and that the paleontologists don't work the Wapiti site in bad weather."

"Sedimentary argillite," Benton says to us and not her. "River clay. The aboriginal people made tobacco pipes out of it, and it cakes on shoes and clothing like cement. After digging at the bone bed the last day Emma was seen alive, no one had cleaned up, including her. They'd walked directly to the chow hall, and when she finally headed to her trailer she would have been extremely muddy, dressed for the weather, including a blue hooded rain jacket that appears to be the one the body has on."

"At night," Hahn tells us, "the campground is so dark people use flashlights if they're walking around because you can't see a thing unless the moon is full, which it certainly wasn't that night. Just a soupy darkness described by her colleagues as noisy, like a shower going full blast."

"It would have been very easy to park a vehicle nearby," Benton says. "And grab her."

"Especially if she were incapacitated first," I point out.

"Unless we're talking about a person she would go with willingly," Briggs suggests, and it appears he's reading and initialing reports.

"I doubt that was possible without her colleagues knowing," Benton answers him. "Without her mentioning something to someone, and based on interviews that have been relayed to us, based on her e-mails, her voicemails, Emma was completely focused on her profession. She wasn't seeing anyone romantically, had only professional associations while she was working in the bone beds or the lab. When she left the chow hall that night, she said she was tired. She was turning in and would see everybody in the morning and maybe they'd get lucky and the rain would ease up. She walked back through the campground alone."

"Any tire tracks or footprints by her trailer?" Briggs asks.

"A sea of viscous mud flooded by deep puddles because of the rain," Benton says.

"So the thought is the killer got her to open her trailer door?" Briggs sips from a mug, coffee, no doubt, and if no one else were here I'd tell him what I usually do.

He drinks coffee all day long and into the night and then complains about insomnia. During my six-month forensic radiologic pathology fellowship at Dover's port mortuary, I managed to get him to switch to decaf in the afternoon and to take long walks and hot baths. *Old bad habits die hard and new good ones don't last, Kay*; he no doubt would say what he always says when I lecture him.

"The thought is he grabbed her before she got inside," Benton speculates. "There's no evidence she ever returned to her trailer, that she actually went inside it. No muddy boots were found, no wet clothing, and the door was ajar, as if she was unlocking it when someone came up behind her."

"They ever find her keys, her flashlight?" Briggs is looking at us again.

Hahn answers that police found them in a muddy puddle at the bottom of the trailer's aluminum steps, which adds to the suspicions she was unlocking the door when she was accosted.

"What we're exploring toxicologically," I then say to my commander-in-chief, "is the possibility of a volatile organic compound like chloroform being used. Possibly some inhalant that would quickly render the person unconscious so he can take his victims wherever he wants, for whatever purpose."

"You'll make sure our friends in Edmonton screen for that and anything else that's in your differential." Briggs looks past his camera, as if someone is in his doorway now.

"An important question," Burke says, "is if he took Emma Shubert someplace first."

"If he doesn't live around there," Briggs replies, and he's distracted, "it seems like that would be risky. A motel or motor inn, and what if she struggled or screamed?"

"More likely he had her in his own vehicle or whatever he'd rented," Benton says. "A van, a camper, an RV that he could park in a remote area."

"We're checking all rentals and purchases in a several-hundred-mile radius for the time frame in question," Burke says to Briggs, who is barely listening. "From Class A's like Airstreams to fifth-wheel travel trailers, in other words towables. Something he could pull up into the very campground where she was staying and it wouldn't draw attention on a dark rainy night."

"It would solve a lot of problems for him if she's unconscious," Benton says to me. "Without the messiness of having to hit her in the head or attempt to force her at gunpoint. No guarantees, and things can go south in a hurry. Far preferable to knock her out with a chemical and get her inside his vehicle and drive away to do whatever he does, to act out whatever his fantasy might be."

"Which seems to include cutting off her ear," Burke states. "Demonstrating a decompensation, a deteriorating self-control, a compulsion that's gaining in force like a hurricane. If Emma's the most recent victim, he's into mutilation, becoming more violent. It's taking more to relieve what builds up inside him," she says, and she's the profiler now, and Benton doesn't comment.

"We're not likely to know if an ear was cut off," I reply. "All that's left of the head is the skull. Unless there's a cut mark to bone, we won't be able to tell."

"It needs to be pointed out that Channing Lott has significant professional and philanthropic ties with this part of Canada." Burke is talking faster and more aggressively. "Specifically, his worldwide shipping company transports petroleum and liquid petroleum gases that are carried by rail from Fort McMurray, the epicenter of Alberta's booming oil fields, and on to various seaports."

Benton is looking at her now, his face expressionless.

"He's made numerous trips to some of the oil refineries." Burke has gotten louder. "And last year one of his subsidiaries made a sizable contribution to the dinosaur museum being built in Grande Prairie."

"Which subsidiary?" Hahn frowns, as if this is information Burke hasn't shared.

"One called Crystal Carbon-Two," Burke says to Briggs.

He is looking down at something on his desk again, and I can always tell when he's done with a conversation.

"*Green* cleaning equipment used in food processing, in paint stripping, for cleaning printing presses and machinery used in the paper industry," Burke says. "No harmful emissions or toxic chemicals. Solid carbon-dioxide blasting, which also is becoming an increasingly popular technique in oil refineries."

"Yesterday was a bad day for our Marines," Briggs says, and Burke has no intention of being silenced.

She tells us that Channing Lott has been marketing his equipment in northwest Alberta, and flight plans filed with the FAA indicate he has flown his Gulfstream jet into Edmonton and Calgary half a dozen times in the past two years. Emma Shubert was a very outspoken environmentalist, and what she was excavating in the bone beds was going to end up in this very museum that he was helping to fund.

"I've got several articles pulled up." Hahn has started digging into what she's just now being told. "Announcements about his donation, five million dollars last year. He was definitely in Grande Prairie."

Briggs nods at someone we can't see, gesturing that he'll be right there.

"Mr. and Mrs. Channing Lott attended a Dino Ball, were the guests of honor, were presented with a proclamation. An announcement was made about the gift from Crystal Carbon-Two." Hahn reads as she scrolls through what she's searching on her computer. "This was a year ago this past July."

"I've got a lot of cases, a hell of a bad day." General Briggs has heard enough. "Another damn chopper, that Chinook that went down in eastern Afghanistan yesterday. The C-Seventeen carrying those twelve fallen heroes is on final, about to land. I've asked Dr. Lopez to call you as soon as he knows more, Kay," Briggs says to me, and he stands up and the LCDs are filled with his teal-green scrub shirt. "So you can see what overlapping there is, if any."

Then he's gone, his webcam disabled.

"What about personal effects? Clothing, jewelry, anything found with the body?" I ask Benton. "In addition to her clothing, the rain jacket? What about her phone?"

"No phone," he replies.

I don't mention what Lucy has to say about Emma Shubert's early-generation iPhone and bogus e-mail accounts and proxy servers.

"I can't figure out what the significance is," Hahn says to Benton, and she knows.

Maybe Benton found a discreet way to suggest what Lucy discovered almost instantly and illegally, but Hahn has found out what she needs to know. She has the information that the video footage of Emma Shubert's last jetboat ride was taken with her own iPhone. I suspect it was recorded by a colleague while the paleontologists were headed to the Wapiti bone bed on a rare sunny morning, a file innocently made and saved and then later looked at by a monster. He probably went through every file saved on her phone, the same phone he used to take a photograph of a severed ear, what we're supposed to assume is her ear.

The same phone that e-mailed the video and the jpg to me.

"He got what he wanted." Douglas Burke pushes back her chair, and no one answers her. "He's out, a free man, right?" She looks incensed. "Channing Lott benefited from what's going on, and in fact is the only individual who has benefited from it."

She gets up and walks to the closed conference room door. She looks angry enough to hurt someone.

"He was in jail when Peggy Stanton vanished." Benton calmly looks at her, and she defiantly stares back at him. "He was in jail when Emma Shubert disappeared. He certainly didn't kill them or anyone while he was locked up in jail."

"Crimes elaborately staged so we're thinking serial murders. Why?" Burke is saying this to Benton, as if Val Hahn and I aren't here. "To cover, to obfuscate the ultimate goal, which is getting rid of his wife and getting away with it."

"He was locked up. That's a fact," Benton says.

"So someone did his bidding," Burke answers him. "Someone makes sure Peggy Stanton's body shows up exactly when it did and is filmed and he gets acquitted. Genius, I have to say. Amazing what money can buy."

"This killer acts alone," Benton says. "Elaborate, yes. But not so we'll *think* serial murders. They *are* serial murders."

"You know what, Benton?" She opens the conference room door. "You're not always right."

thirty-eight

I WANT PASTA OR PIZZA AND HAVE ASKED BENTON TO stop on his way home, which won't be anytime soon, he warned me, when we were leaving the CFC separately.

Both of us alone. Prepossessed and preoccupied. Off to where we need to go, and that is the sum of us individually and together. I know full well when something isn't important to anyone but me.

"Food," I told my husband, as I was driving alone out of my parking lot. "God, I'm hungry. I'm starved," I said on my way to handle what no one else can be bothered with, and I check my rearview mirror again and the dark blue Ford LTD is right behind me.

I follow the Charles River as it bends and snakes, curving like the corridors in my building, taking me where I've begun and ended, where I've been and will go, past the DeWolfe Boathouse again, past the Morse School playground again, heading in the direction of Howard Roth's neighborhood again, on my way to Fayth House. The dark blue Ford is on my bumper, and I see the face with dark glasses in my rearview mirror.

Watching me, daring me. Brazenly following me.

"Food and wine," I told Benton over the phone a little while ago, when I didn't know this would happen, and I'm shocked.

I'm incensed and disbelieving, and at the same time not sure why I'm surprised.

"We will eat together, be together, all of us," I said, alone and hungry and beginning to feel worn down by it all, a single question burning on the dark horizon of my dark thoughts.

I watch the car behind me, my heart turning hard like something vital dying and petrifying into my own bone bed of emotion. *Now you've gone too far*, I think. *You've really gone too far*, and I imagine dinner with Lucy, Benton, Marino. I'm hungry and angry and want to be with people I care about, and I've had enough, because it's too much now. I turn right on River Street, and Douglas Burke turns, too, her dark glasses staring.

I pull into the parking lot of the Rite Aid at the intersection of Blackstone and River Streets, letting her know I'm aware that she's been on my tail for the past ten minutes and I'm not going to be harassed by her and I'm not afraid of her, either. I roll down the window of my SUV, and we are driver's door to driver's door like two cops, like comrades, which we're certainly not.

We're enemies, and she's openly letting me know it.

"What is it, Douglas?" I've never been able to call her Doug or Dougie.

It's all I can do to call her anything.

"I wasn't going to say this in front of them." Her glasses are dark green or black, and the sun is low, the old low buildings of Cambridge casting long shadows, a low late-afternoon well on its way to the lowest time of the year around here, a New England brutal winter.

"Out of professional respect, I didn't bring it up with them in the room," she says.

"In front of *them*?" I ask, and she has no professional respect for anyone, least of all for me.

Her dark glasses stare.

"You mean in front of Benton," I assume.

"I know about your niece." She pushes those words out like animals shoved, herded, moved with aggression.

I don't answer her.

"Exploiting vulnerabilities in websites, harvesting information." She talks snidely, as if she's convinced she knows how to hurt me. "I love the way hackers describe what they do. Which in your niece's case is nothing short of a brute-force attack on whatever server she's interested in for the express purpose of obstructing justice."

"'A brute-force attack'? I wonder who's really doing that." I look at her.

She points two fingers at her dark masked eyes and then points at me.

"I'm watching," she says dramatically. "Tell Lucy she's not so damn smart after all, and you're a co-conspirator to go along with her stunts, and for what? So she can find out something five minutes before we do? Before the FBI does? Because she's jealous."

"Lucy's not the sort to get jealous." I sound perfectly reasonable. "But I think you might be."

"I'm sure it must be awful to be fired by the very thing you're constantly surrounded by."

"Yes, that must be awful," I say pointedly, because Douglas Burke is constantly surrounded by Benton and reminders of him, and she's fired.

She's fired as his partner and he wants her transferred to some distant place, and he may be suggesting more than that behind the scenes. Special Agent Douglas Burke isn't fit to serve. She shouldn't be carrying a gun or arresting anyone, and I advise her as diplomatically as I possibly can that it might not be wise for her to engage Lucy. It would not be prudent to simply show up on my niece's property or to drop by unannounced or to follow her the way she's just followed me.

"You know her history, so I think you understand what I mean," I say to Burke, who likely is aware of every firearm Lucy owns, every handgun and large-capacity weapon she has registered in Massachusetts and she has a license to carry.

"Are you threatening me?" She smiles, and that is when I am certain that she is profoundly unstable and unwell and possibly violent.

"It's not my style to threaten people," I tell her, and now I'm very concerned.

"I'm not afraid to solve this case, you know," she then says. "Unlike others, it seems. I'm not afraid, and I can't be bribed."

I'm concerned about her, about her safety. I'm concerned about other people, too.

"I'm not intimidated or influenced by someone's political connections or money," she says, "not in bed with federal judges and U.S. attorneys, not stupid enough to believe that someone in jail doesn't have people on the outside doing his bidding. A small price to pay. Locked up half a year in exchange for getting rid of the wife you've grown to hate."

"And you know that. You know he hated her? Where did you get that?" I stop myself from arguing with someone who can't possibly be logical.

"I just want to know why you're protecting him. It's obvious why you'd protect your niece, but why Channing Lott?"

"You need to stop this," I reply, because she is beyond being reasoned with.

"What has he promised you?"

"You need to stop this before it goes any further."

"He came to see you," she says. "Now, isn't that just perfect. What else did he say to you, Kay? The missing dog? How scared his wife was and on and on, pleading his case with you while your niece is crashing through firewalls and you're trying to run me out of town, trying to ruin me? And you think you can?"

"I don't want you to ruin yourself."

I warn her she's going to have a serious problem if she continues to follow me, continues to make inflammatory and accusatory statements, that I'm the one feeling threatened.

"You need to go back to your field office," I say to her, because I have a strong feeling about what she intends to do, and I remember every word Benton said about her and the way she used to act around Lucy, and at the same time I know better.

It isn't just pseudoephedrine, whatever drugs she's on. It's what Douglas Burke has to prove, and she's not going to listen because she can't.

"He's so much better off with me." She means Benton is.

The ultimate case Douglas Burke must solve in her life isn't a bank robbery or serial murders but the crime of her own existence. I don't know what happened to her, probably when she was a child. I also don't care.

"He knows it, too," she says to me, through the open window of her Bureau car. "It's a shame you don't want what's best for him. Trying to sabotage me isn't going to help your pathetic excuse for a marriage, Kay."

"Go back to your office and talk to someone." I am careful not to sound provocative. "Tell someone what you just told me, share the information, maybe with your SAC, with Jim." I say it clinically, dispassionately, almost kindly. "You need to talk to someone."

She needs help, and she's not going to get it, and I have a strong feeling about what she's going to do, and when I drive away toward mid-Cambridge, I let Benton know.

"I think she intends to confront Channing Lott." I leave him a voicemail because he's not answering his phone. "She's over the edge, and someone needs to intervene. Someone needs to stop her immediately to protect her from herself."

I pull into a Starbucks to get a coffee, a double shot, black, as if that will help me collect my thoughts, as if caffeine will calm me, and I sit in my car for a few minutes and try Benton again. Next I text him, making sure he somehow gets the message that he needs to intervene without delay before Douglas Burke does something foolish, dangerous, possibly irreparable. She's unstable and obsessed and armed. I drop my unfinished coffee in the trash and drive off, wondering if I should warn Lucy and decide against it. I'm not sure what she might do.

It is dark, the sun below a blackened horizon when I reach Fayth House, a brick complex, tidy and relatively modern, with deliberately placed flowerbeds and trees. A silver SUV is pulling out as I turn in, leaving very few cars in the parking lot, and I suspect most of the residents in the retirement community don't drive. I walk inside a pleasant lobby with blue carpet and blue furniture and silk flowers, and Americana prints and posters on the walls that remind me of Peggy Stanton's checks.

The receptionist is a stout woman with frizzy brown hair and thick glasses, and I ask her who's in charge.

"Which resident are you here to see?" she says, with a cheerful smile.

I ask her if there is a director. I realize it's after hours, but is there someone in administration I can talk to? It's important, I let her know.

"I don't believe Mrs. Hoyt has left yet. She had a late meeting." The receptionist picks up the phone to make sure, and I notice a fall arrangement of fresh flowers on a table behind her, burgundy Asiatic lilies, purple lisianthus, orange roses, and yellow oak leaves.

A floral delivery with no card. Someone, possibly the receptionist, has taped to the vase a piece of paper from a Fayth House memo pad, a name with a room number written on it that I can't make out from where I stand. But I recognize *It's her Bday* written in large print and underlined.

"Cindy? There's someone here to see you? I'm sorry," the receptionist says to me. "What's your name?"

I'm directed to an office at the end of a long hallway that takes me past a brightly decorated dining room where residents are finishing dinner, some of them in wheelchairs, a lot of walkers and canes by the tables. The beauty salon is closed for the night, and an elderly man is playing the piano in a music room, and a cleaning cart is parked outside the library. I notice boxes of commercial trash-can liners, a hundred to a carton, the same brand I found inside Howard Roth's house.

I walk on to the administrative offices and knock on the open door of the one at the end where Mrs. Hoyt, young and very pregnant, is putting on her coat. I introduce myself and shake her hand and she seems puzzled.

"Yes, I recognized the name when Betty just told me," she says. "Do you have family here? I saw you on the news yesterday. That huge turtle on the fireboat and then the poor woman. What can I help you with? Do you have family here?" she again asks. "I would think I would know."

She sits down at the desk with her coat on.

"Or maybe you're considering Fayth House for someone?"

I take a chair across from her and reply that my mother lives in Miami and is stubborn about leaving her house even though she probably shouldn't be on her own anymore. What a lovely place this is, I say.

"I'm wondering if you know who Howard Roth is," I begin. "He was local and lived just a few blocks from here. He did odd jobs, was a handyman off and on."

"Yes." She opens a bottle of water and pours some in a coffee cup. "He was nice enough, with some problems, though, and I heard about what happened. That he fell down his stairs. Very sad; his life was tragic." She looks at me as if to say she doesn't understand.

She can't imagine why I'm here about him.

I ask her about volunteers and if they might include a Cambridge woman named Peggy Stanton.

"I don't know what happened," Mrs. Hoyt replies. "She just stopped coming. Why do you ask?"

"Then you knew her?"

She looks at me, baffled, and of course she has no reason to be aware that Peggy Stanton is dead.

"Okay," she says, and she's starting to get upset. "Please don't tell me . . ."

For a moment she looks as if she might cry.

"Well, what a lovely woman. You wouldn't be here if it was nothing," she says.

"When was the last time you saw her?" I ask.

"I don't recall exactly." She nervously types on her keyboard. "I can check. It's easy enough to take a look at our volunteer schedule. We have such a wonderful group of people who make the lives of the residents so much better, people who bring joy and hope where there wouldn't be any for so many of them. I'm sorry. I'm talking too much. I'm just a little flustered."

She asks me what happened, and I tell her Peggy Stanton is deceased. We plan to release the information to the media first thing in the morning, but a body has been positively identified as hers.

"Good God, what a shame. Oh, Lord," she says. "Dear God. How awful. Well, I thought it was the spring, and I'm right. This is terribly upsetting. When the residents know, they'll be heartbroken. She was so popular, had been helping out here for many years."

The last time Peggy Stanton was here was the night she vanished, April twenty-seventh, a Friday, when she ate dinner with a group she was working with, a collage that night, the residential administrator explains.

"It was a true passion with her," she says. "Teaching arts and crafts, working with your hands. Peggy was just very involved in improving self-esteem, reducing anxiety and depression in seniors, and when you actually shape something with your bare hands and watch it evolve into a work of art? There just isn't better therapy," she adds, and she describes Peggy Stanton as a fine woman shattered by personal devastation, by unimaginable loss.

"She had a healing touch, you might say. Maybe because of what she'd been through in her own life. She was just starting the residents on pottery," she explains. "But then she didn't come back."

She assumed Peggy Stanton had gone to Florida, perhaps to her lake cottage in the Chicago area.

"I wasn't concerned, just a bit disappointed, as we'd been investigating kilns," she says, and I think of Peggy Stanton's basement, of work recently done and of the unusual tools on the table down there.

Not for baking but for pottery, and I ask her if Peggy Stanton might have been thinking about installing a kiln in the basement of her home and if she might have hired Howard Roth on occasion to do an odd job or two. Very possibly, she says, but she can't be sure, and she offers to give me a tour of Fayth House.

"I've held you up enough," I reply, and I thank her as a chime sounds on my phone.

A text message from Lucy.

Who is Jasmine? I read, as I'm leaving.

Mildred Lott's missing dog that turned up later, I text her back in the dark, returning to my SUV, which is next to another SUV that wasn't parked there earlier.

A silver Jeep Cherokee with a silver mesh grille right next to me when the whole damn parking lot is practically empty, and I get an eerie feeling, a sensation that flutters.

Missing??? Then why's she outside at night calling it?

About to get in the car & will call, I reply.

The silver Jeep Cherokee that passed me a little while ago when I first got here, it occurs to me. The same one I saw earlier in my own parking lot or one just like it. I point my key to unlock my SUV while part of me wants to run, and another text chimes.

Jasmine! Jasmine! Where are you? Come!

thirty-nine

I'VE BEEN TAKEN BY PIRATES.

The boat I'm in has a metal hull with carpet. It is moving fast on a heavy surf. It is cold and claustrophobic, and I'm groggy and in pain. I want to sleep.

Don't sleep.

I'm going to be sick, motion sick, vertigo. My stomach lurches as if it wants to climb up my throat, and I wonder if I was hit on the head, if that's how they got me here, dumped me in the cargo area of an old boat. On my back, a fishnet wound around me, I'm nauseated, about to gag. My stomach has nothing in it, and I don't want dry heaves, mustn't start retching uncontrollably. They can't know I'm conscious, and I focus on every part of me, not sure if I'm injured. I don't feel pain, just my pounding head.

"Are you awake?" a man asks loudly.

I've heard his voice before.

I don't answer, and my head clears some. I'm in a car. In the cargo area in back, lights from oncoming traffic illuminating him intermittently. Surrounded by boxy shapes behind the front seats, I do the best I can to gather the darkness around me. To hide in it.

Make him think you're dead.

"You should be awake," says the man driving what I thought was a good idea for the CFC, a small crossover SUV.

I struggle to remember his name and envision his complete lack of empathy when he sat across from me. Soulless. Empty. Emoting nothing.

"Don't fake it," he says.

Play dead.

"Your fakery can't save you anymore."

I recognize the textures of the clothes I put on this morning, I think it was this morning. The corduroys, the cable-knit sweater, and a down jacket I wore because the temperature was freezing.

I rub my feet together, and they are bare and very cold, and I push them against the net and they find the resistance of something hard and square. It is completely dark, and I hear traffic. While I don't remember what happened, I am beginning to be certain I know. Then I think I'm dreaming.

This is a bad dream. I need to wake up. It's a terrible dream, and you're fine.

I take a deep breath and choke back bile as my head throbs, and I take more deep breaths and realize I'm awake. I really am, and this really is happening. I mustn't panic. I push the hard square shape with my netted bare feet, and whatever it is moves very slightly and feels like plastic.

A scene case.

He speaks loudly from the driver's seat, asking if I'm awake, and again I don't answer, and I know who he is.

"Now you won't have to figure it out anymore," Al Galbraith says, and I can tell by the sound of his voice, the fluctuations in the volume of it, that he continues to turn around, looking in my direction.

I don't move in a way he can see, the entire back of the SUV outfitted as a cargo area, the backseat permanently folded flat, and I try to envision what is in here. It is difficult to think, difficult to breathe. My hands are free. He didn't tie me but wrapped the net around me, and it is quite tight, and oddly I think of creatures entangled, of the huge leatherback and what I was told. They run into something like a vertical line and panic and spin themselves up in it and then they drown.

Don't panic. Slow, deep breaths.

My phone is gone. He has my phone. He has my shoulder bag, unless it and my phone are on the pavement of the Fayth House parking lot and he left them there.

He wouldn't leave them.

My hands are pinned against my chest, and I move them, poke my fingers through what I realize is the cargo net we use to secure our equipment, and I feel a knotted tie-down and try to loosen it but I can't. My fingers are stiff and cold; and I'm shaking as if I'm shivering, my teeth about to chatter, and I will myself to calm down.

"You should be awake," he says. "I didn't give you that much. I've always wondered if they could smell it coming. The sweet smell of death coming."

I don't remember anything at all, but I know what he did, probably keeps a bottle of it in his car, in that silver Jeep Cherokee, for when the urge strikes. His murder kit.

You son of a bitch.

"Of course, everybody reacts a little differently," he says. "That's the danger and the art. Too much and the show ends early, which is what happened to the lady in Canada, had to keep knocking her out because I was driving."

I can tell from the sound of the pavement under me and the change in pitch of the engine that we are going through a tunnel.

"Her head was in my lap, and I knew she was going to fight me if I didn't keep the cloth handy. Then she wouldn't wake up anymore. I didn't get a chance to tell her what she needed to hear. Stupid as hell, such a waste. She never heard a word. Not one."

I wiggle my fingers through the net and feel the rough plastic side of another case.

"She had no idea. Keys out, opening a door in a downpour, the last thing she ever knew or did, and that's just a waste. A real waste after all the trouble I'd gone to, so I had to make something of it. I mean, I didn't want it to be a complete waste. I made it interesting, at least. It's all about timing and I know how to wait. But some things aren't preventable. See what happens when people interfere?"

I can't envision which scene case this is.

"How did you know it was dear Mother's birthday? Maybe

you didn't. Did you go to see her? Probably not. Wouldn't matter. She can't talk."

I'm trying to remember exactly how the cases were arranged back here.

"You have to admit I made it interesting, sending you what I did. Look what it caused."

He says it bitterly.

"It's probably best if your boss isn't in jail unless you're the one who put him there. But the end result wasn't the plan. You need to know that, and some of it's your fault. I never intended for him to win the way he has. He should rot. It was just a really perfect time to get everybody's attention, and it's a pity he won't rot in a stinking cell that he can't furnish comfortably with all his money."

He would have moved things back here to fit me inside.

"I confess I was a little squeamish at first. I'm not talking about the disgusting old carcass you were all over the news about. An old carcass even when she was still alive, such a Goody Two-shoes teaching Mother to make a collage and other mindless hobbies and not appropriately polite when I'd show up. She was earlier than the bone lady, and I wasn't as daring because I didn't need to be. I had plenty of time for our little chat, for her to realize the error of her ways. I'm talking about the other one who was a waste. A damn waste."

I'm not sure which plastic case is what. Some are orange, others are black, but it's too dark back here to make out colors.

"It actually turned my stomach, the sound of the knife going through cartilage. And I'm thinking, if this doesn't wake you up, lady, you really are dead."

He laughs. It is a quiet chuckle that has no joy in it.

"Lend me your ear. Play it by ear. Think of all the lame clichés with the word *ear* in them. You never listened. If only you had listened. Why did God give ears to people who don't listen?"

I don't want to open the wrong case.

"Well, now you have to listen. That's all you can do. Isn't it something the way things turn out?"

Please don't let me open the wrong one.

"Are you awake yet!" he yells. "The best part you won't smell. Well, sort of an ozone smell. You ever heard the old saying about someone sucking all the air out of the room? You're about to find out it's true."

I'm pretty sure what I want will be in a Pelican transport case, what Marino calls a sixteen-thirty.

"Are you listening to me? Wake up!"

I feel a fold-down handle, and that could be a good sign, but it's hard for me to remember.

"How good I've been to you, and this is what I get. I bring you flowers and hold your disgusting hand." He continues talking to me, and he's talking to somebody else.

Very, very slowly I push up a plastic clasp, working my fingers along the side of the case until I feel another clasp and then another.

"Dutiful, perfect, really, and put you in the best place when what I really should have done is spit in your face. You know what it's cost me all these years because you had me late and I was raised by a disgusting old hag? By the grace of no one but me. Fayth House, and you aren't gracious or grateful. A damn hypocrite, and it's time you admit it. Well, you will. In a little while, you're going to apologize."

Please don't let there be nothing but gloves and protective clothing in here.

But the size seems right. A Pelican case, what feels like a large toolbox. The cases we keep disposable clothing and sheets in are more like utility dry boxes with steel bar latches. I'm pretty sure. I'm trying so hard to think straight. My heart is flying like a terrified bird.

"You're a cold-blooded bitch, and I could have let you die, which is what you really wanted. And that's why I didn't. A squash for a brain, nothing but a fruit or a vegetable lying there or sitting up in the chair, staring. And you can't speak for yourself anymore, not the silver-tongued phony anymore, the virtuous do-gooder anymore. I've let you live because I enjoy seeing you this way. For the first time, I actually enjoy coming to see you. Pissing yourself, shitting in the bed. Getting uglier, more sour-smelling, more revolting every day. Who's the hero now?"

I work up the lid several inches, feeling inside the case without opening it all the way because it's heavy and I don't want to make noise. I feel convoluted foam inside.

"I know you're awake!" he yells, and I freeze. "Tell me the password for your phone!"

I slowly, gently move my fingers inside the case and feel marking pens and a stapler. Evidence packaging supplies, and I know I've found the right one. I feel the looped steel handles of small scissors and pull them out, and I begin to cut the netting, and the SUV is going much slower. I see tall streetlights and broken windows and corrugated aluminum siding flowing past the tops of the dark tinted windows, some of the buildings we pass boarded up.

Moving as little as I possibly can, I work my arms and head out of the netting, and then my feet are free of it, and they feel frozen, as if they've turned to stone. I slip my hand back inside the case, feeling for the metal handle.

"Wake up!"

Plastic and glass, and I recognize pillboxes and vials, and a steel scalpel handle. He is going very slowly over rough pavement in a dark, deserted area with old abandoned warehouses.

"I know you're awake. I didn't give you that much," he repeats. "I'm going to stop in a minute and get you out, and it's no good for you to try anything. Another little nap and then I'm going to show you something you've never seen before. I think you'll be fascinated."

I find the foil pouch of disposable scalpel blades.

"The perfect crime," he says. "And I came up with it, not you."

I slowly, quietly peel open the pouch.

"A way to put someone to sleep that can't be detected. Not by anyone. An environmentally friendly way. You will go out *green*." That mirthless laugh again. "They all go out *green*. Except the bone lady didn't. Really too bad. I honestly don't feel good about that one. This didn't have to happen, you know. It's all your fault. Showing up and poking your nose in what's none of your business? Timing's everything, and yours is up."

I lock a blade into the handle and steel against steel makes a soft click, and I worry that he heard it.

"Well, well, what's this?"

He stops the car suddenly. His door opens.

"I don't know what you think you're doing," he says, as he gets out.

He heard me safety-lock the blade, and I don't know which

door he's going to open, it occurs to me on a fresh rush of panic. I don't know if he'll open a back door or the tailgate, and I'll have to move very fast because he's going to see I'm not in the net anymore.

"What the hell do you think you're doing?"

I'll go for his head, his neck, his face, his eyes, but it will be hard to see him. Where we are is very dark, and the interior light in my car is off. He turned it off to get me in and out without anyone seeing, and it enters my mind that he hasn't shut the engine off, and he must have left his door open because the car is beeping. The engine is rumbling loudly, and it sounds different, as if he's got his foot on the gas but not like that either, and he's not inside the car. I don't understand what I'm hearing, and I grip the steel handle in a way I've never gripped a scalpel before.

Like a knife for slashing, for stabbing.

"This is private property," he says, and I realize he's not talking to me.

I sit up and have the scalpel ready, and I notice a lot of trucks, white trucks of different sizes with *Crystal Carbon2* and a logo painted on them, and in the distance are runway lights and Logan's air traffic control tower.

We're directly across the harbor from the airport, on a peninsula of the Marine Industrial Park where the U.S. Naval Hospital Ship *Comfort* is dry-docked, its white stack with the red cross on it proud against the black sky, and then I see him in the headlights, washed out by the glare, scowling, enraged. He's holding a small bottle, and a rag that's as big as a diaper, and he's backing away from the SUV and the bottle smashes to the pavement and the rag flutters off like a ghost as he runs.

I open the back door and step out unsteadily, my bare feet numb, and the tarmac we're parked on suddenly is a confusion of strobing emergency lights, cars marked and unmarked roaring in, and he is running toward an old brick warehouse on the water, and Marino and Lucy are on top of him.

He falls, tumbles headlong, as if he's diving into the asphalt, or maybe Lucy kicked his feet out from under him, I can't tell. But Marino is all over him, punching and yelling, and then a young woman appears as if she's been conjured up. For an instant, I wonder if I'm dreaming again.

forty

SHE MATERIALIZES OUT OF FLASHING BRIGHT LIGHTS and darkness, emerging from behind my SUV, where I realize a black Maserati is parked, its big engine rumbling throatily. She asks if I'm all right, and I tell her I'm fine, and I don't know her and I do.

"He might just kill him. All right, Marino. That's enough. Not that I blame him." She's staring in the direction of the warehouse, and I'm staring at her face. "You sure you're okay? Let's get you in the back of a cruiser and I'll find something for your feet."

She's cut her hair quite short, and it looks more blond than brown, still very pretty but older, mid-thirties, about Lucy's age. When I saw her last she was barely twenty, and she puts an arm around me and walks me to Sil Machado's Crown Vic as he's boiling out of it. I climb into the backseat and sit with the door wide open, and I rub my feet.

"I guess someone will explain things," I say to Janet.

The last time I saw her must have been fifteen years ago, when she and Lucy were sharing an apartment in Washington, D.C. Lucy was ATF and Janet was FBI. I always liked her. They were good together, and nothing's been all that good for Lucy ever since.

"I notice you don't seem to have a gun handy, don't seem to be looking to arrest anyone," I say to her, "and I'm sorry if I'm bleary. If only my head would fall off. Maybe then it would stop hurting."

"I'm not with the Bureau anymore, not even a cop," Janet says. "A lawyer, one of those awful people, only worse. I specialize in environmental law, so I'm pretty much hated."

"Just don't adopt a pig. Lucy's been threatening it. And it will be me taking care of it when she's out of town, which is often."

"I guess you don't know what he did with your shoes."

"There should be a box of boot covers in the back." I point at the SUV I was just held hostage in, and it occurs to me that all the CFC vehicles are equipped with satellite locators. "The ones with PVC soles so I can walk around in them," I say to her. "You followed me here. But why?"

"You texted Lucy you would call her as soon as you got in the car," she says. "And you didn't."

"And that was enough for her to start tracking me?"

"She does it more than you think. Tracks you, me, pretty much everyone. And she could see you were at Fayth House and then were heading toward Boston instead of toward home. Plus, you'd left some rather urgent messages for Benton."

She explains to me that they were very close to Fayth House anyway, taking Marino back to his Cambridge house, and were talking about the significance of Mildred Lott going out in the dark.

"She thought she heard Jasmine in the backyard," Janet says. "She was calling out the name of her dog."

I'm aware that Lucy has been working with British and German researchers on computer-based lip-reading technology, and Janet says the software is now good enough to use when people are turned as much as a hundred and sixty degrees sideways. In other words, you can barely see their mouths moving but the computer does.

"And she was turned away from the camera, looking in the direction of where she heard whatever she heard," Janet says. "The security camera caught her from the side only, and it sort of does look, a little bit, at least, like she's saying her husband's name."

I'm searching for Benton, wondering if he's here. He must have alerted agents, the police, and if so, I know what that means. He found out what I feared is true. Douglas Burke came here to do battle with Channing Lott, whose shipping headquarters looms in the distance beyond the dry-docked hospital ship, a huge white prewar building with hundreds of windows, most of them dark at this hour.

"I could see someone like a prosecutor thinking that or wanting to think it," Janet is saying. "Not *Channing* but *Jasmine*. She was calling her dog and looked really happy, thrilled and excited but frantic, and now we know why."

My feet aren't numb anymore, and now they're itching.

"Not exactly," I reply. "Why did she think her dog was out there?"

"Either he had the dog with him or more likely he had a recording," she says. "If he stole the dog days earlier and recorded it barking."

I continue to rub my feet as Janet walks over to the SUV and opens the tailgate.

"Try one of the big orange cases," I call out to her, and police are everywhere, and Al Galbraith is in cuffs and is being placed in the back of an FBI sedan.

I look around at Boston cops and agents and Machado, and then I see Benton with uniformed officers who are breaching the entrance of the warehouse. What I don't see is any sign of Douglas Burke. Three loud thuds of a lightweight battering ram and the door gives and is opened, and there are lights on inside a cavernous open space where I can see rows of shiny steel machines on wheels and coils of hoses and hundreds of wooden barrels stacked against a far wall.

Benton and the others approach a shut metal door, and I can make out the reddish tint to the floor and hear what sounds like steam blasting. I remember Burke's accusatory comments about Crystal Carbon2, a *green* way to do industrial cleaning. Solid carbon-dioxide blasting, she said. Compressed air propelling dry-ice pellets at supersonic speeds, and carbon dioxide is one of the simplest and most common asphyxiants known.

Colorless, odorless, it is one and a half times heavier than air, so it flows downslope and settles, displacing oxygen. In a confined space at a concentration of ten percent a person loses consciousness in less than a minute and will asphyxiate, and Al Galbraith was right.

Nothing will show up on autopsy, not a damn thing, unless the person is burned. At more than minus one hundred degrees Fahrenheit dry ice causes frostbite, is so cold it may as well be hot, and I think of the strange hard brown areas on Peggy Stanton's arm and feet and her broken nails and ripped pantyhose.

He locked her in that room behind that shut metal door and turned on a machine, and she knew she was going to die if she couldn't turn it off. She got close to the white fog blasting out of the nozzle, reached for it, kicked at it, and it burned her. I imagine her darting about, banging on the door, clawing at the nylon hose that weren't hers, maybe wrapping her hands in shreds of stockings to protect her skin as she tried again, and the concentration of CO_2 rose.

Janet returns with boot covers, and I pull them on, frustrated that I don't have my phone. I get out of the car and awkwardly trot, my feet still not quite belonging to me, it seems. I head toward the warehouse, where all the trucks are parked, and the sound of compressed air blasting is coming from behind the closed metal door, and it must be locked because the police have the battering ram ready.

Red woody fibers are like a fine coating of soil or dirt on wire shelves arranged with accessories. Hoses, nozzles, insulated gloves, and the fine debris coats stainless-steel surfaces of blasting machines and scores of hard case insulated coolers and containers, what the dry-ice pellets likely are shipped in.

"You're going to need to take serious precautions, people lose consciousness incredibly fast, don't even feel it coming," I say to Benton, and I put my hand on his arm. "We need to make sure all the CO_2 has been vented outside."

"I know," he says, and I see it in his eyes.

He's afraid Douglas Burke is in that room.

"She came here," Benton says.

"He must have been here and then went to Fayth House to see his mother, to leave birthday flowers for her. His mother must be a resident there, and he must have spotted me pulling in."

"Everybody back!" The cop takes his stance and swings the battering ram behind him.

"A secretary told Doug that Channing Lott was gone for the day and directed her to his chief of operations. To this place. It was around five-thirty," Benton says.

The iron ram slams the door.

"Not long after I saw her," I reply. "When she was following me and I left you the messages."

"Why are you holding a scalpel?" Benton asks, and I realize he doesn't know.

He hasn't a clue what I've been through.

"I got a ride here I didn't ask for," I reply, as the battering ram swings back again and slams again, and wood splinters.

Deadbolt locks break loose of the wooden frame, and the metal door swings in, and the blasting noise is louder. Frozen carbon-dioxide vapor condenses the humidity in the air, and we are enveloped by a cold white cloud.

two nights later

LUCY HAS BEEN HIDING MORE THAN ONE DECEPTION AT her country home, and I remind Marino that a dog is a problem if it's not taken care of rather constantly.

"I've seen my share of neglected pets." I sauté crushed garlic in olive oil. "Having a dog is like having a child." I wish I'd started the sauce earlier.

But there's been no earlier time to do anything civilized, the last two days a relentless ordeal that didn't include cooking or sleeping or eating decent food. I keep wondering how it would have turned out if Lucy hadn't insisted on installing GPS trackers on all CFC vehicles, if she hadn't followed my SUV. A part of me is haunted by what didn't play out.

"Dogs require a lot of attention," I'm saying to Marino, as I stir fresh basil and oregano into the sauce. "Which is why Bryce and Ethan have always had cats."

"You're kidding me, right? We know why the hell the Odd Couple has cats. Gay guys are into cats."

"That's a terrible stereotype, not to mention ridiculous." A few pinches of brown sugar would be nice, and some red pepper flakes.

"You know, that same guy who played Felix Unger also

played Quincy. You ever stop to think about that and how long ago it was?"

"Jack Klugman played Quincy. Not Tony Randall," I reply. "A dog is a lot of work, Marino."

"I don't know. It's just weird, Doc. Where time goes. I remember watching that show before I knew enough to realize how damn stupid it was, like that episode when cancer mutated and started killing everyone? And the guy who had his arm reattached and then his good one went bad after that? Jesus, at least thirty years ago, and I was still boxing, just getting started with NYPD, had never even met a real Quincy, and here I am working with you. People think getting old happens to everybody but them. Then you hit fifty and go *What the fuck*."

I remove a damp cloth from a ceramic bowl and check on the dough, and Marino is sitting on the floor. His big legs are stretched out as he leans against the wall, at home inside my kitchen with a rangy-looking German shepherd puppy, a rescue Lucy airlifted out of a pig farm she and Janet shut down the other day. All paws, with huge brown eyes and cocked-up ears, black and tan, maybe four months old, curled up in Marino's lap, my greyhound, Sock, on the rug next to them.

"Cambridge was all set up to get a K-nine, and then they didn't approve the budget." Marino reaches for his beer, and he's different with the puppy.

Marino's gentle. Even his voice is different.

"The problem's paying overtime for whoever has the dog, but in my case I can do it for free and it's not a union problem or whatever because I don't work for them. You want to grow up to be a cadaver dog?" he says to his puppy.

"What an ambition." I divide the dough into three balls.

"Then he could come to work with me. You'd like that, wouldn't you? Come to my big fancy building every day," he says to the puppy in a voice that can't be described as anything but silly, and it licks his hand. "That would be okay, right, Doc? I'll train him, take him to scenes, teach him to alert on all kinds of things. That would be really cool, don't you think?"

I don't care anymore. Sleeping over in an AeroBed, a dog in the office, none of it seems important anymore. I've played it out so many times and can't answer the most fundamental question. Would I have cut him badly enough to save myself? It's not that I wouldn't have tried, because I have no doubt I was going to slash at his face, but a scalpel blade is very short and narrow, and can break off from the handle.

I had one slim chance that it turns out I didn't need, but I can't stop thinking about it because it's just one more reminder that the tools of my profession don't save anyone. Even as I'm thinking this I know it's not entirely true, and I need to snap out of this damn mood.

"I've been making myself crazy trying to come up with a name," Marino says. "Maybe Quincy. How about I call you Quincy?" he says to the puppy, and I hate it when I'm negative.

It certainly can be argued that if I help stop a killer I'm saving a life, maybe more than one life, that what I do morning, noon, and night prevents more violence, and Al Galbraith wasn't finished. Benton says he was just getting started, that his elderly mother, Mary Galbraith, who has been a resident at Fayth House for years, suffered a stroke about ten months ago and has never recovered cognitive functions. That seems to have been the trigger, as much as it is possible to explain what can't be explained.

The youngest child of a philanthropic Pennsylvania family that dabbles in farms and horses and wineries, a graduate of Yale, never married, and he hated his mother that much. She was a scholar, a member of the Society of Civil War Historians, and a consulting archivist for the Girl Scouts, and he couldn't kill her enough.

"What kind of wine?" Lucy walks in with several bottles.

Janet already has helped herself to a glass, and I wipe my hands on my apron and inspect labels.

"Nope." I return to the dough I'm working, flouring it, pressing it, gently stretching it into a circle. "Those pinots from Oregon." I move the dough, using my knuckles so I don't poke holes in it. "That lovely case you gave me for my birthday, the Domaine Drouhin down in the basement."

Janet says she'll get it, and I move my knuckles apart and rotate the dough, stretching it for the first pizza, this one mushrooms, extra sauce, extra cheese, extra onion, double smoked bacon, and pickled jalapeños. Marino's pizza. I ask Lucy to get the fresh grated Parmigiano-Reggiano and whole-milk mozzarella out of refrigerator two, and I suggest Marino take both dogs out in the backyard.

"You see?" I say to Lucy when he's gone. "I have to ask him. This is what worries me. It should occur to him on his own that it's time to take his puppy out."

"It's going to be fine, Aunt Kay. He loves that dog."

"Loving something's not enough. You have to take care of it." I start on the next pizza crust.

"Maybe that's what he's finally going to learn. How to take care of something and how to take care of himself; maybe it's time he does." Lucy sets bowls of cheese on the counter. "Maybe he needs a reason to go to the trouble. Maybe you have to want something so badly that you're finally willing to be less selfish."

"I'm glad you feel that way." I toss the crust and place it in an oiled, floured pan, and I know Lucy is talking about herself and what's going on in her life. "I just don't understand why you felt you couldn't tell me. Maybe you could get the onions and mushrooms out of refrigerator one; we're going to need to sauté them and drain them. To get all the water out."

"I was afraid to jinx it," she says. "I needed to see if it could work, and most times it doesn't work if you try to go back to someone you used to be with." She finds a cutting board and a knife. "I know you feel you should be told absolutely everything, but I have to be alone in my life, to feel what I feel by myself sometimes."

"I certainly don't feel I should be told everything." I place a third crust in a pan. "If I really felt that way, I wouldn't have much of a marriage."

I haven't seen Benton since yesterday, when he was with me at my office. I took care of Douglas Burke because I didn't think anyone else should, and Benton didn't look on directly, but he was in the autopsy room the entire time. Mainly he wanted to know if she struggled, if she made any attempt at all to defend herself. Burke was armed with a nine-millimeter pistol, and Benton didn't understand what could have happened, why she didn't fight.

All she did was shoot the damn door and shoot it badly, he said repeatedly.

Based on the dents and holes in the door and door frame, she was aiming for the lock.

Why the hell didn't she shoot him? Benton must have asked that a dozen times, and I've continued to explain what seems obvious to everyone else.

Burke was so hung up on Channing Lott, she was so convicted in her own beliefs, that she didn't know who stood before her. She didn't realize who the killer was until he led her into that windowless room, what Al Galbraith had turned into a death chamber, an empty storage area with walk-in deadbolted freezers and a port in a brick wall fixed with a nozzle. The dry-ice blaster was on the other side of that wall, and that's where Galbraith would turn it on, a heavy-duty aggressive machine with a hopper that could hold enough dry-ice pellets to blast frozen CO_2 for hours.

Galbraith had adjusted the settings as low as they would go, the purpose of this particular piece of equipment not for removing mold or sludge or grease or old paint or varnish or corrosion. He didn't use this monster machine to blast clean the inside of wine barrels but to kill human beings, running at a low pressure of eighty pounds per square inch, consuming sixty pounds of dry ice pellets per hour, the carbon dioxide level slowly rising as the temperature in the room dropped, and the noise of compressed air would have been terrible.

Douglas Burke didn't struggle with him, didn't have a chance. I suspect he tricked her into stepping inside that room and then shut the door and locked it. The best she could do was try to shoot her way out, emptying her entire clip, but she couldn't get the door open, and she likely had very little time to try.

It's really not possible for me to know how long she was alive, but by the time we got to her she was beginning to freeze-dry, was partially frozen inside that frigid airless chamber where one chair had been set in the middle of the reddish fiber-covered concrete floor. Where he sat Peggy Stanton so he could verbally abuse her, is Benton's guess. Where he sat Mildred Lott, whom he didn't know socially and who treated him *like a Lilliputian*, Galbraith told the FBI.

*   *   *

It is almost ten p.m. when Benton pulls in, and Sock gets up and lazily trots to the side door and Quincy bounds after him, and I'm glad they're friends. The moon is distant and small over rooftops behind our Cambridge home, and the French stained-glass window is lit up over the staircase landings, its wildlife scenes bright like jewels from the backyard where Benton and I decide to sit. The low stone wall around the magnolia tree is cold, and I realize it is winter.

"Not even Halloween yet and it's cold enough to snow," I say to Benton in the dark, and he has his arm around me, pulling me close.

"Try not to be so pessimistic," I say to him after hearing about his day, about how badly he thinks the case will go. "I've been telling myself the same thing all night. Don't lecture Marino. Don't lecture Lucy. Don't be so damn hard on myself and assume nothing makes a difference."

"I wish he'd just go ahead and commit suicide in jail." Benton sips straight Scotch. "There. I said it. Save the government a trial. But pieces of shit like that don't kill themselves. Same damn dog and pony show all over again. I can't believe Donoghue's firm is going to represent him, probably will be Judge Conry again, and you'll get dragged through it again."

"I won't be called by her this time." It won't be Jill Donoghue subpoenaing me. "This is the prosecution's case. It's theirs to win."

"Dan Steward is a moron."

I remind him the evidence is compelling. Galbraith killed all of them, leaving partial prints on boxes of trash bags, on a malt liquor bottle and a pouch of cat treats, and the wooden fibers he tracked from what the police now call the *blasting house* were also on Peggy Stanton's body and inside her car, where a fingerprint on the rearview mirror is his, and prints were found on checks he forged to pay her bills.

The same wine-stained American oak fibers were inside an old lobster boat Galbraith kept in a marina, I remind Benton, trying to encourage him. Police found Peggy Stanton's clothing and Mildred Lott's nightgown in a drawer at his waterfront house on Cohasset Harbor, where he stored his once formidable mother's personal belongings. Even a moron can't lose a case like this, I say to Benton.

"I'm confident we're going to have DNA," I assure him. "Paint samples from the lobster boat match the trace of paint on the bamboo pole, the same residue on the barnacle I removed from the leatherback. And that places his boat in the area where Peggy Stanton's body was recovered, where he ran into the turtle, plus he had her cell phone and checks. He had Emma Shubert's cell phone, and a range extender in his warehouse so he could log on to Logan's wireless. And then there's the rather glaring detail of Mildred Lott's body."

I mention that it might be difficult for even Jill Donoghue to explain why Mildred Lott's body was found frozen rock-solid inside one of Al Galbraith's freezers.

"Donoghue will say Channing Lott had something to do with it or is to blame, and what's maddening about it is he can't be tried again." Benton's voice is glum, his chin resting on top of my head.

"Well, that would be a good argument." I feel his heartbeat through my jacket, and I reach up to kiss him. "And I'm glad you're not the lawyer in this case. Let's go eat."

credits

As always, I'm grateful to those who so generously share their expertise during a Scarpetta journey. All of you help make the magic.

Thank you, Dr. Marcella Fierro, for all things forensic-pathological, and as always I'm grateful for Dr. Nicholas Petraco, the guru of trace evidence.

I'm indebted to Stephen Braga for guiding me through legal dilemmas and courtroom scenes, and to Cambridge Police Detective Danny Marshall for letting me tag along with him.

Hugs to Dan and Donna Aykroyd for daring Staci and me to join them on a dinosaur dig in northwest Canada's bone beds, where I found a seventy-million-year-old tooth and the idea for this novel.

What a blast that the U.S. Coast Guard (San Diego) and the Boston Fire Department's marine unit shared their go-fast boats with me.

I'll always owe you, Connie Merigo, the New England Aquarium's rescue director, for teaching me all about sea turtles, and allowing me to get close enough to touch and smell a rare leatherback.

And words of thanks aren't enough for my partner, Dr. Staci Gruber, my muse for technology, for everything.